LOVE YOU
FOREVER

CORTNI MARIE

CORTNI MARIE

Salvisa, Kentucky

LA FLEUR DE LIS TRILOGY

❖

BOOK ONE
LOVE YOU FOREVER
October 2024

❖

BOOK TWO
LOVE YOU MADLY
Late Spring/Early Summer 2025

❖

BOOK THREE
TO BE DETERMINED

This is a story about love and the madness it creates.

To my love, J

I could spend forever with you and it still wouldn't be enough.

AUTHOR'S NOTE

This is a story about vampires and gangs of mafia men set in St. Louis, a city rife with the effects of failed institutions and systems. To the outside world, St. Louis is a "dangerous" place to observe from a far like a troubled teenager or family member going through it. To me, it is home. Ignore what the media says, or even the perceptions of some of the characters in this story. Sure, it's a city of brash, honest, foul mouthed individuals, but it's also a city brimming with culture, sights, history (both horrible and amazing, like all history), and beneath the facade, a community that will support their neighbors (unless your neighbors are brandishing guns at a peaceful protest like they are flinging the carving knife at Thanksgiving after a few too many – you can guess my words for those types).

That being said, I try my best to advertise this book as an adult urban fantasy. Here are a few elements that might be cause for pause before you read.

Some of these might be spoilers:

- Heavy explicit language (the number of "fox" given are 245)
- Drug/alcohol use (which is technically legal in St. Louis)
- Mafia/organized crime
- Vampires
- Misogyny
- Questionable consent
- Mentions of violence against women
- Multiple fight scenes
- Open door/in the bed sexual content
- Blood
- Torture
- Death
- Kidnapping

✦

PROLOGUE

One year ago…

The burn of whiskey did little to nurse the splitting headache plaguing Emilien Dumas. Since walking into the hole in the wall bar, he had battled the steady pulse against his eye as it beat in time to the drums of the jazz music from the band in the corner. The walls adorned in voodoo dolls, shrunken heads, and various other spiritual trinkets screamed "Welcome to New Orleans". He scoffed, catching his reflection in the illuminated mirror behind the rows of bottles. A tall man with a tattoo of a skull on his neck approached, slipping into the seat next to him.

"Hard to believe we've made it this far, boss." The man peeked out from under the pageboy cap adding to his Manchester accent. His words caressed a cold, callous line between them.

"Even if this town is a right piece of French twattery," the man added as the bartender set a glass of clear liquid down in front of him. Emilien watched him smirk as he assessed the crowd behind them through the mirror on the wall of the bar.

1

In his past life, Emilien would have been offended by the remark about his country. But that was a long time ago. Worlds away as far as he was concerned.

In the time it took for everything in his life to simultaneously fall apart and be rebuilt, he found himself in the unique position as one of the most powerful men in the world. And maybe one of the most dangerous. Even so, he felt elusive enough to be sitting at this dusty bar, trumpets blaring from beyond the browned glass door, minding his own goddamn business. Or maybe people feared him and his "Society" enough to leave him the fuck alone. Either way, he grunted a response to the man next to him, his right-hand, while staring into the rapidly melting ice in the amber liquid before him.

"You can't play god, Emil," Adette's lackadaisical Parisian voice haunted into his memories and he nearly choked on his bourbon. The glass clinked onto the bar top. His late wife always had a way of surprising him, even from the afterlife.

"Is everyone here, then?" Emilien asked the man next to him. The man had a name, Emilien just never cared to commit it to memory. Never planned the need to do so. Lead researchers on academic projects rarely knew the names of their assistants. They were only around for four years tops. Research could last a lifetime. Yet what had been a desperate man's attempt at saving his dying wife's life ended up damning the world around them, dragging those assistants by his side into hell. And thus, the business of immortality boomed, despite the unsavory side effects.

The price for immortality? A soul, it would seem, as Emilien had not only cured all that ails the fragile human body but completely deviated them from humanity all together, turning them into bloodthirsty heathens. Somehow in his calculations he hadn't factored in the rate of regeneration. A healthy human body took four to six weeks to replenish its red blood cells naturally. Now, Emilien found himself and his band of men needing weekly replenishments. It used to be biweekly…

Pageboy cap man met his eye in the mirror behind the bar before swiveling around to scan the room. "Almost. I believe Jerry and Finn are finalizing the last blood bank and holding pens."

Well, at least the man didn't sugarcoat what they were doing like his investor.

"Call them rooms, Emil. The communities need affordable housing? Well, we will provide it!" The enigmatic Hugh Magnus had said to him right before having Emilien sign his name thirty times across the stack of paper on his shiny oak desk in the windowed office sixty stories above London's city life. Entrepreneur, marketing genius, and socialite, Hugh took Emilien in when Adette kicked him out and offered a solution to the enormous issue of his newfound blood lust. To avoid the drawn-out process of proper testing, Emilien first recruited his graduate assistants, like the man sitting next to him at the bar. This was before he realized his quick healing cure to mortality also triggered a freak rapid evolution event within the body. Only when he woke up on a couch weeks later, drenched in blood with his friend's cat clenched in his fist, an unquenchable thirst scratching at his throat and fangs poking into his gums did he run to Hugh.

Hugh, who took one look at Emilien, and saw money instead of strife. But compromises had to be made, price tags had to be put into place. A business model had to be put together. They couldn't just let *anyone* live forever.

"Good, *bon*. And *les citoyens*, is everyone ready to put that into motion?" Emilien asked the man with the black etched into his neck. His voice sounded like rolling gravel after his mind's steady assault on him. The last twenty years had been dedicated to achieving what they were about to unveil in New Orleans. Twenty years of memories in painfully vivid detail with no more degeneration to his mind, thanks to his cure.

His infamous "Cure to Mortality" became a hot commodity shortly after Hugh sank his claws into the project; government leaders, narcissistic billionaires, and the social elite who could afford the high markup and subsequent cost of longevity came out in droves. Life was an expensive nightmare to the average human, but to those with a yacht parked outside Monaco every summer, it was a party they never wanted to end. And it didn't have to—for a few hundred million euros and a strong constitution. Or lack of one completely.

There was only one small hiccup in the beginning... It was rather improper to be seen on the streets, sucking the neck of whatever junkie was desperate enough for a quick buck, no matter how much clout they held. Soon special facilities popped up, catering to the new nutritional requirements of the social superiorities. Still fueled by those desperate humans but this time behind polished mahogany wood doors and on sleek mid-century modern furniture, not a stack of pallets next to a dumpster.

"All plans are looking mint," the man said, throat bobbing as he spoke. It was hard to believe this was the same graduate student from all those decades prior. Still looking around twenty-three, all the fine bone and sleek gangly features of an academic replaced by the strength and promise of violence of a honed male body.

Emilien had once been one of those average humans, working tirelessly at Oxford University researching communicable diseases like the common cold, tuberculosis, and even mononucleosis, the keystone disease in his modern-day immortality. He worked tirelessly after Adette's cancer diagnosis to find a cure. What good were all those years wasted in the lab if they didn't save the one person in the world he loved the most? As her health declined, he became desperate, reckless, combining diseases and cures like a mad man. One night, his aberration seemed to work as he found a way to overload the immune system. It exploded into hyper drive and started an accelerated replenishment cycle. The preliminary tests showed promise. Emilien immediately administered the concoction on himself.

"What do you mean you have a cure for me?" Adette had said groggily the following morning as he burst into their bedroom, her accent heavy with the sleep he knew she desperately needed.

Gripping her face between his hands, tangling in the soft brown waves of hair, he had knelt before her on their rumpled bed.

"I mean, mon cherie, I have found a cure for all of it. Not just your cancer but every illness," he had said, voice riding the shimmery edge of delirium.

She had sat up, dizzy by the sudden movement, her pale blue eyes staring wide at him. *"Your research has been approved for testing?"*

Running a hand through his hair, he had climbed into the bed next to her. *"Well, not exactly. But all the calculations make sense. They look promising!"*

Her face fell a bit but she had given him an encouraging nod, *"Then the board should approve it in no time, mon amour."*

The memory washed away with the bourbon he drained from his glass, a slight grimace at the burn, before he signaled to the bartender for another. He turned to his cohort. Pageboy man nodded as two men walked in the front door.

"I think our time here is nearly over, *mes amis.*" His words filled the dingy bar. The crowd consisted solely of Society members. The bar itself acted as a front to their headquarters, which lie beyond an inconspicuous door in the back.

Pageboy man eyed him suspiciously as he spoke. Emilien never let him in on his ultimate plans. The man would never reveal as much to the others though. Besides, they would have time on their journey north to flesh out the details. He glanced to the fleur de lis tattoo inked on the man's exposed wrist, a glass held out before him, ready to drink to whatever command came from Emilien's lips next. Loyal till the end.

Would there ever be an end?

His mission, since saving the love of his life had been futile, was to make this world his own and watch it burn. That symbol tattooed on the man had led them all to New Orleans. And it would act as a beacon, steering them to their next destination. Their work here was nearly complete; the rich and powerful were converted and the rest… well they knew their place.

"It is time we move on once more. And where else but the gateway to the west itself," Emilien raised his glass to the group, a wicked smile spreading across his face, "St. Louis." His accent held the long –e sound, his smile widening, and as glasses silently rose in kind around him, the building exploded.

✥

CHAPTER ONE
Izzy

St. Louis could be a real bitch of a city.

In truth, the entire middle of the country could be blamed for the unseasonably warm day in October that had Isabella Ciampi scowling as beads of sweat rolled down her back on her trek toward the Washington University campus in the heart of downtown. Whoever decided to plant a major city in the most unpredictable and volatile-weathered land was a damn fool. She tucked a stray red curl behind her ear as she strode across Skinker Boulevard, the cathedral-like buildings of the university looming before her.

"Fuck you, Lewis and Clark," she muttered under her breath as her foot hit the sidewalk on the other side of the surprisingly empty street. As soon as the sun rose most days, people often scurried out onto the streets, like hoards of rats when a light shines on them. Daylight was no guarantee for safety but it tasted like sweet reprieve after an evening of being locked inside.

A red flag intersected by elongated navy tildes, outlined

in white to represent the rivers, with a golden circle around a blue fleur de lis in the center, lay stagnant on a pole outside the building she approached. Could they not have earned a slight breeze today?

Having grown up here, she was well aware of the haughty seasons this god forsaken city endured, but it didn't make her any less disgruntled. She stewed on it as the castle-like presence of McMillan Hall rose before her, its own magnificent piece of history. Its intricate architecture, giant courtyard, and lush green balcony garden brought her back to a time long passed. Her shared anthropology lab dwelled in the space underneath the native flowers and grasses. The garden had been a beautiful place to sit and watch the sunset before the promise of night held more dangerous connotations. She padded down the steps into the basement corridor lined with thick, metal doors, gridded windows offering snippets into what happened in the spaces beyond. A quick tap of her key card on the lock pad and the dark room welcomed her in with the sweet embrace of air conditioning on her damp back. A groan of pleasure escaped her lips.

"Keep it in your pants, Izzy," Barry called from behind one of the floor to ceiling bookshelves to her right. Humanities research labs were always a disappointment to prospective students touring the campus. Expecting to walk into a replica of Indiana Jones's office, instead, they found themselves in a repressive mix of library chic meets mad academic hideout with chaotic scribbles on papers strewn about the room next to random tagged artifacts of mysterious and peculiar uses. This *had* been a chemistry lab in its past life so there were work benches with sinks, the faucets long since removed along with the gas connections. Thank God for that. The last thing they needed was another reason for Dr. Beechum to deem them unworthy of having the "museum quality pieces" in their own workspace.

"The month of October has no right to see temperatures above sixty-five degrees, Bear. No right."

Her lab partner rounded the corner with a devilish smirk on his face, "That's no way to treat a lady like Mother Nature."

"What? By taking away her rights?" Giving him a wink as he chuckled, she dropped her black leather bag and emotional support water bottle off on her desk below the single line of windows along the back wall. Windows being a generous term. They hadn't been lucky enough to snag one of the street-side labs with its illuminating floor to ceiling panes. Those had gone to the *historians* so they wouldn't strain their eyes reading their repetitive texts or some shit like that.

"Same shit, different century. What new information do they think they are going to uncover from another white man in a wig?" Barry's statement got them both fully ostracized at their first staff meeting together, and every meeting since. To bring the *good vibes*, Barry's phrase, to the space, they installed various twinkle lights around the room after a holiday clearance blowout one year. But there was only so much that could be done when they were practically working in a cave.

Barry came to sit at the desk next to hers. He had wisely dressed for the wretched weather in a pair of leather loafers, plaid golf shorts, and a short sleeve cream Henley t-shirt. His dark brown hair remained flawless in his signature pompadour, further accented by thick framed glasses—a necessity for his blind ass. Barry held a self-proclaimed "goddess-slay physique" and exuded enough confidence that it had slowly rubbed off on her over the past three years of them working together.

"You know your weather app is free and accessible every morning before you leave for the day," he said pointedly at her paper bag style trousers and short sleeved mock turtleneck sweater. Sweat dried on her skin and an unreachable spot between her shoulder blades began to itch. Lovely.

Sticking her tongue out at him, she turned to the various items that had been delivered to her the day before. Requests for grant funding information, fliers for upcoming conferences, and a box with some funky customs clearance stickers on it.

Puzzled, she asked, "What's this?"

Barry glanced sideways over at the box and returned to the text in front of him.

"I don't know, some courier was waiting for me with it this morning. He got out of here real quick after I signed for it." His eyebrows went up to accentuate the "quick".

Peculiar. There was no return address. Just her name scrawled across it and the building address. How had they even known to come down here? This building had several floors above the basement, plus a giant archives library. Why wouldn't they have just taken it there? That's where most packages get dropped off anyway. Dr. Beechum didn't trust them to even open a cardboard box on their own.

"Weird," she sighed, reaching for the dagger strapped to the harness around her chest. Partial style, partial purpose.

When the world went to shambles twenty years prior, people first stockpiled all the guns and ammunition they could get their hands on. Until they learned their average human reaction times were nothing compared to immortals. A close contact weapon became much more beneficial. Welders and blacksmiths, once tossed aside as irrelevant, masters of a dying industry, suddenly found themselves quite popular as people looked to the past and started acquiring swords, daggers, and other weapons assumed to be meant for a museum or a souvenir from their local renaissance faire. Izzy had inherited a collection of the real deal from her grandfather but also commissioned a couple items that she felt more comfortable carrying on a daily basis than those priceless artifacts decorating her bookshelves at home. One of those commissioned pieces being the dagger in her hand: the seemingly ordinary hilt a dark, almost black metal with a blade etched in violets to honor her *nonna*, Viola. She stopped to admire the blade in the glowing light their measly windows and discount twinkle lights offered before sliding it effortlessly through the brown tape keeping the box closed. It unceremoniously popped open.

Within lie layers of linen and lambswool wrapped around a book.

"This better not be another fucking bible," she grumbled to Barry. He snickered. They had seen every rendition of the holy text and studied the rather brutal and bloody history of them all, none having a happy ending. How many times would they have to sit through another stuffy dinner where the tenured professors of yesteryear would argue verses and complain about how the younger generations no longer attend church and how *that* was what was wrong with society these days and where could they find some decent assistants for their research? The thought alone had Izzy rolling her eyes.

She grabbed a pair of nitrile gloves off her desk and picked up the small book. It fit well in her hand, not much heft as she lifted it in the air a few times like a dumbbell. It was jewel-bound on what appeared to be a mix of calf and lamb skins. Strange for such a small book. A crest with a half an eagle's body painted over a gilded background decorated the cover. The crest split in half to a royal blue background upon which sat three golden fleur de lis, each with a large sapphire sparkling in the middle. She swallowed. While seeing objects worth more than she cared to imagine was a daily occurrence, it still made her a bit nervous. The corners were embellished with gilt fleur de lis metalwork. She gently flipped the book open to one of the thick pages, beautiful Old World scroll across the well-preserved skin in breathtaking inks of blue, red, yellow, and black. Goosebumps pebbled her arm as she stared at the text before her.

Barry let out a low whistle from where he now stood next to her, drawn in by the ancient wonder of this artifact. She jumped, snapping the book shut and winced. Maybe Dr. Beechum shouldn't allow them access to this stuff.

"Where do you think it came from?" he whispered, as if merely speaking too loud would disperse the illusion of what they beheld.

"No idea," she whispered back, examining the details of the cover once more. "There was no return address or note. Look at what it was wrapped in too. All this material alone probably costs more than my paycheck." She peered back into the box, searching for any clues to its origin. "Who would send such a beautiful book without at least information on how to return it?" Someone had to want this back; it was worth well into seven-figures. That thought alone choked her as she became hyper- aware of the true weight of the book in her hands. Her eyes scanned her desk, hands now desperate for a place to set it down.

"Maybe its haunted," Barry said matter of fact, shrugging his shoulders and walking back to his own desk.

She rolled her eyes at him. For all the ancient texts and artifacts they dealt with on a daily basis, she had never encountered anything that made her look over her shoulder. Though that didn't stop her from wearing the small golden cross around her neck, a gift from her grandparents.

"*Straight from the hands of il papa al vaticano,*" her nonno would announce in his thick Italian accent to anyone, whether they asked about it or not.

The gentle weight of the charm on her chest put a smile on her face as she opened the book back up, being gentler than before. The language looked to be old. Like medieval times old with its ornate letters and tight spacing. And she couldn't decipher a lick of it. Being trilingual had been born out of necessity, first as translator for her grandparents. They knew some English but not enough to understand contracts and legal documents. Then when she came to university, she learned French. A great deal of St. Louis history was also French history. It wasn't her strongest language but she could get by. But this text before her? It might as well be from a different planet entirely.

Setting the open book back in its nest of fine fabric and wool, she grabbed her phone out of her bag and snapped a few pictures before fishing out a plastic protective sleeve from her desk to slip over the tome. As she walked over to unlock the antique black safe in the back corner of the room, she said to Barry, "I think I'm going to go ask Dr. Beechum about this."

"Oooh, good luck on that solo adventure. I send my thoughts and prayers," he sniped from his desk. Spinning in his chair, he became suddenly enthralled in his work.

The old professor sat as director of their college and as such, oversaw the archive of curios and important research volumes that came in. He also happened to be the least amiable person on campus. One semester at the department holiday party, someone slipped him a weed brownie and no one had been able to tell a difference. If anything, it had made him even worse to be around as he droned on and on about the merits and shortcomings of the Dewey Decimal System. Unfortunately for everyone, he happened to also be quite knowledgeable.

"If any more mysterious packages show up while I'm gone," she grunted, hauling the safe door shut with a loud clank, spinning the giant brass wheel lock shut, "try to get some semblance of information from them, okay?"

Barry waved a hand in the air and said, "Yeah, yeah, ask more questions, don't accept scary demon packages without a notarized letter of acceptance. Got it."

CHAPTER TWO
Izzy

Climbing the stairs to the archives top floor library tested her wills, especially after the grueling workout she endured earlier that morning.

She stopped on the gray concrete landing before the double door entrance to the archives, taking a moment to catch her breath as the lactic acid started to set in her leg muscles. Maybe this daily climb was what made Dr. Beechum an ornery man. The image of the old codger gasping for air every morning put a smirk on her face as she pulled open the heavy wooden door, welcoming the dry, cool air of the library. Kept at a crisp sixty-five degrees year-round with humidity no more than thirty percent, this room offered a popular escape in the summer months and became deserted in the winter. The in-between months like this scorched of an October were a daily toss-up. Luckily for her, the space seemed relatively empty. The welcoming cool temps did little to offset the prickly company though.

She quietly made her way over to the large circular desk

in the middle of the room, taking in the architectural details of the stained-glass windows and domed ceiling with its intricate details carved into the dark mahogany wood. The magic of this library was never lost on Izzy, even if it required confronting the crotchety vibes from its inhabitants, like the elder woman before her. Even while sitting, the librarian peered down her nose at Izzy with a face that looked like it had never seen amusement. How did she do that?

Izzy cleared her throat, "Is Dr. Beechum available?"

"Do you have an appointment?" the woman sniveled, eyes still peering down her nose, her croaking voice sending chills down Izzy's spine.

"Well, no, but I received an interesting book in the mail and wanted to ask his thoughts on it."

"Has it been cataloged properly, Ms. Ciampi?" A bored yet demanding voice called from the back of the room, behind the lines of shelves around the vast space.

The woman at the desk rolled her eyes and waved a hand in the direction of the voice, her annoyance at Dr. Beechum's interjection a noted new layer to the dynamic up here. Izzy jumped on the invitation before it could be revoked and stalked in the direction of that question.

"I, uh, just received it this morning and... have not gotten around to cataloging it yet, Professor," she called out in the abyss, a touch too loud, as she weaved her way through the overcrowded bookshelves. She cringed.

A heavy, disapproving sigh sounded off to her left. This was becoming the worst game of Marco Polo, but she followed the weight of displeasure clinging in the air. As she rounded another tall bookshelf, she had a near collision with the broad, muscled chest of a man that very much did not belong to Dr. Beechum.

The surprise on her face mirrored in his golden hazel eyes as she looked up. Pink began creeping up her neck and she looked away with a roll of her eyes. Figures. All these private school assholes came from old money where proper bloodlines mattered to more than just horses and hounds. Pretty boys were banal around here. She needed to get a grip.

The man reached a hand up as if to catch her then let it drop. "I'm so sorry," he said in a thick southern accent she couldn't place. Her brows rose. That was new. Most of the southern prep school asshats would never stoop so low as to come to this city. He quickly stepped to the side and motioned for her to continue on to where Dr. Beechum sat at a table behind him.

"Ms. Ciampi, you know the protocols and those protocols are in place for a reason and that reason is, of course, to track and protect the longevity of these priceless items we deal with in our most fortunate roles to do so as esteemed academics," Dr. Beechum sneered, looking up at her over his glasses. God, was that also a protocol for this library? Stare at all research fellows with unfiltered disapproval until they ran away? They were absolutely killing it in that regard, if so.

She glanced sideways at the man she bumped into as he stood off in the shadows of the shelves next to the table. Was that a... smirk? Tossing a glare at his stupid handsome face, she said to Dr. Beechum in the sweetest voice she could muster, "I agree with you wholeheartedly, and in order to accurately catalog this item, I need your expertise to help me with, um, identifying what it might actually be."

Dr. Beechum's stare narrowed on her, his lips folding into a thin line of displeasure at her faltering constitution. If there was anything the man despised more than scatterbrained women in his library, she hadn't learned what it was yet, but she was certain to catalog that right to her fucking brain the moment she did. She swallowed the mix of anger and fear that bubbled up, stepping forward to fish her phone out of her back pocket. Pulling up the photos she took in the lab, she handed her phone over to Dr. Beechum. A moment of panic coursed through her veins as she rooted through her memory to make sure he couldn't happen upon any photos that might categorically put her in his bad graces forever. Fuck, or what if they put her in his good graces? She started to pull the phone back toward her but the old man snatched it from her hand and held it within range of his bifocals. The smirking idiot in the shadows strolled over to Dr. Beechum's shoulder to look at the photos as well, like they were just the best of friends gathering around to shoot the shit. She narrowed her focus on his face, studying it while he looked at the pictures on her phone. His hair was an unruly set of dark waves that his hand glided through, the sienna tone of his skin warming the intimidating features of his face. His eyes widened a fraction as he took in the images, but then his expression vanished to boredom as he shot a quick glance up at Izzy before stepping back from the professor.

Dr. Beechum's brows furrowed. "Hmm… where did you say you received this artifact from?"

"I didn't. Can you tell what language that is?" Deflecting the question seemed a better tactic than admitting a potential error in her record keeping, such as the complete and utter lack of one.

"Hmm, hard to tell with the lettering…" And then to her absolute shock, he passed the phone to the man next to him. The ocher of his eyes flashed to her, his expression still unreadable, before he zoomed in to the text on the phone and studied it closely.

"It looks to be… an attempt at Old English." His thick brows bunched together as he scrolled down the picture but his accent… was that Creole?

He looked up again and met her inquisitorial stare, tilting his head to the side with a questioning smirk. God, he was hot. Where did Dr. Beechum find him? And, fuck, since when did the professor defer to someone else on a historical matter? On any matter? What the fuck was happening? She scanned the ivory walls, searching for confirmation she was in the archive's library and not an alternate universe.

Dr. Beechum took the phone back in his hands and passed it across the table to Izzy. She quickly pocketed the thing before the photo could spontaneously switch to one of her more nefarious ones instead.

"Looks to be a school notebook or journal of sorts. Fairly well made and must have belonged to someone well known by the adornments. Be sure to get that cataloged well, immediately Ms. Ciampi, as I'm sure it's quite missed from wherever it came from." He glared at her with a sneer and turned around, back to whatever task she had rudely interrupted by her sheer presence.

The southern beefcake next to him—his new assistant? Fellow comrade in the hatred of women in universities? Companion in the boredom induced by the dull existence of knowing everything in a world of idiots?—rubbed a hand over the back of his neck, the muscles of his bicep pulling on the sleeve of his black t-shirt and gave her another one of those little smirks that suddenly grated on her nerves. Like he was in on a joke with Dr. Beechum. Like he and Dr. Beechum joked. *Like Dr. Beechum joked.* Ugh.

Hot, he may be, but who the fuck did he think he was? She glared at him one more time for good measure before turning on her heel and heading to the exit. Pushing open the heavy doors, she stopped on the landing to pull those photos back up to examine them again herself. A school notebook. A fancy, fucking school notebook. Probably belonged to a medieval prepshit. "Same shit, different century," alright. Who would have sent her a bedazzled, middle age school notebook without a return address, wrapped like it was the Queen of England's crown?

"You should be careful who you show those photos to, you know," a southern drawl said from behind her. His voice was quiet yet she nearly jumped down the stairs at the sound of it.

"Is that supposed to be some sort of weird threat?" she snapped back, pushing her phone into her pocket as she turned around to face him. He stood a few inches taller than her five-foot eight stature and looked like he was no foreigner around gym equipment. And those golden eyes. They pierced through the clouded look on his face. A look almost like... concern?

"No. Not from me at least but—"

Her gaze withered on him, "That definitely sounds like a threat."

"It's not, I promise." He raised his broad hands in surrender. That accent almost had her believing him. God, she needed to get a grip.

"I'll keep your *warning* in mind," she derided as she moved to start the relentless descent to her basement lab where she would promptly inform Barry that Mercury must be in retrograde because shit had just gotten real weird around here.

The shuffle of shoes on the concrete landing and the soft click of the heavy wooden doors closing at least meant she could brood down the stairs in peace.

❖

"And then!" She paced across their crowded laboratory,

regaling her experience to Barry, who sat drinking the tea for all it was worth. "He handed my phone to that, that, smug little pretty boy!"

Barry's brown eyes perked up. "Oh? Pretty boy? How pretty are we talking?"

Her blood simmered, ready to boil over from all her pent-up frustration over the continued misogyny of working in academia and here was Barry, calculating out his next conquest. She huffed out a sound that bordered on a scream before snatching her bag and water bottle off her desk.

Barry whirled around and said, "Hey, wait. Where are you going?"

The building reeked of male entitlement and she needed to get away. She needed space to breathe. To think. Even the thought of staring at some ancient rich kid's diary set her blood pressure into overdrive.

"Out." Preferably far from McMillan Hall. More like McMan Hall. A smirk toyed on the edges of her lips at her own joke. Fuck, this place made her feel senile and she was only twenty-six.

"Okay, are you going to be around for the staff meeting later?"

Each month, the faculty and staff met for a special luncheon. The food represented a patronizing bribe, otherwise none of the faculty and staff within the anthropology and history departments would come listen to Dr. Beechum's dictations on standard operating procedures. Being a historian himself, his speeches were often riddled with back-handed comments to the anthropology crew. His favorite referred to them as a lower subclass of history, like cavemen before fire.

"Absolutely not," she answered over her shoulder as

she made her way to the door. Some days, she questioned why she stayed in this city. Her real family left her years ago with the death of both her grandparents. The rest of her family were nothing more than tormenting memories best left forgotten. But the Ciampi family bloodline ended with her.

Pausing in the doorway, she turned back to her coworker and friend, "Make an excuse for me?" She had a pang of guilt for leaving him behind but she wouldn't be able to keep up her restraint when this new golden boy introduced himself. She needed to clear her mind.

The cogs started to turn in Barry's mind as she watched him begin curating a fantastical scenario for her absence. It was, after all, his specific brand of pastime entertainment. She couldn't wait to hear what he came up with later.

"Oh honey, will I ever," were his sultry parting words.

She smiled and exited the room. Maybe she no longer had a real family to lean on, but her new one wasn't so bad.

⚜

Hitting Throop Drive with a huff, Izzy made an immediate left, heading straight for the University City blue bus station a short walk away. Public transit had never been the city's strong suit but in recent years, it had been one of the few local services to step its game up to provide safe transport for the residents of the metropolitan area. A small blessing in this ruined new world.

As she sunk down into the hard bench, the bus lurching forward down the road, she couldn't shake the interaction she endured in the library. Since when did the know-it-all Dr. Beechum defer to the knowledge of another, let alone someone younger than him? She could've sworn she heard the old man refer to her generation as the "absolute swine of this earth" which felt extra icy all things considered. And who was that guy? He had been on campus all of three seconds and Dr. Beechum treated him better than his tenured staff. How much money had his family donated? The internal stewing coursing through her as the bus lumbered along the rough roads must have started to creep onto her outward expression. An older woman with a pink scarf over her hair a couple rows ahead gave a look of reproval.

Righting her face, she shifted to peer out the window, taking in the city as they drove past the opulent homes along Forest Park. How many of the residents within sold their soul for forever? As a kid, her grandparents got their money's worth from the free zoo and art museum within the park - keeping her curious mind busy from the fact that most of the other kids were there with their parents, their actual, younger parents. Izzy had never thought of her grandparents as anything less than but it didn't stop others in her grade from commenting.

"Junkie Junk"—the nickname kids from more affluent families coined for her. Those from the lower income homes only peered at her with sympathy. The obvious lack of interest in hanging out with her sent the message home though: nobody wants to play with the kid whose parents overdosed on opioids. Or that's the story her grandparents shared anyway. While cleaning out their home, she had come across the police report. Photos of their bodies, mangled in a heap behind a dumpster outside a seedy dive bar, throats practically torn out, heads hanging at unnatural angles, seared into her brain. It was an image she tried to erase every night before she closed her eyes.

The fact she ended up in academia came as no surprise after the ostracizing treatment from her peers. Escaping the torment of society and interpersonal communication through books about old worlds and the men who ruled them offered peace in an otherwise ruthless world. And it had always been men ruling. Despite Barry's research on human sexuality that suggested women historically held the most power within societies—usually in their hands, and usually around the balls of those powerful men—men still let their voices be the loudest in the room. And women allowed them to do so. Izzy let out a heavy sigh.

The bus skirted around the lush green park and jolted to a stop in front of a giant hospital. Her heart rate increased. While most immortals kept out of the daylight due to their increased photosensitivity, that didn't mean they were entirely nocturnal. A recent news article suggested one in every five doctors in the city were vampires. No further details had been released on which doctors and what hospitals to avoid though as the journalist who authored the story went missing three days after it published. Izzy leered at the passengers getting on, mostly weary looking people in scrubs. When the bus launched forward again and no one got up to start ripping into people's necks, she let out a breath.

The driver made quick work of getting to The Hill, the Italian neighborhood on the other side of the interstate and the place she had grown up calling home. Stopping at Shaw Avenue, she shuffled off and onto the familiar streets of her youth. The years hadn't been kind to the neighborhood as many of its older inhabitants had either died off, moved out, or worse. As she walked toward her favorite deli on Macklind Avenue, she took in how times had changed. It had been over seven years since she visited this neighborhood.

A chef stood outside a restaurant, smoking a cigarette while a delivery truck driver unloaded boxes. Ashes flew precariously as the man spoke to the driver in quick Italian. Izzy started to smile when the chef tossed his head back in laughter and she saw the two red puncture marks on his neck. She averted her eyes and quickened her step. A city built on hustle and grind meant the blood business boomed, offering a fast cash option for anyone willing to be drained of a pint or so of blood. If the facility monitors were doing their job, that is. Making a "donation" came with known risks, and everyone knew it could result in death. The contract donors signed clearly spelled out that detail. They didn't care.

Gioia's Deli with its green awning loomed ahead and she had never been more grateful to see a restaurant before in her life. At least this place hadn't changed.

❖

As she took her order outside to sit at a picnic table looking across the street to Berra Park, she thought back to the book sitting comfortably in her safe back at the lab. The lab she had run away from, leaving Barry to clean up the mess of her absence all because she couldn't handle some adversity. She let out a heavy sigh.

She had walked into that library knowing what to expect from Dr. Beechum and his evil counterpart but that guy? He had thrown her off. For so long, she worked hard for Beechum's respect. Wanted nothing more than for him to talk to her like the intelligent human being she knew she was and not like a waste of university dollars. Hell, at least her research provided some benefit in the grand scheme, as she studied human responses after traumatic events. Like the very one they were living in. For three years, she played by his rules, remained nice and civil in his horrendous presence, took the insults with a smile on her face. For three years, and yet he still addressed her as Isadora in his emails. Her email address was her name.

But this guy just walked in off the southern streets and the professor defers to him? She took an aggressive bite out of her sandwich, her cooled blood temperature rising again. She should have stayed. If anything, to learn his fucking name so she could spell it wrong in an email. He probably had some pretentious one like Prescott or Bennett.

Smiling a little, she glanced across to the park as a couple kids ran out with a bat and ball, men that looked to be about their parents' age following behind, talking. It brought her back to the many afternoons she had spent on that field with her *nonno*.

"Keep the ball in front of you, bambino." His strong Italian accent added vowels where they didn't exist and left consonants lost to the wind.

Her grandparents had been her everything and they had looked to her like the sun rose and fell only for her. In their minds, she never did anything wrong. Even when she snuck out after dark in high school to see a lunar eclipse, her grandmother had simply said, *"Al cuore non si comanda, we can deny it no more than we can deny our lungs breath."*

The heart can't be tamed. Unless, of course, it was broken. Thankfully, her *nonna* hadn't lived long enough to see that happen to Izzy.

The death of her grandparents had been expected, they had both lived long, beautiful lives, but that didn't lessen the shock of it for Izzy when that fateful day came. The moment she stepped into the empty row home on Daggett Avenue, the weight of their loss came crashing down on her and she sank to the floor, weeping and alone. Alone. So alone.

She had only been eighteen, when she inherited their entire lives: the old print studio in the back of the property, her *nonno*'s Alfa Romeo she had parked in the basement garage of her apartment building, and the house... the home that had shone with the light of her *nonna*'s laughter, the smell of *sugo* simmering away on the stove, and the melodic sound of The Rat Pack playing from her *nonno*'s old record player.

"Nonno, they have all this music online now, we can get you a better player," she pleaded to him one evening.

"Tsk, mia bella, there is no better than this bellisimo machine." He sang the words as he held the player between his hands on the buffet it sat, a gleam of pride and affection for the old sound machine. It was one of the few items they brought with them when they had immigrated in their early twenties, seeking that American dream.

In the end, Izzy supposed they found it. They had the home, the family, the community—even if it hadn't always been a romanticized version of a dream, it had been a full, happy life. Even when immortalization entered the world two decades prior, when Izzy as a small child moved in with them. Sold as a cure for those hopeless romantics, to "Spend eternity with your soul mate".

That's what the advertisements said. A hefty price tag and damning consequences didn't deter many though. The world's power players devolved into bloodthirsty billionaires while the rest of humanity clawed for an existence in the rapidly regressing political hellscape. In a way, Izzy found gratitude in the fact her grandparents barely had to see St. Louis succumb to the inevitable immortal downfall.

"Time running out is a gift, mia zazzera," her grandfather had mused to her one evening when she asked if they would ever consider the cure. A hypothetical everyone toyed with at family dinner.

He tugged on one of her curls and smiled a warm, comforting smile. *"It reminds you to live."*

She tore her gaze from the park, tears pricking the

edges of her eyes. Her time on The Hill had run out. Her life here ended years ago, standing in the hollow pit that had once been a home. She needed to face her demons, not run from them. She stood from the picnic bench and began her trek back to the bus station, taking a detour to avoid walking past the restaurant with the smoking chef again.

❖

CHAPTER THREE
Izzy

The condensation from her glass had long since created a small pool atop Lando's immaculate, giant live edge oak table and frankly, she did not care.

Lando Denalo, former Italian heavyweight champion, brutal personal trainer, and current mob boss for the once renowned *Campi di Fragole*—the Strawberry Fields. The old man could be heard singing…

> *Niente è reale*
>
> *E non c'è niente di cui preoccuparsi*
>
> *Campi di fragole per sempre*

Usually from behind his closed office door with a chorus of mechanical buzzing mingled with screams of terror. Izzy tried not to be within earshot when that happened.

Even if the crew fell out of glory two decades prior, nobody would dare laugh in the face of the main man. His crew had once kept St. Louis in check, filling in the holes where the local government and police force did little to nothing for the community, like preventing actual crime and keeping the real bad guys off the streets. But when the world fell into chaos, Lando's one weakness set the organization on a downward spiral: his fear of death. Laughable for a man who had taken the lives of others for decades. However, the thought of being drained of all his life force by a savage, bloodthirsty immortal had him shuttering the doors to his upscale gym on The Hill and reinforcing the protections around this warehouse turned luxury apartment building he owned near campus. He moved into the penthouse and never left. The small band of soldiers he led now, a meager shadow of the hundreds he once ruled over, kept him informed with the dealings of the city and provided uncompromising protection to the residents in the building. Residents that were mostly his own crew, along with some older generations from The Hill, and Izzy.

"Of course, the first person to garner any respect from Beechum is a fucking man," she grumbled to the table of…well, men. Their typical Friday night routine consisted of Lando's business recaps from Charlie and Vahagn, his second and third respectively. Izzy usually found a reason to be late so she didn't have to hear any of the gruesome details. Instead, she waltzed in an hour after the official start time to provide them a necessary dose of reality outside the guise of organized crime. Occasionally, they were joined by Lando's daughter, Gio, a guest appearance by Barry, or some of his other city gremlins. But without a doubt, it was always Izzy, Lando, Vahagn, and Charlie.

It was part of the reason why she got tangled up with Charlie Valentini in the first place. A mistake made after too much whiskey. But then that mistake became routine until she couldn't get him out of her thoughts and he became consumed with his possession of her. She glared down the table at the offending man, oblivious to her thoughts weaving her current disdain for him, before she turned to Vahagn sitting across from her.

"Are you sure that's the reason Beechum never warmed to you and not because of your sparkly personality, Z?" Vahagn flashed her a mocking smile under his gruff beard. Vahagn Krog looked like he walked straight out of Norsemen lore with his shaggy, pale blonde hair that fell to his broad shoulders. He had the kindest heart of any person she had ever met but hidden behind a strong jawline, intimidating brow, and that ridiculous facial hair. He was also the only one who dared call her Z, the nickname her grandfather gave her when she was three.

"*Isabella, mia zazzera,*" he would say as he roughed up the mess of tight dark red curls. She would burst into a fit of giggles. The nickname stuck, evolving to a simple Z when she became a teenager and no longer wanted to be referred to as a mop, no matter how endearing it sounded in Italian.

Throwing a sweet smile at Vahagn, she said, "I don't see what you find wrong with my personality, V."

Charlie snorted at the end of the table. A flash of fury passed over Vahagn's face before he swallowed it and said, "Lando, would you consider your first encounter with Ms. Ciampi to be… genial?"

Lando smirked. "Not in the slightest, and that's what made it all the more captivating." His deep brown eyes sparkled as he rose his half full glass to Izzy before taking a sip of the amber liquid within.

She smiled, thinking back to that day.

Charlie, being Lando's right hand for the past ten years, had told her the story of the "golden years" when Lando's crew had kept some of the smaller, crueler gangs at bay while he reigned supreme over the city. When he finally pulled the last of his men out, there had been riotous aftershocks around the metro-area. It all sent Lando into such a rage, he nearly set his penthouse, and the whole building, on fire.

Coincidentally, that happened to be the same day Izzy met him. His masculine temper tantrum had disrupted her peaceful night of research in her much smaller studio apartment a floor below. She had marched her not-so-happy ass up the stairs to his guarded front door, right past Charlie and Vahagn. They had both been so used to not a soul daring to approach, they simply watched her walk by as she hauled her fist against the rather heavy doors to the penthouse. Her anger blinded her to the men's presence looming toward her, arms outstretched to grab her when those giant doors opened and a rush of smoky air mixed with the scent of whiskey wafted out.

"Who the fuck are you?" Lando had shouted at her in his throaty Italian accent.

"Who the fuck are you?" she had shot back, watching as the glare on his face quickly shifted to shock.

"Boss, I'm sorry. We didn't—" Charlie started in before Lando raised a hand and stepped aside as an unspoken invite for her to come in.

Startled by the fact she suddenly had two rather large men flanking her sides, hands still within inches of her arms, she walked forward and turned to look them both in the face. The remnants of surprise stared back at her, though Charlie's expression shifted as his eyes made a pass over her body and back to her face, smirking like a frat boy at a bar. She scowled in response and offered a middle finger to both for good measure.

Lando retold that story to every single sparring partner she had since that day. Turned out, she had arrived at Lando's at the perfect time. Having polished off half a decanter of whiskey, he had shattered the fucking thing into his ridiculous cast iron fireplace hanging from his vaulted ceilings, right in the middle of the room. This devolved into a crazy notion to start chucking nearly everything within reach into the goddamn fire. He had been coming out the door to request more whiskey and some lighter fluid when he found her standing in his doorway instead.

"I've never heard such a dirty word come from such a sweet face," he had said to her later that night, after Charlie left to fulfill the request for more whiskey, thankfully *sans* lighter fluid. He indulged her rage-filled tangent about his lack of respect for the other tenants of this building, his utter stupidity for tossing God only knew what into his fireplace, and his cowardice for having such a ridiculously huge door.

"Where does someone even find a medieval furniture shop these days, anyway?" she had screamed at him.

Rage morphed into amusement on the rugged man's face as she finished, catching her breath while he said simply, "Would you like some pasta?"

And how the fuck was she supposed to say no to pasta? So, there she found herself, in the penthouse of a notorious mobster, eating his delicious lamb ragú while he grilled her about her work and general life outside the building. Charlie and Vahagn had joined them at the table, occasionally asking their own questions. They finished the night with amber whiskey in their glasses and poker on the table, where she robbed them all of over a thousand dollars.

Then Lando had said, his voice brutish, "So, what does your research say about warriors?"

As an anthropologist, people often asked her about all sorts of questions—usually in an attempt to gauge how they would have fared in the brutal past.

"It says no matter what happens, there will always be a

bunch of violent pigs around," she quipped back at him, taking another sip of her whiskey.

Charlie had chuckled to himself as Lando smiled at her in that way he only did when he was proud of someone, she would come to learn.

"Let me train you," Lando said. A demand rather than an ask.

"Sure," she drawled back to him, taking another sip and letting out a half giggle.

One of his eyebrows shot up and he clicked to Vahagn. The Viking man smoothly took the glass out of her hand on its journey to her lips. When she gawked at him, mouth partly open, he shrugged and mouthed the word "sorry" to her.

Her attention snapped back to Lando as he said, "Great, let's start tomorrow."

He then looked to Charlie and next thing she knew her chair was being pulled back as Lando's second in command went to reach down and pick her up. She slapped his strong arms away. When he didn't even flinch, she doubled down and elbowed him in the chest. This yielded a grunt and he stepped back, granting her the opportunity to stand up on her own volition.

Mistake, she had thought before the sight of the floor quickly approached.

"Oh shit." Charlie's words sounded muffled in her mind. Her descent stopped as tan muscled arms wrapped around her.

"I'll take it from here." She heard Lando say. The last thing she saw was Charlie rubbing his big, stupid chest, a look of concern across his face as he ran a hand through his hair.

The next morning, it had been Charlie knocking gently on her front door at precisely five o'clock.

"Boss says it's time to train." His tone flattened as she blinked up at his face.

Tall, tan with the broody black hair and matching scar through his eyebrow that women wrote books about, all above the bluest eyes she had ever seen. This was a man who broke hearts.

Six years later, she sat there at that same table, next to the city's most dangerous mob boss, drinking his expensive bourbon, and watching his lackeys roll a joint of the finest California weed.

This certainly was not the life her grandparents planned for her, but life for the past two decades never followed anyone's plans.

The immortals had trickled their way up the big Mississippi River from the hell hole that was now New Orleans, taking over various cities along the way. However, they met significant resistance in St. Louis.

A damned city, per Lando's judgment, where no one willingly came to stay but rather, they found themselves trapped within. The Society, as the immortal group went by, currently had a small gathering of members spread throughout the greater metro area. But between the city's gangs and the general haughty nature of the average St. Louisan, a full overtaking never happened.

The citizens still experienced their fair share of attacks and immortal zealots though, making a curfew more than necessary, and kept Lando's small crew in business. But it hardly inconvenienced a city that only the strong survived in, even before there were vampires to contend with.

Sliding his tongue along the seam of the hemp paper and gently pressing it down, Vahagn finished rolling the joint and got the smoky ember started before passing it to Charlie, who had moved to the seat at his left.

"You could try being a little nicer to be around, you know." Vahagn winked at her, leaning forward and setting his elbows on the oak table, preparing for the battle he incited. Another round of his favorite smoke session entertainment.

Izzy shot daggers into his warm brown eyes, twinkling with ardor, and quipped, "You have been sleeping on my couch the past two nights because we've been up until like three a.m. playing Grand Theft Auto. Tell me again how much you hate being around me." She batted at his arm as he reached across the table to tug on one of her braids and smiled.

Vahagn became the brother she never had and as such, they spent the last six years catching up on the childhood she never really got, complete with late nights staying up to play mind-numbing video games, laughing until they nearly pissed their pants, and binging on whatever junk food they could find. The supply chains had dwindled over the years as lower paid workers found better pay as private living blood bags for the rich and powerful, so options for said junk food had become limited. Being a strong arm of the most infamous boss in the most dangerous city had its unconventional perks though. Tears were shed the other night when Vahagn dropped a pack of Oreos in her lap. Double stuffed. Her favorite.

"So that's where you abandoned me to last night," Charlie spoke at last to Vahagn as he tried to nonchalantly pass the joint to Izzy. She took it from his grip and tried not to recoil too visibly when their fingers touched.

"Yeah, Izzy and I have been trying a new way to play the game."

Izzy happened to be inhaling as she envisioned their new 'tactic' and snorted into a relentless cough-laugh fit. Passing the joint to Lando in mild panic, she took a healthy gulp of her bourbon—which offered minimal reprieve—and her voice croaked as she started to explain.

"If by 'new way', you mean we drive around, following traffic laws, and soliciting prostitutes respectfully rather than punching their lights out and robbing them, then yeah. We were killing it."

Lando chuckled as Vahagn shook his head, no doubt remembering how she had also rear-ended him in the game because she became preoccupied timing to perfection how long to dunk her Oreo in the re-hydrated dry milk she had fished out of her pantry to achieve ultimate flavor ecstasy.

"Well, you missed a great time at Gio's. Those twins from South County were staying with her. I was kinda glad for the empty apartment when we got back actually," Charlie said to Vahagn but didn't take his electric blue eyes off Izzy the entire time, rubbing his chin with a grin that made her feel violent.

What a fucking tool, she thought while giving him a look of pure indifference. She added some more bourbon into her glass, trying to remember if she had finished off that container of Oreos last night or not.

Vahagn whistled, "Phew—those twins are hot as hell. Did you know they used to dance for the ballet company? Wait… did you say we? You took them both home?"

Charlie's smile widened, eyes still on Izzy waiting for a reaction that never came, before winking at Vahagn.

Lando snapped his fingers from the head of the table. "Enough of the doghouse talk. We've supposed to be helping *mia bambina*, Isabella, gain the respect and appreciation of the old crotch at the university."

Both of the men parted from their shared fantasy of gorgeous women with insane flexibility and turned to their boss.

Lando's ability to command always impressed her, especially with block head, alpha men like Charlie and Vahagn.

"Well, did you talk to this wonder kid who holds Beechum's reverence?" Vahagn spoke as smoke poured out his mouth. The vision embodied one his many "quintessential gangster" looks she often mocked him about.

She thought back to those golden eyes, toned arms, silky dark auburn hair she could imagine running her fingers through… and then remembered his weird "not" threat.

"Sort of. He seemed to think whatever this weird package is, I should keep it secret. He's also hardly a kid. Might even be able to hand you your own poetic ass for breakfast." What kind of a word was reverence?

"Ah, and what a meal it would make," Vahagn purred as he leaned back, tilting his head up and closing his eyes. Charlie snorted.

"What was this mystery package anyway?" Charlie asked before taking a quick drag on the joint between his fingers. He passed it over to her.

Deep down, something told her she should probably heed the pretty boy assistant's warning, but between the bourbon and the weed coursing through her system at the moment, she couldn't actually remember why she wouldn't fully trust the group of men in front of her. They were basically family to her. Sure, a family of criminals. But a family. Sucking in another drag, she pulled out her phone and once the photos were glowing on the screen, slid it across the table to Charlie. He picked it up and squinted at the photo while she studied his face.

It would always be unequivocally unfortunate how goddamn attractive Charlie looked in that traditionally Italian way. The way that had made online dating apps lots of money back in the days before they became vamp blood orgy networks. It would make hating him much easier if she could just forget the way her hands felt sliding through those soft black strands with ease or the heat that radiated off his sculpted chest and stomach as her hands traveled down them to his—

The predatory gaze that met her own as he passed her phone back made her concerned he could read her thoughts. Her core heated as his fingers brushed her hand, his thumb casually grazing the back of her knuckles. But then that devilish smirk appeared on his face and she felt a phantom pain from the bruise that had marked her for weeks that summer. All fantasies froze over.

Vahagn conveniently woke from his stupor to say, "Wait, so what was in this package? Anything interesting like that package of old school condoms you got one time?"

She rolled her eyes at him and let out a breath, "That package was Barry's and it came from the Smithsonian, I'll have you know."

She passed her phone to him, the photos pulled back up, as she explained the odd conditions by which she received the book.

"What language is that?" Vahagn asked.

"Beechum's lackey said Old English, like medieval times old."

Vahagn put his fists on his hips. "Ah, the language of my ancestors."

Lando rolled his eyes as he grabbed the phone out of Vahagn's hands.

A slight panic rose in Izzy's chest as Lando looked at the photos on her phone, but then the heavy, comforting blanket of her high pushed it to the back of her mind.

"What kind of research are you doing that involves Old English novels?" Lando asked, his deep gaze inspecting the image on the small screen.

She held her hand out for her phone, momentarily gaining some clarity that screamed at her to go back to her apartment...*now*, but she hid the sudden wave of panic with a shrug.

"Honestly, I have been researching women's roles in and after World War I so this applies to none of that. I'm wondering if it wasn't a donation that just got misdirected to me?" She kept her voice cool, even. At least she thought she did. Fuck, she really needed to leave.

"But wasn't it addressed to you?" Charlie still had that heated look in his eyes when she looked to him.

How did he know that?

Oh right, she fucking told him. Didn't she?

Fuck, she needed to go.

Looking at her phone, her eyes widened dramatically, she said, "Holy shit, I have to go. Can we push tomorrow's workout to six, Lando?"

"Absolutely not, Isabella. Five, sharp, every day, *giornaliero*," he answered, looking bored again.

Flipping her middle finger to him, she stood and started toward his ridiculously ornate Gothic door.

"Night, fuckers," she called to them without turning around.

"Night, slut," Vahagn called from his resumed napping spot, hands in his pocket and a grin on his face. At least she would be able to get to sleep before midnight tonight, even with only a few minutes to spare.

CHAPTER FOUR
Izzy

Another numbing wave hit her as she descended the marble stairs to the floor below Lando's penthouse. She had to check her hand six—*it was six, right?*—times to ensure she did, in fact, have her front door key pulled out so as not to disturb any of her neighbors by clinking through the assortment on the ring.

Thoroughly distracted in a mind loop that had her checking her keyed hand every five seconds as she swayed down the hallway, she didn't catch sight of the figure at her front door until she was a few feet away.

"What do you want, Charlie." She really didn't want a response so it wasn't a question. Her instincts flashed through the haze of her high enough to tell her to just open her door and promptly smash it in his face.

"I just want to talk, Z." She rolled her eyes and shot him a glare.

"It's just Izzy to you now. You lost special nickname privileges months ago." Asshole. She watched him cringe.

"Please, Izzy. Just talk to me. That's all I want."

"Is that how you got those ballet twins to come home with you last night? So you could just talk with them?" She eyed the door behind him.

He ran a hand through his black hair then stepped aside to let her start working through the multiple locks on her front door.

"It wasn't like that. It meant nothing."

She let out a hollow laugh, ignoring her earlier attempts to be quiet. No way this man could be serious? "What every girl wants to hear. Such a fucking charmer, Charlie." She finally unlocked the last bolt before turning around to face him, one hand on the handle behind her.

Agony clearly weighed on him and it gave her a sick sense of satisfaction to see it manifest on his beautiful face.

She squinted at him for several heartbeats before she sighed.

She was an actual idiot.

"Fine. We're just talking… but I don't think there is anything you can say in the three languages I know that will change my mind or erase what happened between us."

He flashed one of those smiles that used to stop her ability to think. Fuck, it still did.

"I can at least try, right?" And try he could because he fluent in all those languages. Hell, and then some more.

Rolling her eyes, she turned the handle and stepped backward into her apartment, giving him space to follow her in. Closing the door involved a methodical latching of her elaborate lock system, and enough time to reconsider what she was doing with Charlie Valentini in her apartment.

Before she could even turn back to tell him to leave

though, he started on his plea, pacing slowly in the small dining area behind her couch as he spoke. His azure gaze clouded, as if searching for his words.

"Izzy, you know I'm beyond sorry for what happened. It has been gnawing at me since that day. Every time I look at you, it feels like the knife in my heart gets twisted again and again." He paused, running a broad hand down his face. "Fuck, this isn't coming out right."

He stopped his pacing and turned to her, taking a tentative step in her direction. She took one back, putting a crestfallen look on his face.

"Izzy, I love you. I've been in love with you, from the moment you walked into my life. Please. Tell me what I can do to fix this." His hand outstretched to her and his breathing quickened, but all she saw was the memory of his face in a snarl as he raised a hand to her. She scowled at him.

"You love me? You love me, Charlie? Are you fucking serious?"

She might as well have slapped him with the look of shock that appeared on his face.

"Please, Izzy."

"No, Charlie. You don't hurt the people you love. You don't control their every move. You don't leave them emotionally and physically bruised! And then!" Now she paced, feeling her heart begin to race. How long had she wanted to say these words to him? Would she even remember this in the morning? "And then, after everything, you don't get to walk into their home and claim to love them when less than twenty-four hours ago you were tangled in the sheets with two other women! Do you even remember their names?"

Each word hit like a bullet to his chest and as she

watched them aim true, she couldn't find an ounce of sympathy.

Until he fell to his knees and started weeping into his hands.

Gods above, she was too fucking high for this.

"Charlie, I—" She what? How was she supposed to respond to a tatted-up gangster sobbing on her living room floor after he just professed his love for her? Kneeling before him, she pulled his hands from his face so she could cup his cheeks and look into those sorrow filled ocean eyes. He was truly heartbroken.

"I never deserved you." The confession came out on a rough whisper and she felt the deep frequency of those words reverberate through her hands and into her core.

What was she supposed to say to that? Had he ever deserved her? Had it ever been good? Or was it just convenient? It had always been hot and cold with him, and her heart felt made of glass, ready to break with each drastic temperature change.

"I don't know if that's true. But it doesn't matter anymore. This…thing between us ended months ago. I can't go back, Charlie." Back to his inconsistencies. Back to the emotional torture. Back to the fear of her oblivious missteps. She wasn't strong enough to take this loving, caring man one minute only for him to be screaming at her the next.

His fiery gaze heated through her as he growled, "Then how can you still look at me like you did upstairs? How can it be over if every time I look at you, even if you're glaring me to hell, my thoughts are drawn straight to you? To us? To what we had? To the way we used to be?"

He had a point. Their problem had never been a lack of attraction or passion, but more of what came after those embers died. The rubble of a smothered house fire always looked grimmer than the raging blaze.

Dropping her hold on his face, she stood up and offered a tentative hand to him. He took it but didn't release her grip once he stood before her.

"We can't go back, Charlie." Her plea came out half-hearted as he slowly pulled her to him, placing her hand over his heart, a steady beat against the chest she had been fantasizing about running her hand down an hour ago.

"I don't want to go back, Izzy. I want to be here. Now. With you." His gaze slid to her mouth as he tilted his head and slowly leaned in, giving her plenty of time to make a rational decision.

But rational decisions were damned when you stood in the strong, warm arms of Charlie Valentini. Especially after partaking in some of Lando's luxury vices.

She met him halfway and the moment their lips touched, fire erupted between them. One of his hands combed into her hair as the other became a firm grip on her waist. She pressed into his hard chest, nails digging into the soft fabric of his shirt. He groaned into her mouth as she slid a hand under the waistband of his pants, pulling him closer to her. She smiled into the sound.

"You've always been one to enjoy the torture," he said, pressing his brow to hers.

It was true. Nothing was hotter than bringing a big, burly man to his knees with mere touches and words.

Her gaze met the heat in his eyes, moonlight reflecting in the blue pools, and any thoughts of stopping evaporated. Idiotically, she wanted this. Wanted to remember what it felt like to be worshiped by a damn near God.

Pushing against his chest, his muscles tensed beneath her touch. He took the few steps backward to her bed, never taking his eyes off her as she followed. Stopping right at the edge, she stepped away from him, taking in the full view.

"Take off your shirt, Charlie Valentini." He held her stare as he obeyed the command.

His body displayed an enviable canvas, adorned in a mosaic of vines and flowers entwined with slithering serpents. The ink ran up his neck, across his chest and down his arms with two matching skulls on the back of his hands. She knew the design continued onto his back. She used to trace the indigo wolfsbane petals there under the moonlight as it shined in through her windows.

"Now your shoes," she commanded. He smirked. This was the game they always loved to play. He kicked off his leather boots.

"And your pants." A muscle in his jaw flexed as he continued to hold her gaze while he unbuckled his belt, pulling it through all the loops in one go. The sound of him unzipping his jeans filled the space between them. Denim shuffled as he pushed his pants to the floor. His eyes fluttered closed briefly when the fabric rubbed against his bulge. The temperature in the room rose the second they opened again. She glanced down, knowing why, but couldn't help the confirmation. God, he was more than ready.

"All your pants, Charlie," she purred. He bit his bottom lip, grinning as he hooked his thumbs under the elastic waistband of his boxers, working them down with a patience she didn't possess.

Then he stood before her, fully nude.

"Put me out of my misery, Izzy." His words filled with a plea to her as he gripped the base of his cock. A few silent seconds passed where she shamelessly gawked at him. He had no fucking right to be this hot.

Or maybe it was just the bourbon and weed. She knew

it wasn't but it did ease the guilt hanging over her head for what she was about to do.

Stepping forward, she pushed him into a seat on her bed then began her own slow torture of unbuttoning the oversized flannel she wore over her baggy sweatpants. Not the most attractive after work apparel choice, but she hadn't exactly foreseen this scenario unfolding when she slipped it on. Clearly, it wasn't as unappealing as she thought as her favorite muscle on his body twitched in his hand.

Once that final button released, she let the shirt drape over her bare breasts. She took her time pushing her sweatpants down, reminding herself she wanted this. It was totally natural to want this despite their convoluted history. Stepping out of her pants, she stood before him in nothing but a thong and her open shirt draped over her.

He swallowed. "You're fucking beautiful."

She looked down at herself. "Oh, this old thing." Looking at him from under her lashes, she threw him a cocky smirk. Because damn, she did look hot. She needed to remember this look.

Fuck! For what? What the fuck was she doing? This couldn't happen again. This shouldn't be happening again.

That mental weighted blanket doused her fleeting panicked thoughts as she boldly stepped in-between his bare legs.

His hands slid up the back of her thighs, pressing into the muscles, and sending a wave of goosebumps across her skin and up her spine.

He swallowed again as he peered up at her through ebony eyelashes, a shade of sorrow flickered across his face.

"Tell me you want this." A hint of nerves crept into his voice.

She answered by straddling his lap, feeling his heat between her legs as she kissed him. He wasted no time as he picked her up, flipping her gently onto her back. Kneeling between her legs, he pulled away from their embrace to look at the image of her sprawled out before him, the open flannel having fallen off her shoulders, providing zero coverage.

"I've missed you, Izzy."

She closed her eyes as she arched her back. Her silent request for him to kindly shut the fuck up. Bending down, he began kissing her between her now exposed breasts, stopping to lick one nipple and then the other before pressing those anguishing lips on a path down the middle of her stomach. Over her belly button. Traveling further and further south…

He pressed one large hand against her lower abdomen and she felt his warm breath against her as he whispered out a swear. His other hand slid under her thong, pulling his heat away from her as he dragged it down. It disappeared to the floor with the rest of their clothes. She groaned and that was his undoing. He was back on her, his tongue licking fully up her, briefly grazing her sensitive apex before placing an irresistibly irritating kiss against her inner thigh. She felt him smile into her olive skin and she opened one eye to see him staring up at her. As soon as their gaze met, he went back in to repeat his tormenting game. This time he took a moment to suck gently on her clit before placing that evil kiss against her other thigh.

She couldn't stop the breathless squeak that left her body and before she could think too much about it, he went back in, fully licking up her entrance. He let his tongue slip inside her, groaning. The feel of the sound alone nearly sent her over the edge.

Fuck, she felt sounds. He settled his tongue back against her clit, keeping his licks flat and slow.

Her muscles tensed, her thighs clamping against his head. He gripped them both with his hands, gently pushing them apart before switching to a sucking motion that had her amongst the stars she saw from her window. She moaned loudly and would've thought to be quiet if it didn't feel just so goddamn good.

One hand gripped the sheets behind her head as the other slipped into his hair, pulling those silky black strands slightly. He answered by giving a playful nip at her thigh, sending her into another orbit. Every muscle in her body tensed as he sucked faster and harder, flicking her with his tongue. She barely registered one of his hands had left their grip on her thigh until she felt his two fingers slip in, hooking up and release exploded within her. Her moans escaped without control and he gently coaxed everything from her as she descended back into her body. He pulled his fingers from her, placing a tender kiss on each thigh, before starting a trail of them up her body. When his soft lips were at her neck, his low voice vibrated through her as he said, "I have really missed you, Izzy."

And just when she opened her mouth to say something real fucking stupid, a savior banged on her door.

"Z, whoever is in there better have a really fucking good reason for interrupting our G.T.A. time."

No savior. Just Vahagn with his impeccable timing.

⚜

Izzy immediately snapped out of her drunken high, sitting up and taking in her apartment like it was her first time seeing those warm stone walls.

She groaned. And this time, not in a good way.

Her wide gaze met Charlie's and dread sunk deep into her stomach. Recognizing her look, dejection flooded his face that moments ago looked so content. Quickly, he climbed off her bed and put his clothes back on in silence, running his hands through his hair several times. She did the same, avoiding his gaze as she put herself right again.

Fuck, her bed looked like sex. Her apartment smelled like sex. Before she could start to formulate an excuse, Charlie stood at the door, expertly working through her intricate locks and swinging it open. Vahagn's fist was raised, about to knock again.

Fury replaced the mirth on Vahagn's face the instant he recognized who stood before him.

"What the fuck are you doing here?" he barked.

Charlie rubbed the back of his neck. "I wanted to talk to Izzy more about that book."

Vahagn looked ready to murder Charlie as he stepped into the room and to Izzy's shock, Charlie took a step back. Vahagn was the only one who knew what had really happened between them and that gave him power in their dynamic, even if Charlie outranked him as Lando's second.

Vahagn looked to Izzy, "Is that true?"

Stunned to near silence, her resounding panic struck her hard enough to formulate a response, "Um…yes. He wanted to know more about what Dr. Beechum said about it."

Vahagn wasn't buying a cent of her lies as he looked from her to her rumpled bed before turning back to Charlie.

"Get the fuck out of here, Charlie."

Charlie's hands flexed into fists at the command coming from someone below his rank, his jaw tightening. He looked back to Izzy and that haunted look in his eyes nearly cracked her heart.

Nearly.

Pushing past Vahagn, he stopped at the threshold like he had something else to say. Instead, he shook his head, and strode out the door.

Izzy would've let out a long breath if Vahagn's gaze didn't target her next.

"Do I want to know the real story?" His eyes searched her face and body, no doubt looking for red marks.

Her breath exploded out of her shakily. Vahagn might be protective of her but he also wasn't a dick about it.

"I'm going to bet you don't."

"Good." He nodded his head once, "Now, light a fucking candle so I can sit in here and not be forced to put my own pieces of the puzzle together."

She chuckled as she went to the kitchen to find a lighter and lit a candle she had snatched out of a back closet of the lab. Pumpkin pecan pie.

Vahagn sat down on the ivory leather couch and froze, eyes wide in horror.

"It didn't happen… here… did it?"

"Oh my fucking God no, Vahagn!"

His shoulders relaxed as he worked to turn on the TV and get the game queued up. Settling down next to him, her thoughts reeled as she considered the peculiar series of events in her life: one minute her world was being rocked by one of the most dangerous men in the city and the next she was about to rot her brain out on a video game with…well, another one of the most dangerous men in the city. Where was the room for gray area?

Vahagn must have sensed her apprehension because he reached over and put a hand on her knee.

"Hey."

She looked at him.

"Are you okay? Was it consensual?" His brown gaze comforted her, not a single ounce of judgment on his face. She always told him he chose the wrong line of profession because he did a much better job at putting people at ease than inflicting them with pain. He argued he could be better at one because of the other. Fortunately, she never learned how that could be true. In her mind, he was always this version. A kind soul. A beacon of hope in a world of turmoil.

She nodded slowly, "Yeah. I'm okay."

He looked at her a little longer before squeezing her knee and turning back to the glow of the TV screen.

"Good, then let's beat up some innocent bystanders and steal their cars."

She laughed out loud. "No more law-abiding citizens?"

He grinned. "No, fuck that. Some bitch rear-ended me and now I've got a vendetta." He grinned sidelong at her and she slapped him on his arm. Their laughter chased away the haunting moans that filled the space prior.

She didn't stumble back into her bed until 2:46 a.m., crashing into the memories of the evening as the citrus and pine scent of Charlie in her sheets enveloped her senses.

$$\maltese$$

CHAPTER FIVE
Izzy

Chaos. Everywhere Izzy looked sheer chaos unraveled. Screams threw her heart into a rapid-fire pace, fear hung in the air thick and acrid. She whirled in place, taking in the brutality she found herself in. There were people everywhere. Some crowded together like livestock at auction, some bound with chains on their hands and feet, some kneeling in the soggy ground, their sobs wrenching through her. In the gray mist and smoke, she tried to pinpoint some landmark to tell her where in the depths of hell she had woken up.

A figure emerged from the fog on horseback, shrouded in white linen with a red cross on their chest. They galloped through the horde of people, shouting in a language she couldn't place. She barely had a moment to question if she could still be asleep and not insane before the hot steam radiated off the horse as it passed, knocking her back a step. Her heart hammered in her chest.

As quickly as they had appeared, the mist swallowed the rider again. The rattle of wood and metal followed, cutting through the misery in the air. Crowds made reluctant attempts to move out of the way, barely able to shift from the places the earth had started to consume them into their eventual graves. The thunderous sound of hooves slowly drowned out their moans. A carriage grazed past Izzy as she peered to the darkness within. Her eye caught on the gaze of its regal passenger, a predatory shadow cast over him. Then he leaned forward and sank his teeth into the wrist of the man seated across from him.

Holy fuck!

She bolted upright, heart thundering in her chest. She gasped for air as the familiarity of her apartment sluggishly registered in her brain. Meager bits of moonlight peeked out from the clouds and in through her paned windows. She was in her bed. She had been asleep. It had all been a dream.

Vahagn's bone jarring snore from the couch confirmed it along with a flood of memories from the night before. A new panic crept into her bones.

Oh God.

Slamming back into her pillows, she rolled to her side and peered out onto the dark, empty street below. Streetlights had been decommissioned several years back to lessen the draw on the electrical grid as workers sought higher wages elsewhere. Horror rattled through her weary constitution as she watched a woman, around mid-forties and dressed in a tight green mini dress with ankle breaking heels, stumble out from a parking garage across the street. Movement in the shadows had Izzy gripping her pillow as she leaned toward the pane, pressing a hand to the glass.

Her breath fogged the window as she breathed out, "No".

The woman fumbled with and then dropped her keys outside the door to the building. Not once. Twice. Izzy wanted to shout, scream, something. Why was this woman out there? Curfew existed in the city for a reason.

In typical St. Louis fashion, when news spread that vampires were haunting the streets in the newfound darkness of the night, no one believed it. One guy, exuding frantic energy through the television screen, held his Glock up to the news camera after a reporter asked him if he planned to change his routine with the new reason to fear the dark.

"Fuck 'em all!" The man had exclaimed and then fired two shots into the air, screaming the whole time.

The news stations brought all their reporters off the streets after that. Street artists filled the walls of abandoned buildings and overpasses with the image of the man: whites of his eyes bulged and his mouth screaming, spittle flying from his feral expression. The caption a profound, collective sentiment: fuck 'em all.

That was until Claudia King.

Claudia King owned a small restaurant downtown. During the day, she would serve the most delectable slow cooked meals to paying customers. Eating there felt like being invited to a friend's house as a kid, sitting at their dinner table with their family, and experiencing some amazing new dish that danced on the palette. Every plate at King's restaurant was left empty, an echo of forks scraping for every last remnant played on steady repeat throughout the day. At night, she closed down the register and turned her kitchen over to the homeless community, feeding them, and even giving them lessons in the kitchen if they wanted. Years ago, someone donated several washers and dryers so the patrons could do some laundry while they cooked or ate.

Claudia King was a queen in the city. Lando even donated two of his men to her to keep the peace after the sun set.

One summer evening, ushering the last person out the door and toward their shelter of choice with a brown bag of snacks, a wave, and a smile, she turned to close up shop and came face to face with a man standing before the bodies of Lando's men. Blood dripped down his hands and mouth.

Footage recovered from the cameras on the traffic lights outside revealed Claudia faced her death not in fear nor in anger. No, she lifted her hands to the sky and began praying, smiling, as the man jumped on her with inhuman speed and ripped her throat out.

A week earlier, he had sat at her table, eating her gracious meals and marveling at her use of beets.

That event marked the threshold for the city. After that, an undeclared curfew blanketed the city. Mortals stay inside after dark. Or else.

On the third attempt the woman across the street made it into her building, safe and alarmingly placid. Izzy gasped, rolling away from the window to look over at the clock above the mantle of the fireplace.

4:45 a.m.

She curled further into the soft warmth of her pillows and comforter, vying for a few minutes of peace. Between the stress of the dream and the idiocy of one of her neighbors, she felt exhausted. But her attempts at rest were futile. Her mind whirled and her heart never ceased thudding in her chest.

Cold awoke her senses as she tossed back her comforter and threw a small pillow at the oversized gnome on her couch.

She said groggily, "Get up idiot. It's time to pretend we have our shit together," as she pushed through the old church confessional door in the middle of her floor to ceiling bookshelf. The details of her apartment were like little snippets of her soul spread throughout, but this closet was her *magnum opus*. Tucked behind the bookshelf, it felt like a secret escape, dark and separate from the rest of the space.

Vahagn groaned his protests from the ivory couch, curling in around the pillow she had thrown. She closed the closet door behind her and absentmindedly changed into her workout gear.

If she was going to be miserably awoken by ridiculous dreams and kept up by the antics of bat shit people on the streets, she was dragging him down with her. Besides, he carried part of the blame. Never again was she to tango with the botanical abomination of Lando's weed supply. Those dreams were weird. Really fucking weird. And what was that thing with the vampire? She shivered. *Just a dream*, she reminded herself as her pulse started to throb heavily in her neck. She rubbed a hand over her chest. Dying of a heart attack at twenty-six seemed ridiculous.

As she pulled her form fitting cropped tank top over her chest, a dark stain of coal dust on her forearm caught her eye. Nausea roiled through her as she stepped toward the mirror. Furiously, she rubbed at it, watching it disappear into an angry red mark. Meeting her own gaze in the reflection, she recognized the fear undulating through her before she swallowed it down and threw her mess of curls into a bun.

Emerging from her closet to see Vahagn still in the fetal position around that pillow, she delivered an overly aggressive slap to his ass as she walked toward the kitchen for much needed coffee. More protests bellowed out but a reluctant return to life soon followed.

"You're a cruel woman," he groaned.

She smirked. "Save it for Lando, V."

✦

Izzy and Vahagn both stumbled into the custom-built gym in Lando's ridiculous penthouse apartment. His clients had been more than willing to continue training with him when he turned reclusive, so the room featured everything imaginable for a luxury gym run by a mob boss: weights, cardio machines with a spectacular view of the city, a sauna, and a sparring ring with a selection of weaponry fit to arm a band of medieval warriors. Fitness had been his primary focus as a trainer but his popularity grew with his self-defense classes. Business boomed after the immortals came to town.

"What a *bellisimo* morning, yeah, Isabella? Vahagn?" Lando gave a wide smile from the middle of the sparring ring that took up a good quarter of the large space. He worked through a familiar series of stretches. It was a routine Izzy knew well. Its tedious movement soothed her on a good day and set her nerves against grates on a bad one. Based on the steady pound in her temples, the morning's start was not looking optimistic.

Vahagn responded to Lando with a grunt and a middle finger as he walked over to a set of mahogany lockers to the left of the entrance. He kept an emergency supply of clothes stashed here for the occasions when his loyalty to his duty within the organization outweighed his desires to stay in bed after a late night.

Following Vahagn to drop off her own bag, she thought, *Those late nights used to be spent raising hell with Charlie and sleeping with every woman in the city.* Then she entered the picture and it was Izzy by his side when he stumbled into the gym each morning, still half drunk, or high, or both from the night before.

She shook her head, grimacing at the movement, and squinted at the bright lights overhead, reflecting off the shiny finish on the lockers. She nearly jumped out of her own skin as Lando's soft, smooth Italian accent floated into her right ear.

"Isabella, *mi amore*, you look as though you've seen a ghost."

She whirled to find him standing within arm's reach of her. Yeah, ghost was right. The man floated around like a silent whisper.

"Jesus, Lando. Just tired. You know it is rather cruel to subject us to your vices during the night and torture us with the consequences before the sun even starts to peek out in the morning."

His melodic laugh warmed her heart some. It reminded her so much of her grandfather.

"It builds character," he said simply, patting her shoulder before turning to walk back to the sparring ring. Vahagn emerged from the back office in his workout gear, blonde hair and beard dripping wet. Likely from splashing his face with cold water to either wake up or sober up before the misery Lando was about to dole out.

Based on the insane dream that woke her up, Izzy wondered if she might still be high. But no excuse had ever caused Lando to go easy on them. She learned that early on. If anything, his inner sociopath came out those days and it seemed his one and only goal became to either break your soul or watch you vomit in the corner while he laughed.

"Alright *bambini*, let's warm up, no?" Lando gestured to the floor in front of him with the point of a short sword held careless in his hand. They got to work, mindlessly going through the same motions they saw Lando performing when they had arrived. Hip openers, spinal twists, even rotating their wrists around to prepare for the sword work they practiced every session.

They moved in silence for a few minutes before Vahagn seemed to finally come back to the land of the living and said, "So, you want to talk about it?"

She kept her gaze on the gray matted floor in front of her as she leaned over her butterflied legs. The weight of his stare pierced through her. She knew exactly what he was talking about. Last night, he had been happy to let her forget for the time being. But that was last night. Now? Now, he needed answers, and victims, for the storm brewing in his eyes.

"Not particularly." It was a half-hearted grumble. Regret and embarrassment had her shifting, uncomfortable as the flashbacks flooded through in cloudy spurts. She cringed at the wraith-like memory of Charlie's hands pressing into her thighs, as if she could still feel them there.

An exasperated sigh came from Vahagn. "Look, I don't have to tell you what a colossally stupid move it was because you're an adult. You make your own choices." His tone softened as he added, "And because by the look on your face, you are already eating yourself up over it."

His words prompted Izzy to look up and see him studying her with the same concern and caring that had initially sparked her innate trust in him. She gave him a grim smile.

"It was a mistake. It won't… it can't happen again," she finally admitted.

He shrugged and went back to stretching.

"That's the magic of being human, Z. You make mistakes. You feel all the range of emotions of every decision you make. And then you keep going." He smiled up at her as he slipped into his rather pathetic Italian accent. "Builds character, *mia fragola*."

A laugh burst out of her and with it the weight pressing on her shoulders released.

It all came crashing right back down as Charlie and a few more of Lando's crew came in through the gym door.

"You're late," Lando chastised as they set their stuff in their lockers and shuffled into the sparring ring. Charlie's steely blue gaze seared into her skin as he found a spot in the back of the ring, right behind her. Goosebumps crawled up her spine as she continued to stretch in silence. Vahagn tensed from his spot across from her, his jaw set as he glared at the man behind her, presumably envisioning crushing his skull.

"Partner up. We are working on defensive tactics together so try to pick someone who is your opposite in some way or another," Lando instructed, weaving between the bodies on the mat, tapping someone hunching their back with the flat of his blade.

Charlie began stalking toward her, a lion on the prowl, setting the panic alarm off in her brain. The conversation she saw brewing in his eyes would not be happening today and definitely not here. Before he could reach her, she grabbed Vahagn's wrist.

"Oh look, big, dumb, and ugly. All my opposites. You're my partner." Her eyes pleaded, but deep down, she knew he needed no explanation for her request.

Vahagn's chocolate eyes narrowed on her as he replied, "You're incredibly unkind for someone who is about to get their ass handed to them." His mischievous wink reassured her he knew exactly why her grip tightened on his wrist.

Charlie stopped his pursuit, a tint of anger and sadness cast over his handsome face. He reluctantly turned toward a scrawny looking man with glasses and tattoos of robots on both his hands, lines of binary inked down his neck. Data, Lando's hacker turned mafia tech guy.

"Thank you," she whispered to Vahagn, releasing his wrist. He captured her hand and squeezed it.

"Always, Z." His warm smile wrinkled the edges of his

eyes.

She returned it as they took their positions and started working through Lando's instructions. It only faltered when the eerie feeling of Charlie's persistent gaze raised the hairs on the back of her neck.

❖

CHAPTER SIX
Izzy

Hours later, having showered and changed into her "uniform", as Barry put it, a ruffled white blouse tucked into vintage trousers tapered to heeled leather boots, she made her way across the short stretch of city before hitting the park that would lead her to campus. While not the quickest route —*nor the safest*, Lando's voice rang in her ears—the walk served as the therapy she couldn't afford. Besides, these days therapists were just undercover headhunters for the luxury blood catering services.

She didn't normally go in on the weekends, but she wanted to study the details of the mystery book sitting in her safe right that moment. And clear her head of nightmarish flashbacks, both real and figments of her imagination.

Despite its ruthless reputation, St. Louis was beautiful. A city built on the backs of immigrants meant a rich culture evolved to create a unique sense of unity. Albeit, a prickly and sometimes unusually savage sense of unity, but enigmatic and endearing nonetheless. Her grandparents used to regale her with stories of how they stayed here because the community felt so similar to the one they left behind in Italy.

This memory had her smiling even as she rubbed at the shoulder Vahagn had damn near twisted out of socket while sparring. Lando had them working on their hand-to-hand combat that morning. To escape Vahagn's hold, she had stomped the bridge of his foot hard enough to force him to release her. This opened up a beautiful opportunity for her to elbow him in the sternum. Remembering him gasping for breath made her smile grow as she turned down the dark stairwell to their little hidden lab in the basement.

"Well, well, well, what a beautiful thing to bump into," a smooth British voice said as she stepped onto the cool concrete of the bottom landing. Her smile faded as a tall figure emerged from the shadows, peeking out from under a tweed pageboy cap with a sly smirk, one eyebrow raised. He would be charming if not for the creepy ass opening line.

Suspicion flooded her senses, and she instinctively reached for the onyx hilt of her dagger. The only people with a good enough reason to be down here were Barry, Donnie, the ancient caretaker of the building, and the occasional lost freshman looking for Anthro 101 and getting Barry's ancient butt plug collection instead.

"Can I help you find something?" Izzy said, allowing distrust to seep into her tone.

"Now, now, no need to be alarmed. I believe I'm looking for… you. Isabella Ciampi? Anthropologist extraordinaire? Keeper of my wildest desires?" His smile splashed like a bucket of ice water down her back.

The shock must have been printed across her face because that smile morphed into a full-on beam of wicked delight.

"Yeah, I figured as much. Bartholomew provided us

with such invaluable intel last night when we paid him a little visit."

Shadowed figures she hadn't noticed before started to shift into focus. Three more men emerged from behind presumably the leader of this little group. A blink and her brows furrowed as his words registered in her mind.

"Last night?" Barry never worked during the night…

A muscle flinched in the man's jaw as his smile faltered and he glanced at the floor before meeting her gaze, piercing her through the darkness with their silver hue.

Silence.

Fuck.

Her hand tightened around that dagger right as those shadowed men started moving quickly, too quickly, toward her. She narrowly got the chance to drop her bag before the hilt connected with a jaw as her uppercut met its first target. Stumbling back, he spat out dark crimson blood onto the gray floor and let out a chilling chuckle.

Fuck, fuck, fuck.

A second man slowed momentarily on his approach after seeing his friend get jacked in the face and she took the opportunity to dive into his space.

"Aim for the heart; it's their weakness after all," Vahagn's voice from their workout this morning repeated in her mind, a flash of his wink before she had punched him the stomach.

So that's precisely what she did. Dagger met heart. The vampire hissed his fangs at her as she withdrew her weapon and her eyes widened as she watched him crumple to the floor.

All the other men approaching stopped as heartless laughter filled the dimly lit hallway. The skull tattooed on his neck bobbed in time with the sound.

"Oy, am I in love? Boys? Is this what love feels like?"

the man with the cap said, hand on his chest, depraved joy and amusement dusted over his words. It sent bile straight into her throat.

"What the fuck do you want from me?" she snarled, taking a tentative step back. A door to an empty lab stood a few yards behind her. Donnie had granted her access to it a couple years ago for nights when she got caught up in her research and he hadn't wanted her to brave the trip home in the dark. If she could get there, the door would lock behind her and she could call Lando.

"Oh, it's definitely love." Those silver eyes sparkled as he continued, "It turns out, love, you have something that just doesn't belong to you, I'm afraid." He tsked at her, taking a step forward.

Her stomach clenched but she kept her words sharp. "Then why not simply take it and leave? Why do you need me?"

Anger flashed across his eyes and his voice took on a new edge. "Because it's just. Not. That. Simple." He bit each syllable out at her.

With each snap of his words, she took a step back.

"What can be so important and difficult to get from me that you need a small army to corner me in a hallway for? This seems like overkill." She gestured to the group of men with the point of her dagger, hoping it would serve as a distraction. She only needed to make it about ten more feet.

"A little," he clicked his tongue between his teeth, "birdy suggested you might have found yourself in possession of The Ramblings."

Curiosity caught her mid-step and her brows furrowed. "The Ramblings?"

"The very ones, deary." Condescension coated his

statement.

His eyes shot down to her foot, still partially in a step back, and flew back to meet the confusion in her gaze. It quickly morphed to fear.

FUCK.

Not giving another second of thought to The fucking Ramblings, she took off for the door, pulling the key card from its retractable lead at her hip. Crashing into the heavy steel while simultaneously scanning the key card, terror ripped through her bones. A normally mundane click sounded like a symphony in her ears as she ripped the door open enough to squeeze in before yanking it shut behind her with all her force. Another beautiful click sounded in her ears and she gasped out a breath.

Locked.

Safe.

Hands smacked the sides of the reinforced glass window, jolting her attention to it as the man's feral snarl hissed at her, white fangs becoming visible. She slid back onto the floor, dagger held out in front of her, her chest panting as the adrenaline coursed through her blood.

"There's no need to be such a tease, darling," he purred.

She raised an eyebrow to him.

His harsh laugh haunted the space around her as he blew her a kiss. She glared in response.

"Another day, boys. Another day." He whistled, pushing off the door, and spun his fingers around in the air before they disappeared, out of sight.

She collapsed onto the ground, breath shaking while the chilly concrete floor brought her back to equilibrium.

The fucking Ramblings.

A supposed myth from Charlemagne's reign—

presumed to be a journal of his "ramblings" about events of the time. Essentially a mad man's manifesto. Made more mysterious by the fact the ruler had never actually learned to write. At least according to history. But no one had ever seen the damn thing so it was labeled as conspiratorial bullshit and left to internet forums and tabletop role playing games. No way that bougie ass notebook randomly sent to her could be The Ramblings.

Her heart started racing. Why would the immortals want The Ramblings?

Immortals. Vampires.

Holy fuck.

She had just come face to face with a bunch of vampires. On campus. During the day. What the actual fuck.

Her hands scanned over all the potential locations of her phone before she dropped them to the floor and groaned.

It was in her leather bag. Still in the hallway where she had dropped it.

Legs shaking, she hauled herself up and crept over to the window, scanning the daunting hallway on the other side. It looked brighter than it had moments ago. And, thankfully, a lot less empty. Even the man whose heart she had stabbed had disappeared. She needed to update Vahagn that his theory proved false.

Her eyes zeroed in on her bag. It looked untouched. She scanned the hallway one last time as her hand hovered over the handle.

Where did they even go?

Who were they?

Why were they here?

Why did they need her?

Shaking those thoughts away, she took a deep breath,

closing her eyes to ready herself for the task before her. Snapping her eyes open, she pressed down on the handle. This time the click sound sent an icicle through her heart, but she pushed the door open and hauled toward her bag, diving to the floor to fish out her phone. Punching Lando's stupid name on her speed dial, she frantically looked up the stairs as the phone found signal and rang. That stairwell happened to be the only way in or out of this section of the building and there were only a handful of labs down here, all behind key card locks.

"*Ciao mia bella?*" Lando's Italian accent shouted melodically on other end of the call, the familiar sound of feet smacking sandbags in the background.

"Hello my fucking ass Lando. I was just ambushed."

A whistle sounded on the other end and the background noise went silent.

"What do you mean ambushed?"

"I mean," she seethed through clenched teeth, "I was fucking AM–BUSHED, Lando!"

The familiar heavy thud of the gym door cut through her growing anger.

"Charlie is on his way and he is calling Vahagn. He should be nearby. Do you have somewhere safe you can wait for them?" His tone had shifted to the all business one she actively tried to avoid hearing.

"Yeah, I'll be in the old supply lab, to the right of the stairs. He better call me when he gets here. I'll have a damn heart attack if he knocks." She gathered her bag and stood up, heading back toward her room of rescue.

"Good—" and that was the last she heard of Lando's voice as she dropped her phone, the pressure of a hand on her shoulder mainlining adrenaline back to her heart. Whirling around, she grabbed a fistful of navy cotton with her left hand as her right hand, still gripping the dagger, shoved the blade against the dark tan neck of her attacker. The momentum sent his back into the stone wall behind him, arms held up in surrender, and alarm in his eyes. Golden wide eyes that danced between her death stare, the dagger at his neck, and her fistful of his shirt.

"Izzy! Isabella! ISABELLA!" Lando's frantic yelling on the other end of the phone that now laid on the ground behind her filled the corridor, the distance muting what had to be a deafening volume.

Those gilt eyes glimpsed the phone before jumping back to her gaze. They held each other's stare.

"Who the fuck are you?" she growled, pressing the knife's edge further into his neck. Bright red blood started to bead to the surface.

"Not the enemy," he breathed out quickly. "I saw those guys slinking through the shadows out of here so I came down to see what the hell had The Society lurking about." He spoke in a deep, calm voice with a slight drawl.

She scanned his face, suspicions still on high alert, as recognition clicked in.

Beechum's new assistant. The golden boy with the golden eyes.

She frowned at him and he raised a dark brown eyebrow at her. Well, he didn't look like he wanted to drink her dry so that put him a step above her most recent company at least. He glanced back down at the dagger still at his neck and she gave him a little shove before stepping away.

He bent over, breathing deeply, as his hand casually went to his neck. He pulled it away, examining the blood on it.

"Was that truly necessary?" he muttered.

"Uh, yeah!" She spun around, motioning to the empty hallway and her things strewn on the floor. "What do people not understand about being fucking ambushed in this goddamn city?"

His smile was grim as he stood back up and said, "It's Noah, by the way. My name. I believe you were wondering who I am. I work upstairs in the archives with—"

She glared. "Dr. Beechum, yes. I remember you."

He pursed his lips then looked around the hallway. "So, the question becomes who are you and why does The Society have a target on your back?"

The Society. The fucking Society. That's who had been down here. She swallowed the rock that suddenly lodged itself in her throat.

Concern flashed across Noah's face, probably in response to every ounce of blood draining from her own, and he took a step toward her, arm outstretched as if to catch her. His mouth opened, starting to form words that never came. Instead, he was interrupted by the hasty sound of boots pounding down the stairs toward them. He barely had a chance to see Charlie massive form approaching before the gangster hauled him back against the wall.

CHAPTER SEVEN
Noah

Oxygen rushed back into Noah's lungs long enough to recognize the emerald eyes staring a promise of death into his soul. Then he found himself right back up against this damn wall, face to face with a rather large and rather angry looking man.

"Based on your equal propensity for violence, I'm guessing you know her," Noah coughed out, his eyes glancing over to her. An impressive glower looked back. He cocked a brow.

"Nice job, you big idiot, but wrong fucking target." Her voice maintained its ire but he swore those eyes twinkled as she looked to the behemoth of a man, whose tattooed forearm pressed into Noah's sternum harder. The skull on his hand looked menacing. The man stood only a couple inches taller than Noah but looked like he benched his weight as a warmup.

The giant grunted, a flash of annoyance and relief passing over his otherwise hardened face. He dropped his hold on Noah and walked over to the woman, amusement twisting her rosy lips into a smirk.

Noah coughed again, rubbing his chest as he looked at the two of them. His eyes roved over her tall, athletic frame. He had the proof she could hold her own in a fight. His hand absentmindedly slipped to his neck. Standing next to that giant though, she looked small. Until she opened her mouth.

Plucking the phone off the ground, she said with a mocking sweetness, "Don't worry, Lando, *Charlie* has it all under control." She rolled her eyes at the bear of a man, Charlie. He responded with another grunt, scowling at her. She returned his malcontent with a sunny smile and a middle finger. Murderous and beautiful—a deadly combination, even in this day and age.

"Yeah, yeah, yeah, I'll be there eventually, I need to take care of some stuff here first… No, I won't lose his ass this time… Oh, look! Reinforcements are arriving in St. Louis timely fashion—after the action and with all the wrong suspects. I think they can take it from here, Landy." She glanced up to the top of the stairs, stuffing the phone into her back pocket. Noah's gaze followed to see the shadow of another burly man. How did every gargantuan man in this city know this woman?

"That's no way to talk to your elders, Z," the new burly man said as he descended the stairs, catching Noah's confused stare, before looking back to her and Charlie, the bear man.

"Apparently, we aren't worth much in the eyes of the princess. Did you call me a big idiot?" Charlie said, giving the woman a sideways smile.

"Next time," she stepped toward him and poked him in the peck with the tip of her dagger, causing him to wince slightly, "leave your workout at the first mention of ambush, Charlie." Charlie gave a light chuckle before all three turned to a bewildered Noah. He raised both hands before stuffing them into the pocket of his jeans.

Charlie would've been an effort to fight off, though Noah thought he could use some speed against his brawn to get out of here unscathed. But two of them? And a woman yielding that dagger with far too much comfort?

They had him at their mercy.

"Let the record show all hands have been placed on me and not the other way around," he said in a desperate attempt to buy his freedom.

The burly man started to open his mouth but the woman stepped forward, tilting her head a little, and said, "How did you know that was The Society?" Both men next to her blanched and opened their mouths to speak, but she held his gaze. He became the sole proprietor of her attention.

"You didn't notice the gold?" he blurted without second thought. The words continued to fall out, "They were all wearing it in some way or another. Goes back to the eighth century when there was a shortage. The theory is it marks them as something valuable and rare. It's a quick identifiable piece to verify if the large group of men stalking toward you is friend or foe." His historical tangent slowed as he watched a mix of curiosity and anger cross their faces. Rambling never saved a man in a fist fight.

The burly one faced him, puffing his enormous Viking chest out.

"Where did you say you were from?" The man growled, actually growled the words at him.

The curiosity in those beautiful green eyes standing next to the Norseman nearly ignited as she shook her head, pinching the bridge of her nose and leveled the man with a look that would've brought Noah to his knees.

"Wow, okay, Vahagn. Down boy." She whistled at him.

Whistled. Noah couldn't help the smirk on his face. It quickly fell as she continued speaking though. "Just because someone has an accent like that and information like that does not mean they are from…" As she turned back to face Noah, he could see the pieces of the puzzle click into place. The crinkled nose, the closed fist, the slight hitch in the eyebrow.

"Where *are* you from?" It came out her lovely mouth as a demand rather than a question.

Taking a breath, Noah weighed his options, studying those emerald eyes. They were like getting lost in a dense forest, dew kissed leaves filling the air with a damp, sweet scent. He looked to the stone wall leading up the stairwell and let out a ragged exhale. Running a hand over his face, he decided fuck it.

"Uh," a nervous laugh escaped him as he heard his own accent, thick and languid as it drawled through his lips, "yep—New Orleans."

Charlie and the man she called Vahagn, he could've sworn they shared a snarl as they both started stalking toward him. He backed a step toward the stairs, having played out each of the potential endings to this scenario in his head and justified fleeing as the best path, dignity be damned.

"Well," the woman quipped from behind them, "as entertaining as this Magic Mike show down would be, I actually have more questions and don't need to kick your ass to get answers… hopefully." She walked between the two men toward Noah, sticking her hand out. He snapped out of his shock and tentatively took her warm hand in his own. Her grip tightened and a flash of a bright smile nearly stopped his heart as she said, "I'm Isabella Ciampi, but please just call me Izzy. The overgrown bull dogs are Charlie and Vahagn, respectively based on their horrendous arrival times."

His eyes widened. His life had been threatened at least twice in the past fifteen minutes and here she was, referring to men with murder in their eyes as canines. What had he got himself into?

"Good, that's that," she said. Noah had no idea what he agreed to with that handshake but she dropped his hand and leveled a serious look on her face. The moment brought him back into reality, as she asked, "So, Noah, why do you think The Society is going all Peaky Blinders on me before nine a.m. on a Saturday?"

He glanced between all three of the people with their attention honed on him.

"If I had to take a well-educated guess, I would say it would have to do with a certain ancient book you have in your possession that a certain research partner might have been gossiping about to the director of archives before our staff meeting yesterday."

Staring up at the yellowing ceiling, she growled, "Fucking, Barry."

"In his defense," Noah cut in, "it has been pretty empty up there. I don't even think he knew I, or anyone else, were in the shelves when he came in." Noah also happened to have been eavesdropping pretty heavily but that detail felt best left out.

Snorting a laugh, she suddenly met Noah's gaze, eyes widening in a mix of terror and concern as her face paled.

"Barry." She breathed out his name and in a flash, she was down the hall, slamming into the lab door. She fumbled with her key card on the reader, swearing before it clicked open. Charlie and Vahagn appeared right behind her as she pushed in then stopped. Noah arrived behind them a moment later and stared in shock.

The room was trashed.

"Barry? Barry, are you in here?" Izzy crawled over the

disaster of papers, boxes, and chairs strewn across the floor. "Bartholomew?!"

Jesus, The Society had even ripped the clock off the wall and the curtains over a small window in the back hung off kilter. No response to her calls sounded within the small lab room. She made it to the back of the room in impressive speed and turned to face Charlie, the agony on her face matching the agony on his own.

"Iz, he might not be here," Charlie implored her, his voice deep and smoky.

She started to open her mouth, a retort undeniably forming on her soft rose lips, when the high-pitched whine of a door hinge cut through the room. Vahagn said tensely, "Um, guys. You're going to want to come see this…"

Noah gulped down the fear wrenching his throat shut as he appeared in the doorway of a large supply closet. Old papers and files covered every surface, some splattered with something crimson. Blood. Charlie stood next to him when Noah heard the man take a sharp inhale before turning around to grab Izzy by the shoulders, blocking her view.

"You don't need to see this."

She scowled up at him. "The fuck I don't."

They both stood there for several heartbeats, eyes narrowed on each other, neither moving. A whole conversation went unspoken before the man huffed and stepped aside, releasing her into the doorway.

Fear painted her features as she made a slow climb through the wreckage, careful to avoid the red spots.

"Barry?" she whispered.

Silence.

She glanced up at Vahagn's pained expression as she

passed him, her hands trembling slightly. She worked her way to a collection of boxes in the dark, back corner of the closet.

"Barry, for the love of God, please don't be dead," she pleaded through a slight sob.

One of the boxes in the stack shook slightly. Rushing to it, Izzy started ripping them down. Charlie appeared beside her a moment later, placing the discarded boxes to the side in a more orderly manner. As she discarded a box about waist high, she paused. Breath caught in her throat, coming ragged and quick as she slowly brought it to the floor beside her and approached what appeared to be a black hole within the pile of boxes.

"Barry?" she whispered again.

Inching forward a step, she leaned into the darkness. Suddenly, a feral face of frantic fear popped up out of the hole, shrieking and covered in blood, glasses rimmed eyes wide and scanning the room with a butcher knife in hand.

"HOLY FUCKING SHIT BARRY! WHAT HAPPENED?" Izzy screamed, wheeling backward with her dagger in hand.

Vahagn cracked his knuckles, bouncing on the balls of his feet as he shook out his arms, while Charlie let out a choked cough and ran a hand through his black hair. The clear reactions of surprise around him prompted Noah to become acutely aware his lack of a reaction probably rose a red flag. Quickly, he slapped then fisted against his chest and grumbled out a half-believable cough. Fortunately, all eyes were on Barry.

Barry's hands started trembling something fierce as he stared into Izzy's face. The butcher knife clattered to the floor and the man wailed a blood curdling sob.

"Oh God, Charlie help me get him out. We need to take him back to Lando," Izzy implored as she climbed back toward the box hut, pulling away more to free the weeping man.

Nodding, Charlie stepped up next to her. He grabbed her wrist as she started reaching within the hole and she paused her motion to look up at him. Pushing a strand of her wine-red hair away from her ear, he leaned in to whisper something to her. The simple act seemed too intimate to observe so Noah glanced around the room. When he looked back, her forest eyes bore a hole into him. Blinking once, she turned to Barry, his sobs overcoming his whole body at this point, shuddering through him in violent waves.

"Bear, Charlie is going to get you out and we are going to take you to Uncle Lando where we will give you a long hot bath and a stiff spritz. Does that sound good?" He answered with a brief pause in his sobs before they resumed, albeit less violent. Izzy nodded to Charlie and then she started stalking toward Noah.

Oh shit.

"Listen, I see this has clearly gone beyond my scope of assistance," he began his plea, hands up as he backed toward the door, "I was genuinely just curious and then when I saw you kneeling on the ground, I wanted to make sure everything was fine. I'm going to head back to my dusty old records now."

Tilting her head as he spoke, she flashed him a half smile. Vahagn started to walk toward him as well but she held her hand up and kept her pursuit.

"Unfortunately, I think you're going to need to let the director know you won't be in today. I suddenly find myself with even more questions. And I think you have the answers." A cold stare settled on her face.

He glanced to the burly man next to her—God, was he like a direct descendant of Thor?—and sighed, letting his hands drop to his sides as he stopped moving.

"I'm guessing the answer is no, but do I get a choice in

the matter?" he drawled, already resigned to his fate.

"There is always a choice, but in this moment, do you think the best one would be to run?" she replied, hands spread to the dismantled chaos in the closet and subsequent laboratory behind him.

He took in a deep inhale and dramatically let it out, "You might have a point."

"I usually do." She winked at him. His heart pounded in his chest.

"Alright, then I guess I choose to answer your questions."

"So agreeable, such a hard quality to come across these days." She glanced over at Charlie. The man huffed at her as he hauled a limp Barry up against his shoulder, steadying the trembling man. Barry was about the polar opposite of his human crutch, shorter, stockier, glasses. His hair in a destroyed pompadour. His fingernails painted a crimson hue that rivaled what splattered on the floor.

"Right," Vahagn nodded at the scene, "are we all ready to go then?"

Noah balked. "Go? Go where?"

Izzy's eyes twinkled up at him. "The most ridiculous place you've ever been."

CHAPTER EIGHT
Noah

She wasn't kidding.

The apartment—a loose description because the space around him consisted of the entire top floor of the massive building—was absolutely ridiculous. The door alone looked straight from a medieval castle. It had to weigh as much as the two giant men who ushered Noah through it when they had arrived at the converted warehouse on the other side of the park.

His mouth must have been open as they walked in because Izzy glanced over her shoulder and let out a small giggle. Snapping it shut, he tried to play it cool, taking in the rest of the luxurious penthouse. A giant black fireplace suspended from the rafters held court in the middle of the vast living room. Leather couches placed thoughtfully around the centerpiece looked plush enough to sink into and never want to leave. A door to a small, in comparison, room built off to the left of the entrance caught his eye and he peeked in to see enough equipment and weaponry to train a small army. They passed through to the gourmet kitchen situated to the right of the grand entry. The smell of expensive espresso and buttery pastries wafted through the air. A tan man with soft curly black hair peppered with gray and an unnerving air of confidence sat at the ebony stone counter. A porcelain espresso cup dwarfed in his scarred hands. The hands of a fighter, Noah noted. And he would heed that warning as the heavy doors closed behind him.

What kind of an idiot walks right into the viper den?

The same one who would walk into a hallway after The Society.

"A series of poor life choices"; that's what his headstone would read. If anyone bothered with one. Though these days, most of the dead were burned in batches and scattered about fields, unmarked, forever forgotten. Nothing more than fertilizer to feed the living. The circle of life, or some shit.

His gaze flicked to the fireplace. It did seem suspiciously large.

The man at the counter tossed his espresso back in one quick drink, and said in an accented voice, "Isabella, *mi amore*, you had old Lando so worried." Ah, Italian.

Wealthy Italian. With bodyguards. A lot of bodyguards.

Noah groaned internally. Fucking hell.

"Not worried enough to climb out of your ivory tower though, huh?" she retorted, patting the older man on the cheek and garnering a stifled grunt from Charlie and Vahagn. They both stood behind Noah, ready in case he made a run for it. The idea tempted him, even with the hulking obstacles to contend with. Barry, much more mobile than before, still clung to Charlie's sculpted chest. Which left Vahagn as the main hurdle to overcome. Noah sized the man up again.

Lando's hand went over his heart and he said with a

touch of theatrics, "You wound me. After everything I've given you, you wound me so. Oh, Isabella."

She rolled her jungle eyes, "Only one of us was almost wounded today. Well, besides Barry. He was actually wounded, though—" she glanced back at Barry, one eyebrow up as she caught his hand against Charlie's chest, "it would appear he might have found his cure."

Barry jumped a little as if waking from a trance, petting Charlie's chest a couple times before backing away from the man.

"Please, rescue me anytime. I'm begging you," Barry said to Charlie, straightening his coiffed hair as best he could.

On the ride over, he had regaled the explanation for the blood that still coated his face and the front of his shirt. As he went to leave the night before, a little closer to sunset than normal, he saw The Society lurking in the hallway. He panicked, crashed into the closet door, and knocked over a pile of records while scrambling into the makeshift panic room he had built the first week working in the lab. The butcher knife had been hidden within for that exact type of scenario.

"But what happened to the rest of the lab then? It was in shambles. How were they able to get in?" Izzy had grilled him, an incredulous look on her face.

"What do you mean? I... I think I might've blacked out. I ate like five edibles I had stashed in there to prevent the heart attack I felt looming in my chest."

Her gaze had narrowed and shifted to Noah, a tight line across her mouth, before she turned to stare out the window and the city streets flashing by. Their drive hadn't been long and they parked in a guarded underground garage off a secluded back alley.

Lando gave Izzy a lazy smile then looked to Noah, his gaze turning predatory.

"How is New Orleans looking these days?" His playful accent turned criminal. Someone must have tipped him off about his visitor then. Interesting.

"I… wouldn't know. It has been a while since I was there." Noah became hyper aware of his own accent again. Like a death note stapled to his chest.

"Is that so? So, you left New Orleans a while ago," he stood from his seat at the counter and started making his way around the island to where Noah stood, "and then you what? Have family here? Threw a dart at a map? How does someone just end up in St. Louis?" The man studied Noah's face before he leaned in to whisper, "None of the souls damned to this city came here by choice." He shifted back to stand a couple feet in front of him, holding the wrist of his left hand, a loose fist opening and closing. Noah felt the men behind him tense in anticipation.

"I, uh, actually work at the university. In the archives," Noah started, glancing to the man's hand. He calculated the number of people who could break him like a pencil in this room and the lack of easy escape routes. "That's actually how I came to find Isabella in the hallway."

"Please call me Izzy," she remarked from the golden light of the crystal bar over by a giant window overlooking the city. A massive live edge table sat in front of it, at least twenty chairs situated around it. He noted the amusement in her tone. Somehow this seemed like a game. One he didn't know the rules to or even the objective of. He felt certain he had been brought to the home of a mob boss. Which meant everyone around him was part of his crew, even the trembling man at the table, eying Charlie like he was his last meal.

He gulped and amended, "When I found Izzy in the hallway."

"Did he hurt you?" Lando's fiery dark brown gaze went to Izzy.

A devilish smirk flashed over her shoulder, and she gave Noah a wink before saying, "Actually, I hurt him."

Lando blinked. Then he erupted into roaring laughter that shook the air between them. He bent over, mirth rolling through him. As he looked back up at Noah, pointing, a smile cracked across his face again and he keeled over in another fit. Noah remained still, a muscle ticking to his steady pulse in his jaw. Abruptly, Lando went silent and the face of a lion peered at him.

"If you ever get the notion to hurt her, just know she has already plotted your death. It likely occurred within the moment she laid eyes on you, if I trained her right." Intriguing. Noah glanced over to Izzy as she walked back, several glass bottles balanced in her arms.

"Oh God, Lando, I can't take the dramatics anymore." She gently set the liquor on the counter and went back to grab glasses. "Barry needs to be medicated and after that display, so do I."

Bourbon, a red liquor Noah couldn't place, and a chilled bottle of prosecco were laid out.

"Where's Gio? She will kill me if I open this prosecco without her present," Izzy asked as she came back with a couple crystal lowballs and a rose-tinted champagne flute. Everyone broke apart then and found what appeared to be their assigned seats at the tremendous table.

"Out. For the foreseeable future," Lando said. Izzy's expression fell as she mixed a bubbly drink and took it to the table where Barry sat. Noah followed her movement, catching on the view from the massive window with a surprisingly clear view of the silver arch along the river. Noah glanced to the table with its wooden groans and scrapping chair legs. Lando stared at him.

The older man gave Noah a once over, clicking his tongue against his teeth, before walking toward the head of the table. He sat down, resting his elbows on the table and pressed his hands together as if about to pray.

He called out coolly, "Come, boy. Sit next to me."

Lando waved a lazy hand in the air and patted the spot on the table to his right, currently occupied by Charlie. The man stood and walked to the other end of the table, next to Barry nursing his fizzy concoction.

Noah took his time walking over to the oak table and sat down. Izzy breezed behind him and set a pour of bourbon down, first in front of Lando and then himself. He caught the brief scent of her, vanilla and spice mixed with the smoky liquid in the glass, and watched as her hand brushed his arm as she stood back up. He looked up to see Lando watching him with murder in his eyes.

Swallowing, Noah grasped the clear glass, a single ice orb clinking the sides, and said, "Thank you." He looked the man straight in the eyes and held his drink up toward him. Lando's gaze narrowed before he did the same and they both took a sip, neither dropping the other's stare.

Izzy slid into the seat across from Noah. He watched in his peripheral as she closed her eyes, taking a healthy gulp of the amber liquor, head tilted up with a small smile of satisfaction on her wet, rose lips. A smile he was sure would've been his absolute undoing had he not been preoccupied holding onto his life in a silent staring contest. Her emerald eyes popped open and she looked down her nose between them, before sitting upright. A moment later, she rolled her eyes and set her glass down with a thud that had both men shifting their focus to her.

"Would you like us all to leave you two alone then?" she quipped, eyebrow raised.

The older man barked a hollow laugh at her and took another sip.

"No, *furbacchione,*" he grumbled lowly.

She pursed her lips at him before turning to Noah.

"So, what exactly do you do up there?" she asked.

"You mean the archives?" he replied.

She sighed, leaning back in her chair, studying him. "Yes. Beechum has never had an assistant as far as I know, besides the witch hag at the front desk."

Noah smiled into his glass before taking another sip, holding her gaze as he said, "Organize, mostly. And sort. Rearrange the many boxes of materials. Occasionally, find a request or answer questions for a fellow or researcher... like yourself?"

She smirked, "Observant. Yes, anthropology. You know, the science of humanity." She emphasized that last bit with an expressive flourish of her hands, staring off in fake wonder. Vahagn snorted from down the table. "Which is why I'm truly baffled by The Society ransacking our lab room. We barely have anything of real value in there."

Barry let out a stifled cry into his nearly empty flute. "Says you. Those seventeenth century nudes are priceless."

She pointed a look to Noah that seemed to say, *See, no real value.* He wiped his mouth to hide his smile.

"Did they say anything to you?" Lando croaked to Izzy, leaning back more casually in his chair.

She turned her gaze to the man, eyes lighting up, "Actually, yes! They mentioned something about The Ramblings! But that's just a myth, right? 'A diary of a mad man' or whatever? What would they want with that?"

"Isabella, I do not know why you ask me these kinds of questions all the time," Lando responded, flitting his hands about in the air as if trying to shoo away the academia from the table.

Noah coughed and rubbed a hand across his left forearm, "There are theories…"

Her gaze crashed into him, along with everyone else's at the table, all leaning forward.

"Go on," she purred at him, her eyes narrowing a little. They reflected the twinkle of the Edison bulbs artfully strung above the table. He looked to the clouds outside the window behind her to avoid getting lost in them.

Letting out a deep breath, he continued, "The Ramblings, it is theorized, were essentially what you said, the diary of a mad man. However, that mad man happened to be Charlemagne and the diary's last known whereabouts were on a French merchant ship destined for the New World. That was in 1852, a couple months before Napoleon III became emperor. The trail goes cold from there so it was assumed that the ship likely sank and the book was lost to the sea."

She surveyed his face, brows furrowed, nose wrinkled slightly. He dropped his gaze to his drink. He wondered how deep this hole he dug would get before he fell in. Or ended up kicked in.

"But Charlemagne wasn't considered a mad man?" she pressed.

Leaning softly back in his chair and pushing his hands into his pockets, he said, "That's exactly why it's considered so valuable and also part of the myth. The man was revered by church and people. What could he have written to end up having his diary called The Ramblings?"

Everyone studied him for a few heartbeats that thundered in his ears before Vahagn broke the silence with a loud whistling exhale.

"Well, shit. And you have this book, Z?" the burly man said.

Izzy threw her hands up in exasperation and slumped to the side of her chair, hand under her chin. "I didn't think so, V. I thought that was just a rumor and the fancy old book that arrived in our lab one day was just like… a princess's ledger or a king's black book." Her green eyes glazed over, as if she were searching for answers in her mind. Noah reminded himself not to stare but couldn't look away. A cough sounded from the other end of the table and he broke his trance.

"Well, like I said, it was last seen in 1852 on a ship and last I checked, books and water don't mix well," he offered with a shrug.

He glanced at the clock above the bar.

2:00 p.m.

"How do you know this much about The Ramblings, Noah?" Using his name felt like a threat on her lips.

"New Orleans, remember? French history is our history," he answered.

"Seems like a really in-depth education." Her eyes narrowed some more.

"Well, I did go to college as well… to study history. We do have those in Louisiana," he added, a grin tugging on his lips.

Vahagn laughed and Noah became faintly aware of Charlie's ever-present attention on him.

Izzy raised her eyebrows at him, "Hmm. Seems like a useless thing to study."

He smiled. "About as useful as anthropology," he said before taking another sip of bourbon.

Vahagn doubled over on the table now and even Barry

was smiling, a giddy look on his face as he took a sip of his fizzy drink. Charlie's face remained cold, shooting steely daggers down the table at him. He swallowed. Izzy started to lean forward, a vicious glare, her lips parting for a retort when Lando held up his hand.

"This would make for the most boring dick measuring contest," the man said. Izzy pivoted her glare to the old Italian as he droned on, "And while I'm sure there is some winner in that, I would rather like to know how you came face to face with The Society and walked away, *mi fragola?*"

She cringed at the man before recounting the events of the morning. Noah noted she ended up leaving out the part of holding him against the wall, dagger to his neck. He tilted his head, mouth parting to question her when she skipped over that detail but she only quickly glanced to him, before turning her attention back to… her father? She and Lando didn't look related but their relationship seemed so paternal. She finished her story with them hauling Barry's near lifeless yet conscious and willing body into the big SUV.

"And you know the rest." Taking the last swig of her bourbon, she eyed the bottle on the island.

"How did you know they were The Society then?" Lando asked.

Slumping back into her seat, she gestured across the table. "Noah told me."

A hard pit formed in his stomach. Before Lando could question, he said, "It was the gold, sir. They all had some gold something on them. That and the slinking about in the shadows felt like a dead giveaway."

Izzy sat up, assessing him. He resisted her gaze.

"Gold you say? They teach that in your university

studies then?" Lando asked.

Noah rubbed the back of his neck.

"Um, no, that information came from the streets. Most mortals in New Orleans learned that one quick."

The gold ring flashing on the hand of The Society group leader this morning almost sent Noah fleeing the city. Almost. Looking around the room at what was clearly a group of questionable morals, he probably should have listened to his gut.

Go home, pack up, keep moving North.

But he knew Isabella, Izzy, worked down there. They hadn't actually interacted beyond that day in the archives but he remembered her. It was hard to miss that mess of wine-red curls or those soul piercing eyes on campus. Harder still to forget them too.

Her questioning glare made him realize he was staring again. Swallowing, he looked back to the clock and then out the almost floor to ceiling window to the bright daylight beyond.

"Well, this has been… a conversation." How else was he supposed to summarize an unplanned meeting with a table of mobsters? "But, Mr. Ciampi, and company," glancing around the table, "I really need to get home before it gets dark. I've seen enough of The Society for one day." And he likely needed to go plan his escape of this city now that he was on the radar of the men in this room.

He started to stand when Lando erupted in a fit of booming laughter that spread to everyone else in the room. Everyone except Izzy. Her stare sliced into Lando and she cleared her throat loudly before growling, "Lando is not my father."

Lando began to reel it back in as he glanced at Izzy, snapped once at the rest of the group. The room immediately quieted, though the grin across Vahagn's face held firm.

"No, as much as I love my Isabella like a daughter…

she is not," Lando sighed.

The man acted as if he wanted to say more to that but thought better by Izzy's unrelenting gaze drilling a hole into him.

"I'll walk you out," Izzy said as she pushed back from her chair, green eyes smoldering into Lando the entire time until she stood. Her gaze shifted to Noah, and the fire within cooled marginally.

"Don't go too far, boy. We might have some more questions," Lando commanded, pulling his near empty glass to his lips. Noah could still feel the piercing blue stare from the other end of the table as he made the journey to the elaborate door.

"If anything, we just need the entertainment," Vahagn added, throwing a smile to Izzy. She stopped halfway to the door and threw him a middle finger before continuing on. This only made the man at the table smile bigger.

A room of questionable morals Noah gladly left behind.

⚜

Noah met Izzy in the hallway. She leaned against the wall opposite the doors, her strong arms crossed over her chest.

"Sorry for assuming," he said, trying to do damage control as he pushed the heavy mahogany door shut behind him, throwing all his weight into his back to do so.

She gave him a soft smile and stepped away from the wall.

"In a room full of men who could, and would, tear you in half with their bare hands, plus Barry, I would say you handled yourself surprisingly well. Most men don't have the constitution to even look Lando Denalo in the eye, let alone sit next to him in his own home and drink his bourbon."

Curiosity flicked on her face as she looked him up and down, a slight tilt to her head. Sunlight from the paneled window behind her glinted off her curls, the color of black cherries in the summer.

Noah felt heat rising from his chest under her scrutiny so he started towards the stairwell they had come up earlier. He felt her gaze for a couple steps before she glided up next to him. Glancing sideways at her while she studied the stairs intensely, they climbed down them in silence. She kept the bottom half of her lip held under her front teeth in the most distracting way. He finally got the nerve to say, "You know—" just as she started in with, "Do you think—"

They stopped to grin at each other before he said, "Go ahead."

Flashing a brilliant smile at him, peppered freckles across her nose scrunching, she asked, "Do you think they will keep coming back? Like would they be there now? Tomorrow?" Fear edged her words.

He huffed out a long breath, "Possibly. I wouldn't put it past them to be on a relentless pursuit. Why?"

She looked a bit ghostly then and said, "The book is still in the lab."

His step faltered.

✢ CHAPTER NINE
IzzY

Izzy reached for his arm on instinct as she watched the fear momentarily freeze him mid-step down the marble stairs. A beautiful touch to the building, thanks to Lando, but a hazard when trying to convince a stranger to help rescue a stupid old diary from a basement room recently crawling with bloodthirsty immortals. His forearm muscles flexed under her hand but he remained upright, instead stopping to look at her hand around his arm. What was she doing? The words had just spilled out. Why was her guard so let down around this guy?

Pulling her grasp away quickly, she rubbed her right arm as she started to explain herself, "I have this incredibly old safe in the lab, most people think it's just some artifact along with the rest of the weird shit we have in there. But I actually use it. The skills to crack it are basically archaic and it must weigh like three tons so I've never been worried about someone breaking into it."

A nervous glance up revealed his attentive gaze homed in on her, though his arm muscle remained flex, a sinewed sculpture. Her gaze shot back to the floor as she continued, "We, I mean, that is, I only have a couple more hours of daylight and the —book—the potential copy of The Ramblings—is inside that safe. And they clearly don't know where it is based on the state of the lab this morning. But…"

Lifting her gaze back to him, she hoped her face wasn't a blatant reflection of the fear painted on his own. This half-baked plan was insane. A torrent of thoughts unleashed in those hazel eyes as his lips parted slightly, and then he said, matter of fact, "You want me to go with you."

"Yes." She chewed on her bottom lip again.

He exhaled, releasing the tension in his body, fist unfurling to run through his wavy hair, the color a confused shade of dark chocolate, "Why me?"

Great fucking question.

Holding his gaze for a couple seconds, she tried desperately to reckon with her perception of him. He felt trustworthy, safe. But how could she convey that to him without sounding delusional? It would involve explaining why she didn't want any of those fools at the table upstairs knowing about her secret hiding spot. That as much as they had done for her, given her, she still couldn't trust them with every part of her. It had been what infuriated her by Lando's ridiculous barking at the Mr. Ciampi comment. But staring, assessing those hazel eyes as they searched for an explanation from her, she felt the flood gates threaten to open. She faltered and looked away before saying, "You said you're from New Orleans? And clearly know a thing or two about The Society and those goons upstairs," motioning with her head to the penthouse above, "are liable to shoot first and never ask questions so I thought you might be my best bet."

A muscle clenched in his jaw as he regarded her and the

explanation she hoped would convince him.

A heartbeat passed.

Then another.

God, this had been a mistake. He would leave this building, go straight to Beechum and tell him she needs to be reviewed. Investigated for her ties to two gangs and a lurid collection of associates. As well as searched for weapons. And charged for assault.

She felt a bead of sweat roll down her back.

"Okay," he said calm, assertive, and continued his descent down the stairs. She nearly fell down the stairs as she started off behind him.

"Okay… okay. Thank you. I, uh, know this is a big ask for someone you've literally just met and who might have held a knife to your neck earlier."

He glanced back, a smirk on his beautiful face. "Yeah, now that you mention that this *does* feel like a big ask." His hand brushed over the small cut on his neck, the blood having dried and been cleaned up on their way to Lando's earlier.

She blushed a little but he thankfully missed it.

"Small casualty for the state of the world."

A low laugh escaped him. "I'll consider myself lucky it was only small then."

And she could've sworn that smile was still on his face as he pushed through the heavy door out of the stairwell and into the lobby of the building.

❖

She hadn't bothered to let anyone sitting back at Lando's table know where she went. Or with who. The bourbon bottle still open on the island had a few more rounds left in it and she knew the rest of the crew would be swarming back soon before the dark set in to report to their boss while Vahagn painted a colorful depiction of the morning's developments. They hopefully, probably, assumed she had gone back to her apartment below them, dissociating with some work of fiction or staring hopeless out her window.

The apartment building sat a short walk from campus, the primary reason she had moved there after taking on this research role. Plus, Lando offered a discount for university staff "to keep the riffraff down"—a laughable statement now that she knew about his dealings within this city, both before The Society and still to this day.

She and Noah kept in silent contemplation for a while before she asked, "Do you live nearby?"

She must have snapped him out of some deep thought because he looked blankly at her and then around before giving a small grin, "Yeah, not too far. I never wanted to get stuck on campus with nowhere to feasibly go. Just in case." He smiled at her.

Just in case a deranged woman pulled him from his reality and into the chaos that was her own life to join on a quest for a very old, very important bedazzled journal.

She nodded in understanding, "Yeah, it's sort of my security blanket, being this close." She continued as they passed onto campus, heading back towards their mutual building. "You know, we've met before."

He raised his eyebrows at her but didn't add anything.

"Yep," she said, giving him a smile that hopefully didn't make her sound anymore unhinged given the situation. "I typically just send Barry upstairs because your director..."

"Dr. Beechum," he provided.

"Yes, Dr. Beechum is a lot. And while I study

anthropology, I don't actually want to spend every human interaction dissecting the sociocultural impacts of our conversation matter."

He laughed. "I could see that." He glanced over, then added, "I remember. You came to ask questions about this very book."

Anger briefly flooded her senses as she remembered how Dr. Beechum fawned over Noah's opinion that day.

"You've quickly attained golden boy status with a man I assumed liked nothing in this world." She smirked.

Grinning at the ground before meeting her gaze, a twinkle in his golden eyes, he stopped walking and nodded to the building before them.

"We're here."

Peering up at the building, the memory of this morning fresh enough to cause some trepidation, she glanced to her left at the sun now making its slow descent to end the day and knew it was now or never. She doubted she could convince Noah to join her on a different day, if she even ever saw him again after all that happened. And she really did not want to make this trip on her own. Or worse, with a tail. A dark haired, overbearing tail.

A hand quietly took hers and squeezed, a small gesture of reassurance from a stranger that sent a flutter through her heart. She looked at their intertwined hands and up to his eyes as he stared into the courtyard before them. Feeling her gaze, he looked to her then and quickly pulled his hand away. "Still have that knife on you?"

She smiled broadly, pulling it out from its holster at her side. She twirled it between her pointer and middle finger before gripping the handle with her right hand. Rolling his eyes, he whispered something along the lines of, "Devilish," before walking toward the stairwell down to the little hallway of misfit labs. Trailing behind, the smile on her face willed her to not turn and run the opposite direction. Despite the steady thrum of blood she felt in her neck.

The hallway looked normal. Lights on. Nobody around. She led them to their laboratory toward the end, her heart rate steadily raising with each step. Noah flanked her left side, practically floating along even though he took sideways steps to keep an eye behind them. She pulled her key card from her pocket as they stood back-to-back in front of the door. The heat radiated off him into her skin chasing away the haunting sound of that click a bit before they shuffled into the room. She hadn't fully taken in the damage to the room this morning but it was a fucking disaster.

"Did you remember Barry saying anything about talking to The Society?" she mused, climbing over the debris.

Noah took in a three-hundred-and-sixty-degree view of the room. When he slowly turned back to face her, brows furrowed, he said, "No?"

"Hmm… that demented Thomas Shelby wannabe this morning said they had paid him a visit last night but he never mentioned that?"

Why would Barry lie about something that likely would've sent him into cardiac arrest?

Noah's eyebrows furled, "Maybe they were bluffing?"

She pursed her lips and turned to continue making her way into the room, "Maybe."

They stepped over endless papers and artifacts that would require her to grovel to Dr. Beechum in an attempt to prevent him from making her pay for them. Though she knew Lando would handle it, she didn't like making a deal with the devil himself.

"My God, you weren't kidding when you said this thing was ancient," Noah remarked as they approached the giant, antique safe.

Sliding her hand over it, she smiled a little. This thing had held her dearest possessions and memories all these years without fault. Barry once talked about having it removed from the room because "it put off the vibe." However, the maintenance crew said there was no way it could ever be moved. So, it stayed. Barry assumed it would be locked forever, taking away prime real estate in their small space, but she had cracked it within the first week of working down in the lab. She couldn't remember the last time something felt truly safe in her life and this ridiculous hunk of metal provided just that.

"Okay, please turn around." She turned to Noah, waving her hand at him to emphasize.

"You can't be serious?" He raised an eyebrow at her.

"I actually am." She stared him down.

He put his hands up and began turning around, "Fine. Keep your secrets, Ciampi. Just don't get any ideas with that knife again, please."

She smirked at his broad back, this position emphasizing the muscles of his upper body and lower. Peeling her eyes away, she got to work opening the safe. The metal components clunked and clanked together, grinding and whirling until a satisfying click followed by sweet silence announced it was unlocked. Heaving the door open with a grunt, she didn't take a moment to marvel in the artifacts of her life before her, instead she zeroed in on the old, leather-bound book enclosed in its protective plastic in the back. She snatched it up, putting it under her arm as she heaved the door back closed. She whirled the lock around and turned back to Noah as it clicked into place.

"Okay, let's go."

He turned, arms still raised, and glanced to the package under her arm, eyes widening. She nestled it into her leather bag. His arms dropped then met her stare before gesturing to the door. "Ladies first."

Her brows rose, "Oh, a gentleman? You must not have been in this city that long then. That shit's usually the first thing to go."

She thought she saw what looked like dread run across his face but then he smirked at her and let his accent drawl heavily as he replied, "A Southern man is always a gentleman."

She laughed as she pushed the door open and started down the hallway back towards the steps. Hearing the door click closed behind her, she started to turn to make a joke about how history suggested otherwise. But her opportunity for comedic timing disappeared as a hand gripped her arm and hauled her across the hall, into the shadows.

ARE YOU FOREVER

❧

CHAPTER TEN
Izzy

She opened her mouth to begin a ruthless verbal assault featuring some of her favorite curses when Noah pushed her into the deep alcove further. He placed one hand over her mouth, the other caught the wall above her shoulder as her back softly thumped into it. She glared up at him but the fear in his stare softened her gaze. He dropped his hand from her mouth and slid it to the holster at her side, his fingers grazing across her stomach before finding the hilt of the blade she had stashed there to open the safe. Pushing off her, he started backing out the darkness in the alcove, glancing over his shoulder toward the stairs.

Cold followed the space he previously occupied and fear pressed into her, trapping her within the stone confines of the alcove. Trapped. In an alcove. Without a weapon. While a man she literally just held that very knife to this morning goes off to protect her.

Fuck.

Noah glanced one last time to her, though she doubted

he could see through the shadows. But she saw him, the fear creasing the edges of his eyes, pulling his plump lips taunt. She also saw the fiery gaze of a man about to go to battle. She had seen it enough times on Charlie's face to recognize the look.

He started toward the stairs, leaving her to stare into the hallway, unsure who would be the next face she saw. Heart racing at the prospect that it wouldn't be him, she glanced to the door they had exited across the way moments ago. Too far. Too exposed. She couldn't make it. Especially unarmed.

Fuuuuuuck.

She stared up at the dark ceiling of the deep alcove. So, this is where she would die. Would Lando come to her funeral? Would Vahagn cry? Would *Charlie* cry? Barry would definitely cry, enough for all of them. She blinked back these thoughts, rage started blooming inside her chest.

This would be a supremely stupid way to die.

She started to charge out of the alcove, destined to not die like a damsel in distress when she heard what sounded like a fist hitting flesh and a grunt.

A familiar grunt.

Hurrying toward the stairs she took in the scene before her, footsteps faltering to a stop. Noah stood defensively next to Charlie. Who was hunched over.

"What the actual fuck Charlie? I was sitting here planning my own goddamn funeral and you're out here... *why* are you out here?" she barked at the groveling man.

He glanced up at her then to Noah before releasing a loud groan as he straightened, a hand over the left side of his stomach.

"I went by," he tossed a glancing glare in Noah's direction, "your apartment. But when you didn't answer I... let myself in. Just to see you weren't there."

"You broke into my fucking apartment?" Her blood started to boil. The audacity. The fucking audacity of this man.

"Yes, because you didn't answer. So, then I ran upstairs and had Data track your phone to here. I thought you were crazy Izzy but not enough to warrant a death wish."

"You tracked my phone?" Was there enough sunlight left in the day to go dump a body in the river?

"I thought you were in trouble." He tried to plead his case, gesturing to Noah for emphasis. "Are you in trouble?"

"Are you fucking delusional, Charlie?" she seethed, pacing back and forth. Noah even backed up a step, dagger in his hand but arms raised innocently. She tried not to notice how the motion caused his shirt to pull tight across his chest. Ugh, fuck men.

Charlie's gaze turned to her, glowering. "No, Isabella, I am not delusional. You were gone, no note, nobody knew where the fuck you went. The last person we all saw you with was him. Was I just supposed to accept that?"

"You certainly weren't supposed to track me down like a lost dog."

She stalked toward Noah. This conversation was over in her opinion. Fuck Lando and his protective ass cronies. Fuck Data and his genius boy tech skills. And fuck Charlie and his delusions.

Noah flipped the dagger and handed it to her, hilt first. As she went to put it back in her holster to leave this shit show, Charlie reached for her arm and whirled her around to face him.

"Izzy…"

Too goddamn late. The tip of the dagger pressed into the lump in his throat before he could finish his sentence.

"When does it end, Charlie?" she asked through

clenched teeth, her voice a smoldering whisper. "When do I finally convince you I don't need you? I never needed you and I no longer even want you."

Charlie's eyes burned with anger and she saw that muscle in his jaw twitch. Just as it did that night, right before… She held her ground and pressed the knife further into his skin, lips snarling. He glanced behind her to where Noah waited and stepped away from her knife, letting go of her arm.

"Not here, Z."

She backed away a step, flipping her knife into her holster. Giving Charlie a final glare she hoped conveyed her visions of bursting him into flames, she started up the stairs without a word. Footsteps sounded a couple steps behind her and instinctively knew they weren't *his*.

He may be delusional but he wouldn't be stupid enough to risk her shoving his giant ass down these concrete stairs.

Keeping her pace as she walked out of the courtyard and back onto campus, toward that old warehouse she called home, she only stopped stewing long enough to glance to the sky. The sun had started to paint the sky in the beautiful brush strokes of sunset. A time she missed the most since before The Society and its immortality corrupted everything good in the world.

Still brewing in her thoughts, she heard Noah say gently, "Izzy?"

She slowed but didn't stop. An invitation, though thin, for him to approach.

Striding up next to her, he matched her pace and asked, "Are you okay?"

She glanced to his hazel eyes. They were striking at this time of day, the painted sky reflected within those golden shades. She gave him a half smile.

"I have been better. But I'll be fine."

She looked to the sky, reaching up to slide the golden cross along the chain around her neck, and then glanced back to his face, the concern and care in that beautiful face. "You need to get home soon."

He didn't break his gaze as he said, "I know." But he made no effort to move in any other direction than with her.

She sighed.

"Charlie and I have… a complicated history." To put it lightly. Fuck, she could still feel how his hands pinned her thighs to the bed, his breath between her legs...

But as easy as it was to enjoy Charlie in bed it was just as easy to hate him outside of it. He was possessive and controlling, never trusting her to be able to exist without him. She knew he thought he was being endearing, the protector every girl fantasized dating a gangster would be like, but she felt smothered.

When she told him as much, he had smacked her to the floor and torn her front door off its hinges as he left in a thunder. No one saw him for two days after that. Vahagn helped put her door back on and Barry pulled out some inspirational "fuck men, drink vodka" energy in an attempt to make her feel less sad. It worked. For a while at least. Except now her sadness had been replaced with a callous fury.

"I gathered as much," Noah said, finally looking ahead. She watched him swallow, his jaw set, creases in his forehead as if deep in thought. Rotating the onyx ring on her thumb, she began weighing that intuition in her heart again. How much did she want to say to this man? How much should she say to him?

"That was juvenile comparatively." Regret coated her mouth at the confession.

He raised an eyebrow to her but bit back the response

she could see floating to the surface.

She sighed.

She really wished it would've been anyone but Charlie. But who would've even noticed she was gone? Why had he even gone to her apartment? He lived on the first floor of the building with Vahagn.

Another fight for another time.

Lost in her thoughts again, she didn't realize they were right back in front of her building until Noah stopped walking. She surveyed the dwindling sunlight in the sky and the shadows it cast on the street around them.

"Are you sure you'll be fine getting back to your place? It's not much but my couch..." she said, not sure why she willingly offered her home to this stranger. She had officially lost it.

Giving her a sideways smile, those hazel eyes twinkling in the amber glow of the incoming night, he turned to face the building across the road then glanced back to her, "Yeah, I think I'll be okay."

Stepping off the curb, he jogged across the desolate street that no one dared to find themselves on after dark, and typed a code into the keypad at the front door of the similarly refashioned warehouse-turned-apartment-building. Right across the street.

He turned back to her, flashing a smile in response to her gaping mouth, before raising his voice enough for her to hear him drawl, "See you around, neighbor."

He didn't give her a chance to contemplate a reply before he closed the door behind him, giving her one last glance from behind the thick glass door. Then he turned and disappeared into the building.

A blush crept up her face as she entered her own

building, clutching her bag close to her body. She hoped for his sake none of Lando's crew saw him. Rule number one of surviving this city: don't let the mob know where you live.

CHAPTER ELEVEN
NOAH

Noah should have left as soon as he got back to his apartment. To his credit, his bags were packed and then promptly abandoned on the floor as he sat back on his mattress, running hands through his hair. He had been fully prepared to leave, even after uncovering that book with Izzy. But then that brute of a man showed up and the anger and the hurt in Izzy's face... His mistake was watching her pick through her words, to tell him it's "complicated", sending a fucking dagger to his heart.

He shouldn't care but he knew that feeling. Knew what it felt like to wake up from the accepted turmoil of life, no longer convinced it was deserved. But also, unaware how to escape it either. It was bold of him to infer about her situation but he knew that hurt in her eyes. Recognized the look he stared at in the mirror every morning all those years…

Insistent knocks boomed across the apartment as he played emotional Battleship with himself.

No one knew him here. At least they hadn't until today. Jumping to his feet, he had enough sense to kick his bags under his bed and shut the bedroom door before unlocking everything but the security chain. A scowling face of the man he just sat seething about stared back at him.

"Charlie, was it?" Noah snarked at the man.

Charlie huffed out a humorless laugh and said, "We come to offer a proposal courtesy of Lando Denalo." His attempt at a smile would send a child screaming.

Noah raised an eyebrow and gazed around his ridiculously huge frame, "We?"

The slightly shorter but equally large man he remembered as Vahagn stepped off to the side and waved, his smile a stark contrast to his burly blonde beard.

"Ah." Fuck. "And this meeting couldn't just be an email?"

Nothing but blank stares peered back.

"Of course not," he muttered under his breath, as he tossed the door closed long enough to pull the chain off and swing it back open, arms splayed dramatically.

"Welcome. Please, come in."

Charlie simply grunted at his mock hospitality as he sauntered in but Vahagn clapped Noah on the shoulder as he passed and said, "I like you, kid."

Noah rolled his eyes. At thirty, he would hardly call himself a kid but he also still looked like any one of the students on campus. So, fuck it, let them believe he was a young, idiot academic. It presented an easy facade to slink back into.

Locking the deadbolt, he walked into the small living room right off the entrance. The apartment itself wasn't overly special with a small kitchen, simple living room with a brick fireplace, a small bedroom and bathroom jutting off of that. Quaint but what really sold him was the giant floor to ceiling industrial steel window with its many vertical panes and old-world wonder. Plus, it came fully furnished.

The night sky spilled into the space, a beauty he had fully disregarded until it suddenly became a symbol of terror. Apparently it even drew in the wonderment of these idiots now in his apartment as they peered out it, toward the building across the way. The view Noah knew too well.

The walls felt closer now with the three men standing within. He had never had guests before.

"Please, sit, make yourselves comfortable." He gestured to the tufted leather couch in front of them while casually sinking into one of the two matching armchairs to the side of the fireplace. Vahagn hopped over the back and sat down with such force Noah couldn't hide his cringe. Charlie raised an eyebrow at his comrade, walking around to sit down in a less aggressive, albeit still uncomfortable, manner. Resting his elbows on his knees, he clasped his hands between his legs and said, "Lando wants to work with you."

Alarms blared in his mind and he was back, sprinting through the streets as dust and blood stuck to his sweat, in his throat, devastation erupting around him.

"Work with him, how?" He feigned ignorance. Another table, another set of strong arms seated across from him, Benji at his side. He blinked. He afforded himself that one reaction.

"Well," Charlie sat back, hands still clasped together, now at his chest, "he would have to assess you first."

"And if I don't want to be assessed?" The words came out with more bite than Noah intended.

A muscle in Charlie's jaw tightened.

"It can't always be easy finding a way out of this city."

A statement and a crystal-clear threat.

"Huh, well it seemed pretty easy to get in." Noah tried to quiet the roaring of explosions and buildings crumbling in his mind, instead setting a steel gaze on Charlie. Vahagn observed the back and forth with the same amusement as someone watching Serena at the US Open.

Charlie broke first and sighed, "That's the wicked curse of this city, I'm afraid. So easy to get in, so hard to escape." Escape. Because leaving wouldn't be willing at this point. "Like any good woman," he chipped in with a wink.

The chaos in Noah's mind swiftly turned to rage as the image of those agonizing emerald eyes pushed aside the visions of fire and brimstone. His jaw throbbed with the pressure of his clenching teeth when he finally growled, "Fine. When is this assessment? I'm assuming it's across the street since your boss can't be bothered to step pass his medieval barricade."

Loathing flickered across Charlie's face, enough to make Noah smirk. Target hit.

"6:30, tomorrow morning. I'll come get you," Charlie said curtly as he and Vahagn stood up, starting back toward the door.

"I don't need an escort." He followed them to the door, not wanting to waste a second in locking their asses out.

Vahagn undid the deadbolt and walked into the hallway but Charlie paused halfway through the threshold, tattooed hand on the door.

"I would warn against starting off on Lando's bad side with your smart comments." An unnerving kindness.

"The key to an assessment is to be the smarter than the test, right?"

Charlie simply glared back at him before walking out, pulling the door shut with more force than necessary. Noah immediately went to work on the locks and bolts but couldn't resist saying just loud enough to echo into the hall, "Could've been an email."

The growl he heard in response did little to quell the storm of memories and emotions that flooded back in their wake.

❖

The rest of the night was spent rattling his sanity as he toyed with staying or going, his packed bags mocking him from under the bed. By the time his alarm went off at 6:00 a.m., he had already been staring at the ceiling for the past hour, the familiar chime deafening in the silence threatening to bury him.

He pulled on a t-shirt and gym shorts, went to the kitchen to brew a quick cup of coffee in an attempt to garner enough of his soul back to reality. As far as he saw it, there were only two options for this *assessment*: fight or flop. Fight, for real. Or flop, showing a lame hand, which meant he would probably be exiled to researching secrets in the extensive library he possessed the key to but that also risked revealing his own secrets in the process. Fighting, that was easy. Get the other guy on the ground, preferably dead but at the least, incapacitated for an extended period of time.

That he had trained for, knew like the back of his hand.

That would be his safety blanket for as long as it took to figure out his moral dilemma and get the fuck out of this city.

An unnecessary boom of a knock rattled him back to the present. He would fight. That's all he knew at this point. Downing the rest of his coffee with a wince, he made his way to open the door.

"You know your knock is entirely unnecessary. I mean," he gestured to the hallway behind the man, "I can hear you breathing halfway down the hall. Knock, unnecessary." He pushed past Charlie. Stealing one last glance to those captivating windows he adored, he sent a hopeful wish this wasn't the last time he would see them and locked the door.

Charlie merely grunted in response and trailed him down the stairs, across the lobby, and out to the first beams of sunrise.

❧

CHAPTER TWELVE
Izzy

Trudging up to her apartment that night, Izzy had triple checked her locks to ensure Charlie couldn't disturb her fleeting peace then all but passed out on her bed, fully clothed, with the book still in its protective plastic next to her.

She woke with a start, glancing outside to see it was still dark out. Rolling over with a groan she checked the clock on her phone: 4:45 a.m.

Perfect.

Even as she felt the fatigue set deep in her bones, she needed whatever torture Lando had in store for her in the gym this morning. If for any reason but to imagine Charlie's stupid face on a punching bag while she repetitively kicked until satisfied it would wipe the smugness off the real thing. Hopefully as he walked in.

She quickly traded her clothes from the previous day for a matching black set of leggings and a cropped tank top. She chugged a large glass of water, pouring a little out to the hydration gods to prevent the headache she felt creeping up the base of her skull, and pulled on her tennis shoes. Working through her elaborate locking system to her door took a hot minute, and as she heaved the door open in a rush, she walked right into Vahagn standing there, fist raised, mere seconds from knocking.

The surprise on his face would've been insulting if she didn't normally need a full body shaking to wake up in time for the 5 a.m. workouts Lando *insisted* on daily.

"Not my preferred morning visual and not required today. Sorry V."

He dropped his fist and ran the hand through his scruffy hair, "Always lovely to see you in the morning too, Z."

She rolled her eyes and pushed into the hallway as he stepped back, closing the door firmly behind her and making a dramatic show of locking *every* padlock she had installed when she first moved here. Vahagn raised an eyebrow but didn't say a word as she finished, turning toward the stairs at the end of the hall. They climbed that cool, marble staircase, in silence, walking into the hallway before Lando's grand entrance.

Stationed across the hall from the door, Charlie only glanced sideways as she walked past him, his jaw jutting out slightly – the only tell that her words from the previous day still stung. The burning ember of anger gave her the momentum to heave that ridiculous fucking door of Lando's open, Vahagn following behind her. She gave Charlie's sad, stony gaze a glare before hauling the door shut behind them, closing it with a satisfying clunk. Vahagn witnessed the whole thing and said as she stalked off toward the gym, "He didn't mention why he was in such a pissy attitude last night but I'm going to guess he didn't exactly woo himself back into your bed... again?" She scowled at him. He just raised an eyebrow. "Or maybe he did."

She made to kick him behind the knee but the old

bastard was too fast and twisted, catching her ankle instead. He dropped it to the ground and calmly said, "Save it for Lando."

She held up both middle fingers to him as payment for his unsolicited advice.

❖

Lando's paranoia for The Society and her close call with them fueled the most intense workout of her life. He had brought out a broad sword, *a fucking broad sword,* towards the end when she was already dripping sweat, dry heaving in a corner.

"This isn't the Battle of fucking Troy, Lando," she barked at him through heavy breaths.

"No, Isabella, it is much worse and we need to be prepared to defend ourselves in all ways possible," he insisted, pushing the handle of the sword into her hand. His mood had been foul all morning and she wondered how much Charlie had told him about her little side quest.

God, the sword was heavy. Her arms trembled just trying to keep it up.

"Honestly, if it comes to this, I'll just surrender."

Lando attacked her then, holding a sword she hadn't seen him grab. Sneaky bastard. Throwing her own hunk of steel up across her body to block, she grunted against the effort, a grimace on her face. Lando glared angrily at her face.

"Don't you *ever* say that, Isabella." Jeez, he really had woken up on the intense side of his mulberry silk sheets today.

She glared back, "What does it even matter to you, *Lando?*"

He pushed back and attacked in the other direction. She stepped quickly to defend, grimacing again as her muscles burned, beads of sweat rolling down her forehead.

"We bow to *no one.* You especially. Understood?" he

growled to her.

Her eyes widened a little. Lando had always been protective of her but never in a coddling way. He taught her to respect and defend herself, something she had truly appreciated more than she could ever express to him. It was what kept her around despite the rest of his many fatal character flaws.

She stared back at him, her arms trembling slightly as she pushed back against his weight, wondering how much he even knew about her and Charlie. The thought gave her an extra spark and she growled, shoving against his weight. The movement sent him stumbling back several steps. Taking the opportunity, she charged forward on burning legs, swinging the heavy blade behind her then down across from her right side.

This time Lando grunted as he raised his own blade to block, a proud look of shock on his face. A smile slowly creased the edges of his dark brown eyes as he glanced to the entrance to the gym. She didn't dare let him deceive her, instead taking the moment of distraction to push herself under his raised arm. She whipped her body around to kick him in the back of the knee and he fell forward onto them. The dagger at her thigh was in her hand, pointed into his chest in seconds. She palmed the flat side of his blade, pinning his back to her. Only then did she chance an eye to the doorway and a new type of rage boiled to the surface as she locked eyes with Charlie. Snarling, she kneed Lando in the back while releasing her grip on the sword, pulling her dagger out of the way. The older man dropped his sword to catch himself, hovering inches above the floor, smiling like a fool.

"Take a fucking picture, Charlie." She made no attempt to disguise the bite in her voice.

Charlie's eyes narrowed slightly and his lips pulled into a tight half-grin before he stepped aside to reveal Noah standing behind him. The rage threatening to explode from her veins went ice cold. *Why was he here?*

She gave him a questioning look but he gave nothing in response. Charlie gestured for him to walk over to the lockers and he did, dropping a duffle bag off his shoulder.

Lando let out a soft chuckle as he pushed off the ground and hopped up onto his feet in one fluid movement. Showoff.

"Well, that sure shut you up, *scalmanato*. Wish I would've found the kid years ago had I known it was that easy." She picked her sword back up and pointed it at the old man's chest.

"Is he here against his own will?" Her arms begged to tremble with the weight of the sword balanced off the edge of her extended arm but she didn't dare yield to him.

His returning smile sent goosebumps down her spine. "Now, Isabella, you know I would never *force* anyone here." He winked and she glared at him. "But we did take some liberties in… convincing him to come."

Noah snorted from the bench he sat at, forearms resting on his thighs as he watched this whole conversation unfold.

"Were these legal liberties?" The heat of her anger raged anew in her chest.

"By what laws?" Lando chimed, his stupid Italian accent grating on her nerves.

She glared at him until her face turned to a grimace, no longer able to hold that sword up any longer. It fell to the floor in a clatter and she bent over, breathing heavily while Lando started over toward Noah.

"Welcome, boy, to your first day."

Cursing under her breath, she hurried over to step in front of Lando's extended hand. Noah sat up, surprise in his hazel eyes, and she searched his face. He tilted his head, an inquisitive look passing over him.

"Why are you here?" She winced at the accusation in her tone. He flashed a sheepish grin, rubbing the back of his neck before glancing at Charlie then back to her.

"You want the long or the short end of this tale?" His drawl came out slow and gravelly with the early hour, sending shivers down her spine.

"Whichever version is the truth."

"Ah, I'd never dare lie to you, Izzy." Amusement twinkled in his eyes. So, these liberties Charlie and Lando took couldn't have been that bad if he was willing to blatantly flirt with her in front of these jugheads. She glanced at Charlie and pursed her lips.

"The short version is fine," she quipped.

He followed her gaze and understanding flitted across his face. "Turns out Charlie knows one of the night doormen for my building so he and Vahagn decided to stop by for a visit last night with an offer I just couldn't refuse."

Her brows furrowed together, "What *kind* of offer?" *Surely to God he knew who he was dealing with…*

"Don't worry, Isabella, he's not working for me exactly," Lando chimed in from behind her.

She whirled around, fire blazing at him, "What does *that* mean, *Orlando*?" The cut to Lando's ego was deep enough to garner a glare from him. Learning his weakness had been an early survival tactic and using his real name happened to be one of them.

Family issues stick with a person.

His voice seethed, the accent coming on thicker, hinting at the vicious nature that made him the most prominent mob boss in this city, "It *means* he has information I want and in return, I train him how not to let a little *girl* slice him to bits in a dingy hallway."

At this point, a headache threatened from her failed attempts to ignite these idiots in flames with her gaze. Noah snapped her out of the murderous fury coursing through her blood by contributing, "To be fair, I can defend myself. I also don't make it a point to fight first when I'm trying to ensure someone hasn't been harassed by thugs." She snapped her gaze to him and he simply shrugged at her.

Admirable. Idiotic but admirable to display dignity and honor in a room full of actual thugs.

"Fine, but he trains at the same time as me," she announced to the room, eyes still focused on him.

All eyebrows shot up at her declaration, all for different reasons.

"To make sure you don't kill him or vice versa." The excuse tumbled out as she tore her gaze from Noah's.

Charlie grunted at this but a raised eyebrow was all she deigned to waste on him, remembering exactly who had handled the situation last night in that dingy hallway.

Lando looked from Noah to her a couple times before responding.

"Fine, but we start later so the poor guy doesn't have to play Frogger with those monsters out there before the sun rises."

She tamed her excitement at hearing this. The 5 a.m. wake up calls were truly getting old. "Fine, 7 a.m.?" She glanced to Noah. He gave her an approving nod. "Okay, 7 a.m. And call off your dogs, we don't need escorts. Just give him a code to the building."

Surprise flashed across Noah's face and it was understandable. She literally *just* had a knife ready to slice open his jugular yesterday and now she was what? Advocating for him to have full access to her place of residence? That feeling in her chest surged again, her intuition to trust him. When had she last had that feeling? Her gaze flicked to Vahagn who gave her a 'what the fuck are you thinking' stare. A smile etched on her face but it quickly fell when Charlie walked up to whisper something in Vahagn's ear.

Maybe her heart couldn't be trusted either.

The battle of will played across Lando's face as she mentally questioned her decision before he finally sighed. "Fine. He gets a code, no escorts. 7 a.m." He looked at the other two men in the room, "Anymore requests while I'm feeling amiable?"

She would hardly call any of this amiable. Neither man spoke.

"Good, then let's get to fucking work."

He clapped a hand on Noah's shoulder and he stood, following Lando toward a power rack in the back of the room. He glanced back at her and she swore she caught a smile play at the corner of his lips before he turned his focus back to the exercise Lando demonstrated.

The small action didn't go unnoticed by Charlie. He stepped up next to her, following her gaze.

"I considered killing him last night." His tone came out unbothered, like he conveyed the weather forecast and didn't just admit to conspiring to commit a crime. A heinous crime.

"I thought I said my peace the other night," she turned to him, "and again last night. But I'm really starting to think you don't listen to me because here you are, fixated on being jealous of a man I *actually* almost killed yesterday." His ocean eyes seared into her, steely against his dark features. It infuriated her.

"Let me remind you, Charlie," his name seethed like a curse across her tongue, "the only reason Lando doesn't know the truth about us, about what actually happened, is because I *know* it's a death sentence for you." A muscle tensed in his jaw, as he glanced over to where Lando demonstrated another exercise to Noah. He seemed to be humoring the old man by listening intently. Neither glanced their way. "So next time you want to start this bullshit, be prepared for how thin my patience is wearing."

She didn't give him a chance to respond before she stalked off toward a section of the massive room designated for stretching, right next to the sauna and cold plunge tank. Golden eyes caught her gaze as she flicked open a mat a little too aggressive, his eyebrows furrowing under loose waves of dark auburn hair as he glanced back to where she had left Charlie standing. Staring straight ahead, she tried to forget his presence and the presence of every other man in this room. When she first walked into this gym years ago, she was weak, mentally and physically. Yet she willingly walked into the lion's den. She hadn't even known her own strength until the night Charlie's anger had detonated. And now look at her? Her sheets still held his intoxicating citrus scent, mocking her fortitude every time she laid in them.

That same fortitude broke as she heard a grunt of pain from the sparring ring.

Watching Noah's workout was brutal… for Lando. She knew the old man restrained himself with her. But she had never seen him breathe so hard, not even sparring with Charlie or Vahagn. Noah was strong, though not nearly as bulky as the other two men, but he was also *fast*. He looked like the one holding back a few times.

She tried not to gawk while working through a cool down routine but eventually she found herself mouth open, eyes fixed on the carnage while steaming like a crown of broccoli in the sauna. Vahagn strode in with just a towel around his waist, closing her mouth with a single finger under her chin. She quickly scurried out of the small box before he could joke about her objectification of men.

Bracing herself, she plunged into the ice bath, fully clothed minus her shoes and socks unlike the heathen still chuckling to himself in the sauna. The chill went straight to her bones, clearing her head. Eyes closed, she focused on her breath, calming the urgent pressure signaling for her to seize up. She willed herself to stay in as long as she could. Time slowed until there nothing but her inhale, exhale, and the numbing water pressing against her. She slipped under, gasping as she resurfaced and pulled herself from the tub. A warming cabinet stuffed with luxurious fluffy towels sat against the mirrored wall, and she ripped one out to wrap around herself. Warmth enveloped her body, as she shivered from the four minutes in the tub. Four minutes that had felt like a lifetime.

She finally opened her eyes to meet Noah's gaze in the mirror. He sat on the other side of the tub, legs stretched out in front of him on the padded floor. They had finished sooner than she expected, probably so Lando could save face before his other clients arrived for their self-defense class. Grinning at the thought, she watched Noah's head tilt sideways at her. She padded over to him, dripping water as she went. His curious look tracked her movement and his spine straightened as she approached.

"You promise they didn't force you here?" She kept her voice hushed by the towel, pressing it to her trembling lips.

He tracked the fabric as it shuttered from the touch and chuckled. His gaze fell to the floor then he looked back up at her with a half-smile, one eye closed.

"I wouldn't call it forced. I was given an option but do

you feel like you actually have options when those brutes are delivering them?" He gestured to Vahagn, asleep in the sauna, and Charlie, glowering from a bench in the back of the room as he curled a dumbbell.

"Not usually," she said and her face must have revealed too much of the truth behind those words because the amusement quickly vanished from Noah's face. She spoke before he could question her further on the topic, "Are you almost done?"

His eyes darkened at the quick detour in conversation but he didn't press her on it.

"Almost."

"Cool, I want you... I want you to come look at this thing." A group of middle-aged professors and bankers came in through the doors, causing her to tiptoe over her words.

"Um, sure. I don't have to be on campus until 9 a.m." The clock above the mirror showed it was almost 8 a.m. Not a lot of time to look at a historical artifact of great significance but it would have to do. In truth, she just needed him to either confirm the book was nothing more than a glorified school notebook and she was paranoid or that it was in fact The Ramblings and she could justifiably spiral into a pit of despair.

"Okay, I'm going to finish drying off some. Meet me in the hallway, one floor down in fifteen."

He glanced at the puddle she had created before him and smirked.

"Whatever comment you're about to make, shove it."

His hazel eyes gleamed up at her, "I would never. Southern gentleman, remember?"

His quiet laugh followed her as she stalked back to the towel warmer to grab another, a smile pulling on her own lips.

"Hallway. Fifteen minutes. Noah, what's your last

name?" She whirled back around at him.

He glanced around for a second and said just loud enough for her to hear, "Broussard."

An eyebrow rose on her face and she replied at the same volume, "Broussard... fifteen minutes."

His returning smile momentary took her back to his body pressed against her in that alcove, before she had recognized the fear in his eyes. His full lips so close to hers she could smell the bourbon on them. The press of his broad hand against her stomach as he searched for her blade.

She shook her head, rolling her shoulders to play it off. Such a shame all these gangster types had to be so damn good looking. Even Vahagn wasn't an eye sore, fulfilling every Viking fantasy. But she didn't need another one of Lando's men warming her bed. Besides the obvious that she didn't even know this guy, Charlie already threatened to murder him. Hell, he probably will if he finds out she invited him to her apartment. The same apartment she had let him climb between her legs in only a couple nights ago.

Noah didn't deserve the shit storm that came from knowing her, let alone fucking her. The Society practically knocked at her front door.

She glanced up at the clock, threw her used towels in the basket and headed over to her locker to put her socks and shoes back on before leaving.

Noah walked out the door as she pulled her second sock and shoe on. He was good. Or he got smart and truly left. She halfway hoped he did. Save himself before she ruined his life. She let out a full breath before heading out the door, not bothering to say goodbyes.

CHAPTER THIRTEEN
NOAH

He should have left.

He thought about leaving.

His bags were still packed and under his bed. But that face... her face as she refused to back down to Lando in the sparring ring popped back into his mind. That's how he found himself pacing in the hallway one floor down from the penthouse, frantically trying to put together a plan. He could help her, just this once, and still disappear into the night. He could escape this before he got in too deep. The sound of a latch opening stopped him in his tracks and he shoved his hands in his pockets.

This was such a mistake.

Emerald eyes met his as she pushed through the door, her wet hair hanging past her shoulders, already starting to curl into perfect little ringlets. He swallowed and looked away as she said, "I'm surprised you actually decided to meet me."

Me too, he thought.

He shrugged and tried to maintain a cool timbre in his

voice as he said, "Curiosity plays cruel games on our better judgment." He glanced at her as she walked past, a smirk creasing her pretty rose-colored lips.

"Ain't that the truth."

A smile tugged at his lips as he trailed behind her. She stopped in front of a light blue door, the same door as the other five doors on this floor, each marked by a beautiful medieval sconce and bronze numbers. The only difference on her's were the number of locks. There were at least four visible ones but he would bet good money there were some deadbolts only able to be opened from the inside. Locking the world out. Or keeping her demons in. He glanced up at the ceiling, as if he could peer back into that room above, right into the eyes of at least one of them. She finished unlocking her fortress and pushed the door open, motioning for him to go in.

"Welcome."

Her apartment was small, a kitchen and bathroom off to the left of the main room which served as both bedroom and living room. A small white couch and coffee table faced a television with a healthy layer of dust over it. A queen-sized bed sat in the farthest corner from the door, pressed against large industrial paned windows facing his building across the way and a wall of shelves that stretched from the floor to the ceiling. A little ladder on casters reached the top. He vaguely registered the door closing with all the clicks of locks following: seven total. Walking toward the television, he ran his finger across the top, the dust quickly bunching up on the tip and turned back to her, one eyebrow raised.

She shrugged and worked her way out her shoes before heading toward the bathroom.

"Feel free to make yourself at home. Hell, clean it if you want. I'll be right back."

The door shut behind her and he shook his head, wiping the dust off on his shorts. The apartment clashed with touches of modernity next to eclectic, old artifacts. Her television was perched on an old wooden chest with leather straps and handles. The ladder had ST. LOUIS PUBLIC LIBRARY burnished into the wooden railing. The shelves themselves housed everything from books to weaponry. An ornate wooden door bisected the middle of the bookshelf and his fingers itched to open it when he heard her voice behind him, "Now, now, usually I at least get a drink out of the deal before someone starts snooping through my unmentionables."

"You told me to make myself—" He turned to see her in a soft cotton robe, a towel in her hand as she scrunched the water from her dark ruby curls. He swallowed. "—comfortable."

Her eyes met his before he whirled back to the bookshelf and added, "Not every day you see a copy of *Sapiens* above a collection of horseman picks." The weapons were museum quality. Authentic?

Her laugh brought his focus back to her, that smile on her face catching his breath.

"I would hope Yuval Noah Harari would appreciate my cataloging methods." The words came out breathy as she ventured into the kitchen.

He could barely stand to be the receiver of that smile, so thank the gods above he spotted a familiar little plastic package sitting on her bed. A lifetime had already passed between them and yet it was really only a day. A day since she held a knife to his neck and threw his entire world into orbit. He shook the thought away and grabbed the package, heading over to the couch. She joined him, passing him a pair of disposable gloves. He tried to ignore the smooth skin of her thigh exposed from the slit in her robe. Tried.

Failed.

"Thanks" was all he could muster as thoughts rollercoastered from how that skin would feel under his hands to the very old, very important, pretty much impossible piece of history occupying them at present.

He should have left.

Slipping the gloves on trembling fingers, he reached into the plastic package to grab the ancient text. It was small, easily held in one hand, and bound in a thick leather he couldn't quite place, exquisitely adorned in jewels and metal accents. A whistle escaped his lips as Izzy took the plastic bag from him. He held the book between his hands, watching the lights sparkle off the gems and gilded accents. The physical weight of it didn't remotely represent what was held within its thick parchment pages. He could feel her leaning into his shoulder, sucked into the same out of body experience at what they were beholding.

Her breath tickled his neck as she exhaled slowly, "So, did I happen upon The Ramblings or can I go to sleep in peace tonight?"

Steeling a sideways glance at her, he relished the awestruck wonder in her eyes as she studied the fine carvings in the leather binding. He took a deep breath and carefully opened the front cover. Unsteady script appeared on the parchment.

BLÔT ELE MÆCE

The words repeated over and over on the page, the handwriting getting marginally better down the page. Marginally. He heard Izzy gasp quietly while his own heart thundered under his shirt.

"They, uh, they say he couldn't write but tried to learn later in life so kept various journals around to practice. But every one discovered was illegible, suggesting he never truly learned." He could barely form the words as he stared at the page before him.

"I mean, it isn't neat by any means but I wouldn't classify this as illegible. Do you know what it says?"

He studied the words carefully, "By the blood of the... *mæce*"

Izzy's studious eyes centered on him. "By the blood of the mace?"

His shoulders shrugged and he let out an exhale, "It's not a great translation, but it's the best I can figure. I haven't ever seen *mæce* though. I'll have to look into it." He could feel his plans of escape faltering.

Her eyes narrowed on him a bit, but she seemed to bite back her comment. Instead, she looked back to the book in his hands, "But if he could barely scribble out a logical sentence, what does The Society want with this? It's truly just a collection of random thoughts? What the fuck even is a mace?"

The faint sound of screams rang in his ears.

"That I don't have the answer for, unfortunately." He rubbed at his neck and looked to the line he had left in the dust on the top of the TV.

She huffed out a breath and collapsed back against the couch. "Fuck me, so it really is The Ramblings, then?"

His grim glance provided answer enough. "Do you have a safe place to keep it?" *Preferably not where you sleep,* he wanted to add, but didn't want to have to justify why he cared.

Another exasperated sigh, "Without telling Lando I have it? You're looking at my safe place." She gestured to the apartment.

"Why not tell Lando? I'm sure he has a pretty impressive safe with an extra bodyguard to watch over it."

Her lips pulled into a thin line as she stared into the

fireplace next to the TV. Her silence left him haunted with questions. Questions that were about to escape his lips when she finally breathed out, "It's… complicated." Her eyes shot back to his and he saw the mingling of fear, anger, and something else he couldn't place.

He glanced back up to the ceiling separating her from *them*, his own lips thinning as he tried to puzzle together the situation. "So it appears." Glancing back at her, her bottom lip sucked under her upper teeth, her stare shifted to the book now resting on the coffee table.

"How did they find you?" she asked softly.

Peeling his gloves off, he tossed them onto the table next to the book and rubbed his hands together. "I'm not entirely certain we were alone on our walk back last night. But how they were allowed in by the doorman was on my to-do list to figure out today." Along with delving deep into his inner debate on the idiocy of his life choices.

Her stare still trained on that book, she asked, "But they didn't make it *in* to your apartment?"

He studied her face, quizzically. "Not until I opened the door for them." She couldn't possibly be considering…

"How good are you at hiding stuff?" Her eyes finally met his, a pleading in them.

Fuck. *Get out Noah. Get out of the city, get out of this country if you can.*

He sighed, burying his face in his hands as she quickly continued, "I'm not fully convinced Lando doesn't have keys for the locks on my door and even if he didn't, Charlie has been here enough times and clearly knows how to get in without them. They would never suspect I gave it to you but I don't want it in his possession. Not until we know what makes it so special. So valuable The Society is willing to ambush me during the day to get it."

He lifted his face from his hands, his jaw tight. They stared at each other for a moment, studying each other.

"You've just met me, Isabella." A flash of anger speckled across her beautifully freckled face. It quickly disappeared.

"Please," her voice rattled a bit, "call me Izzy."

"That doesn't change what you're asking me to do. What you're *trusting* me to do… you've just met me." That anger reappeared and did not leave this time.

Her voice remained cool and calm, deadly, as she said, "You're right, Noah. Why *am* I trusting you?" She stood up, surveying the scene as if she had just woken from a trance, the book on the table, him sitting on the couch, *her* couch in *her* apartment while she stood there in nothing but a robe. The flames of her rage radiated off her as she took a step back and looked to the door.

"Get out."

The words were a cool dagger right into his chest. *Get out Noah.*

"Izzy, please, I just meant…" He stood up, reaching a hand out to her, to explain himself. His idiot self. The rage and disappointment in her eyes stopped him dead in his tracks.

"Get. Out."

He straightened his spine at the finality of her command. Heading to the door, he grabbed the bag he had dropped by the entrance and made quick work of her locks. His breath felt heavier in his chest with each click. Before he turned the final one and walked out, probably forever, he had to know the answer to the question that had been haunting him, keeping him on the fence between logic and insanity.

"Are you safe here?" He didn't dare turn to her, his voice barely above a whisper.

Her responding laugh shot across the room, hollow and short.

"Are any of us safe anymore?"

He dared a glance back over his shoulder to see the pain etched on her face, the fear that danced along the details, banking the fury he saw raging there before.

"Just get out, Noah." The words weighed her down and his stomach sank at the sound.

Then he left.

$\maltese$

CHAPTER FOURTEEN
IZZY

She didn't even bother putting on clothes after Noah left. As easily as she took each breath, she locked up her door behind him, hopefully while he was still in earshot, and collapsed face first on her bed.

Where she still laid, staring at the stupid book on her coffee table. She had let Barry know he would have to work on cleaning up the lab by himself today but as soon as the message sent, another went to Vahagn asking him to keep a casual eye on the lab for her. Just in case.

As annoying as Vahagn could be, he was the closest thing she had to a sibling. Or at least what she assumed having an obnoxious older brother would be like. While only a few years older than her, he was the only man in Lando's crew who hadn't leered at her the first time she met them all at family dinner. But the rest of his men? Fuck them.

Including Noah. Maybe she had been a little quick to trust him, but she thought with him sitting in her apartment, he had wanted to help her. A stranger, sitting next to her while she sat fully naked underneath her robe. What an idiot she had been. She scoffed and glared at that book, his discarded gloves still next to it. Rolling onto her back with a groan, she stared at the bronze coffered ceiling instead.

Lando had done a brilliant job renovating these apartments, updating with a sophisticated taste that blended modern comfort with the beauty of tradition. It was what drew her to this building in the first place. Like a mosquito to that beautiful mystic glowing blue light. She only had herself to blame in getting involved with Lando's crew. She had been the one who hauled her cranky ass up those stairs. She was the one who stormed past Charlie and Vahagn as if they were mere field mice. She had slammed her fists on Lando's obtuse, ornate door. She had been the one to slip into Charlie's bed that first time. And so many times after that.

Her grandpa said that the fire in her blood came straight from the Tuscan sun of their heritage but it came with no warning that she would continuously find herself in hot water as a result.

She sighed and looked back over at the book. Grandpa. *Nonno.* It had been about seven years since he and her grandmother had passed, grateful they didn't have the opportunity to choose between forever or fighting for survival in this world damned by some scientist named Emilien Dumas. And for what reason? Money? Love? Some speculated he was a lover scorned but no amount of heartache had ever made Izzy want to actually watch the world burn.

Regardless, pain still ripped through her the moment she walked through the doors of their shotgun home on The Hill to nothing but silence. A shadow ache of that cleaving pulled on her chest and she rubbed it, scanning her apartment for a place, any place, to hide The Ramblings.

The fucking Ramblings.

This apartment used to be her last bit of sanctuary, her only refuge from the outside world. Even from the crew of criminals above her. She bought this apartment outright from Lando and immediately changed all the locks, adding a few more for good measure.

She rolled off the bed and pushed through that antique confessional door separating the main room from the closet she had hidden behind the bookshelves. It was only a walk-in closet in the sense that one could physically walk in, but it was barely as wide as a hallway. With the dim lighting and the once annoying loose floorboards, an idea emerged. She danced around, bouncing on a few until she found one in the corner against the brick wall on the back of the closet. Running back out to the living area to grab a dagger and the book, she made sure to carefully seal it up. Dr. Beechum's disdain for her actions crept into her thoughts. As she floated back into the closet, she grabbed a scarf on a second thought and wrapped it around the book in its plastic. Using the dagger, she pried up the loose board and peered within. Nothing more than dust and more wood.

Perfect.

Double checking the plastic seal held tight, she tied the scarf and gently placed the rather priceless parcel under her freaking floorboards.

This is insane, she thought. She didn't get a chance to second guess her hiding spot though as the three beat knock Vahagn used to let her know it was him echoed into the small space.

"Fuck," she whispered as she carefully slid the floorboard back into place, making sure not to make a great deal of noise and ran out to open the door.

Only when she made it to the last lock did she remember the dagger in her hand. She quickly shoved it into the sleeve of her robe and then flung the door open.

"Took you long enough." Vahagn gave her a once over, raising a brow at her robed attire, hair still in a towel. It was going to be unruly once she released it.

"Sorry I wasn't planning on hosting company." She shut the door behind him as he strode in and sat down on the couch, sprawling across the whole thing.

"Shoes, fucker."

He gave her a sly grin but started undoing his boots. "People would like you more, Z, if you weren't so uptight."

"I'm not uptight. I just never see you cleaning around here and having seen your home, it's probably for the best." He smirked as he pushed his boots off to the side of the coffee table. "Besides, what people do I need to like me when I've got you to fill my time?"

But he wasn't listening to her. Instead, he picked up the discarded gloves still on the coffee table and turned to her, both brows raised.

Panic choked her.

"You… interrupted me cleaning." She added a measure of annoyance to her voice, as she snatched the gloves out of his hand and went to the kitchen to throw them away.

"Do you want anything?" She opened the fridge, searching desperately for a place to hide this damn knife as well when he replied, "And what cleaning involves hiding a six-inch throwing dagger under the sleeve of your robe?"

Observant bastard. She closed the door to see him leaning against the threshold, staring at the offending hand that did in fact hide that exact dagger under it.

Panic revved in her heart again. She could never seem to hide anything from Vahagn. It was part of why Lando kept him employed. The additional benefit of being a moral sounding board for Charlie helped as well. For the most part…

The silence drew out between them and her opportunity to lie vanished, so she slid the dagger out, catching it swiftly by the handle before setting it on the countertop next to him.

"There is a perfectly good explanation for this…"

"Uh huh, and are you going to tell me what it has to do with that Noah kid slipping out of your apartment after your frozen Baywatch show upstairs? That resulted in you waltzing around in a robe?" His voice grew more irritated as he tried to put the pieces together himself.

She opened her mouth to argue but then shut it. Pieces that made a great story. One she could lean into.

She studied the floor, uncomfortable under his scrutiny. Glancing back up at him, she paled slightly.

A modicum of rage flickered across his face as he threw his hands up, "Come on, Z. You don't even know this kid and you're fucking him?"

"Ew, Vahagn, what does it matter to you? You didn't care when it was Charlie tangled up in my sheets?" The blow was low and she felt the shame that flooded his face. But she gave nothing away, wouldn't bend.

"We both know that was different and *had* I known sooner what had been happening, I would've been just as upset." It was true. She was actually surprised Charlie lived through the beating Vahagn gave him. Bruises to match her own, blood for blood, and then some.

"Well, it is different, V."

"You just met him…"

"So what? Because I'm a female I have to be courted over weeks? Months? I can't just *enjoy* someone else's body after a sultry glance across the room like every other man in this damned world?" The snap in her words might have been overkill but fuck it.

He glared but couldn't argue. He had been someone's actual brother once upon a time. Though he never fully told her the story, she knew enough bits and pieces through Charlie to know how cruel her words were now. His sister had been a stripper and Vahagn, being the good guy his persona defies, supported her choices when their parents didn't. Until they found her body raped and murdered behind the club by a thwarted rival gang member who felt he had been slighted in his private lap dance because she wouldn't fuck him.

Vahagn had spent three days torturing the piece of shit and probably would've kept going had the man not had a heart attack under his hands.

He stalked back into the living room area and sat down on the couch, face in his hands. He looked at where he sat then and back up at where she stood in the kitchen threshold. "You didn't… you know… here?" He gestured to the couch, his face still torn.

She glanced toward the bathroom and shook her head.

He glared at the bathroom door and back at her.

"This is reckless, Z. And not just," he held up a hand as she started to open her mouth in protest, "because you know nothing about him. But you don't know *anything* about him and he has just gone through an assessment with fucking Lando Denalo where I'm pretty sure he could've killed the old man if he wanted to. There's more beneath the surface there." He was right. Noah had barely broken a sweat today and those weren't skills attained organizing historical records in a stuffy, old library.

"I understand, Vahagn." Her eyes shone with a shameless plea to him.

He ran a hand down his face, staring at the ceiling, and his voice calmed, "I know. I know you do. I just can't go through another asshole treating you…"

Like she was nothing but something to control.

She sat next to him and put her hand on the arm resting on his knee, the worry and shame etched deep in his face. God, she felt like an absolute asshole.

"I know. I know how to protect myself this time." Thanks to his special training after she healed from Charlie's wounds, mentally and physically. "I promise if I need your help, if I need you for *anything*, I won't hesitate this time."

Grabbing her hand, twisting the onyx ring on her thumb, he met her gaze, his expression so pained and full of sorrow she wanted to vomit. "That's all I can ask."

The tears that sprang to her eyes weren't faked. "Thank you."

He let go of her hand and that signature sly grin softened his expression as he glanced back toward the kitchen behind her. "So, you want to explain the dagger then?"

She smacked his arm. "Absolutely not, Vahagn!"

He laughed. "What? I want to know if maybe I'm not exploring enough in my endeavors."

"You're a fucking dog."

He winked at her. "So, besides playing nookie hookie, are you feeling okay? Barry gave me fifty percent less attention today when I nonchalantly came by 'looking for you'."

Oh, Barry. Lando's entire crew was all devilishly handsome in their own ways and Barry never missed an opportunity to eye them up when they were around. Vahagn especially. An unrequited dream but Vahagn relished in the attention regardless.

"Yes, I'm fine. Just tired. Before yesterday, I didn't foresee being attacked over a book but here we are."

"Speaking of said book…" He scanned her face, the lie detector ticking away in his mind.

"Still locked up in the lab. Figured if they didn't find it the first time around, they wouldn't come back."

"Pssh, hopefully." He let out a breath and sat back in the couch. "Let's try to limit our interactions with immortal gangsters for a while though, okay?"

"Aye, aye, captain. Keep it to mortal gangsters only," she mocked with a sweet smile and a salute.

He stood up, putting his boots on, clapping her on the back.

"You're going to give me a fucking heart attack, kid."

"We wouldn't ever be that lucky, Vahagn."

He grinned at her, such a surprising thing to behold on his burly, bearded face, and headed to the door.

"At least get some fucking fresh air, okay? Laying around like a French whore all day doesn't suit you."

She tossed him a middle finger in response as he shut the door behind him, laughing.

❖

Unfortunately, he was right. She dressed quickly after he left, chancing one last glance at the corner in her closet as she pulled on an oversized Wash U sweatshirt. The sun beamed high in the sky as she pushed out the lobby door onto the street below.

Shooting Barry a quick text to meet her in the archives, she made her way toward campus.

B: Only if that hot little beignet is up there

She rolled her eyes.

I: See you in 15

The day was crisp, the air holding the cool promise of colder days to come as autumn kept its persistent descent to winter. Taking in a deep breath, she closed her eyes and tilted her head to the sky, the warmth from the sun a mere tickle. Everything felt right and truly fucked so the least she could do was relish in her favorite season. St. Louis vibrated on a different frequency this time of year. Barry and Lando once concocted a stoner theory that it had something to do with the spirits present in this city. That the arch was a true gateway but to the underworld. Quite frankly, she didn't take in many of the details of their logic because she and Vahagn sat reeling at the image of the most dangerous man in the metropolitan enthralled in conversation with a man in pink frame glasses and a pink feather boa around his neck. Had the cannabis not taken such a deep root in their brains at the time, they might have been smart enough to snap a picture.

For now, the mental image would do.

Seventeen minutes later, Izzy pushed into the library, gulping air. A library on the top floor of a university. A concept for torture. It was probably poor, little undergraduates who had to stock the thing when it was completed.

Barry gave a wave fit for royalty from a table in the back, by the window. This was their typical research spot so they could bask in the sunlight they were so deprived of below ground.

"You're late," he managed, matter of fact as she tossed her leather backpack into the chair next to her and slumped into the seat.

"Actually, I was on time. Then I had to climb Mount Vesuvius pre-eruption to get up here." She always underestimated how many stairs there were, and how fast she could climb them. Lando would murder her on the stair master if he knew.

"Well, let me catch you up to speed." Barry closed the book in front of him slowly, removing his glasses and marred her with the cold-hearted look of a man scorned. "The laboratory was trashed. I'm talking, t-r-a-s-h-e-d, Dr. Cannon after her five shots of tequila at the holiday party trashed. I contemplated setting it on fire. Thrice."

Izzy winced. She needed to atone hard for her all around wrongdoing this morning.

Barry continued, "But I stumbled upon something interesting I think you might want to see."

A burnt piece of paper slid across the table to her.

"What is this?" Her brows furrowed together, studying the scrolling script on it.

"A ship log." Her eyes widened as she searched the page closer. "But not just any ship log…" He pointed to a line of text at the top.

Le Charlemagne, 1852

The blood in her veins chilled a few degrees as the image of the man in that carriage sinking his teeth into the flesh of another, eyes peering into her soul, flashed across her memory.

She blinked it away and her eyes scanned the catalog of items on the ship. Clothing, goods, a fucking horse?

She said, "This can't be…?"

"The ship our delicious new southern comfort mentioned yesterday? It most certainly can be. So, it started to make me wonder, what do the French love most?"

"Uh, baguettes?"

He rolled his eyes. "Poetic details." His devious smile spread as he put his glasses back on and opened his book, flipping it around to show her.

"According to history," he motioned to the library like it was the representative of the subject, "*Le Charlemagne* was destined for the states with some noble immigrants and dignitaries but it never made it to port."

Izzy read the words before her: *Destined for port in Charleston, South Carolina, Le Charlemagne never showed and was assumed lost at sea. The crew, passengers, and cargo were never recovered. Many theorized the ship was wrecked in a storm.*

The ship never made it to port.

The cargo was missing.

The cargo that could've theoretically had The Ramblings on hand.

"Where did you find this?"

Barry examined his ombre nails in the natural lighting. "Adrift with the rest of calamity in the lab, near that hideous old safe you insist on keeping."

She rolled her eyes, "Barry, they said we can't get rid..." her words trailed off. By the safe. The safe that had The Ramblings in it.

Fucking hell, how had they known?

The hair on her neck stood up suddenly and Barry peered over her shoulder as a deep, slow southern voice tickled her senses.

"Dr. Beechum will want that properly cataloged."

Before she could turn to face him, Noah slipped into the chair next to her. He had showered and changed since she saw him this morning, those dark strands still damp on the end of the soft billowy waves he had brushed back. A smoky apple scent intoxicated her for a moment before she came to her fucking senses and glared at him.

She shuffled the log into the book and shut it. "This is a personal artifact so it won't need to be cataloged. Charlie found it in a storage box in the basement and thought I, uh Barry and I would find it interesting." She smiled to Barry, trying to convey a swift *shut the fuck up* while he looked to her, eyebrow raised and hands ready to start slow clapping her performance.

Bravo, he mouthed to her then snapped into his role seamlessly.

"I'm looking into the history of importing women to the new world and how it relates to the myths of sirens."

Noah blinked between them but his face remained completely unreadable.

"Your research sounds fascinating," he finally drawled to Barry, a statement that likely sent his toes curling. His batting eyelashes confirmed it.

"Oh, you have no idea." He reached across to briefly touch Noah's arm. Noah smiled ruefully down at the touch before turning his focus to Izzy.

She revived her glare and began packing her things.

"Izzy, I…"

"Anyway! We were just leaving actually." She looked to Barry. He nodded once, swiftly putting all his things together and headed toward the door without her. Abandoning her. That was not the plan they silently agreed upon. She mentally face palmed. They needed to sit down and work out their telepathic communication.

Noah placed a hand on her elbow as she finished throwing things into her bag to go chase after her traitorous partner.

She whirled on him, the sincerity in his golden eyes nearly had her staying to hear him out. But the last time she let a man speak his bullshit, she had abandoned every ounce of common sense and let him right where he didn't deserve. No, not this time.

She ripped her arm out of his grasp and he rubbed behind his neck, glancing out the window before looking back to her.

"Please, Izzy, I just…"

"I just don't want to hear it, okay."

She didn't give him a chance to say anything more as she spun on her heel and fled.

⚜
CHAPTER FIFTEEN
NOAH

Izzy was already dripping sweat by the time Noah made it into the gym the next morning. By the look on her face, she still wasn't happy with him. Their whole interaction haunted him the rest of the previous day. Often he found himself standing in an aisle, clutching a document, and staring angrily at the shelf in front of him. After the fifth offense, Dr. Beechum coughed at him and Noah spent the rest of his shift apologizing. Once he left for the day, Noah thought he saw a look of relief on the old man's face. A rarity for someone he was certain had no emotions.

Noah started toward her, to explain himself, explain his reaction had nothing to do with her. Provide the typical male explanation, "It's not you, it's me". He groaned internally. What had him acting like such a tool around her?

As he neared her, she slowly shook her head at him, glancing over his right should as Lando marched up and clapped him on the back.

"Welcome back, kid. Glad we didn't scare you off

yesterday. Can't promise it won't happen today though." The old Italian man winked and walked away to let him warm up on his own. Not to be deterred, Noah started once again toward Izzy before he was intercepted again. This time by a rather put off Vahagn. He wasn't much taller than Noah and this close, he wasn't much bigger either, but the Viking aesthetic did add a *je ne sais pas quoi*.

The man smirked at him in a sly, violent way. "Why don't you walk me through the warmup you do to be so nimble in the ring?"

Noah glanced behind him to where Izzy sat on the ground, a slightly amused expression on her face as she watched them. Then Vahagn stepped back into his line of sight, another devilish grin on his face.

"Um, sure, but I don't know how much of it is credited to my warmup routine..."

"Yeah, doesn't matter. Still think we should have a little chat."

Shit, did Izzy tell him about yesterday? What would she have even said?

Hi, Vahagn, the idiot from the bayou balked when I suggested I trust him to hold onto and protect a priceless, believed-to-be-myth historic artifact. Kill him.

Keeping it together as best he could, Noah asked, raising a brow for emphasis, "What kind of a chat should we have?"

The man scoffed at him and stepped close enough Noah could feel the bristly hairs of his beard on his cheek. Only loud enough that he could hear, Vahagn growled, "The type of chat where I remind you the number of ways I can and have killed a man so you can keep that image in your mind while you wet your prick in my sister."

He couldn't help the choking cough that escaped his lips. "What?" The question came out louder than he anticipated.

Hearing the outburst, Izzy scowled at them.

Vahagn turned and began walking away. He said over his shoulder, "Maybe you're right. The warmup routine has shit to do with it."

⚜

Standing outside the sparring ring, Noah watched Lando walk Izzy through disarming him while simultaneously making her attack.

Vahagn's words tumbled through his head. What the fuck had Izzy said to him to make him believe they were sleeping together? Or did he just presume Noah had slept with her? Had she let him believe that? Why would she do that?

He found himself watching her when Lando said, "NOLA, your turn. You and Izzy, partner up."

Noah climbed into the ring and walked over to the weapons table, stiffening as Izzy stepped up next to him a moment later. The space between them disappeared and he felt every electric inch as it did. Reaching across him to a pair of short swords, she whispered, "We are going to need to talk in more detail later but for now, I need you to follow my lead and trust me." The last words came out clipped.

"Izzy, I…" he started in but her gaze caught his as she shoved the swords into his chest, grabbing her own pair off the table.

"But now is not the time for talking." Her whole demeanor changed in an instant as she winked at him, turning to saunter away. His heart pounded in his chest. This woman was dangerous. And this game they were about to play even more so.

And yet he found himself trailing behind her, taking in the glorious sway of her hips. She stopped at a spot in the ring off to the side to make space for Vahagn and another behemoth of a man to join them, each holding a pair of daggers that dwarfed in their hands.

"Izzy, will you let me explain now?" He felt determined to say his peace while they paced in a circle around each other. Her face became unreadable, the cool calculations of a predator stalking its prey, as she studied him. The intensity of her stare made him want to simultaneously cower away and slam her body into the floor.

"The rules of the sparring ring are simple," Lando boomed from the middle, looking at each of them as they prowled each other, readying for an attack or defense, "don't kill anyone and more importantly, don't stab me. *Inizio.*"

Noah barely had a moment to inhale before Izzy struck his left side, a weakness somehow gathered from their seconds of perusal. He flicked his right sword in a cross behind his left to defend and as they locked weapons, he took his chance.

"Please, just hear me out." His voice went low, his accent rolling around the vowels.

Anger flashed vividly in those green eyes as she grunted and shoved him back. A breath and then she came at him again, to the other side. He blocked, holding her there.

"I'm sorry for whatever I did or said." There was a slight growl to his voice this time.

Apparently that was the wrong statement because her anger intensified and she practically roared when she shoved him off again. She followed her push with an attack straight on. Another block, another hold. This time she spat a response.

"You don't even know what you're apologizing for.

Pathetic." Her green eyes burned with overwhelming fire. He smirked.

She gritted her teeth as he shoved her back, surprised by how difficult it was to move her. God, she was strong.

Following his attack, he took the blades over his head, coming down on her defense of crossed swords.

"You're right. I don't know what I said or did but *Vahagn* has some idea of what happened between us. A better idea than even I have."

He glared down at her. She glared back up at him. He stepped back and they paced around each other again, panting. His next attack went for her right side, the one she seemed to be guarding more.

It had been a decoy. She leaned into his attack, just as he had watched her do the day before to Lando. She ducked, sliding behind him, but not before slicing ever so slightly into his side. The cut stung.

A reminder.

A promise.

He rolled before she could kick him to the ground like the old man. He rose a few feet away, crouched and staring at her. He didn't dare glance at his side but the nagging twinge told him enough.

"That was naughty." The words purred out of him.

She responded with that sweet little smile that stopped his heart. Fucking hell, he was in treacherous water.

"Some might say it was earned," she purred back, biting her lower lip as she began pacing around him again. The sword swung lazily in her hand.

"And the cold shoulder yesterday? That was earned too?," he said, taunting her. Her eyes sparkled and she took a powerful step toward him before launching herself into the air. There was just enough time for him to throw up a block but the momentum of her slamming on top of it had him falling backward, taking her with him. She landed in a straddle over his midsection with his arms locked, pushing his blade against her own. As she leaned in, pressing her weight into her sword, he felt the cool blade of the other one slide up his chest and rest at the hollow of his throat. A mercy killing.

"Don't get confused. Beyond this room, this ring, this ruse—we are nothing." He felt her whisper on his lips, the anger coating every word.

"You don't trust me, remember? So, I'll explain myself. Once. And then never again. Understood?" She added. The sword slid closer to his neck. He felt his skin yield to the sharp edge, begging to break.

"Understood," he growled back at her. As she hopped off him, he added, "As long as you offer me the same. An opportunity to explain my apprehension." What that explanation would entail was beyond him. How could he explain he didn't want to get wrapped up with The Society because he was practically a dead man walking in their ranks? That handing the book over to him further chummed the water. That his bags were still packed in his room while he spent every night debating the merits, or lack thereof, in the decisions he has made in his life, because he was too stupid to separate his heart from his head.

Her stare followed him as he rolled back to his feet and she glanced over to where Vahagn and the ogre were crouched in a standoff. Noah hoped the Viking missed their whole show on the mat.

"Fine," she growled before stalking off toward the table of weapons.

"Good work everyone. Stretch it out and let's call it a day. Stay hydrated, *mia familia*." Lando walked toward Vahagn, still crouched, each man waiting to see who would get the last move in.

Noah walked over to the weapons table where Izzy stood, watching the two men decide when to yield.

"You know where to find me," she said, before stalking off to the lockers, grabbing her stuff, and walking out the door. He tried not to stare but the memory of her strong legs wrapped around him was too fresh. The shape her lips made as she threatened to stab him if he so much as breathed in her direction beyond this room. A flash of bare leg under a robe and the memory jolted him to move. He worked through his cool down routine twice, even going as far as to hop in the cold plunge long enough to forget the heat building in his core before he stalked out the door and down the stairs to his ruination.

❖

The thundering of his heart must have been louder than he thought because only one soft knock and the door swung open, Izzy dragging him inside as she peered up and down the hallway.

"Did anyone see you?" she asked, before slamming the door shut, working quickly through the locks on the inside.

"I, uh, I didn't see anyone but what is this about? Yesterday you made it clear you didn't want me in here or even near you again. And now?" He spread his arms out, studying her face for an explanation.

She had showered and changed in the time it took him to finish his extended cool down. She stood before him in jeans and a simple sweater that plunged precariously to the middle of her chest. Not that he was staring at her chest. She glared at him and he returned the sentiment.

"I don't have time for games." He dropped his hands

with a slap, pushing his way back to the door. There was no point in staying in this room. This city. Decision made.

He didn't have to be in this moral limbo because of a deranged stranger. That's all she was – a stranger. A stranger who clearly found herself stuck between a rock and hard spot based on the company she kept. Fear flowed beneath the surface and her words about Charlie… *It's complicated.*

He didn't have to imagine, he knew. It was complicated and he was leaving. The end.

A hand on his arm stopped his escape and his stomach dropped. He knew what he would see when he turned around. Knew it would redirect his entire trajectory. And yet, still, he turned. Still, he looked into that pleading, ashen face. Still, he ruined his own life.

"I'm sorry. I just jumped to a million conclusions yesterday." Her words came out slow and shaky, like they were grating their way out. "I should have never asked you to take the book or even let you get in this deep. I just thought since you felt so trustworthy I could, well…" She held his gaze as she spoke to him.

"Can you also explain why your werewolf of a brother thinks I'm sleeping with you? With vivid detail?" His jaw ticked as the words fell out in a bite.

"He's not technically my brother." She let go of his arm and walked to the bed a few feet from the couch. "And things got a bit complicated after you left."

Right, complicated. He might have to adopt that as his new life motto.

"After you made me leave," he growled.

She glared up at him. "Yes, when I made you leave *my* home."

"That doesn't explain how he now thinks I'm fucking you." His voice stayed a steady volume but there was a force behind it.

"Is it such a horrible thing for him to think?" A challenge in her voice that had him setting his jaw in response.

"I'm not playing games, Isabella."

She exhaled, looking to the floor as she explained, "He saw you, somehow, yesterday. He's a sneaky bastard for being the size of a tree and he has… he was concerned. But I couldn't explain the book to him, not yet at least. So, I might have let him jump to his own conclusion."

"And you didn't correct him? Or come up with a more logical explanation?" He pinched the bridge of his nose.

Emerald eyes narrowed up at him. "What other *logical* explanation was there?"

He ran his hand down his face and let out a long exhale. The room felt warmer, the sunshine blinding through those windows.

"Fuck if I know. Why can't you just tell him about the book?"

Why drag him into this? Those words died on his tongue.

She studied his face, his whole presence, so thoroughly his skin tingled under the assessment.

"I have my reasons for not involving them."

He couldn't bear it anymore. He had to know. If anything, so maybe she would offer him a reason to grab those bags under his bed and leave this god forsaken city. One last mercy. He wasn't in too deep now. He could head west this time. The Society hadn't reached those remotes stretches of desert yet.

"And me?" *Why me*, his eyes pleaded.

Her brow furrowed. "I haven't figured out why I trust

you yet." She bit her lower lip and looked out her window, to the building across the street.

An exasperated sigh escaped his lips. "Fine."

"And what about your reasons? Why were you so quick to balk at my trust? My motives to involve you? Why are you still *here*?" She motioned toward the ceiling, to the crew of men above. Fuck.

He started pacing slowly before he decided it was better to just sit on the couch, turning to face her.

"If I were to say I have my reasons, would you accept that?"

She scanned his face for a moment then said, "Only if you give me one of them. Something to hold onto so I know you're not another shady ass man."

The shock of her statement rippled through him. One reason? All his reasons were damning. "It's just," fuck, "a lot to take in, in a new city."

She nodded her head slowly, her damp curls swaying with the movement. A faint smile creased her lips. "Okay."

Keeping his breathing steady as they found themselves on a rocky truce he said, "Okay. So, what now?"

As she moved next to him on the couch, he tracked her. When she sat, she turned her body to face him.

"Well, Vahagn does think we are sleeping together and honestly, I had no better cover story for why I had you in my apartment. I don't exactly let anyone in here." She gestured to the locks on the door. "So, if you're comfortable with it, I figured that's a good enough story to explain why you'll be in here."

He raised a brow. "And will I? Be in here, that is?"

She grimaced. "I need your help."

A laugh choked him. She ignored it and started into

him.

"I started researching everything I could on Charlemagne yesterday and there is *nothing* about The Ramblings. No mention of it. No explanation of what on earth is in it and definitely nothing that points to why The Society of all things wants its dirty immortal hands on it. All Barry found in the ruins of our lab was an old ship log for *Le Charlemagne* in 1852 but when he looked it up, the ship never made it to port. With no mention of a fancy journal on board. That's not even something that would've been in our lab. It doesn't relate to any research we do."

What was The Society getting at?

"And you're trusting me with this?" he asked.

She let out a sharp laugh. "God knows why I am. I think I might actually hate you a little but I have limited options and even more limited time so I'm compromising."

"Just what every man wants to hear." A smirk played at her lips. "So, where is this enigmatic book?"

"Ah, that information falls outside the purview of my faltering trust in you. Besides I need to get to the lab soon so Barry doesn't feel abandoned and starts hiding my things. But I'm free in a couple days for us to look through it together, if that works for you?"

There it was, his absolute last chance to back out. To run from this city and The Society and whatever hellhole they were imagining next.

"Yeah, okay." Idiot. "I'll try to dig up anything I can on the ship log and The Ramblings until then." Absolute fucking idiot. Hopefully he didn't rattle any Society trip wires while he researched.

"Okay. It's a date then." She winked at him and slapped his knee before standing up to go open the door. "Now get out, for real this time."

Following her to the door she held open for him, he stopped next to her, whispering into her ear, "Tomorrow, try to make it harder to let you win, will you?"

Fury blazed in those emerald eyes but he saw her skin pebble across her chest, and he strode down the hallway before the murmurs of profanity followed in his wake, punctuated with the slamming of her door. He smirked at the camera positioned in the corner of the hall as he pushed into the stairway doors.

❖

That evening Noah sat at his dining table next to the grand window view of the street below and the building across the way. Her building. He sipped his bourbon, watching the constellations take their shapes in the sky. No matter how far he traveled beyond the giant oaks and sticky humidity of Louisiana, he always knew those stars would be there, reminding him how big the universe was and how small his issues were in the grand scheme of things. Even if those issues found him in a city notorious for being anything but welcoming, entangled with multiple gangs and a woman who might get him killed. Or kill him.

He sighed and looked at the ice floating in the golden liquid, swirling it around.

Just as the image of those green eyes that had been haunting him lately flickered into his mind, a familiar looking apartment lit up across the street. He watched as she strode across the living room, Vahagn stalking behind her with what looked like bags of junk food. She threw her head back, laughing at something Vahagn must have said before tossing her stuff on the bed and taking a seat on the couch next to him.

A pang of jealousy coursed through him. Not at Vahagn but at the both of them, together. He had been alone for over a year now, his heart thumping hard as the familiar ache of loss crept in at the thought of his brother. He still couldn't bring himself to say his name, not knowing when he did if it would be the last time. If his existence would disappear in that moment. It was irrational.

Noah drained his glass, stealing one more glance into Izzy's apartment. She stood in the kitchen now, mixing up drinks for the two of them. As she poured them into salt rimmed glasses, smiling, her gaze drifted across the street… to his building.

Mortified, he quickly set his glass down, examining the grain of the wood table beneath it. His heart galloped in his chest and what the fuck was wrong with him? There was no way she had seen him, she didn't even know if his apartment faced the street. Steeling the courage to stop being an absolute coward, Noah peeled his eyes from the table to look back to her window. Where she still stood, smiling softly, with a glass in her hand. When his eyes met hers, she raised her drink. He did the same, lifting his empty glass. Her shoulders shuddered a bit as her smile grew. Taking a sip, she turned and walked back to the living room, the other drink in hand to pass off to Vahagn. Mario Kart flashed on the screen, the burly man smiled broadly up at her, a smörgåsbord of candy and chips laid out before him.

Noah looked away, his own smile shifting down a bit as he turned to head to his kitchen. Movement near one of the back entrances into Izzy's building caught his attention at the sink as he set his glass inside. His heart rate quickened. Was someone breaking in? No one dared walk outside in the dark anymore. Unless—

Charlie emerged from the door, turning to quietly close it before stalking off down the alleyway, deeper into the shadows.

Was this guy insane? Even Noah knew not to tempt fate with the immortals that roamed this city.

A million scenarios raced through his mind. The sound of the ice cube cracking in the glass below snapped him back to reality. He surveyed the street, seeing no sign of Charlie or anyone for that matter. He glanced back up to Izzy's apartment where her and Vahagn had switched to a movie. Vahagn appeared to already be asleep as Izzy rose to walk toward her closet door. She left it open some and he could just barely make out the flash of her bare skin in a mirror. He blushed and turned away, tunneling his vision as he stalked back to his bedroom and turned on the lights to see his bags sitting sentry on his bed.

Leaning back against his closed door, he let out a deep sigh.

"What the fuck am I doing?" he whispered to no one.

CHAPTER SIXTEEN
Izzy

"Maybe we should invite Noah over some night," Izzy kept her tone nonchalant as she passed Vahagn his margarita, a sour candy straw hanging out the side of his mouth.

He grabbed the drink and said, "I'm not having a three way with you."

"Ew!" She slapped him on the shoulder as she sat back on the couch, reaching for a tortilla chip. "That's not what I was suggesting, you pervert."

He shrugged but looked at her quizzically, "All I know is that you're fucking him. But now you want him to join family gather time?"

She rolled her eyes and took a sip. Barry's family had the best tequila hookup in the city. "I just don't know if he has any friends and I mean, he lives right across the street. Just seems silly to waste all my charming personality and impeccable gaming skills on you."

He snorted, as the game on the screen started its countdown. Izzy's character, a little green dinosaur named Yoshi, careened around a corner, narrowly missing a banana peel Vahagn's character, the Princess Peach, had thrown out from ahead of her.

"Plus," she grunted a little as Yoshi spun out a bit on an oil slick in the game, "if we befriend him, it keeps him out of Charlie's scope. Or at least, protects him some from it." Hopefully.

"And do you feel like he needs protecting?"

Yes. No. She didn't know. She barely knew why she cared so much. All she knew was every time she had something to share about The Ramblings, no alarms went off in her head when it came to telling Noah. She hadn't even trusted Vahagn with that information.

"Maybe not protecting but you know."

He glanced sidelong at her. Yeah, he knew. He knew perfectly damn well what kind of a monster lived in Charlie's core. Where Vahagn had fallen into a life of crime merely by circumstance, Charlie had chosen it. Given up his full ride and family home in Webster Groves to join Lando. He had worked his way up the ranks pretty quickly, motivated to succeed as a gangster. For what end, she never learned. It's not like they had spent much of their time together talking.

GAME OVER

Vahagn didn't celebrate his victory though. Instead, he switched the screen over to the movie they had been trying to finish watching for the past three nights.

"Look Izzy…"

She rolled her eyes, tossing her controller on the coffee table as she slumped back on the couch. "Oh, please, I didn't want this to start a lecture."

His deep brown eyes narrowed on her but he persisted,

"As I was about to say, I think it might be a good idea. Gets him out of his lonely boy apartment. Did you know he has basically nothing in there? And gives me a chance to get to know him, and his intentions, a little better."

She resisted the urge to roll her eyes again, settling on a beaming smile instead. "Okay, I'll set it up."

This time he rolled his eyes. A shark flew across the screen as a giant tornado ripped through what appeared to be rural Texas. A line creased between his eyes. "What the fuck is even happening in this movie?"

Another shark appeared on the screen and then the sharks started… battling in the tornado?

"You had last pick," she said. He had also been blazed out of his mind at the time.

"What a mistake," he groaned.

She snorted a laugh and set back to watch the movie progress. As the sharks whirled around, biting at each other's tails, Vahagn already fast asleep beside her, her mind wandered to planning out a night to come. Where she could get to know this mysterious neighbor of hers. Where she could maybe figure out why she trusted him when she barely knew him.

❖

"What do you mean you don't remember what happened, Barry? No one even touched you!"

Izzy had been trying to get the details of the attack-turned-assault in their laboratory the next day but all attempts had been fruitless, despite buttering him up with his favorite pistachio flat white with the cinnamon dust picture of a cat on the top.

"It means, Isabella, that I. Don't. Remember." He took a sip of his drink, peering over his glasses at her.

She sighed. He had been rightfully annoyed that she

abandoned him earlier this week in cleaning up the lab and thus, doled out his punishment by being dodgy.

"How many times will I have to grovel and apologize before you will forgive me?" She had been incredibly late that morning, making the detour for his drink and accompanying pastries.

He sighed, closing his eyes and pushing his glasses up his face before he looked to her and said, "Fine. You are forgiven for your transgressions. Don't let it happen again."

She rolled her eyes. "Thank you, Your Highness. Now, can you at least tell me what the hell those goons were talking about when they said they had talked to you the night before they attacked me?"

Another sip and he swiveled his chair back to his desk, scanning the documents before him.

"I truly have no idea what they were rattling on about. I talked to no one that evening. I only barely made it to my safe room because I heard them checking all the doors in this creepy ass hallway. For some reason our door was unlocked. It was all so *peculiar*." The word looked like it tasted of vinegar.

This conversation wasn't helpful.

"What can you tell me about Charlemagne?" she tried, willing the man to say something, anything of use.

"Whoa, honey. Give me a warning before you swerve to a new direction." He pivoted his chair back to face her. "What do you want to know? How many lovers he kept? When he kept them? How many were male versus female?" He winked.

Right. Asking Barry historical questions yielded only the secrets many of the most important figures of distance pasts thought would die with them.

God, she hoped she ended up being no one of

significance. Her sexual history would be burned to ash along with the rest of her.

"None of that, Bear. But thanks for fueling more questions than answers."

She turned back to the laptop on her desk, opening the browser to continue digging through everything the internet had to offer. Which consisted mostly of accolades for Charlemagne's success in uniting kingdoms and ruling for such a long time.

No one was this perfect, Izzy thought. She learned long ago through her years of anthropological research and sitting next to Barry that humans were notorious for nefarious acts of cruelty and repetitious mistakes. Everyone had their dark secrets. They were the ones who dug them up.

For a moment she thought back to that bizarre dream that woke her in a panicked state the other night. The man within, he had to have been Charlemagne. Who else would be transported in a royal carriage led by a crusader escort? And it had looked he was *drinking* the blood of the man in the carriage with him.

Maybe she truly had gone insane. Maybe The Ramblings were a figment of her imagination. Maybe this whole ordeal was a really long dream she would wake up from any moment. She closed her eyes and pinched herself just in case.

Ow!

She scowled at the reddening spot on her arm, rubbing it gingerly before turning her scowl to the laptop before her.

This doesn't make any sense, she thought. No one simply rules an entire empire without pissing off at least one person.

Sighing, she pushed back from her desk and stood, gathering her laptop and the rest of her things strewn across it.

"I'm going up to the archives, if you need me," she said to Barry.

"Ah, a little mid-morning rendezvous with a certain Southern gent?" he purred, peering up from behind his paper drink cup.

"You're insufferable, Barry." She hauled her bag onto her shoulder and stalked to the door.

"Character assets, darling. Character assets," he called out after her as the door shut. The lock clicked into place automatically. She paused a moment when she heard it.

The door was unlocked.

She shook her head. It had to have been a silly mistake. A jammed lock or something. This building was ancient after all. She continued her path out of the depths of their basement condemnation, mentally preparing for the ruthless ascent to the archives, and forgetting the fluke in their rusty security.

❖

"Charlemagne was marveled by many for his ability to unify the kingdoms and for ruling the Holy Roman Empire, a feat by which few could ever be compared, especially in a time of such separation between the ruling classes and the common people." Izzy rolled her eyes as Dr. Beechum droned on, repeating everything she had already read online.

"Yeah, but how?" she asked, wincing at the annoyance creeping into her voice. He had been talking like a one-man fan club for the Frankish emperor for the past half hour. She couldn't take it anymore.

Beechum balked, either at her tone or her question. "Well, he formed an alliance through marriage with Desiderius, the kin—"

"The king of the Lombards, yeah, yeah, yeah. Women must have been a high value currency back in the day to be able to unify entire kingdoms. But weren't there people who opposed his reign? Surely his brother's heirs had a problem with it. But were there any commoners who wouldn't have voted for him if it had been a democracy?"

"Well," Dr. Beechum's lip tightened, "he was fairly successful on the battlefield as well, spreading the Frankish culture and ideology—"

Her eyes drifted over the collection of old, weathered books on the shelves behind the professor as he spoke. She sighed loudly. "Yes but how?!"

As if on cue, Noah appeared in the doorway of the professor's office they were sitting in. Whether from witnessing her outburst or knowledge of the professor's subsequent disdain toward human emotion, he knocked softly on the door frame. Izzy had left the door half open, one of the many things Vahagn had ingrained in her.

Always have an escape route. Don't ever let someone lock you in with them.

Noah glanced to her, a curious look on his face, before he said to the professor, "I managed to find those Olympic tomes you were looking for, sir." His southern drawl soothed like honey in her ears and she hated herself for it. It was just a freaking accent.

She turned away from him and looked back to Dr. Beechum.

This Charlemagne madness grated on her nerves.

"Mr. Broussard, let me borrow your younger mind. Isabella here is asking a great deal of questions about Charlemagne and apparently my answers are not *sufficient*." He peered down at her as he stood. "Where did you say you found those tomes?"

Noah cleared his throat and turned to the professor, "I left them on the circular desk for you."

"Thank you. Please, take my seat and assist this poor

girl will you?"

Noah ran a hand through his hair and walked to the large, leather chair behind the desk, opposite Izzy. She tracked his steps with wide eyes. No one had ever sat in that chair besides Beechum. He had sent a mass email out to the whole department one summer accusing someone of stealing it and could they *"Please return it as soon as possible!!!"* Turns out it had been removed so maintenance could repaint his office. He never apologized.

"Yes, sir."

"Excellent. Good day, Miss Ciampi," the professor quipped at her, not at all suggesting she have a truly good day.

And with that he left the office, closing the door behind him.

Izzy instantly rose, opening the door back to its previous halfway point. When she sat back down and looked up at Noah, he watched her with one eyebrow raised.

"Assurance," she said simply.

He leaned back in the big chair, putting his hands behind his head as he did so.

"Harassing the old professor often on your to-do list, *Miss Ciampi?*"

Her eyes narrowed on him. Smug.

"I don't need this." Her patience was a bridge made of matchsticks at this point. Her temper a steady building flame. She made to gather her things and leave when he leaned forward, offering his hand to her.

"Wait, I'm just messing with you. Please, sit. Ask your questions." His drawl thickened and she ground her teeth. Insufferable.

Plopping back down in her seat, she sighed. "I was asking how Charlemagne became 'Charles the Great'?"

Noah tilted his head at her. "Well, he unified the kin—"

"Holy fuck, we all know!" She threw up her hands in exasperation. Did they train this irritating skill up here in their staff meetings?

He smirked. "Then tell me what you want to know." Light twinkled in his eyes, more amber than golden today. Not like she marked the color of them every day. Fucking Christ, she needed to get out of this library.

"How was he *so* successful? No one is universally well liked enough to garner unanimous support to the point of ruling an entire vast empire for decades. So, I want to know how?"

He gave her a quizzical look but didn't answer.

She looked around the room, "Jesus, you too? Am I speaking a made-up language?"

"This has to do with the book, doesn't it?" His words rolled slow off his tongue, as if testing them in open air, waiting to see if they spontaneously combust.

"Possibly."

He lowered his voice, hitting an octave that sent vibrations through her skin. "You're riding a dangerous line asking these questions here." Goosebumps sprung along her forearm and she rubbed at them.

"I'm getting nowhere on my own. It's like no one wants to do anything but marvel about the man who hasn't been around for centuries. No one person was this revered." He studied her as she spoke, intently following her every word. Was this what it was like to be heard by a man? Was it the first time it had happened in this room? She looked around at the stark white walls and precise organization of the book spines in their wooden shelves.

"I don't disagree with you but I repeat my sentiment. This is dangerous talk here." He settled a stern, serious look on her.

For a heartbeat, they stared at each other and as she began to feel the heat creep up her chest, threatening to blush her entire face, she looked away.

"Then I guess this conversation is over?" she said to the bookshelf to her left, this one organized by what look to be age of book.

"It doesn't have to be."

Her gaze shot back to his. "What are you suggesting?"

Mischief put an annoying smirk on his face. Her heart thudded despite it.

CHAPTER SEVENTEEN
NOAH

"I've never been here before and I grew up in this city," Izzy said quietly as she spun around in a circle, mesmerized by the tall roof of the cave above them. Noah watched her, marveling at how her dark red curls shifted in the amber light of the underground room. When she stopped spinning and looked to him, he turned his focus to the cave walls.

"These were originally used for brewing when German settlers came to this city, but now I think they mostly lie vacant. A forgotten attraction with all the grandeur above." He motioned to the ceiling with his hands, tossing her a sideways grin.

An internal lighting system had been installed ages ago, likely for tours, and still functioned. A lucky find with his first discovery of these caves almost a year ago. And thankfully, one The Society had yet to come upon as well. Or rather they didn't care to further separate themselves from their humanity by secluding to the darkest of shadows within.

Either way, they were safe down here. And no one

could hear them.

"I'm breaking all the rules Vahagn has ever taught me about self-preservation but oddly, I think it is worth it." Wonder coated her words as she continued to scan the vast underground corridor.

Studying her face another moment longer, Noah said, "So, you wanted to know how a man becomes one of the greatest emperors in history?"

She turned to face him, a smile creeping on her face. "Correct."

"Simple. Money."

Her frown felt like someone cut the lights, drenching them in darkness.

He chuckled. "Yep—the age-old decider of our fates as measly peasants. Those with the money wanted change in their favor. So, they bought it."

Her frown deepened, "Yes, but how?"

"Now I see why Beechum nearly sprinted out of his office earlier." His soft laughter bounced off the walls of the cavern.

She glared up at him. "Money doesn't always win wars. *How* could one man be so successful?"

Noah rubbed the back of his neck with one hand, looking at the stalactites lit across the way and glanced sideways at her, "I don't have an answer for that."

She let out a long exhale.

"And," he continued, "I'm not entirely sure it isn't hidden in that book of yours."

Her eyes glowed a tortuous emerald as she looked to him.

"Go on," she urged.

An exhale blew out his lips. "Oof, where do I begin? The mystery of Charlemagne and *The Ramblings* is such a convoluted one. It's shrouded in secrets and intrigue, very Nicholas Cagey. And because of that it also became popular with conspiracy theorists and… I'm putting you to sleep with my explanation." He added the last bit in haste as he watched her attention drift to the walls of the cave. There were symbols and sketches, words written in an old, Germanic language he didn't know.

She didn't break her concentration, a wrinkle in her forehead as she studied the drawings around them. As she stepped toward one of the walls, raising her hand to the markings, she said, "No. Go on. I just… what did you say these caves were used for again?"

He followed her, a moth to the flame. "Brewing. Stable temperatures being good for slow fermentation and all."

"Hmm," she hummed as her fingers brushed across the rock. His eyes followed their path, his own hand twitching at his side.

He rubbed the back of his neck. "Anyway, no one knows exactly how Charlemagne amassed such a grand fund nor if it was used to buy off his opposition or convince communities. All that is known for a fact is once he acquired his Paladins, he became an unstoppable force."

She whirled around quickly and he stood so close behind her, she braced her hands on his chest to steady her momentum. The touch burned like fire and electricity through him, igniting his senses. And all too soon, she ripped it away.

A faint blush twinged her cheeks as she asked, "The Paladins?"

He tilted his head, studying the color for a moment. "Well, well, well—you anthropologists don't study political structure then? Just embarrassing facts about kings and queens and the like to torment them from their graves?"

That beautiful pink disappeared as she scowled at him and turned back to the carvings on the wall.

"Just tell me what you know, Broussard." The words had a bite to them. He smiled. What a masochist he was around her.

"The Paladins, or Twelve Peers, were essentially the knights of the round table for the Carolingian Empire. The knights themselves fluctuated, or so they say, but it was always twelve."

"The perfect government. Divine order." Of course, she knew this much.

He nodded enthusiastically, nonetheless. "Exactly."

She turned back to him. "But that number, twelve, it exists across religions and cultures. Beyond the rule of Charlemagne and his Paladins." Her eyes glazed over as her mind worked behind them, putting the pieces of the puzzle together.

"Correct."

"It even corresponds to astrology." She no longer spoke to him as she pushed past to start pacing in the dusty sand floor.

"Twelve months, twelve stations of the moon and the sun, the twelve zodiacs—"

"It's derived from Old English. *Tuelf.*"

That caught her attention. Her emerald eyes went wide.

"Like *The Ramblings?*" she said quietly.

He gave her a slow nod. "Exactly like *The Ramblings.*"

She stared off into space, nodding. Then she pulled out her phone and said, "Oh my god, I need to get back to the lab. Barry is going to *kill* me."

He tensed.

As if sensing it, she glanced to him and smirked. "Not

literally. At least I hope not. But he has been abandoned a lot in a time of need lately so I have to get back." She pocketed her phone and looked nervously to him. "Um, thanks. For this. And the information slash history lesson."

She stepped up to him, close enough to touch.

"You're welcome." His accent came out thicker than he planned. Her smirk turned devious as she reached a hand up and patted him on the chest.

"I've had enough mansplaining for today though." On that note, she started toward the stairs they had descended from, leaving him to ponder what the fuck it meant to mansplain.

❖
CHAPTER EIGHTEEN
Izzy

The following morning Lando sent a text at *5 a.m.* to let her know workouts would be canceled for "business". She had squinted at the screen with one eye open long enough to read the message before falling right back to sleep. Her extra slumber time disappeared as she woke in a panic an hour later to remember none of them had Noah's phone number. Hell, she didn't even know if he had a phone number to have. She grumbled her way out of bed to shower and get dressed so she could intercept him in the hallway. Steam clouded around her as she stood in the hot water, still reeling from the cave experience yesterday. She remembered learning about the caves early in school but that was nothing compared to experiencing them firsthand. The fact The Society hadn't taken them over as some sick torture dungeon felt like a miracle. But as they climbed the steep stairs out of the ground, she brimmed with questions for Noah. How had he found them? When had he found them? What did he do underground, cut off from the world above? All those curiosities vanished when she got back up to the lab to help Barry sort a collection of letters between a founding father and his mistress.

Throwing on some leggings and an oversized sweatshirt, she tossed her mess of unruly curls into a bun and trudged into the kitchen to make a quick coffee. The purr of the little espresso machine had her nodding back to sleep, eyes heavy. Snapping out it, she grabbed her mug, tossed the appropriate amount of cream in and made her way out the door, down the stairs to the lobby.

In the grand entrance, it was just her and the doorman on duty, Larry. She set her mug on his counter to grab one of the newspapers stacked beside a golden bell. Good lord, Lando, a bell? Really?

Media somehow became worse with the advent of immortality, spearheaded by the fear fuel that naturally coursed through any sane person's body these days. She sighed at the terror mongering headlines and folded the sheet back up before turning to Larry. "Do you read this stuff, Lar?"

Larry was an older gentleman with a kind brow and soft smile. He also turned out to be a retired S.W.A.T. officer. It put her down a rabbit hole when Vahagn clued her in to the fact that sweet old Larry gave up the right hand of the law to work as Lando Denalo's personal bellhop. He used to volunteer at the animal shelter back in the day and ran many different after school programs for kids around St. Louis. Basically, he was a saint that could kill you.

"Of course not, Ms. Ciampi."

"Larry, please just call me Izzy."

"I could never, Ms. Ciampi."

She rolled her eyes and peered back out the glass doors of the entrance, taking another sip of her coffee. Her eyes drifted closed as the caffeine took its sweet time rebooting her system and when she opened them, Noah strode through the door. In jeans.

She tilted her head and frowned.

"Vahagn shot me a text about workouts but figured I could come… er," he glanced at Larry, "finish our discussion from yesterday."

Larry grinned like he knew exactly what type of *discussion* they were having and she rolled her eyes again. This charade was already getting old.

"And here I was thinking I woke up kind today. Guess I should stop." She winked at Larry then turned back toward the stairwell, coffee mug cradled in her hands. She didn't bother to check if Noah followed.

Once they were in the stairwell, she slowed to let him catch up to her. Glancing sideways at him, she asked, "So, you and Vahagn? Sharing numbers? Texting?" Vahagn rarely texted her more than one-word responses and that annoyingly smug emoji with the sunglasses.

His laugh rumbled up the echoey chamber. The coffee in her mug seemed to shake too. Or were those her hands shaking?

"More like forced surveillance, I think. He conveniently found me in this stairwell when I left the other day and we exchanged numbers, just in case." He tossed her a half smile and she caught herself before she tripped up the stairs.

It really was cruel how the world made all these shady men so God damn attractive. Why couldn't looks be ruled by a moral compass?

"He never mentioned it to me." She frowned at the thought. Vahagn rarely kept secrets from her, often to the point of disgust. Why would he keep this secret?

Noah shrugged as they pushed through the door into

her hallway.

"Are you jealous, Izzy?" That melodious accent coated his words, sending a shiver down her spine as he said her name.

Despite the traitorous coiling in her stomach, she scoffed. "Hardly. Though had I known you were already informed, I could've slept in this morning for the first time in decades." A bit dramatic, maybe just a few years. Since she found herself alone in her grandparents' house on The Hill, with a scary world closing in on her bubble of safety and no idea how to be an adult. No eighteen-year-old did.

Noah raised his eyebrows but didn't push the subject as they stepped up to her door and she got to work on her locks. A few clicks later they were in.

"Make yourself comfortable," she quipped as she beelined to the kitchen, mug desperate for a refill. "Would you like a cup?" she called over her shoulder, turning around as the espresso machine purred away. Noah leaned against the threshold to her small kitchen. Their eyes met fully for the first time that morning and she bit her lip to keep from gasping. His eyes were breathtaking in the morning light starting to pour in through her massive windows. Like pools of gold, with shimmering specks of green.

This was a cruel, cruel world.

"I'd love one," he said, his words drawling out. Why an accent, too? What in the Hallmark Hell did she get herself wrapped up in?

"What?" Still in a trance by his eyes, she had started to assess the rest of him in her sleep deprived delirium when he nodded his head to her waiting mug in the machine. "Oh shit! Yes, of course! Cream? Sugar?" Bustling around the kitchen was a better alternative. Less insane.

Completely fucking insane, as she ripped open the cabinet that held her collection of junk food. Like she didn't live here and know where her cups were kept.

You can't actually sleep with him, moron, she thought, as she went over to the fridge and reached for the half and half within. One of Lando's clients happened to be a dairy farmer across the river, thank fuck. It was a dark time in the beginning when she forced herself to use powdered milk, else be forced to drink her coffee black like a sociopath. A mark in the pro column of knowing Lando Denalo and all his connections.

"Just a splash of cream, if you don't mind."

Shit. Who would mind when he asked so nicely?

She shook her head and got started on his cup while doctoring up her own, needing something, anything, to busy her thoughts and hands with. This was all Barry's fault. When she had walked back into the lab, he presented a slide deck titled: *The Merits of Sleeping with Southern Men.* It ended up being all pictures of the entire cast of True Blood in various stages of undress.

"Did you not watch True Blood, Izzy?" Barry had said when she asked when the merits would be listed. His point was, unfortunately, inarguable.

Focusing on the swirling of the cream in the dark espresso, she said, "Well, I'm glad we had the same plan today about the book. I think I have more questions than answers after our excursion yesterday."

He walked past her into the kitchen as the machine finished its ministrations and grabbed the cream she had left on the counter.

"I'll be honest, I have some of my own as well." He gave a well measured pour and returned the bottle to her fridge before grabbing the mug. He leaned against her counter to take a sip, his muscled arm flexed with the movement.

Barry would be jizzing himself.

"Right, well, stay here a moment and I'll go grab it." Not bothering to explain herself further, she shuffled to her closet and her expert hiding spot. Prying the floorboard up, she grabbed the precious parcel and smiled to herself. She replaced the floorboard and started back to her living room to see Noah already seated at her couch, studying the windows behind him.

She joined him and he broke his assessment of the rising sun to raise an eyebrow at her. "Do I want to know where you decided to hide that?"

She smirked. "Probably not."

He sighed and held up his mug. "Right, let me finish this cup and then we can pull it out."

Right. Smart. Coffee plus centuries old, borderline mythical, bedazzled diaries of major historical figures that have not been properly cataloged did not mix.

She glanced back to the kitchen and frowned before turning to the coffee table to see her mug before her.

"Oh, um, thank you?" She gave him a grin that bordered on deranged grimace.

Why did she act so awkward around this guy today? So what he did something nice. Men can do nice things. Say thank you and move on.

He smiled softly, "So, while we wait, what's the story about the bookshelf?"

She blinked at him a couple times before it dawned on her.

"Oh! You mean that thing?" She gestured to the massive floor to ceiling bookshelf to their left. "As you can see, this apartment isn't exactly huge and I wanted both a library and a closet. Lando compromised by giving me both, in typical Lando fashion." She smiled at the result of his overzealous gifting.

Anything for you, mia bella. It was always a bit unnerving, the juxtaposition of the man.

"The ladder came from the basement of the old public library and the shelves themselves were hidden in some forgotten room of one of those insane houses on the way to The Loop."

Noah's brows scrunched, "The Loop?"

She laughed and she swore his cheeks turned a shade pinker when she did.

"It's just another area of the city. It has lots of eclectic stores, food, and the best concert venue in the city. Well… used to be." God, when was the last time she went to a concert? Most had been reduced to blood orgies these days. Rockstars always chasing the next high.

"What type of concerts?" he asked, taking another sip, and relaxing back into her couch some more.

Letting out a long exhale, she replied, "Gosh, just about anything I could get my hands on tickets to. It's one of those really intimate, standing room only type places so even when you're going to see a bigger name band or artist, you feel like you're part of a special club. It's the only place I could consistently find myself in the front row."

He watched her intently and she became acutely aware of how much she talked about herself.

"Did you ever go to any concerts in New Orleans? Or did you just follow the banjos into the woods?" She peered over her mug at him, taking a long sip of coffee.

He smiled and the room brightened a notch

"I actually used to play guitar in a band. The Whip Pets. We thought we were clever." The smile never left his face as he spoke and he shook his head, tousling his dark waves, as if remembering a precious memory before taking another sip of coffee.

Her features scrunched. "The Whip Pets?"

He chuckled, "Yeah. Our lead singer's mother bred whippets and we always enjoyed just saying the word." He smirked. "So it stuck."

"And what kind of music could you expect from The Whip Pets?"

He exhaled, "Oh, you know, the angsty grunge of teenage boy youth." His eyes twinkled as he grinned at her. "But like you said, it's been decades since I picked up a guitar. Who knows what kind of music you could expect from us now." Clouds smothered the smile she had been losing herself in and she wondered how many members were in The Whip Pets... and how many remained today.

But why would she care? This guy was a stranger to her not that long ago. Still was. Another know-it-all to add to the tower of know-it-alls in the archives, destined to make her regret her career choices daily. Nothing more.

She drained her mug as he did the same and grabbed his from him to return to the kitchen.

"You know, you never really did explain why you left New Orleans? Seems like you had a pretty deep connection there," she called, as she grabbed some disposable gloves from a drawer.

Noah's words came out stiff. "Yeah, born and raised there. What do you know about New Orleans?" The question was hesitant.

She barked out a laugh, "That it's an absolute nightmare and the city is completely overrun by The Society and fanatics who..." she stopped talking as she walked back into the living room to see all the color had drained from Noah's face. "Oh God, I'm sorry. I should've realized… I just… I didn't know…"

He turned to meet her gaze, the sorrow in his eyes ripping through her soul. "It's okay, really. We, uh, we were fortunate for a long bit but luck has to come to an end at some point, right?"

"Right…" she whispered and sat next to him, fighting the urge to reach a hand out to his. Instead, he grabbed a pair of gloves from her grip and clapped his hands together.

"Alright, let's crack open the most ridiculous diary I've ever held in my life."

She shook her head and put on her gloves.

"Yes, let's."

CHAPTER NINETEEN
NOAH

"So, how much Old English do you know?" Izzy asked from her spot on the couch next to him. The space between them had steadily decreased over the past hour and a half. Not that he had noticed.

They had been staring at the text, carefully flipping from page to page, jotting down ideas here and there in a notebook she had dug out from under her bed. But mostly they had been gaping in wonder at some of the *worst* handwriting either of them had ever seen.

"Well, typically I'm reading it from books that were printed by paid scripts who wrote with meticulous detail," Noah sighed, "so in this book? It's not much."

Izzy threw her hands up and crashed into the back of the couch.

"I think we need a break," she sighed. Noah agreed with her statement. His eyesight had long since gone crossed and his brain felt like reheated mush.

He took care as he placed the book back into its plastic bag, wrapping the silk scarf around it.

"And what do you have in mind for this break?" he asked, turning to face her.

She peered outside. Rain came down in consistent waves, droplets splashing against the panes of the window every now and then when the wind picked up. It had been like this for the past forty-five minutes, not a reprieve in sight.

Turning back to face him, she asked, "Have you ever played Mario Kart?"

He raised his eyebrows at her. "I'm older than you but not that old."

She laughed. "How would you even know? Besides, you don't look a day over twenty-one." She winked at him as she stood. "Let me put this book away and I'll get it queued up."

Grabbing the small, wrapped parcel, she jogged off to her closet, leaving Noah to follow her path before running a hand over his face. They had been at it for so long and it felt like they really had no answers to why The Society wanted this book, or why anyone would for that matter. With his basic translations, it appeared to be a simple journal of observations: *cat, bird, blade, parchment.* Not even in sentence form. Groaning into his hands, he nearly had a heart attack as a soft knock sounded at the door.

"Z, I know you're in there. You would melt in this rain."

Vahagn.

Noah's heart pounded in his chest. What was he doing here? Did he see him come in with her? Footsteps softly padded past him and he registered the clicking of the locks coming undone but didn't blink out of his panic until he heard her softly coo, "I'm busy, go away," before slamming the door shut and rejoining him on the couch.

"Are you okay?" She peered down at him, a slight frown on her lips.

His face must have looked like he had seen a ghost and his voice came out gravelly at first before he coughed to clear it, "Uh, yeah. Yes. Let's play this newfangled Mario Kart." He winked at her to play off his irrational behavior.

Her laugh wrapped around his chest and squeezed it. "How old are you anyway?" she asked, as she turned the television on and powered up the gaming system. She passed him a game controller.

Rubbing the back of his neck, he took the control from her hand and tossed a glance at her as she sat back down. "Thirty," he said.

"Oh man, you are old," she said it like she was delivering a terminal cancer diagnosis, hand on her chest and a mock look of concern on her face.

Noah snorted. "As if you're far off these greener pastures."

She gave him a dismissive scoff but smiled broadly as they got to work choosing their characters on the screen. "I'll be twenty-seven here soon. You get held back?" The menacing grin on her face was too much for him to handle so he kept his eyes on the screen, selecting Bowzer, a big, burly character often depicted as the villain. Noah always felt the guy was probably just misunderstood.

"No, just chose a degree with limited career paths so I found academia to be a comforting place to wallow in the sorrow of decisions I made as an eighteen-year-old."

Izzy selected Yoshi, the little dinosaur character looking sweet and innocent, and set her controller in her lap to look at him.

"I can relate to that," she said earnestly.

He raised an eyebrow to her as their eyes met.

"You mean the world of anthropology is not ripe and lucrative? Those within finding themselves so lucky to be a part of it all?"

Her laugh came out hollow this time.

Between pauses and grunts as they raced around the track on the screen, she said, "For some, I'm sure it might be. But the majority of us find ourselves in dusty basement workspaces, shared with random individuals of equal fate, chasing our ideas and theories until we either burnout or get promoted to another level of insufferable." Like Dr. Beechum.

He grinned and with the screen distracting them enough to boost his confidence, he asked, "This is not the life you had imagined for yourself?"

The little dinosaur on the screen swerved to the right but quickly recovered as she said quietly, "Not in the slightest."

Chancing a glance at her, he felt sudden responsibility for the anguish on her face.

"I didn't mean to pry," he said softly, not taking his eyes off her, surely to Bowzer's demise.

She quickly glanced between him and the screen before locking her gaze with his, abandoning the game as well.

"I'd love to meet *one person* whose life has gone according to their hopes and dreams," she admitted to him, an edge of defiance in her tone.

His gaze softened and dropped to her lips, how they were slightly parted. A storm of emotions danced on her face: anger, sadness, intrigue. Clearing his throat, and realizing he was staring, he rubbed the back of his neck and gestured to the screen.

"I believe I have crashed." His accent dusted with that

Southern aristocracy of a born and raised Downtown New Orleans boy.

Her gaze lingered on him a moment longer before trailing back to the screen.

"Shit, you and me both. Are you hungry?"

She set her controller on the coffee table and started toward the kitchen, not waiting for him to answer. His stomach grumbled in response.

"Um, yes. Actually. But I can go. I have already taken up enough of your time today and…"

"Just accept the kindness, Broussard. Can't promise it'll come around often," she hollered from the other room, the sound of cupboards opening and plates hitting the countertop.

A smile tugged at the corners of his mouth, and he didn't hide the blush that crept up his neck since she wasn't there to witness it. Instead, he walked over to explore the bookshelf.

It was a gorgeous focal point for the small apartment, the wood marked and worn from centuries of use, renewed with a simple satin finish. And the books. The genres spanned the breadth of literary history and there was weaponry speckled throughout the volumes in equally vast collections. There was a Crusader helmet, a display of riding crops, and… was that a sica?

"That one is just a replica," she sighed from the doorway to the kitchen, leaning against the threshold.

He looked over his shoulder at her before continuing his survey of the artifacts, coming to the ornate door that he knew led into her closet. His fingers trailed over the intricate carvings in the wood, depicting a man kneeling on the ground, hands clasped behind his back, face turned up to what looked like the sun.

"The congregation complained it looked like the man was worshiping the sun and not 'thee son', so they sold it for pretty cheap at a neighborhood yard sale a few years ago." She made her way to his side, her shoulder brushed against his arm, causing him to pull his hand from the dark mahogany wood. "I personally like the idea of a sun worshiper getting a bunch of Catholics up in arms," she added, mischief twinkled in her eyes.

"Seeing as the sun inspired the original December twenty-fifth celebration, I do like the irony of it all." Her smile broadened at his typically useless wealth of historical knowledge.

"Ah, a cynic. Not the stereotypical bible belting Baptist of the South then?" There was a note of honky tonk in her words, mocking him no doubt.

He turned to face her, assessing as he said, "There is hardly anything typical about the religions of New Orleans. Surely an *anthropologist* would know that." The side of his mouth quirked in a grin.

Only a couple inches shorter than him yet with an attitude that screamed she would take no shit, he felt intimidated under her open appraisal as she turned to face him. Hell, she had planted his ass on the mat the other day. An image that played on repeat in his mind.

"I will admit you have been rather… unexpected."

Snapping out of his memory, he tilted his head, crinkling his brow.

"Unexpected?"

Breaking their gaze, she strode back to the kitchen, her hips rolling dangerously side to side. Was she doing this on purpose?

"Food's ready." A moment later, a beep sounded from the oven and the smells woke him from his trance.

Was that lasagna?

He walked up to the small seating area at the counter

that separated the kitchen from the living area.

"You really didn't need to go through all this trouble," he said, sliding into the tall chair.

She glanced up at him as she lifted the pan from the oven, two mitts on her hands.

"Oh, I didn't. Lando did." She smirked. "He is rather mother hen-like for a grumpy old murderer."

Noah choked on the water he was sipping from the glass in front of him.

She rolled her eyes. "Did you really forget he was a mob boss?"

He lightly smacked his chest, "I actually really didn't know. Just assumed he must be a part of something suspicious to keep company with men like Charlie and Vahagn."

She started dishing out portions into ceramic plates and passed one to him. "He's not apart of it. He is it." She walked through the threshold to join him at the counter. "He once ran this entire city and really, it's best to pretend he still does as not to hurt his ego. To your credit, I didn't know who or rather, what he was when I first met him either."

He raised a brow before digging into his food.

Oh fuck, that's delicious.

She took a bite, nodding her head as she chewed. "It's true. Marched right up to his ridiculous front door and chewed him out like he was just a spoiled prick who had never been told no, not a fighter from the streets who had worked his way up the ranks to oversee one of the biggest crime conglomerates this city has ever seen." She took another bite and said with her mouth full, muffling the words, "And that's saying something."

Jesus Christ, how could he possibly be this big of a magnet for these organizations? He swallowed the choke in his throat with a gulp of water.

"Anyway, once the immortals came around, his biggest fear became reality—not having control. Don't tell him I told you. But to become a vampire who could be so overcome by blood lust, he could murder his own family? Hard pass for him. So, he took the gym he used as his front and personal passion project, brought it here to his fortress of a housing complex, and never left. Before you get too concerned about his vitamin D intake, he has roof access and I recommend never going up there in the summer." She shuddered.

Noah finished his plate and drained the rest of the water before he asked, "So, how did you end up here?"

She stopped eating, straightening her spine and set her fork down.

"That story is a bit more complicated and a lot less entertaining." The words threw ice on their conversation.

Yet he couldn't stop himself saying, "Ah yes, complicated." Fucking idiot. Why did his thoughts fall out of his mouth in front of her?

Her eyes pleaded with him not to press her on it.

Grabbing both their plates, she shuffled back to the kitchen sink.

"So, thank you for your work today on the book. Um, I think we should get each other's phone number so my precious sleep can be garnered whenever possible and maybe I can send you some pages that look legible?"

She smiled at him but her eyes held a haunted chill, no longer giving that reckless twinkle of mischief.

Way to kill the mood, Noah.

Fishing his phone out of his pocket, he slid it across the countertop as she did the same. A text message from his number popped up on her phone with a book and mind blown emoji. He smirked and sent back a sun and a man running away. She grinned at the screen and to his relief, it stuck as they exchanged phones again.

"I can't promise I'll be any more successful at deciphering what it says but I'll give it my best go," he said.

Her shoulders relaxed and his heart gave a damn near audible pump.

She led him to the door and he put his shoes back on as she worked on unlocking it. She pulled it open for him a few seconds later. As he started to walk out of her apartment, her hand grazed his arm lightly and she breathed out a whisper, "Thank you."

He turned to her and as their eyes met, she added, "Truly."

His brows scrunched, "For what?"

She looked away, rubbing her arm with the hand she had just placed on him. His skin burned where she had touched him, ingraining the light feel into his mind.

"For listening and not… prying." The look in her emerald eyes froze the breath in his chest. So, what did he do?

He fucking winked at her and said, "Anytime." And before he could embarrass himself any further, he was out the door, nearly halfway down the hallway when she hollered, "I'll hold you to that, Noah."

A smirk plastered on to his stupid face as he pushed into the stairwell and walked straight into Charlie.

❖

A vein throbbed in Charlie's forehead and he raised a scarred brow to Noah.

"You've been rather frequent in this stairwell lately," the

man grumbled, icy blue eyes spearing daggers at him.

Noah tilted his head before brushing past Charlie to continue down the stairs.

"Figured that would be the case after your *proposal,*" Noah quipped, smoothly descending the stairs.

The air vibrated with the anger radiating off Charlie as he was forced to follow Noah if he wanted to continue this conversation.

"Workouts were canceled today. I thought you got the memo," Charlie barked down to him, trailing behind in no hurry.

Noah smiled ruefully and couldn't help glancing back at Charlie as he said, "Yeah, I did."

Charlie paused his pursuit, a tension growing in his jaw that both silenced him for a moment and removed his ability to walk. Noah continued on to the exit.

Fuck whatever this guy has to say.

"You know," Charlie called after him, a slight growl in his voice, "the sex is the easiest part with her. Especially with an ass like that. It's the bullshit for the rest of the hours of the day that you'll find less than ideal."

The words hit their target and exploded in Noah. He stopped in the middle of the stairwell, taking deep breaths before he slowly turned around, fists clenched.

"Only delusional men think its solely the woman who was the problem. Did you ever think she might have found your rutting between her legs not worth the shit you likely put her through?" Each word came out strained as he held back the fury roiling inside him. He didn't know the full story between Izzy and Charlie but he could put the pieces together well enough. *It's complicated.* Yeah, fuck that. It seemed pretty fucking clear this guy was the worthless scum he expected in a thug.

Charlie held the wrist of his own clenched fist, puffing his chest out as he stared down at Noah. Noah just smirked at the gesture and turned to continue walking down the stairs. As he went to push through the door at the bottom, Charlie called out once more, "She'll never love you, you know?"

And despite himself, despite his better judgment, despite everything in him that said *shut the fuck up and leave now*, he couldn't resist saying, "Who said anything about love?"

Charlie turned a veritable shade of red, mouth twisting into a snarl as he opened it to say something but Noah was already through the door. The satisfied grin on his face tasted bitter as he continued across the lobby and out onto the street.

CHAPTER TWENTY
Izzy

There were few images that surprised Izzy these days but there was something about Vahagn leaning against Barry's desk, holding a bulbous shaped stone while her lab partner eyed the burly man with unadulterated hunger that caused her brain to short circuit.

"So," Vahagn rotated the object around, measuring it in his hands, "explain how this works again."

"Oh, with pleasure," Barry purred as he pushed back from his desk to stand and take the jade stone from Vahagn's hands.

"This smooth object was often used at the end of a massage by inserting it into a person's—" Barry caressed the stone as he spoke, his words heavy.

"I know how a butt plug works," Vahagn chimed in. Izzy choked on her coffee. The men both ignored her as she fought for her life.

Barry raised an eyebrow, "Oh? We will explore *that*

nugget of information a little later. Anyway, to justify its use as anything other than pleasure, the nobles would say it helped prevent the loss of 'vital essences'." He gave the object another obscene stroke before passing it back to Vahagn, leaning in. "I can think of a few men whose essence I would want to prevent the loss of…"

"Okay Barry, thank you for the unnecessarily graphic history lesson!" Izzy interjected, plucking the paraphilic stone from Vahagn's hands and placing back in its red velvet box.

It was Wednesday, apparently a slow day for organized crime because it was also the day Vahagn often came to hang out with them after his morning rounds, with coffee and bagels in tow, and always to the feral delight of Barry.

"V, I've been thinking about our little dinner party idea," she said, as she sat back down in her chair, salacious instruction over for now.

"*Your* dinner party idea, Z. I don't recall anything about it being dinner or a party though." He gave her a wary scan, a hesitant look in his eye.

"Did someone say party?" Barry rolled over in his chair, a whole two feet.

Izzy turned to him, fully taking in his outfit *du jour*: a burgundy velvet blazer over a puffy white shirt straight from the French renaissance with navy plaid slacks and some brown loafers. Likely vintage. Definitely Italian.

"Yes, I was going to see if you wanted to come. I figured we could do it at my place and then Barry could stay over after."

"Oh, thank god, I love your bed," Barry said, feigning a dramatic faint, but Vahagn gave her a quizzical glare.

"And what about Noah?"

"What about him?" she said.

"Wouldn't it be awkward to share your bed with Barry and your fuck buddy?" Vahagn clipped back.

Barry nearly fell out of his chair in a choking cough fit. She had failed to mention her charade to him. To be fair, she hoped it would be over before he ever found out.

But then what would her excuse to see Noah be?

Barry pulled her from her thoughts when he sat up, eyes watering and voice croaking as he snapped his fingers and said, "Go off, queen! Get that debonair dick!"

Fuck, she hadn't thought about the sleeping arrangements. It would be an asshole ask to send Noah back across the street after dark, even if it was less than fifty feet. Any distance in the dark was treacherous on these streets now.

It also would be suspicious as hell, and just as dangerous, to ask Lando to let him stay in his guest bedroom. And staying with Vahagn? She might as well be inviting him over for his last meal.

"Oh, right..." She had to think fast. "Well, I couldn't just assume you would let Barry stay with you, so I figured he could crash with Noah and I." She swallowed the unease building in her. There was no way Noah was going to agree to any of this deranged idea.

Vahagn held his glare on her but said in his rough, authoritative voice, "Barry can stay with me."

This time Barry did fall out of his chair as he feigned another faint. Or was that a real one? She was concerned until he raised his hands to the ceiling.

"Sweet lord baby Jesus, I know I have sinned but I will open one of those bibles after this all-holy blessing." His preaching sounded like a Southern Baptist woman on her knees. All he was missing was a beret, white gloves and a lace fan.

Izzy raised her brows but looked to Vahagn, clasping her hands together, "Well then. That's very kind of you. Thank you, Vahagn."

He hadn't stopped his open judgment of her. "You're welcome, Izzy."

They held each other's gaze, a torrent of words passing between then unsaid. She broke first and clapped her hands together once.

"Right so I'm thinking Friday night so I don't have to work with hungover Barry the next day. I'm going to commandeer Lando's kitchen to cook in, but we can meet at my place before sunset. I'm thinking sugo, antipasto, and a couple bottles of vintage from the Denalo Den." Gio kept Lando's wine cellar well stocked with her frequent flights to Europe so she doubted the old man would notice if a few bottles went missing.

Vahagn finally broke his death gaze on her to smile. The promise of his favorite meal tended to improve his mood. "I'll make a cheesecake," he said.

Barry smiled up at the man, "Okay, daddy, and what about dessert?"

Izzy rolled her eyes. "If you don't toss him out on the streets by the end of the night, I'll be surprised."

Vahagn smiled at Barry, the near heart attack it gave the man was palpable in the air. "At least someone appreciates all that I have to offer around here, Z." Good, he was done being suspicious of her. For now.

Smacking her laptop shut and throwing it into her leather bag, along with a notebook and her phone, she stood, "Well, with that sorted, I'm off to invite the guest of honor."

"Before you dishonor him in your sheets!" Barry

cackled in her wake. He was on a different level today with his latest shipment of Ming dynasty sex toys.

"Please save it for after we leave though," Vahagn quipped in from her chair that he had stolen as soon as she stood.

She rolled her eyes as she pushed through the door.

❖

"All I'm asking for is a few minutes to browse the sections and see if anything looks promising." For some reason, she had this same exact conversation with the circulatory desk assistant every time she came to the archives without an appointment or materials request.

"Ms. Ciampi, the rules are clear. No admittance without an appointment or materials request on file." The woman pointed a crooked finger to a sign that said the exact same sentiment on it.

"But you know me. I'm here at least once a week. If you had a frequent flyer program, I'm sure I would be top of the list." She gave the woman her best *sorriso confettato*, as her nonna would say.

The clerk slowly pushed her glassed up her nose, the thick, golden chain that kept them around her neck jingled against her mess of gaudy bracelets. Then simply turned away from Izzy. The audacity.

Izzy let an exasperated sigh, contemplating the merits of beating up an old woman.

"Izzy?"

She turned to see Noah behind her, a cart of books in front of him with several additional tomes in his hands. His hair looked darker in the dim lighting of the library and a few wavy strands had fallen across his forehead and why the fuck was she still staring at him with her mouth open?

Then she snapped her finger, "Oh, just the man I had

an *appointment* to see!" Her words were loud and clear, but her gaze pleaded with Noah to play along.

The old woman's eyes must have been shooting daggers into her back as Noah grimaced but said, "Um, yes. Right this way. That collection of war admiral's final diary entries is just over… here." He nodded over his shoulder, taking off toward a dark study nook with a couple desk lamps and a few discarded textbooks on the table. Izzy didn't hesitate to follow after him, not resisting a smile and a wave over her shoulder at the cranky old witch. No doubt a curse on her family line would be dealt after this. Izzy's smile faltered at the thought. A grimoire or two probably sat in the restricted section only accessible by Dr. Beechum and his circulatory assistant.

Noah had continued on and now sat at the table, looking over the books. When she approached, he stood quickly and looked her over with… concern.

"Is everything okay?" he asked, scanning her body. For what? Injuries?

She waved a flippant hand at him and slumped into a chair, "Oh, yeah. I'm fine. Please, sit down. Unless, of course, you're busy?"

He collapsed into his chair, running a hand through his hair. Had he been concerned for her?

"No, no, I'm not busy. But what's up? Why are you here? I don't usually…" His words trailed off as he looked away, back to examining the books on the table.

Fuck, she was an idiot. Who was she to think she could waltz up here and talk to him like he wasn't at his job?

Her nerves skittered on a new frequency, so she sat on her hands to keep her erratic Italian gestures in check. "I, um, I'll be quick." Why didn't she just text him like a normal fucking human? It wasn't like she hadn't opened that stupid emoji text chain several tens of times already. "I'm having a small get together Friday night—just dinner, drinks, a little friendly competition." She felt herself rambling, fuck. She huffed out a breath to compose herself. "I was going to see if you wanted to… join… us. It'll be Vahagn, Barry, and me, obviously." She finally looked up to see him watching her, his gaze unreadable.

"You came up here to invite me to a soirée?" Even confused, his accent stroked a nerve.

She rolled her eyes, "Okay, calm down NOLA. This is not the French Quarter. It's just pasta and really good wine I will steal from a mob boss without repercussions, hopefully."

He smiled at her, genuinely smiled, and said, "Okay."

For some reason this shocked her. "Okay?"

He stood, gathering the books on the table and turning off the green lamp that had been left on.

"Okay, Izzy." Such a matter-of-fact response.

"Okay." She couldn't do anything but sit there as he started to walk away. "Wait, don't you want the details?"

He turned slightly, those unruly strands of hair executing another escape across his brow. "I know where to find you."

⚜

The sweet smell of stewing tomatoes with seasoned ground lamb, using plenty of additions from Lando's luxurious spice collection, and a healthy pour of red wine, mirrored in her own glass, simmered on the gold-plated gas stove in the penthouse. Izzy hummed to the Sinatra playing over the house speakers while she kneaded the dough for the bread tonight. A garlic and rosemary Italian loaf, crusty on the outside, chewy in the middle. Perfect for dipping into sauce.

Sipping her wine, she swayed to the melody, unable to not feel excited about tonight. For this meal. For *cooking* this meal. She placed the dough ball into a bowl, covering it with a damp cloth and sat down on a stool at the island. Opening her messaging app, she pulled up the thread between her and Noah. The stream of their silly emojis popped up, all from their quick exchange the other day in her apartment. This was only the fifth or sixth time she had opened the message chain today, writing and rewriting a rather basic text. Definitely one that shouldn't require so much contemplation.

I: Hey, we are meeting at my place before sunset but come whenever works for you!

Her thumb hovered precariously over the Send button.

What a coward.

She took another sip, glowered at her phone, and pressed the stupid button before throwing it, screen down, onto the counter. Barry had granted her leave, since no one else really cared what happened in their little lab, to come home at lunch time to get started on the sugo, her family's pasta sauce recipe.

"From the old world, for the new," her nonno would say as he stirred the pot while her nonna rolled out her pasta dough.

The sauce was a life lesson in patience and trusting the process. Pull the sauce before the required four-hour simmer period and it would taste borderline disgusting. But let it stew for longer and the reward was the most complex depth of flavor, transporting the diner straight to the streets of Venice.

A drop of crimson wine splashed on the black marble countertop as her phone buzzed, snapping her out of the mouthwatering daydream. Ignoring the mess, she grabbed her phone and saw the reply. His reply.

N: Ok should I bring anything?

N: Beside my irresistible southern charm

Izzy smirked and started to type out her reply.

"I know none of the goons around here have you smiling like that," a sultry female voice said from the doorway.

Izzy set her phone down and squealed, "Gio!" before hopping off her stool and running to embrace the woman. Shorter than Izzy, Gio possessed the Italian curves and rock-hard muscles that screamed Denalo genetics. Izzy's fingers tangled in her long, black wavy hair as she squeezed her cheeks between her palms.

"What are you doing home?" Lando sent Gio over to Italy a few times a year to handle the *familia* business, a.k.a. rub elbows with other predominant families around the world to swap notes and share concerns.

Gio glanced behind her to the gym and subsequently, Lando's office. "Papa said there was reason to come home early." She peered back at Izzy. "But I brought goodies." A devious smile spread across her red painted lips as she held up a rather full duffel bag.

Izzy clapped her hands together. "Perfect timing! I'm having a little dinner party tonight. You'll have to come by and see Barry and Vahagn and…" She trailed off, taking the duffle bag from Gio, ignoring the incredulous look on the woman's face as she walked back to her seat.

"And?" A dark eyebrow raised as Gio followed her. No detail got past anyone around here, Gio included.

Izzy focused on the various treats, spices, cheeses, and cured meats Gio had brought back with her. It would mostly be gone within a week or two so it was a treasure to be the first to see it all.

"And," she elongated the word, "Noah. A new research fellow at the university."

"And lackey for my father?" Izzy's eyes snapped to Gio, the woman giving an all-knowing smirk. Of course, Lando had told her. She was the only true family he had anymore and thus told her damn near everything. Nothing was secret around here once someone joined the ranks. Every bit of news became family news. Gio followed up, "And that's who has you grinning at your phone like a teenager?" She gave Izzy a wry smile.

Izzy glowered in return. "No! Yes but no—I was just organizing when everyone should arrive and what to bring, that's all." She fumbled with the wrapper on a hazelnut chocolate bar.

Gio's brown eyes scanned her and she nodded once before stepping up to the large pot on the stove, stirring the sauce, "Okay, if you say so."

Time to turn this conversation around, "Does Vahagn know you're here?"

Gio stopped stirring for a moment before tapping the ladle on the side of the pot, replacing the lid as she turned back to Izzy. Murder in her eyes. Game, set, match.

"No. And I hadn't planned on telling him until absolutely necessary." The words were venom in the air.

Gio and Vahagn had been on and off about as often as, well, as often as she left for Italy. Izzy had never been able to find the right potion of drugs and alcohol to get the truth about their relationship out of Vahagn. The man either grumbled nonsense about Izzy being too nosy or got real silent, staring off into space like the wall could explain it for him.

So, it seemed they were off.

"Well, you don't have to come tonight then. But I will be bringing this with me, thank you," Izzy said as she grabbed a wedge of parmigiano reggiano and a jar of strawberry preserves. There were at least five jars wrapped within since it was one of

Lando's favorites. His taste of home.

Gio gave a tight-lipped smile and said, "We'll see." She peeked under the damp cloth and said, "So, tell me about this Society attack."

"What's there to tell? They came, they pillaged, attempted to plunder, and then skittered off into the shadows like the cockroaches they are."

"This is serious, Z. Those aren't the type of— That's not who you want to be on the radar of." Gio's eyes offered a warm but firm reprimand. Few questioned her authority in the crew and fewer still told her if they did. She was the big sister Izzy never got to have, part of the normal family she fantasized about as a teen when her peers would make fun of her living arrangements.

Wonder if she was born addicted to something? No way her mom stayed sober for nine months, the girl behind her in study hall would not-so-quietly whisper to her friend next to her.

Definitely would explain a lot, her friend would reply and they would both burst into disgusting laughs that reverberated through Izzy's memories to this day.

"I am taking it seriously, Gio. But I can't just hole myself in this building because some Oxford blood bros came knocking on the lab door." She lifted the towel on her dough baby, pressing a finger into the smooth lump.

Gio gave her a pointed look but didn't press. "And what about Noah? Where did he come from?"

Well, fuck. She replaced the towel and wiped her hands together, inspecting the ebony countertop. "New Orleans."

"Are you fucking serious? He just pops up from New Orleans right around the time The Society makes a move in this city?" Gio exclaimed, drawing Izzy's attention back to her with a wince.

"It's not like they haven't been here this entire time. It just feels close to home because it's me."

"Yeah, Z, that's home!" Izzy's heart clenched at her words but Gio didn't relent. "And this *guy* just happens to waltz in after the attack and weasel his way into this organization? You don't think that's suspicious?"

Yes, she thought it was suspicious. Very fucking suspicious. But every time she talked to Noah, her gut told her to trust him even when her brain said run fast and run far away. The confliction had her in a constant state of uncertainty.

"Well, come over tonight and meet him yourself before you make any final judgments." There was a bite in Izzy's words that felt bold in present company but she didn't care. She was getting real sick of everyone telling her they could make a better judgment call on her life than herself. Like she hadn't been fucking doing it since she was eighteen, long before Lando or anyone else entered the picture.

"*Mi orgoglio, Gio!*" Lando beamed from the gym entrance, arms spread.

A switch flipped in Gio as she turned to her father, returning his blazing smile with a matching one and she ran to him, arms outstretched.

"Come, let's talk about your trip. Isabella, do not steal all my vino or my strawberries, *si?*"

"*Si, Signore!*" Izzy called to them as the man ushered his daughter back to his office in the gym, one strong arm around her shoulders. Another vice gripped in Izzy's chest as she watched them smile and laugh to each other along the way, but she swallowed it and got back to cooking.

⚜

"Are you sure you're fine with Barry staying with you?"

Izzy asked Vahagn for the second time since he had helped her carry all the food down from Lando's. A caprese salad, the pot of sauce, and a bowl of handmade pasta sat on her counter. Several bowls of sliced bread were scattered about on various tables in the small apartment. There were only two dining chairs at the counter so people would have to mingle, find a seat where they could.

Vahagn rolled his eyes at her, tugging a curl, "Yes, Z. Charlie said he would be 'out' this evening and honestly, I enjoy Barry's company. Highly aggressive passes and all."

"Besides," Barry called from his place on the edge of Izzy's bed, peering out her giant paneled window, "I don't want to interfere. Unless," he brushed an invisible strand of hair back into his immaculate pompadour, "I'm properly propositioned by all parties."

Now Izzy rolled her eyes and pinched Vahagn's shoulder. "Rest assured that won't be happening, Bear. So, enjoy you stay at Chez Krog." She wrinkled her nose as the name clunked off her tongue. Sounded like a disease.

"I can guarantee a two-star experience at best," Vahagn said, smiling as he took his bourbon glass and set up at his usual residence on her couch.

5:45 p.m. A golden glow basked across the buildings outside. This hour always tempted her to run out and capture every last drop of sunlight before it vanished, but instead, she tapped her foot for another reason.

Would he come? Surely he would come. What reason did he have to not come?

What reason did he have to come?

He owed her nothing. They were working together to solve a problem. *Her* problem. Really, she was a nuisance in his life, not the other way around.

As her spiraling started to pick up some momentum, there was a knock on the door.

Vahagn stepped up to unlock and open it.

"Don't you clean up nice," Vahagn chastised from the doorway she couldn't see from her spot in the kitchen and she hurried to the threshold to get a look.

Noah strode in wearing an all-black paisley satin vest over a plain black collared shirt, the first few buttons undone to reveal dark tan skin and hints of black ink. A pair of heathered charcoal slacks completed the look. The clothes looked well-tailored and it made Izzy feel incredibly underdressed in her oversized goldenrod sweater and torn up boyfriend jeans. She tugged at her sleeve.

Despite her best attempts to spontaneously combust, Noah's eyes snapped to her as he replied to Vahagn, "No dress code was given so I went with my usual soirée attire." He winked at her.

"Well color me obsessed," Barry purred from his spot on the bed, taking a sip of wine as he devoured the man with his eyes.

"Right, that's everyone so let's—" Izzy started to say, frantically moving back about the kitchen to do something, anything, when a familiar female voice chimed in.

"Ah, so I'm no one then?"

Gio strode in clad in a leather mini skirt, fishnet tights, and an Italian band t-shirt that made her look as cool as she was. Izzy became vaguely aware of Vahagn choking on his bourbon. Gio noticed too and smiled.

"Nevermind, now everyone is here. *Mangia!*" Izzy clapped her hands and the tension waned off some as everyone suddenly had a purpose to be there.

Noah approached her where she stood in the corner of the kitchen, watching as the others milled about making their plates and found a place to sit.

"A gentleman never comes empty handed," he breathed as a bouquet of wildflowers appeared from behind his back. "Handpicked by myself, of course."

She smiled at the bundle of color popping against the dark shadow he made and said, "Isn't that illegal?"

"Probably but what's a horticulture crime in today's clime anyway?"

She looked up to see him studying her, a half-smile on his face. Who was this guy?

"Thank you, you really didn't have to do all this." To her utter embarrassment, the words came out breathless.

He backed away and she became aware of how close they had been standing. And the number of eyes that had been on them. That were still on them. He must have noticed too as he rubbed the back of his neck.

"Uh, do you mind if I set my bag down in your closet?"

His bag? Oh, right. He had a backpack with him. To stay the night. How had she missed that? She tripped a little as she led him to her closet, like he didn't already know exactly where it was.

She needed to get her shit together and fast. As she made to go back to the kitchen though, he grazed a hand on the crook of her elbow and said, "Thank you."

Crinkling her brow, she turned to him. "For what?"

He looked out the portion of frosted window that made the exterior wall of her closet. His words were sheepish as he said, "For letting me stay here tonight. For inviting me."

She blinked at him and opened her mouth to respond

when Vahagn moaned from the couch, "Z, why don't you make this more often?"

Noah walked further into her closet to deposit his bag before she could respond to him so she turned her focus back to the rest of the room.

"Because it's a labor of love, V, and I only have a finite amount to give you each month. Most of it is spent on allowing your snoring ass to crash on my couch."

Everyone snickered except Vahagn.

❖

CHAPTER TWENTY-ONE
NOAH

The mindless activity of eating helped Noah steady his nerves. Even with the churning in his stomach, he couldn't resist the incredible meal that had been laid out for them.

As he finished his pasta, dragging a slice of crusty bread through the leftovers on the plate, he said, "Did Lando make this meal?"

Vahagn snorted from his spot on the couch, Barry seated between him and the woman he learned was named Gio. Izzy narrowed her eyes on the man before softening her gaze as she looked to Noah, "No, this was all me actually."

Gio coughed from the couch. Izzy rolled her eyes.

"Oh, yes. And Gio stirred the pot."

"And pulled the bread from the oven!" the woman called out, holding her fork up in the air.

Izzy smirked at her back before returning her gaze to him. "Do you like it?"

She sounded uncertain, like his next words carried some weight for her. He gave her a smile, taking a quick sip of his wine.

"This is incredible. Did Lando teach you to cook or are you self-taught?" He spoke soft, his appreciation genuine. It had been a long time since he had a meal cooked for him, even longer since it tasted this good.

Her eyes flickered to the countertop before them, her fingers tracing the marbling in the stone, "That's a... complicated answer. But the recipe is my nonno's, my grandfather that is. *'One of the most important cargo'* he would say, though by the time it was passed down to me, he had it memorized." A sad smile etched on her lips and before he could stop himself, he had her hand in his and he squeezed. Briefly—then sanity regained traction in his mind and he pulled his grip away, rubbing the back of his neck as he studied the near floor to ceiling paned window to his right. The waning moon set a ominous glow on the dark street below. Not a soul in sight.

"You are close to them?" The sudden urge to know everything about her was heady. He studied the way she shifted under his inquisition, tucking a curl the color of his wine behind her ear, and pressed her lips together, as if mulling over what to say next. What to give him. Whatever it was, he would take it all. Drink it down like this vintage in his glass.

And that thought terrified him.

She met his studious observation of her, tilting her head curiously. "Yes. They were... they were my everything." The moonlight sparkled in the line of moisture that threatened to spill over her lower lashes.

Were. You fucking idiot, now you're going to make her cry. His inner monologue smacked him in the back of the head.

"I'm— I'm so sorry. I shouldn't have, I should have

realized," he said, attempting to back pedal out of his own cloud of stupidity.

She smiled at him through the tears, swiping away the errant ones that fell. "Oh no, don't be. They would've hated this world. They did hate the way the world was becoming. A life where they couldn't dance under the moonlight like two madly in love teenagers? That would be enough to send my grandfather into the grave. I just miss them, that's all. And this meal," she gestured to the meager remains in the kitchen, "it always brings back the memories I miss the most."

Noah nodded, "I can understand that sentiment."

Her gaze turned curious again and as her lips parted to say something, Vahagn cut in, "Please save the gross flirting for after we have all properly digested our food and left this floor of the building."

Middle finger raised and tongue stuck out at him, Izzy rose and began collecting empty plates. The mass of long, auburn red curls fell over her shoulder and across her face in unbridled freedom with her hands full. A quirk of a smile played on his lips and he turned to his glass of wine to hide it.

"Who needs drink refills before the fun begins?" Izzy called from the kitchen.

Empty glass raised over her head, Gio purred, "What's the game of the night? G.T.A?"

Coming out of the kitchen, a bottle of wine in one hand and a bottle of bourbon in the other, Izzy beamed as she said, "Charades!"

Vahagn groaned and said in a rat pack accent, "Bar keep, better make it a double."

And despite himself. Despite everything he had gone through to be here, everything he was currently going through to be here… Noah was having fun.

And how dangerous a thing was that.

❧

CHAPTER TWENTY-TWO
IZZY

"You have my number on speed dial?"

"Yes, Vahagn," Izzy said, dismissively.

"And if you can get out, you know how to get to my apartment downstairs?"

A heavy sigh escaped her lips as she pushed the man backward, closer and closer to the open door Barry leaned against, a placid smile adhered to his face for the past hour, ever since his edible kicked in.

"Yes, Vahagn."

Vahagn stopped moving at the threshold and gripped her shoulders, the serious look in his eyes pulling at her heart strings.

"Izzy, I'm being serious. If anything happens, find me. Call me. Get me, please?" His deep voice and brown eyes pleaded with her.

She pulled on his beard and said reassuringly, "Nothing will happen, V. But *if* it does, you're the first person to know, okay?"

This seemed to satisfy the burly man as he nodded once and turned, throwing his arm around Barry and headed toward the stairwell.

Gio had left a while ago when her phone had buzzed. While scowling at the screen, she stood and murmured, "Gotta go." Izzy had marked the look of disappointment in Vahagn's face as they all watched her stride out the door. But Barry, sweet Barry, pulled out a bag of edibles from his pocket and announced it was "time" in a rather prophetic way.

"Time for what, Bear?"

"You'll know," had been his only response as he and Vahagn split a rather innocent looking chocolate chip cookie. Homemade, no doubt.

Weed sales sky-rocketed in the wake of impending doom as people chased happiness wherever they could find it while their loved ones either disappeared in the night or outright sold themselves into the blood trade. Politicians, being savvy businessmen disguised as democratic public servants, invested in their growing operations and made sure that particular supply chain remained intact.

Barry, however, was a master grower all his own. He followed Greek mythology like a religion and his success at having a full ass garden growing in his apartment like some modern-day Demeter almost made Izzy a believer too. Almost.

"He really cares about you." Noah emerged from her closet, a small bag in hand with some comfortable clothes thrown over his shoulder. His satin vest had been removed and he leaned against the small doorway, rumpled with his shirt untucked, a few more top buttons freed like he had started to undress out of habit and realized his location so stopped. What a shame.

Her lips pressed together as she turned to the task of locking the door and said, "Yes. I never had siblings growing up, but he remedied that almost immediately when I walked into Lando's life. In a twisted way, it's been the best decision I ever made, joining a family of gangsters."

Turning back around, she found an unreadable look on his face, like her words were churning in his mind. "Unofficially, of course. I don't do any of the business, just reap the rewards of free personal training and sometimes stellar security," she added, hoping to ease whatever he calculated behind those hazel eyes. Noticing her gaze, he snapped out of it and motioned to the bathroom with his chin, "Mind if I…?"

Her eyes flickered over the things in his hand and to the bathroom and she said quickly, "Oh, God, no not at all. Please, make yourself at home. What's mine is yours. The whole shebang." Her feral Italian hands flitted about the space.

He licked his lips before smiling at the floor as he made his way to the bathroom, "The whole shebang? That's a new one on me."

✦

The whole shebang. The. Whole. Shebang. Izzy scowled at her reflection in the floor mirror in her closet. She had rushed in here to change after Noah had closed the bathroom door, giving her one of those fucking winks that catapulted her heart. Since when did that happen around him?

And now he was about to sleep in her apartment. In her bed. Albeit alone. She would sleep on the couch, but still. The proximity felt suffocating already and they were on opposite ends of the apartment, behind doors.

She threw on her usual sleep attire, an oversized band tee and nothing else, and started to walk back to clean up a bit when better judgment told her shorts, yes shorts, might just be a good idea. No need for Noah to wake up in the middle of the night and see her with one leg hitched up, ass to the world.

Decorum established, she emerged from the closet, and began the task of picking up the empty glasses and cloth napkins strewn about. Once in the kitchen, the menial work of putting away leftovers, filling the dishwasher, and wiping everything down tunneled her in, the rest of the world a steady hum in the background.

That's why she jumped, the rag in her hand falling to the floor with a smack, when she beheld the man leaning against the threshold to her kitchen, arms folded and a coy smirk on his face. No, not just any man. Noah. His wavy hair looked darker than she remembered and she realized he must have taken a shower while she cleaned, a towel hung over one of his arms.

"I hope you don't mind if I used your shampoo," he drawled, his lips still quirked up.

Her words stammered, "No, no, not at all. I can hang your towel up for you. I usually keep them in my closet because," she gestured to the giant window that made up her exterior wall.

His lips curled into a full smile and pink tinted his cheeks as he scanned the building across the street. *His building.* "Yeah, you really never know who might be watching."

Her back straightened and her heart rate quickened.

The color in his cheeks deepened and he shook his head, broad hand running through the damp strands in his hair. "Ah, fuck, that sounded creepy as hell. That's not what I meant, I— I don't know what I meant."

She relaxed. He was…nervous? Good. The playing field was evenly matched then.

"Here," she grabbed the rag from the ground and

handed it to him, gestured for him to give her his towel, "you finish cleaning the counter and I'll go find a spot for your towel in the bathroom." She would have to remove her makeup bag or robe from the only hooks in there.

"Deal," he said, making the trade and meeting her gaze. His fingers brushed her own and she ignored the jolt it sent rippling up her arm. This. This was a charade. It only made her feel all tingly because the warm hug of good red wine had its arms wrapped around her. She shuffled past him toward the bathroom before the rose tinge heating her neck could make it to her cheeks.

"So, I figured I would give you the bed. I changed the sheets this morning," she started saying as she walked back in to see him hunched over the sink, shoulders flexing under his t-shirt as he cleaned the damn thing. Shit, was she supposed to do that more than once a year?

He washed his hands before turning around to lean against the counter, pulling a small towel from his shoulder to dry his hands. "That's unnecessary, I'll sleep on the couch."

The command in his voice curled her toes. Or was it that damn accent again? She needed to get a grip.

"No, I insist. Vahagn is the only guest who gets relegated to the couch. It keeps him humble." She smiled at him. He tossed his towel next to the sink and pushed off, making his way out the kitchen. She had laid out a pillow and blankets on the couch for herself while she had been cleaning up and Noah started making up the makeshift bed. Before her brain could register what he was doing, he laid down, hands rested behind his head as he looked up at her. Defiant.

She glared down at him. "Men are infuriating," she grumbled and turned on her heel to march into her bed, throwing the down comforter open and punching her pillows.

"Consider it a version of equality," he replied, a hint of amusement in his words. She glowered at the back of the couch as she punched her pillow once more for good measure and tossed herself back into it.

Silence descended over the apartment, the only sound the whooshing of water in the running dishwasher. She studied the coffered ceiling. She glared at the coffered ceiling. A sigh sounded from the couch followed by a rustle of feathers and fabric. She glared at the couch. She sighed and turned toward the window, rustling her own bedding.

Normally, the twinkle of the stars could push her to the edge of sleep, the constellations more vivid than before with the elimination of artificial light polluting the sky.

Normally.

"Did you have any siblings?" she said at the same time he said, "Did you grow up here?"

They both sat up and looked to each other, green eyes meeting golden ones. Then they burst out laughing.

"Noah, this is stupid. We are both adults, with deteriorating joints and sore muscles from the torture inflicted upon us at the hands of a Mr. Denalo." She scooted over to the edge of the bed next to the window and patted the open spot, "I think we can handle sharing a bed for a night."

In the moonlight, she could see his nostrils flare, a muscle ticked in his jaw and for a moment she thought he might just lie back down and ignore her. The pounding in her chest had to be audible in the stillness. Oh God, was this a heart attack? If she died of a panic-induced heart attack, Vahagn would burn the city down regardless of the fact it started because she was a nervous wreck over a boy.

The shuffle of fabric jolted her out of her doom. Noah

stood, facing away from her as he first ran a hand over his face, then through his hair and finally rubbed the back of his neck as he made his way to the bed, glancing up to meet her gaze. She offered a smile she hoped conveyed welcome, inviting connotations and not maniacal panic.

Gravity pulled her toward him as he sat down facing her, crossed his legs, and studied her. She resisted the pull as he said, "Happy?"

This time she winked, again praying it came across playful and not deranged, as she said, "We'll see."

He smiled and looked to the books on the shelves above the bed. "I have… had a brother. Benji." He glanced back to her and she noticed him wringing his hands together. "He, uh, died. In the riots last year."

Her heart sank for him. The news of the riots had spread like wildfire across the city and Lando's men worked around the clock to make sure no one got any ideas. The details and cause had been vague or outright missing so everyone was on edge, not sure where the next threat would come from.

She reached across the bed and squeezed his fidgeting hands. They immediately stopped and his golden eyes flickered to her as she said, "I couldn't imagine losing a sibling and all mine aren't even real."

He shifted their grasp to hold her hand between his. His thumb grazed over her knuckles and he played with the ring on her thumb, the onyx stone Vahagn had given her for her birthday a few years ago.

"*Birthstones are dumb, this is cool,*" he had said.

Noah shook his head, a half-smile on his face as he swallowed then looked to her.

"Your turn. Have you always lived here?" He didn't let

go of her hand, nor did he stop toying with the ring. She edged closer to him so she could sit up straighter.

"Yes. I wouldn't be surprised if they cut me open one day and found muddy water running through my veins." Another smirk played on his lips.

"I've had the same thought."

"So, a true born and raised bayou boy?" She pulled her hand from his hold. A slight downturn of his lips and crinkle in his brow showed when she did, but her Italian desire to talk with her hands, especially when nervous, won out as she gestured up and down to him, "This whole southernly gentleman thing is authentic?"

His features lightened and he laughed. "Yes. It's authentic. Trust me, I've tried to hide the accent for years."

"That would be a shame." The words were out before she could stop them and his smile went lopsided.

"You know you're not immune to having an accent either. It's not as strong as this but its noticeable to someone who is not from here."

"Oh yeah? Is it one you want to fall asleep to every night?" *Like I want to yours.* She kept that tidbit of information out.

He ignored her question, thank God, and instead asked, "So, how long have you been an honorary member of the Denalo family?"

"About six years. After my grandparents passed, their house no longer felt like a home. And I was young and alone and scared, so I used the money I inherited to buy this apartment and pay for school. It's not much but the security is top notch and that was my main concern."

He looked to the locks on her door and raised a brow to her. "And you feel safe here?"

She knew he was thinking about her conversation with Charlie in the hallway when they went to retrieve the book from the lab.

She looked to the locks, eyes glazing over a bit. "I've been alone most of my life, so having people in it now, even if they care about my safety and wellbeing, feels… treacherous."

When she looked back to him, he watched her. Studied her.

"What?" She asked, feeling self-conscious under his scrutiny.

He looked away to the sheets then met her gaze again, his eyes glowing in the darkness around them. "I've just never heard someone put how I feel into words before."

❖

The rattle of chains against the wooden box she laid in startled her awake.

The chains. The wooden box.

Her heart rate catapulted into an unhealthy churn in her chest as she banged against the confines she found herself in. She knew it was a dream this time but she couldn't escape it. Panicked breaths filled the space with a palpable heat that sent her adrenaline to a new level.

"Help." The word felt feeble and croaking, but it was her own voice.

She tried again with a shout, "Help!"

The jostling movement stopped and for a second she remained still, listening for clues, hints of what the fuck her imagination had conjured up to disturb what should be a peaceful night of sleep. A knock sounded against the side of the dark panels. She waited to see if someone would release her. After a few moments, she pushed against the top of the box. It gave to the pressure, opening up to a foggy sky, air filled with the scents of smoke, mud, and excrement.

Slowly rising out of the crunched fetal position she was in, she scanned the encampment around her. Tents of dirty canvas sheets and areas with small fires filled the space. Gatherings of soldiers sat around the meager sources of heat. These soldiers had swords, crosses stitched on the breast of their uniforms, above their hearts.

Setting a hand against the rough grain on the edge of the box, she began to lift herself out when a man donned in white linen with a white hood appeared around the side of the carriage.

The crusader.

"*Hie mîn prættig hû êow attain hêore?*" The man's voice came out gruff beneath the fabric draped over his face.

Fucking hell. Noah hadn't gotten to the spoken part of teaching her Old English. She was impressed she could even distinguish it as such after the weeks of translating with him.

"Erm, sorry?" she said. Like that was going to be useful.

The man reached a red gloved hand up to his face. Izzy flinched at the movement. But when he removed the veil over his mouth, it was the shock of the gleaming white fangs curled into a menacing smile that released the scream deep in her chest.

She sat up in bed, panting, sweat sticking curls to her forehead as she took in deep breaths and gripped the soft olive bedding beneath her hands. Her bedding. Her bed.

Slamming back against the pillowy softness of her mattress, she let out a loud exhale and rolled to her side, reaching a hand out to the cool, empty space next to her.

She froze. *Noah.*

Panic roared through her veins again as she sat back up and scanned her apartment. There was really no place to hide in here, with walls only separating the necessary spaces of the bathroom and her closet. As she started to push the blankets aside, swinging her legs over to check those two places, a shadow appeared in the threshold to the kitchen.

Noah's image focused in the blue haze from the moon outside, clutching a glass of water. He stopped dead when he saw her legs hanging over the edge of the bed.

"Are you okay?" she asked, her voice a touch into a shrill frequency.

He padded toward her, his shorts teasing higher with each pull on his thick thighs. When he stood before her, he held the glass of water down to her.

"You were murmuring and tossing in your sleep. And you were absolutely on fire. I thought a glass of water might be appreciated when you woke out of whatever was disturbing your dreams." His golden eyes glistened in the moonlight shining in from the windows behind her. She lost herself in them for a moment while the flutter in her stomach wrenched her speechless.

Snapping out of it, she grasped the water, drops spilling over the edge at the movement and splashing to the floor. The brush of Noah's fingers against her own disappeared as he moved back toward the kitchen.

"Leave it," she commanded. She winced at the tone. His steps faltered and he stopped, shoulders heaving slightly. "You can just come back to bed," she added before downing the glass of water and scooting back to her side of the bed. She pulled the blankets back over his space and watched as he slowly turned on his heel and climbed back into the space. The mattress sighed against the added weight. He laid back against the pillow, crossing his arms behind his head, the movement revealing a small bit of inked text on his bicep. The words disappeared under the sleeve.

As he gazed up at the ceiling, a ghostly look crossed his face.

She positioned herself in a mirror to him, keeping a small distance.

"Do you want to talk about it?" His voice echoed in the chamber of the space between them.

Izzy let out a long exhale. "I don't even know what to say. It was just so weird. And vivid. God, I thought I wouldn't be able to escape."

She felt the bed shift beneath her and a soft caress along the sensitive skin of her underarm. She closed her eyes, savoring the touch that worked to swallow the visions of gray skin and red tinted lips.

"When I was a kid, I had a dream of being a marine biologist." His voice had some distance to it, as if he drifted back into that childlike version of himself. Dreams had before reality ripped open the ugly scar of potential. "I went so far as to declare it as my major when I went into college."

Izzy crinkled her nose and opened her eyes to meet his glowing gaze. "Really?"

He chuckled softly. "Yes, really. It was my first night in the freshman dormitory when the dreams began though."

She rolled her eyes and looked back to the ceiling. "You're making this up to make me feel better. And while I appreciate it, it really is unneces—" His rough finger pressed into her lips, silencing her, though she glared at his amused expression. He released his touch on her lips and she tried not to think about the tingling sensation it left behind.

"Unfortunately, my most embarrassing and traumatizing memory is, in fact, not a lie. I'm not that creative, I'm a historian." He winked at her and she kept quiet to listen to him elaborate.

"Every night, I would fall asleep on that wretched, plastic wrapped mattress and open my eyes to swimming in the depths of the ocean. It would be amazing, crystal clear water with rainbows of fish swimming by, coral as bright as the sun radiating off the ocean floor. Then I would see a fin beneath me, which was no big deal, I love sharks. Fascinating creatures, very misunderstood," he added as she crinkled her nose. "It was an incredible scene, a true dream. But then it morphed. The water would start to turn murky and dark, the coral graying and the fish scattering into holes within the rocks along the floor. I would swim in a circle, searching for the source of the disturbance. And then, before I had a chance to react, a giant great white would appear, barreling toward me at full speed with its jaw wide open. I would awake the moment of impact, coated in so much sweat it looked like I wet the bed, and gasping for air like I had just finished a rough set of hill sprints."

"Oh, sheesh, that's terrifying," she said, scanning his face as notes of shame painted across his brow. He shook his head and his golden eyes set fire to her own as they met.

"Oh no, it gets worse." He grinned. "This went on, nightly, for the entire first semester of freshman year."

Her eyes widened. "Oh no."

"Oh yes. Nothing like sleeping next to your first hook up in college only for her to wake up covered in a pool of some mysterious liquid while you're panting next to her like a crazed dog."

She gasped and covered her mouth. "Oh no," she said from behind her hand.

He ran a hand down his face and groaned. "Oh. Yes."

A moment passed and then they both burst into laughter.

"Oh God," she said between gasps for breath, "I'm so sorry. I shouldn't laugh. That was your life dream! Your whole childhood!"

He leaned back against his pillow, dark brown waves spilling across his forehead as he smiled at the ceiling. "Yeah, I changed my degree path the next semester and avoided that girl for the rest of the year. I got quite a lot less attention from any girl after that, actually."

"Oh, I hardly believe that," she let the words tumble out her mouth before she could stop them.

"Oh. Believe it, Isabella Ciampi. I was scarlet lettered in the worst way: as the weird guy who had wet dreams." He turned his head to smile sideways at her. She returned it, a clouded weight lifting off her chest as she forgot what her own dream was even about.

✦

They spent the rest of the night talking, laughing, and when Izzy woke the next morning, a strong, tanned arm wrapped around her waist, holding her against the solid weight of Noah's chest. When she moved to get up, his hand gripped her and a sleepy groan escaped his lips before he pulled away suddenly. She knew he was pretending to be asleep as she climbed out of the tangle of sheets and made her way to the bathroom. When she emerged, wrapped in her robe, he was no longer in the bed and instead stood in the kitchen, making himself a coffee.

A shade of pink she could never match stained his cheeks as their eyes met and she nearly sprinted the rest of the way to her closet. A steamy mug awaited her on the counter when she came out, dressed in a sweatshirt and leggings, the desire to go for a run overwhelming her. Last night had rattled her. Filled her with a frantic energy she needed to burn off. When was the last time she had just opened up to someone like that? With Charlie? And look how that had ended.

She spiraled and needed to channel that energy somewhere else.

Noah walked out of the bathroom, dressed in jeans and a vintage Saints sweatshirt, a black t-shirt peeking out the bottom. His pace slowed when he spotted her but he kept at his task of packing up his things.

She cleared her throat and said, "Um, thank you. For the coffee and for the company. Last night, I mean. It was… nice." And now had her reeling into a different dimension, but it was too early for all that.

"Yep," was all he said as he put his things in his backpack, zipping it up and stood. "So, I'll just…" He motioned to the door. Her heart sank, the traitorous organ.

"Oh, yeah. Of course, don't let me keep you from whatever." The sun had been out for a couple hours now. He had no reason to be here any longer. And yet…

He stood at the door, shoes on and locks undone, his hand hovered over the handle as he said, "We should probably get together again. To discuss the book some more, I mean. I might have some theories."

She watched his shoulders relax as she said, "Yes, I'll shoot you a message sometime this week."

He nodded his head once and didn't look back as he pulled the door open and left.

Emptiness filled the space in his absence and she took one gulp of coffee before lacing up her sneakers and running out the door before her own demons lurking in the shadows could appear.

$$\maltese$$

CHAPTER TWENTY-THREE
NOAH

An uncomfortable yearning settled in his chest the moment he walked out her door. It didn't leave until later that evening with the welcome burn of bourbon as he sat on the floor of his room, staring at his open, still packed bags.

How had he found himself here?

Benji would've never ran from this. Hell, he probably would've sought out Lando Denalo himself, joining his ranks and divulging everything he knew about The Society without a second thought.

And that's exactly what got him killed, Noah thought as he took another long sip, staring at those bags that haunted him nightly.

Why was he still here? This entire time, he never unpacked. Never put anything of his own in this apartment. Like he couldn't ever commit to this place.

He leaned back against the wall, tilting his head up and

closed his eyes. In his mind, he met a vision of a sleepy emerald gaze, unruly soft curls, and the warmth of her body against him…

A thud sounded as he knocked his head against the wall.

Last night had been a mistake. He knew he should have stayed on that couch. He knew it every second it took for him to stand and walk over to her. Drawn to her like a magnet despite every alarm bell telling him it was a line too far. The line he couldn't cross. Shouldn't cross. And yet, all he wanted to do now is run back across the street and into that bed. It had felt… right. A comfort he hadn't known. Ever.

He narrowed his gaze on his bags again, scowling deeper as he drained the rest of his glass and stood to make his way back to the kitchen for a refill.

He wasn't going anywhere tonight

As the amber liquid flowed into his glass, his phone buzzed in his pocket and sent an electric shock to his heart. The thing was normally a silent weight, often forgotten until Dr. Beechum sent him daily agendas.

"Who the fuck would," Noah mumbled as he pulled it out and saw Izzy's name across the screen. He quickly set the bottle down and looked out the window to that room across the street. He was acutely aware it had become second nature to spot it. But the lights were out and there was no glow of a phone in sight.

Frowning, he opened the text message.

I: I bet you're good at poker.

What the fuck did that mean? He gave his phone a quizzical look as he typed his response.

N: I am but I'm not sure how you deduced that?

I: HA! Knew it.

I: You just look like you're really good with your hands.

Noah choked on the sip of bourbon he was drinking and set the glass down to pound on his chest as he coughed, typing out his response as fast as his fingers allowed.

N: I'm not sure that has any applicability in poker.

I: Sure it does ;)

He couldn't stop the grin on his face at this point, abandoning his bourbon as he moved into a seat at the dining room table, looking out to the clear night sky.

N: Where are you? Your lights are out.

An instant lump of dread dropped into the pit of his stomach as he pressed Send. Even through text message, he couldn't help but fumble his fucking words.

I: Keeping tabs on me? Already obsessed after one night in my bed?

I: Lando's poker night but the company is less than ideal despite the weed

That explained the boldness.

N: Not tabs, just curious. Who else is there?

I: The usual suspects though Charlie was extra pissy and left about half an hour ago before V could finish preparing the bong that his tight ass probably needed

Noah let out the breath he had been latching onto. At least Charlie wasn't there. Anymore. He had a pretty good idea why he might be upset though.

Movement in the street below caught his eye. He scanned the desolate roadway, only seeing a cat perched on the stone railing of the building next to Izzy's, near the same alleyway he had once seen Charlie appear in.

His phone buzzed again in his hand.

I: Where are you?

God, his heart pounded in his chest. This felt like high

school again.

                        N: Why? Are you already obsessed?

                        N: Home, of course.

Home.

Was he home? This wasn't home. He didn't have a home anymore. He hadn't since the beginning. It had always been just him and Benji. And now... He couldn't even remember what their first house had looked like, they had only been placed there three months before being passed along in the system. He vaguely recalled the smell of stale cigarette smoke and cheap beer, the shaking floors and hollow walls of a trailer.

Why had he told her he was home? And why did it spiral him to analyze his childhood?

Shit, you've got to stop drinking bourbon alone. The voice in his head sounded like Benji.

He stood to go back to the kitchen to do the only logical thing and drain the rest of the glass he had poured himself, wallowing in his self-pity until tomorrow. Tomorrow Noah could deal with this. His phone buzzed again from the table as his grip tightened around the glass and he tossed back the rest of the liquid, setting it down with a thud.

No, wait. That thud wasn't from his glass. It came from his room.

Where all his weapons were hidden.

His pulse skyrocketed.

He grabbed the bourbon bottle as he crept toward the partially closed door. He could've sworn he had left that open. Floorboards creaked under his feet and he swore under his breath. This was his home. He never planned to have to defend it like this. From the inside.

He shook his head as that word floated into his mind

on a bourbon fueled boat. Home, home, home.

Focus, Broussard. Now is not the time to get sentimental.

The bedroom door screamed on its hinges in the silence as he pushed it open. He crept into the room, scanning the walls and windows looking for the source of the thud. The bourbon bottle held out in front of him like a trained soldier. Like the trained soldier he was.

The second his eyes noticed the bags strewn across the floor, he whirled around. Pain erupted on the side of his face before he could make out defining features of his attacker. All he knew was rage in those eyes and then a wet cloth caught his mouth as it flew to the side. Glass shattered as the bottle slipped from his fingers and fell to the floor. He gripped the wrist holding the cloth but it wouldn't budge. His strength drained from his grip, his hand slipped from the wrist as gravity overcame him and he fell hard to the floor. Another buzz sounded from the dining room table as his attacker dragged him out the door of his apartment.

His home.

CHAPTER TWENTY-FOUR
Izzy

I: You could be here if you wanted…

I: Oh god, please ignore that. Of course you don't want to be in this shit show.

I: Unless you do! Then you're always welcome.

Izzy stared at the unread messages on her phone. One remained typed but never sent, thank God. A *'Because I want you here'* first thing in the morning before they were in forced proximity of each other for Lando's workouts was an embarrassment she didn't think she could recover from. The rest could just be interpreted as friendly. Because weren't they friends now? Surely sharing a bed automatically put you into friendship territory.

Vahagn groaned from the couch a few feet away and she looked to her phone's clock, quickly deleting that unsent message lest she accidentally hit Send.

6:04 a.m.

She should be savoring her precious extra hour of sleep

before morning workouts but her heart raced. She had *texted* him. Full on flirtatious texting. Like a goddamn teenager. She softly smacked her phone to her forehead a few times, whispering "Stupid, stupid, stupid," before tossing it into the mass of linen and down, and rolling off the edge of the bed to trudge into the kitchen for her morning salvation: coffee.

"Why does my throat hurt so much?" Vahagn croaked from the couch, making her jump the remaining four feet into the kitchen.

She fumbled around for a mug and rattled it into the espresso machine, pressing the button before stumbling to the fridge for her cream when she responded, "I would say it would have something to do with Lando breaking out the karaoke machine and you doing your best Creed impression."

She couldn't help smiling at the hazy memory. Trying to be a responsible adult, she had kept to one vice last night, learning her lesson the last time she tried alchemy with her drugs. Thankfully, Charlie's sour mood had even put himself off and he had left before he could rain on their parade the rest of the night.

"At least tell me I hit the high notes." Vahagn had emerged from his nest on her couch and now stood in the doorway. She snorted.

"Oh, you hit something." She smiled devilishly before popping another mug under the machine, splashing some cream into her own. A moment later, the machine hummed and garbled to announce the completion of its sole task on the planet and Vahagn trudged over to grab it.

"None of that mess in my nectar, please."

"Only psychopaths and serial killers drink black coffee, V."

"Then don't make me angry before I've had mine, Z,"

he grumbled in reply as he strode back to the couch to sit down with his eyes closed while he sipped his coffee.

She smirked and grabbed the cream to return it to the fridge, her memory flashing back to the coffee Noah had made for her before he left. The secondhand embarrassment roiled through her again as the chain of unread messages came haunting behind the sweet thought. Scrubbing her face with her hands, she grabbed her mug and followed Vahagn into the living room. She sat down beside him, leaning against his solid frame as he remained still, eyes closed, sipping his coffee. She studied his profile, the content way the lines in his brow softened. He seemed at peace, despite his grumpy disposition.

The caffeine started to buzz her back to life and with it a steady thrum radiated through her as the tension and anxiety she had been running from yesterday and last night found its way back into her bloodstream.

"Do you mind if we go early to workouts this morning?" she asked Vahagn.

"Shhh," he said, petting her face with his hand, eyes still closed. She leaned back out of his reach and swatted him away. He curled around his coffee in defense and whispered, "Careful."

"You're a menace. Do you mind?"

"Give me," he weighed his mug in his hand, "one and half more cups of coffee and we can go." He popped one eye open, it narrowed on her. "Why in such a hurry this morning? Wanna catch up with your lover boy?"

She blushed and turned to look out the window behind them as the morning sun made its ascent, lighting the room more and more each minute. "No, Vahagn. I just want to do some cardio or run on the treadmill or something."

"Sheesh, okay, calm down you little dingo. What's got

you so wired?"

She bit her bottom lip as she glanced back to her phone on her bed.

"Did Charlie seem extra weird last night?"

Vahagn snorted, finally opening both eyes, blinking the sleep away. He scratched his beard and yawned, his accompanying stretch shaking the couch.

"I mean, yeah, but he's been extra weird for months now. Since you guys…" he grimaced and abandoned his sentence to take another sip.

She pursed her lips. He *had* been extra weird since they finally broke things off. He had disappeared for several days and came back so *angry*. For someone who had nearly beat her to the edge of death, he had looked like the one who had been traumatically wronged.

"I just have a lot going on at work and the pressure is stressing me out, I think. That's all."

Vahagn scanned her thoroughly in the emerging light. "If you say so." But the scowl on his face told her he didn't believe her for a second.

Thirty minutes later, and Vahagn's allotted one and half cups of coffee consumed, they made their way to Lando's penthouse. Izzy tried but couldn't resist the itch to check her phone several times on the short journey up before Vahagn cut in, exasperated, "Is my company not enough, Z?"

She grinned sheepishly up at him and tucked her phone back into the side pocket of her pants.

"I just…"

"That's the same stupid grin that was on your face at the poker table last night. The table where you lost, continuously.

Over and over and it such glorious fash—"

"Okay! I get it!" she sniped as they approached Lando's medieval doorway and Vahagn went to push it open.

"It's that Louisiana boy, isn't it?" he said, holding the door open for her.

She brushed past him and glared up for good measure, "So what if it is?"

He raised a brow. "Already trouble in paradise? Anything I need to handle?"

"No, Vahagn. I can handle my own trouble," she said before mumbling under her breath, "Just can't handle my high."

"Well, if it's just a matter of crafting the best text reply, you know I'm the in-house poet. I'll even offer my services for free, in repayment for all the couch and coffee stealing." He winked at her.

They dropped their bags in their lockers, but Izzy held onto her phone. Just in case.

"I don't need your help crafting anything. I over crafted and now, I'm wallowing in my shame."

Vahagn's face fell as he looked to her. "Oh no, Izzy. You didn't?"

She nodded her head gravely.

"And he ghosted you?"

She nodded again.

A slight grin played at Vahagn's stony expression but he held it together.

"Do I even want to know what you sent him?"

"Absolutely not."

With that, she strode toward the stationary bike near the window, tucked in the corner behind the office. Lando added the secluded little area that housed all the cardio equipment so his clients could get a sense of being outside without actually being outside. In a gym full of meat heads, it stayed pretty much empty, making it Izzy's private little sanctuary. She put her headphones in and the world melted away as she rode, the tension in her muscles easing with each passing mile on the odometer, the bass bumping as each new track pushed her harder.

Eventually she felt a soft tap on her shoulder and she pulled her headphones out to see Lando next to her, a frown on his face.

"It's 7:25, *mi amore.*"

She frowned and looked to her phone.

7:25 a.m.

Still no reply.

"Is Noah here?"

She almost winced at the question but she needed to prepare herself for impending humility if he had been able to sneak in without seeing her. How was she going to make it through an entire workout with him? In hand-to-hand combat of all things?

But then Lando shook his head.

She hopped off the bike, her frown setting in as she followed him out to the main area. There was Vahagn, Charlie, even Gio, but no Noah. She scanned the expanse of the gym, certain she missed something, yet came up empty.

Pulling her phone out of her pocket, she shuffled out the gym entrance and through the main door toward the windows in the hallway that faced his building. Scrolling through the text chain from last night, all her most recent and cringe worthy messages still unread, an uneasy pit settled in her stomach.

Her brows furrowed deeper and she glanced down to the street, like she would see him emerge from his building, hurrying over to join them.

Her fingers hovered over the keyboard on the screen and she bit her lower lip, toying with what to do. She blew out a deep breath and just went for it.

I: Hey, where are you? We are starting soon!

There. Harmless. Maybe he won't even notice the other messages before he gets here.

She stared expectantly out the window for a few more minutes before Lando appeared behind her.

"I don't think he's coming today, Isabella. Let's go ahead and get started." His hand went to her elbow and she turned around with him but not before stealing one last glance out the window. She willed the entrance to the building to open, to see dark waves tousled in the wind and a broad hand running through them.

But there was no one.

Her frown deepened as she made her way back into the gym to join the rest of them in the ring. Charlie seemed down right chipper that morning. Even Vahagn looked sideways at him, an unreadable judgment in his gaze.

"Why do you look so fucking happy?" she bit at Charlie as they all worked through Lando's warm up routine.

He shook his head, smirking at the ground before his steely blue eyes met hers, rogue strands of black hair across his forehead contrasting with the stark white scar through his brow.

"Am I no longer allowed to be happy anymore, Izzy?"

She glared at him.

"No, you've just never *been* happy. It's concerning."

He switched legs smoothly, squatting down on his left and stretching the right out to the side. His devilish grin didn't disappear as he looked to her with one eye closed, head tilted.

"Oh, I think I can name a few times I've been happy."

She flipped him both her middle fingers before rotating away from his gaze. Not only had she been ghosted in every way possible, now she had to deal with Charlie's infuriating smugness? Hell no.

"Okay, let's change it up today. Ladies, team up. We are going to work on handling multiple attackers with a partner."

She rolled her eyes and looked to Gio who did the same. But then the day outside her lab flashed into memory. When The Society had done exactly that. She had escaped, but just barely. If she hadn't been given access to that spare room... That menacing grin on the man's face as he stared at her through the window, both fangs flashing despite the dim hallway lighting. The blood drained from her own.

"Pick your weapons."

❖

They finished the workout an hour later and Noah never showed up. At first it was her ego that was upset but then it evolved to concern for him. Now, it festered as anger.

Why hadn't he responded last night and let her know he wouldn't be here today? Where could he even be?

She was so lost in her thoughts she didn't realize Vahagn had followed her back to her apartment until he appeared next to her as she unlocked her door.

"I need to talk to you," he said in a tone that raised the hairs on the back of her neck.

She started and looked at him curiously. He never talked like this. Normally, he barged in announcing his newest issue, with her or the world, and they went from there. But the look on his face had her a bit alarmed. He looked ready to murder someone, like he busied himself calculating how to do it. This didn't sit well in her already off kilter heart.

She pushed the door open and gestured for him to come in. She followed and beelined to the window to peer across the street while Vahagn put all her locks back into place, then began pacing.

"I think something's going on."

This snapped Izzy out of her trance and she turned from the window to look at him. Anguish blanketed thick on his expression, all contentment from that morning lost. Only hard lines and threats of violence remained.

"What do you mean?" she asked, leaning against the glass behind her.

He stopped and turned to her, rubbing a hand over his face.

"Did you see Charlie today? Like you said, he's *never* happy."

"Yeah, so? I figured he probably convinced some poor girl to come home with him and that's why you stayed here."

"No, see that's the thing. He hasn't been home. Every night for the past week, he has left just as daylight is sinking away and he doesn't come home until early in the morning."

Izzy stared at Vahagn as he continued.

"And then Noah didn't show up at all today and it was like he was *ecstatic* by it. He kept looking to you and grinning any time he saw you frown or check your phone. Like he knew something."

Dread sank into the pit of her stomach.

"You don't think he would do anything to him, do you?"

"That's just it, I don't know how anyone could. Noah is good. Like better than any of us good. You saw him. He was holding back with *Lando* and you know Lando has handed both

Charlie and I our asses several times before. He was a Heavyweight World Champion, for Christ's sake." His words bordered on frantic. It did little to ease her own anxiety.

"What are you saying, Vahagn?"

He looked her in her eyes finally, his face full of the fear she felt.

"I'm saying I think something happened and we need to go confirm it before we go to Lando for help."

Fuck. Going to Lando meant this was serious. Going to Lando meant this was *business.* What had Charlie done? Had Lando asked for this? Surely Vahagn would have been included in the plan if that was the case. But maybe not since he and Izzy were so close? But then why? What did Noah do? Or know?

The questions swirled in her mind, a steady fire fueling the thundering in her heart.

"You've been to his apartment before. What was security like over there?" she asked.

Vahagn shrugged, "About the same here. Maybe less cameras but heavily guarded with multiple doors before you finally get to the residential areas. Why?"

Her brows furrowed.

"If it's heavily guarded, then it would have to be someone they knew or has been granted access in order to get past them, right?"

Vahagn slowly nodded his head.

"Charlie did seem to know the guard on duty when we went there to invite him to his assessment," he said.

The color drained from Izzy's face.

"Vahagn, we need to go check."

He tensed and ran a hand through his burly hair.

"I don't know, Z. Maybe we are overreacting."

Her glare could've set him on fire.

"Are you fucking serious, Vahagn? You came here to all but tell me you think Charlie is up to some bullshit and you suddenly want to back down?"

He winced at her accurate assessment of the situation but didn't relent.

"If we get this wrong. If we march into a situation unprepared and unorganized, we both get killed. Even if we're right, we aren't ready yet." He sighed heavily. "Go to the lab. Go about your day like normal. Maybe Noah is in the archives. Maybe he just got spooked by spending the night with all of us. Or your crazy high texts. But don't raise the alarm. Not yet at least."

She glowered and he answered with an equivalent stare before adding, "I'll look into it, Z. I'll learn what I can while you're on campus and we can reconvene here this afternoon."

He stepped forward to her and grabbed both her hands. She squirmed under the contact at first but met his gaze, "I promise, Izzy."

She nodded, aware of the tears threatening to spill over her bottom lashes. She pulled away from his hold and walked to her bathroom to start getting ready for her 'normal' day. Only when the door clicked behind Vahagn did she let the tears fall, stepping back out to lock it, the choke hold of fear taking root deep in her chest. Something felt wrong, and no matter how right Vahagn was that they needed to be *sure* when they went to Lando, the fissure in her heart threatened to burst the longer she waited to get answers.

✤

CHAPTER TWENTY-FIVE
NOAH

Lightning bolts of pain shot across Noah's face as his brow furrowed, squeezing his eyes open and shut a few times before the space around him eased into view.

"I thought you said pretty boy would put up a hell of a fight, bruv?" a faintly familiar British accent sneered from somewhere in the darkness of his left peripheral. His vision was fucked. "He barely looks able to hold his head up."

A few affirming grunts and snorts orchestrated around him. At least five others, spread about the room. Which, as it came into focus, was more like a storage basement, lines of shelves and various plywood boxes strewn about. Noah instinctively tried to pull his arms in front of him to stand but both his wrists and ankles met resistance. Right. Of course they would tie him up.

"Chemical warfare is cowards work," Noah croaked, the split in his lip stinging against the words. The cut felt deep. Another scar to add to the mix.

The man in front of him regarded his remark with

contempt beneath the pretentious pageboy hat on his head. That hat always made Noah want to punch his fucking face in. Even now his fists curled, the rough rope holding them together groaning with the strain.

The man leaned forward, flashing fangs at Noah before saying, "Ah, then what does that make you and your traitor brother?" Noah's jaw flinched at the mention of Benji and the man's smile broadened into a sick beam. "Sorry, I mean your *dead* traitor brother. My condolences or whatever." He flipped his hands about in the air as if describing the color of a potato and not the death of Noah's only family member. He walked over to another man, whispered something, and then footsteps sounded as the other man left the room.

Silence droned on as Noah contemplated his options and after a few minutes, concluded he was wholly and truly fucked. The ultimate sum of his efforts amounting to dying in a musty old basement surrounded by a bunch of dudes who were sold a lie and wore the jewelry of devotion to prove it. Each marked with a pretty little fleur de lis as a token for their loyalty. A modern-day multilevel marketing scheme. Become a vampire henchman, eternity is yours for the taking.

Noah did the only thing he could think to do in that moment: he laughed. It started small, pained, like it rattled out of his chest to escape. Then eventually it rolled through him, effortless, deranged. The men around him shuffled uncomfortably, glancing at each other as Noah continued his descent into premortem insanity.

"Jesus fucking Christ, someone shut him up." A new voice. Angry. American. Noah recognized that smug undertone before those steely blue eyes leveled on him from around the corner of a set of shelves.

"Hello Charlie, you piece of shit. Got sick of beating women finally?" Noah smiled despite the drop of blood it produced on his lip. The scorned look on Charlie's face was worth it.

Charlie approached Noah, peering down at him. "You were such an easy little mouse to catch, in all your broody despair. I tried to warn you, she's not worth the heartache even if it's the nicest little cunt I've ever been in."

The chair creaked with the tension Noah put against his shackles. He was going to rip this guy's fucking dick off and shove it down his throat. That would be task number one as soon as he could find a way out of these ropes. Hell, it might be the only task he would be able to complete before his life ended but damn, would it be a glorious way to end. A cruel smile pulled on his split lips again, more blood streaming down his chin. God, that cut really was deep.

And about to get deeper as Charlie raised his hand and backhanded Noah, forcing his head to the side. Before he could spit out the pool of blood in his mouth, Charlie clenched his jaw in with his rough grip, forcing his face mere inches from the bastard's own.

"You two would make the perfect couple though," spit glistening Charlie's lips as he snarled in Noah's face, "with those smart fucking mouths you have."

In that moment, Noah could see it. The rage Izzy would have stared into, probably held exactly as he was right now minus the ropes and audience, right before beating her near death and walking away. Nothing but a monster stared back in those eyes. Not an ounce of remorse. Barely a recognizable human. He might as well have joined the rest of the immortal assholes in the room and taken the cure.

Just as the grip on Noah's jaw started to tighten to a point that threatened to crack a bone or two, a buzz sounded from Charlie's pocket. He growled in Noah's face, a promise of the violence he had planned to unleash before this interruption, before shoving his face back and fishing his phone from his pocket. He held up a finger to silence the room and said into the device, "Yes, boss?"

Noah couldn't make out the voice on the other end to hear if it was Lando or someone else. If present company provided any indicator, the alternative would be everyone's worst nightmare. He swallowed, hoping Izzy would be kept out of this.

Charlie nodded a few times and hung up. Turning away to face the rest of idiots in the room, he said, "Leave him here. We need to go."

And just like that Noah was alone, crimson blood sticking the front of his shirt to his chest as it congealed on his skin.

Alone. It was better that way.

The ropes scratched the skin on his wrists raw as he pulled against them. Again and again, until the burn in his shoulders became unbearable.

Tears joined the flow of liquids down his face.

Alone.

It was better that way.

CHAPTER TWENTY-SIX
Izzy

St. Louis and bad days were synonymous.

Today happened to be one for the record books, as far as Izzy saw it.

The entire walk to the lab, she couldn't shake the uncomfortable film across her skin of someone watching her. While working next to Barry, the man oblivious to the torment of emotions wrecking her peace, all she could think about was the unsettling smirk on Charlie's face that morning. And how she still hadn't heard from Noah. The scowl creasing her brow became a permanent fixture.

By the time she trudged up the stairs to her apartment that afternoon, she wasn't sure if she wanted to burst into tears or drive a fucking stake through Charlie's heart. Barely registering Vahagn's presence in her living room as she stumbled in, she beelined for the liquor cabinet in the kitchen. Grabbing the bottle of bourbon, a much cheaper and more bite-y brand than Lando's collection, and two coffee mugs, she trudged back to the couch, slumping next to Vahagn.

A heavy sigh escaped her lips. "Well?"

He eyed the bottle and her nervously as she passed him a mug. "You're not going to like what I'm about to say."

In response, she tilted the bottle into her own mug, allowing a few healthy splashes to fill her cup halfway before passing it on to him. A strong gulp followed by a stronger grimace and she set her mug down, turning to him.

"I'm ready," she said, breathless.

"I went to the building after our morning meeting with Lando just to… ask some questions. The doorman today was different from the one who had been there that night Charlie and I went to visit. So, I told him I was looking for my cousin, saying he was supposed to give me a ride to work. The doorman seemed suspicious when I said which apartment he lived in but he let me in regardless. Not exactly a tight ship over there." He rubbed his bearded chin mindlessly as he thought about all the alarming holes in the security.

Izzy leaned forward, drinking in his words as heavily as she had the alcohol humming through her bloodstream.

Her eagerness seemed to prompt him back into their discussion, his deep brown gaze focusing on her. "Z, the apartment looked like he had just vanished into the night. All of his stuff was still there, a towel hung in the bathroom, hell, even his phone sat on the dining room table."

The burning in her chest felt almost intolerable as she held her breath.

"But something was off. I told the doorman he must have gone out for a second and he would be back soon so just to leave me there. Once he was gone, I searched the apartment. There were fully packed duffel bags in the bedroom, shoved under the bed. It actually looked like he had never unpacked them. Everything in the apartment was generic and impersonal, like it was furnished. And that's when I saw this."

He fished a small piece of fabric out of his pocket and unwrapped it to reveal a thick shard of glass.

"This was under the nightstand."

Her brows furrowed as she took the shard and examined it. It looked vaguely familiar. Her questioning gaze lifted to Vahagn's as he nodded his head.

"So, I went to the kitchen and checked the trash can. Izzy, there were shards of an entire bottle of bourbon in there. How does a man living alone end up breaking an entire bottle of bourbon inside his bedroom, clean it up, and then just disappear without a trace?"

They don't. That's not something that happens to people unless…

Her eyes grew wide.

"Vahagn, we have to go to Lando."

His lips tightened under his beard but he nodded and squeezed her hands.

"I know. I'm so sorry we didn't go sooner." The remorse in his eyes broke her heart.

She squeezed his hands in kind.

"Don't apologize until we find him."

⚜

Ice and amber sloshed around Lando's glass as he swirled the concoction within, peering down at Vahagn and Izzy sitting at his table. They had detailed the entirety of what they knew and what they suspected happened over the course of the last ten minutes. His hand finally stopped moving and he tossed back the drink before setting the empty glass down.

254

A wicked gleam shined in his dark eyes as the words slowly rolled off his tongue when he spoke. "You know, I would almost say you two are being paranoid if it weren't for the fact that I witnessed my second leave almost immediately after our morning meeting and he hasn't been back since."

A pit opened in Izzy's chest.

"So, what do we do Lando?" She didn't recognize the voice from her own lips. It sounded… afraid. She twisted her hands together. Vahagn watched the movement, some conflicted look passing over him before he focused back on Lando.

Ignoring her question, Lando continued, his voice tinted with a restrained anger, "I would also almost say you two were being paranoid if it weren't for the fact that I've been trailing my second for several weeks now because earlier this year, he disappeared for almost a week and came back acting like nothing happened." He gritted his teeth, glaring at the ice in his glass and poured himself another shot.

Her eyes grew wide and even Vahagn's eyebrows were raised as he dared a look across the table to her. *Oh shit.*

"In fact, I would *almost* say you two were being paranoid except a couple days ago, we discovered Charlie meeting up with a group of Society thugs outside a warehouse a few blocks from here, near the river." He took a long sip of his replenished bourbon.

"Why didn't you say anything?" Vahagn growled, turning his gaze to the old man at the head of the table. Izzy froze. He… *knew?* He fucking knew and didn't say anything? Didn't warn them? Her breaths came in faster and faster as she stared at the man who had taken her in, treated her like his own goddamn daughter. Called her as such on many occasions. All for him to use them as pawns? For what end? Just to see what happened? How thi would unfold? What would be the final act of treason against his reign so that he could finally respond to the growing threat in his territory?

But would he act?

Rage coursed through her body as her eyes narrowed on him.

"Are you *fucking* kidding me?" she said, the words a cool, calm whisper as her eyes lit with the inferno burning inside her.

Lando met her stare, his face pure indifference. The face of a murderer, accustomed to the rage of others. This was a business discussion, nothing more.

"You *knew* for weeks? You had suspicions for *weeks* and you warned none of us?" she seethed, both hands braced on the edge of his ostentatious table. Her fingers tingled with the urge to reach for the dagger at her side and shove it through the wood grain underneath her palm.

"It was not necessary information for you, Isabella." The finality in those words sent her anger to orbit. A dismissive statement. *Know your place in this organization,* it said.

"Don't you dare use my name like we're a goddamn family. Like you have my best interests in mind. Any of ours for that matter. Fuck, Vahagn has been *living* with him. You didn't think this might have been *necessary* information for him?" Her fingers curled into fists and she hovered over her chair as she leaned forward, the pulse of her blood a steady roar in her ears.

Lando's gaze narrowed on her, the only crack in his mask.

She stood up, pushing her heavy chair back with enough force she hoped it gouged his precious hardwood flooring.

"And what about Noah?" she asked, eyes narrowing to

a sardonic look of contemplation. "What was he in this scheme? What part did he play?"

"An opportunity," Lando said, matter of fact.

She slammed her fists down on the table, a short, feral scream escaping her throat. Lando flinched slightly while Vahagn kept his eyes on the old man, a cool rage brewing beneath his skin. She had never seen Vahagn like this. She never knew he could look like this, despite his profession and rank. Murder, incarnate.

"You don't get to play God, Lando! You don't get to play all the humans in your life like little pawns in a game, when none of us even know the rules or that we are even playing! And for what end? You think you can take down *The Society?* From your throne in your ivory fucking tower?" She let out a bitter, hollow laugh. "You can't even stand the thought of walking down the *steps* of your goddamn fortress and you think you're going to be able to take down an organization of *fucking immortals?* You're no better than Emilien Dumas." She barked another laugh, pressing her palms into her temples. "No, I take that back because at least he can fucking walk outside." She leaned into his space, tempting him, daring him to show his true colors. It's what she had done with Charlie. Broke him down to his barest core. Pushed until the true man within came out. The color of his soul had been pure black.

What would be left of Lando Denalo when the facade came crumbling down? What color would he bleed?

His face remained stoic as he took another sip of bourbon then snapped his fingers at Vahagn. "Get her out of here," was all he said before he turned to look out the window and into the city.

She'd been… dismissed. Ignored. Vahagn stood up and made his way around the table, reaching for her elbow. She ripped it out of his grasp, searching his face for some guidance on what to do next. He gave a solemn shake of his head, his lips pressed tightly together.

Fuck, she wanted to scream. Instead, she stalked to Lando's absolutely stupid fucking door and paused only long enough to say, "You'll send Vahagn the location of this warehouse and then do what you continue to do best: nothing." A command. Her final one. He was dead to her.

Not waiting for a response, she pushed into the hallway and down the stairs to the only home she had found safety in for the past few years, suddenly repulsed by the idea that could have ever been true.

❖

An old map of the city laid out between her and Vahagn on her kitchen counter, held down by an assortment of weaponry from their combined arsenal.

"So, if we stick to the roofs, we can pretty much go unnoticed until we get there. Getting out will be the struggle. I don't know what kind of security they have on this building or what the immortal activity is like in the area. That's Charlie's territory. As long as we stay out of the Metro lines, we should be okay."

Izzy nodded her head as Vahagn studied the map, drawing lines for multiple escape routes. She sheathed a few more daggers onto her body and started eying the axes before her.

"This is the important part. If we get separated, just go wherever is safe. I'll go back to Lando to report in but if you can't get back here safe, go to the room at the lab or Barry's or somewhere. Anywhere." She could barely stand to look him in the eye, the intensity of his gaze, his words. It was all too much. They hadn't been this serious with each other since that night Charlie held her life in his hands.

258

Her face turned grim as she nodded. Her "safe" options were dwindling in this town but she didn't want to spend too much time thinking about that right now. Her only objective was to get Noah out of there.

Vahagn nodded and scanned the weapons she had strapped to herself.

"Don't forget your training. It's second nature at this point, so leave doubt at the door and trust your instincts. Adapt as needed but you fight like hell." His words resonated through her.

She nodded again, refusing to look him in the eye as she left the axes on the table and stood to sheath the short swords in a cross behind her back, fitting into the harness she wore.

Vahagn grabbed her hands before they could float back to her sides and forced her to look him in the eye.

"We will get him back, okay?" This version of Vahagn she knew, the caring man who would set the world on fire for her.

Silver lined her eyes and she quickly nodded, backing out of his grip. She had been so selfish, wrapped in her own worries and anxiety to not see the signs. She should have known something happened last night. Guilt rested uneasily in her chest and she rubbed at it, her eyes drifting to her bed. Memories that felt like a lifetime ago weighed on her.

Vahagn fixed a heavy sword to his back, the handle peeking out above his head, long hair braided. He looked to her one more time. Man, he looked like a true Viking warrior.

"Are you ready?" he asked, searching her face.

They hadn't discussed the moment upstairs, when he had chosen to listen to his boss instead of back her up. When he had let Lando dismiss her concerns. Vahagn had followed her down to her apartment, his phone buzzing with a message as he stepped through the door. The coordinates to the warehouse, and nothing else.

Determination took a stronghold in her heart, and she blinked away the memories as she met his gaze.

"Let's go."

❖

Cool, damp wind whipped a few curls loose from her own braid as they stood on the roof opposite the warehouse location Lando had sent Vahagn.

Doubt crept into her mind as she surveyed the building through squinted eyes. They were about to break into a secret Society compound and free a man who was still basically a full-blown stranger to them all. One who had never even unpacked his bags since he arrived in this city. She pushed that thought back too, shaking her head. One small, Earth-shattering task at a time.

Vahagn nudged her arm with his elbow and dipped his chin to the solo guard at the door they had been watching for the past twenty minutes. From their best observations, the warehouse was barely guarded, likely due to the fact it was nighttime and no one dare fuck with an immortal at night. They were the apex predators. And also, it was The *fucking* Society. They were a household name at this point. Do not disturb, lest you want to die.

A few shadows passed in the upper floors but Izzy had a sneaking suspicion their mission was going to be taking them down into the depths of the old building. All the bad shit happened underground; life lessons taught by gangsters. Getting out? That was going to be the challenge. She tucked the errant red curl behind her ear and studied potential points of escape.

They had gone over the various paths they knew and guessed were available for them to get out over and over on their way here. Vahagn made sure Izzy had every route memorized.

"Just in case," he had said in a voice she supposed

should be reassuring. It had the opposite effect though.

Nerves started creeping in, causing her confidence to falter. She could do this, couldn't she? They were only going to take on the criminal organization that was the backbone of a world changing revolution that had seeped into the political and economic infrastructure of nearly every country in less than two decades, corrupting the entirety of society in irreparable fashion. All for a man she had just met.

No big deal.

Her breaths came in pants to remind her this was insane, she was insane, she should turn around now and forget Noah Broussand had ever happened. Vahagn's broad hand laid across her forearm, snapping her back to reality. Now was not the time. She could have a panic attack later, hopefully with copious amounts of alcohol and weed to forget what it felt like to feel.

She met his gaze and he nodded. It was time.

Below, the guard at the entrance moved deeper into the warehouse, likely escaping the dropping temperatures the night brought. They made their way silently down the fire escape of the building they were perched on and swiftly crossed the quiet street, hiding with shadows to conceal their movements. They slipped inside. The warehouse was lit by dim bulbs hanging from the high rafters, the entrance only distinguishable from the darkness outside by an eerie yellow glow. Keeping to the interior wall, they crept around to a stack of pallets and wooden boxes off to the left, crouching to remain hidden while they took stock of their surroundings. Lando had provided them a basic layout of the place, another infuriating secret of his, but being inside now they had to fill in the details on the spot.

That's when she spotted it, across the way. A random doorway sticking up out of the floor. The only logical direction it went was down. That's where Noah had to be. She elbowed Vahagn and nodded toward it. He gave her a responsive nod and held up five fingers then pointed up. He had spotted five guards in the upper rafters, metal scaffolding walkways that led to other doors. One more scan of the lower level and it appeared they were alone.

Keeping to the shadows along the edge of the expanse, they made their way toward the door. Fear threatened to rattle her trained composure with every step she took but she pushed on. As they sidled up to the door, Izzy put tentative pressure on the handle and almost let a sigh escape when it gave underneath her hand. Not taking a moment to hesitate, they slipped into the inky abyss behind the metal frame, closing the door quietly and erasing the last slivers of light with it. Her heartbeat thundered in her ears as they felt their way down, the temperate plummeting further with each step. They hit a small landing at the bottom with another door before them, a soft glow peeking out from underneath. Vahagn pulled her behind him as he leaned in to press an ear to the door then cracked it open a hair to peer in. A couple heartbeats passed, panic steadily flooding her senses in the silence, before he closed it and turned to her.

"No guards, from what I can see, but I think I see him past the shelves, tied up to a chair," he whispered. She couldn't see his features in the dark but his pause spoke volumes. "Looks like they've beaten him pretty good..."

Her nails bit into her palm as she clenched her fists but she nodded, even though she knew Vahagn wouldn't be able to see it. He reached out to touch her arm briefly and said, "Remember the plan. See you at Lando's."

Then he turned back to the door, cracking it once more to confirm no guards had arrived before he pulled it open wide so they could sprint in toward Noah. Her footsteps faltered as she rounded the corner of the shelves.

God, what did they do to him?

Noah sat slumped in a wooden chair, hands bound behind his back while his head hung low. Blood dripped onto his gray sweatpants; a once white t-shirt coated in an abstract splattering of dark rust that clung to his chest. He wasn't wearing shoes and his feet were bound to the chair as well. She tried to catalog this all for their escape as she approached him.

Fuck, their escape. Would he be able to make it back across the city? Was he even conscious?

Hands shaking, she knelt before him and got to work cutting the binds around his ankles while Vahagn went to his back to remove the ones around his wrists. Noah's head snapped up, the look within his eyes burned with frantic fury and fear. He drank in the details of the room before those golden hazel eyes locked onto hers, his pupils dilating, his gaze softening as Vahagn freed his hands. In the next breath he cupped her cheeks and she gasped under the touch, a stray tear running down to meet his rough skin. His eyes danced across her face, lingering on her lips before his brows furrowed and he met her gaze again.

"Why are you here?" His voice was hoarse and gravelly, that damned accent nearly making the words unrecognizable.

She flashed him a quick smile, tilting her head to the side. "Saving you, of course." The words faltered a bit as she said them.

His frown deepened but he released her face and she finished undoing the binds on his ankles. Once freed, he stood on wobbly legs, grabbing her hand as he turned to Vahagn.

"They come down about once an hour to make sure I'm still alive. I would say we have maybe ten minutes before they are back for their next check. We need to get out of here. Do you have a plan for that?" The words came out so orderly and practiced, like he often found himself in situations like this. Izzy tried to ignore that thought too.

"I was hoping you might have some insight on that. I doubt we can just waltz you out of here through the front entrance and be on our merry little way." Vahagn smirked.

Noah's face paled as he peered to a door behind him, along the back wall of the basement, opposite the direction they had come in.

"That door goes to the parking garage next door but it's pretty well manned. We might get luck with the hour—"

Footsteps cut him short and they all sprinted back to the dark stairwell Vahagn and Izzy had come in through. Not waiting to see who came in from the parking garage or how long before the alarms would be sounded, they continued up the stairs and huddled behind Vahagn as he cracked the door at the top to check the area before turning back to them.

"There are two guards talking by the entrance. I'll distract them and you guys get out of here. I'll be right behind you," he whispered, as he worked his sword free from his back. There was such surety in his words, like this was the plan all along.

Panic rattled against its cage inside her heart. "*No!*" she seethed the words out in a whisper. This wasn't right. They couldn't separate now.

Unable to see her, Vahagn put his hand on her arm and squeezed.

"Yes, Z. You get out of here. I'll be okay." She heard him shuffle as he directed his next words to Noah, "You take her and get out of here. Go wherever you can that is safe but you take her, you promise?"

Izzy felt Noah's chest rise against her shoulder as he responded, "I'll protect her with my life. I promise."

The world tilted around Izzy. *No, no, no*—she knew getting separated was always a possibility but that was on the streets, avoiding the random immortals who ran this city at night. Not here in the viper's den, surrounded by the enemy set out to kill them.

She shook her head and whispered out her dissent but Vahagn ignored it, unable to see her apprehension as he quietly pushed the handle down. Before he opened the door, he whispered back to her, "You're the best thing to have ever come storming into my life, Z."

And before she could respond, he was gone.

✤

CHAPTER TWENTY-SEVEN
Izzy

Izzy reached for Vahagn as he slipped out. A sob escaping her lips as a strong arm wrapped around her waist and hauled her back against a hard muscled chest. Noah's chest. She felt his breath against her ear as he whispered, "It'll be okay, let him go."

She leaned into his hold, searching for comfort in it as her heart threatened to pound out of her chest. How did he know that? How could he possibly know Vahagn would be okay?

Panic rose in her chest again, her breaths coming back erratic as she tried to grasp onto a plan. What were they supposed to do next? Vahagn was gone. What were they supposed to do?

Below them, the sound of crashing and chaos start to unfurl at the same moment similar sounds echoed from beyond the door in front of them. There were shouts, footsteps running up metal stairs and Izzy snapped back, her training kicking in. This was their chance. Noah dropped his hold on her, feeling the same clarity, and they burst from the door, sprinting to the street exit.

Their salvation.

Vahagn was nowhere in sight as Izzy glanced behind but there was no time to look for him. Noah ran in front of her, a slight hitch in his gait that he didn't allow to falter his steps. He gripped her hand, dragging her down the street in front of the warehouse. They weaved through alleys and side roads, shouts looming behind them, the words muffled as distance between them and the predators grew. Noah ducked them into an old, abandoned building and Izzy skittered to a stop, thoroughly lost. Cursing herself, she looked to him as he turned to her, reaching for her hand again.

She ripped it from his grasp, out of reach. Despair drenched her words as she exhaled, "I have no idea how to get out from here."

He stepped forward, his hand hovering over her cheek as he searched her face, his chest heaving.

Finally, he looked her in the eye and said, "Do you trust me?"

They stood there, gasping for air, on the precipice they had been skirting around. Did she trust him? Hell, did he trust her?

She took him in then, the split lip that looked like it would never heal as it shined with fresh blood, the cuts and bruises scattered across his face, no doubt contributors of the dark red liquid that caked his front and matted his hair. But through the pain, she caught the undercurrent of worry as he stood there, still reaching for her. Worry for her. Through all this, he worried for her.

She reached up, pulling his hand to her cheek as she nodded her head.

He gave her a small smile, a rough thumb traced over her cheekbone and said softly, "Follow me."

Her momentum fought him as he led her deeper into the building instead of back onto the street. He kept a firm grip on her hand. The space in front of them had once been something spectacular, she could tell from the giant windows and columns in the foyer. The ceiling was rounded, with aged, gilded etchings. Climbing a grand stone staircase, they pushed through a cracked glass door to reveal thousands of shelves filled with… books?

"Where are we?" She tripped as she tried to drink in the room while he weaved through shelves upon shelves of dust covered books. For a moment, the brevity of their situation disappeared.

His eyes twinkled as he glanced back at her, a smirk playing on his lips.

"I'm surprised you don't know." Then his expression fell as he turned back, leading her toward the back of the building.

"Just trust me and I'll explain soon."

Panic renewed its effortless flaying through her. Where could they go that was safe? His apartment was clearly the worst option. Her apartment was barely better, housed in the same building as a mob boss hell bent on using them like tokens in his political games. She wouldn't even know how to get to Barry's place or the lab from here. And Vahagn… She choked on the memory of him pushing through that door without her. Noah turned into a blurred silhouette before her and she blinked rapidly to clear the image.

As if he heard her worries, Noah squeezed her hand and pulled her through an old, wooden door, intricately carved in a way that was almost identical to the one on her closet. Only this one looked like the man knelt to the moon. The door opened to a small seating area with benches, beautifully maintained garnet velvet carpeting covered the floor, ceiling, and walls. Her hand went weightless as Noah dropped it but her focus became lost in the pattern on the fabric around them. Crusaders, galloping across fields to battle against smaller armies of people. Farmers, villagers, children. Normal, ordinary people. Her fingers roved over the delicate fabric, tracing their forms. Were these the people she assumed opposed the Catholic rule? She leaned in, brow furrowing. Some detail seemed off. The Crusaders weren't how she had ever seen them depicted. They had… fangs.

"*What the fu—*" she started to mumble as Noah pulled a metal flower on one of the medieval sconces and a portion of the velvet wall parted, opening with a low groan to a cavernous set of stone steps.

He turned around to flash her a half smile before reaching his hand out to her.

"Trust me, Izzy."

Her heart set a merciless pace in her chest as she took one more glance around the crimson velveteen room before grabbing his hand and stepping down into what was, in fact, a genuine cave. Her lips parted in awe as she reconciled the fear trickling into her thoughts, instead focusing on taking each step further down. Noah put the flower right and pushed the secret door closed behind them. Darkness flooded the stairwell, her senses seizing as panic rose to a crescendo right before a match struck behind her, igniting a lamp hanging from the wall above. She turned and raised an eyebrow, desperately trying to silence the blare of alarms going off in her mind.

He gave a nonchalant shrug and said, "I've been here a couple times." Her brows only shot further up as she turned back to continue her descent, now illuminated by the flickering glow from the lantern behind.

"There are a few hundred steps down but once we get

to the bottom, it'll open up and no one should be able to hear us," he whispered.

"And what about immortals? The Society? They don't know about these?" It was one of her million questions she had when he first brought her below ground. Fear rattled the edges of each word as she spoke.

She glanced over her shoulder to see him shake his head slowly.

"No. At least, I've never seen anyone else down here before. I'm not sure if they don't know about them or if this level of darkness is too intimidating to someone with an eternal lifespan."

She scoffed. An eternal life was one thing but to accidentally become trapped in an intricate cave system without knowing a way out did sound like an absolute nightmare.

Fifteen minutes later, the steps stopped and Noah walked over to what looked like a breaker box on the ground a few feet away. A loud click echoed around them before the darkness pressing against them illuminated into an expansive room with an integrated lighting system. Her eyes went wide as she took in the glittering rocks and massive ceiling of the cave. It appeared to go on forever, disappearing into darkness beyond the limited reach of the lights.

She turned to Noah who watched her with a wide grin on his face.

"How did you know this was here?" She winced at the suspicion that crept into her words.

His smile faltered and he looked away from her as he pushed off the wall of the cave, walking over to a wooden box positioned next to the light switch. He opened the box and began pulling out blankets, pillows, candles, and a couple bottles of water.

Gathering the supplies, he handed her a bottle as he passed to set up camp on a flat, sandy part across the way.

"Next question." The words were terse.

She pursed her lips. So much for trusting him.

"So just like that the trust is gone? You drag me who knows how far underground on the principle that I should trust you and now what? I'm here. I trusted you. Where's my explanation?" she demanded.

He paused setting the pillows down on the blanket laid out in the sand and then looked to her.

"No. The answer to your first question comes layered under many others and I don't think the history of how I found myself living in a cave for months is what you want to dive into right now." His jaw set as his eyes bored into her.

She sighed. He was right. The question beating around her mind had been there since he didn't show up to workouts that morning.

Her voice softened as she said, "What happened?"

He smoothed out the makeshift bed and sat back against a large boulder, pillows propped behind him, before patting the space next to him. Izzy approached tentatively but chose to sit across from him. He smirked, rubbing his hands together as he said, "Someone very rudely interrupted the most interesting text message conversation I have had in a while." His hazel eyes reflected the golden glow of the cave lighting, his smile slowly broadening as her gaze narrowed on him.

"Seriously? You're kidnapped, beaten to an inch of your life and you want to talk about a couple flirtatious text messages I sent while high out of my mind?" Her scowl deepened as he started to laugh, the sound both irritating her and lighting a fire in her core.

"So, you were flirting?" He smiled up at the ceiling, running a hand through his matted hair. Her gaze got caught on the split in his full lips. It had stopped bleeding at least, but it had to hurt to smile like that, the raw skin threatening to break at any moment. "I've recently had some free time to sit around thinking about what exactly having good *hands* has to do with playing poker."

She blushed as his eyes met hers again, his smile turning to smolder as his gaze fell to her lips. She swallowed under his scrutiny and the fire in his eyes seem to heat even more.

"Did you see who took you at least?" Her voice came out a bit uneven and the fire quickly extinguished in his gaze before he looked away, nodding.

"And? Who was it?" she asked.

This time he swallowed before looking to her again, a pained expression on his face as he rubbed at the back of his neck before sayng quietly, "It was Charlie."

Her heart stopped and she squeezed her eyes shut.

She knew that would be the answer.

She knew that would be the truth. His truth.

She *knew* Charlie would always be the monster in her nightmares.

But fuck, she had also held onto hope. Hope gathered and tucked away in those moments when she had stared into those sapphire eyes sleepily smiling at her in bed. When he would whisper words of encouragement to her while sparring. When he held her under the moonlight in her apartment, swaying to the invisible music playing around them. Somewhere in her heart, she could see the goodness that had once made-up Charlie's soul. Before this world had ripped it apart and rebuilt him in its cruel image.

She hadn't realized she had started crying until she felt Noah's thumb graze her cheek, whisking her tears away. Blinking her eyes open, she saw him knelt before her, concern washed over his features as he searched her gaze. That's when she really looked at him. Unlike Charlie, he wore his goodness on his sleeve. As if despite it all, he couldn't hide that part of him away, no matter how hard he fought to do so.

His expression shifted as she continued her open assessment of him, her brows furrowing. His head tilted to the side. Gilded eyes drifted to her lips before he took a deep inhale and sat back against the rock. Izzy wiped away her tears, feeling the phantom of Noah's warm hands on her jaw.

He cleared his throat and said, "There is something I need to tell you." He didn't meet her gaze, staring off to the darkness beyond the lighting around them.

She let out a cold, hollow laugh. "What? Besides the fact that a man I gave everything to is actually some weird gangster double agent and attempted to murder my—"

His swift glance to her stopped her sentence short, but he quickly looked away, rubbing the back of his neck, and letting out a long exhale as his eyes closed.

"Yeah, besides that."

The alarm bells she had muffled in her mind began a new relentless torrent. This was it.

He looked to the ceiling of the cave, mumbling what looked to be a silent prayer before he finally met her gaze again, devastation painted through his hazel eyes.

CHAPTER TWENTY-EIGHT
VAHAGN

"**F**uck you, assholes," Vahagn spat blood onto the leather boots in front of him before leaning back against the chair they had bound him in.

He peered at the group of Society scum before him, a smug smirk on his face as he counted the number of injuries he had inflicted before they were finally able to get him down. Blood dripped down the face of the boot's owner, crimson glory. The rest of the men gave him a scowl as they rubbed their various pain points.

He resigned to the fact this was going to be his last fight but it didn't mean he was going to go down without getting in some of his best punches first. A stabbing pain ached in his chest as memory flooded back to that last image of Z before he slipped out the door and up the stairs to end this battle. The hurt in her voice had been nearly enough to keep him standing next to her, reckless abandon, forcing them all to fight their way out. But he knew the outcome of that decision.

This was better.

This was the best plan they could've come up with, even if he was the only one in on it. He had known it the second they had decided to go get Noah.

Swallowing the hard knot of his sorrow, he blinked once to ignite the rage within again. It was easy enough when the man before him opened a blood-tinged mouth to say, "Hardly seems like you're in a position to do any fucking, bruv."

Vahagn growled up at him. He looked like the Thomas Shelby knock-off Izzy had described attacking her. There wasn't enough time left in his life to give this shit ball what he deserved. Add it to the growing list of his regrets.

"Why don't you bend over and see what I'm capable of doing right now?" Vahagn spat on his boots again. The man grinned down before back handing him, sending his head careening to the left. Vahagn laughed through the pain but fuck, that *had* hurt his already broken nose. At least he wasn't leaking blood all down his chest like the fool before him, flashing fangs with an ever-menacing smile.

"Look, we can make this easy enough on you. Join our forces and this stops here. I'll even take you up on your offer," Leather Boots said, winking at him.

Vahagn glared.

"And why the fuck would I join your group of glorified mosquitoes?" he bit out in reply.

The man before him looked over his shoulder and smiled before a familiar voice said, "You would be working with me, for one."

Every muscle fiber in Vahagn's body tensed as Charlie walked around the back of the chair, Leather Boots stepping aside to allow his traitorous roommate to stand before him. Pure rage coursed through his veins as he looked into the steely blue eyes he had known for the past decade, had shared an apartment with, gone out partying with, had sat up late at night talking to about the emotional turmoil of being a brutal murderer for a mob boss who couldn't be bothered to leave his luxury reclusive penthouse to dirty his own hands. Fuck, he thought they had been best friends, as thick as he and Z were before… before Charlie ruined Z's life.

"I reiterate, why the fuck would I join?" he seethed, eyes narrowing.

Charlie sighed, looking away but not before Vahagn caught a glimpse of something… was that regret? Hurt? Sorrow?

Yeah, fuck that guy. It was too late for him to manifest a fucking moral compass and atone for his wrong doings. This had gone too far. He had gone too far.

"Vahagn, I'm going to be straight with you. You know my options here. Hell, the only reason you even have *options* is because of me. So please, for the love of God, swallow your pride and make the right one."

"And what God is that, Charlie? The leader of The Society? The one who ruined any hope for a future in this world as a normal human being?"

Every other man in the room straightened, fists clenching at the threatening tone from him. Charlie held up a hand but none of them made an attempt to look less predatory.

"You don't know what you're fighting, Vahagn."

"Do you?" Vahagn said through clenched teeth. Charlie couldn't honestly believe he was in the right here. Not after everything they had been through together, been through *against* these assholes around him.

"Did she ever mean anything to you, Charlie?"

Charlie's jaw tensed and he looked away again. Yeah, that was shame. Good. Let the fucker fester in it.

"This is hardly the place…" The words escaped Charlie's lips in a snarl.

"Look, if I'm going to fucking die, I at least want to know that while you were beating my sister within an inch of her life you at least felt *bad* about it."

Charlie's gaze bore into Vahagn, revealing the monster within. The last time they had this conversation it involved far less words.

Vahagn took a sharp inhale. "Will you feel bad when you kill me?"

The coward looked to the dirty floor. Unable to even garner enough false courage to look his supposed best friend in the eye before he did it. Vahagn scoffed.

"Fuck man, at least have the dignity to tell her it was you when she finds out. I want to seal your fate in her eyes, once and for fucking all." The words choked out of Vahagn. He hated to give that power to this scum. Another regret.

Charlie glared at him, his lips thinning, his skin going pale. A cruel smile spread across Vahagn's face.

"That's my only request. I'm not fucking joining your band of assholes hell bent on conquering the world. So that leaves me walking into the arms of death. By your hand." The words tasted as cold as he felt.

Charlie continued to glare at him for a heartbeat. Then another.

"Fine," he ground the word out behind clenched teeth.

❖

CHAPTER TWENTY-NINE
NOAH

The air between them crackled as the battle in Noah's mind waged on. Should he continue talking or shut up while he had the chance? Stay or leave? Always the same theme.

But those emerald eyes had broke something in him and he couldn't stop the flood gates opening. Everything he had been hiding for years pressed against his tight lips, begging for release. As the sudden center of her focus, he needed to get this out. It already felt too late. The hollow pit in his chest deepened as he opened his mouth to speak, the words barely coming out. Would they be his last to her?

"Prior to coming to the city, I was in New Orleans."

Fuck, she looked like she already hated him with those simple words, something she already knew.

"I know this already." Her words were ice down his back.

He looked away, the weight of her stare unbearable.

"Yes, but what you don't know is that right before I left, there was a massive riot in the streets after several of the main Society headquarters across the city blew up one evening." He swallowed the rock lodged in his throat. His next words came out hoarse. "It was considered a rebel attack from within and I only know that information because I not only set those bombs in place... But I was inside one of the few spared buildings when they detonated."

Blood roared through his veins, the pulse in his ears near deafening. His gaze flashed back to hers as he watched her put the pieces together. She shifted backward, firing the final arrow into his heart. He couldn't breathe. Couldn't think. That was all it took to make her run.

"You're one of them," she whispered, the words heavy with rage and fear. "That's why they didn't kill you."

He shook his head and glanced to the ceiling, sending a desperate prayer to a god he didn't even believe in.

"Not in the way you're thinking," he replied, mustering the courage to continue talking about this. No one had heard this story before. There had been no one to tell.

Her words turned to daggers. "In what other way are you not quite apart of a gang of murderous vampires? There isn't much room for interpretation there."

He reached back to rub his neck and she flinched. A grimace bloomed on his face. Fuck, now he was the monster in her story. "They, The Society, needed mortals to help infiltrate certain spaces and spread their... agenda... easier." Each word made him want to vomit.

She turned away from him, loosing a disgusted huff as she stared into the inky abyss beyond them.

"You mean you *willingly* spread some bullshit immortal

propaganda to people who I assume trusted you?" His stomach dropped.

An echo of blood wrenching screams tore through his subconscious. "Nobody said anything about willingness."

Her gaze softened a fraction as those emerald eyes shot back to his. God, she could kill him here and now as long as he got to see those eyes one last time before he went.

"So, what, you blew up The Society? Or tried to and it didn't work? And before you could get caught, you ran to this city to do it all again?" Disgust feathered her words.

A hollow laugh escaped his lips. The twisted humor of it all not lost on him.

"Not quite." He ran his hand through his hair, getting caught on the dried blood in the strands, and exhaled.

"My br—" He swallowed down the lump in his throat. "My brother, older by a couple years, he orchestrated the plan early on, when the immortal campaign came overseas to New Orleans. He, Benji," his words tumbled over the name, "was the one who convinced Emilien The Society *needed* to maintain a league of mortals in their ranks to keep the, um, stock in line." Bile rose in his throat at the thought. "Benji brought me in but kept me mostly out of the loop of his grand plans, convincing me to trust him and follow his lead, no questions asked." He scoffed but didn't dare look to her. "I only knew about the bombs the night before I was meant to go set them up. That's when he laid out the information he had gathered about The Society's ultimate plans for the mortals within the city and the revolt to disrupt it."

The intense way she listened to him nearly made him stop there to back pedal out of the shit storm he laid out before her but someone needed to know this. To prevent this. Especially if his time finally ran out.

"They were planning on gathering all the mortals in the major cities across the country and keeping them in encampments like, well, essentially livestock. These encampments would provide feeding and breeding stock for the longevity of the immortals. The more amenable stock," his lips curled around the word, "would be given jobs across the city to keep up the creature comforts for the immortals. Indulging them in the things that make them feel human. But beyond that…"

"Beyond that, it's slavery," her words cut through the space between them and his eyes shot to hers.

He nodded his head slowly.

"So why not blow up all the headquarters?" Her brows furrowed.

"I don't know what happened. If someone sold out Benji or if he wanted to simply disrupt the system and not destroy it. He didn't have a chance to tell me though because he didn't make it out of one of the targeted headquarters when they detonated."

Nausea roiled through him when her expression turned sympathetic. It was too much for him to bare, after everything he had done. He looked away before continuing.

"The city erupted into chaos immediately after the explosions and I ran through the streets, telling every person I saw to evacuate. The Society patrols heard and started to chase me. I managed to lose them in the commotion and hopped onto a barge leaving port. I figured I could easily hide in the cargo since they aren't as heavily manned. Once I saw the arch come into view a couple weeks later, I assumed I was far enough away to get off and make a new plan. I never imagined I would be here long enough to find The Society or get others entangled in my mess."

Her eyes never left him as he spoke. "What happened

to the mortals?"

"What?" He met here gaze then.

"The mortals in the city. What happened to them?"

Shame doused him. He wanted to vanish on the spot. "They started rounding them up that night, slaughtering the ones who fought against them, and imprisoning the rest. A few escaped, according to the conversations I overheard on the barge but… not enough." He couldn't look at her. He scanned the cave. There was a small pool along the edge of the light's reach. He focused on the golden cast it reflected into the clear water, washing away the memories of bloodied faces, coated with dust, features set in perpetual fear.

"Not enough." Her words snapped through him.

Rubbing at the hollow pit in his chest, he stood, starting back toward the box of supplies. As he passed Izzy, he paused and said, "Listen, I know this is a lot to take in. I'll go stand watch if you want to clean up in the pool over there." He motioned to the crystal water. "I have towels and extra clothes down here. If you need anything else, let me know. Otherwise," he paused, testing the words in his mind before letting them free. "I never meant to put you in this situation."

She rose to her feet. "No."

"No?"

She pushed pass him to go to the supply box, pulling out a towel and sweats before stalking back over and shoving them into his hands. "I'll stand watch. You go clean up. You look like shit."

His harsh laugh pulled at the split in his lip that had finally seemed to heal. "Don't be ridiculous." He shoved the items back at her but she backed up out of his reach and sat on the supply box.

She pulled a dagger from her side, etched in floral designs, and drew a circle in the sandy ground. "If you hurry up, I promise not to look." Her eyes twinkled up at him, "But you're not even wearing shoes Broussard."

He looked down and winced. He did look like shit and that was just his clothes. When he made it over to the crystal waters, he stripped down, not daring to glance to see if she kept her word, and sank into the warm pool. A slight groan escaped his lips before her voice echoed across the space.

"What did you mean 'put me in this situation'?"

He glanced in her direction as he scrubbed the dried blood on his chest and arms. She had rid herself of the weapons harness and stared at the stairwell door, her dagger playing carelessly in her hand.

"I meant, I figured the reason they were in this city was because of me," he said.

Her face scrunched as she looked over to him before her eyes widened and she looked away, letting out a cough. She set her dagger down and said toward the door, "The Society was after me before I even knew your name. The way I see it, we were destined to come together at some point as long as you stayed in this city. For some reason, an anonymous package showed up on my desk and I became target number one for a bunch of immortal assholes. But you showing up to play hero didn't seem all that important until about two days ago. So die on your own sword all you want but I don't think you being here is the problem." A pause, "Unless you're more valuable than you're letting on?" She glanced over to him.

His pulse stuttered. He was as clean as he was going to get so he dunked under the water to escape her scrutiny before pulling himself out, toweling off and pulling on his fresh clothes.

When he approached her again, rubbing the towel through his hair, she asked, "Why didn't you leave? When you saw those scumbags slinking around after they attacked me that day? Why did you come investigate instead?"

He swallowed, drowning on the air around him. She knew the answer, her eyes told him she knew this answer.

"I just needed to know. To make sure." Her gaze pressed him to say more. "I needed to make sure no one else got hurt."

"And when you got dragged into the lion's den as well? Why didn't you leave then?"

She stood up, close enough to touch. He dropped the damp towel onto the box.

"I tried to leave. That night. But then–" He looked away, his heart pounding in his chest. "But then I remembered the look in your eyes when you held a dagger to my neck, that same look you had when Charlie challenged you in the hallway, the look... that look in your eyes as we walked back to our buildings afterward and you tried to hold desperately to your humanity and the humanity of others, rationalizing what was clearly a fucked up situation between you and him. It reminded me of the way Benji looked whenever we were working in the mortal communities, even when on official Society business, he would sit with anyone and hear their concerns, fears, rage. He took it all and I think he used that to fuel his rebellion, push him through. Seeing that level of fight and passion again stopped me in my tracks and I just... couldn't leave. Not yet. Not until I got to," He swallowed as she leaned in closer. "Not until I got to know you. Just a little more. Whatever you would give me, I wanted." Her hand laid on his chest and his words dropped to a whisper, "I needed to know."

His heart thundered under the warmth of her touch.

"And do you? Know me now?" Her voice rasped as she studied the fabric under her fingers.

He smirked, eyes dropping to her lips. "Not nearly enough."

Before she could respond, before he could second guess himself, before he could run away, he tilted her chin up, closing the distance between them and pressed his lips to hers. It was tentative and devouring all at once. He winced at the copper tang of his bloody lip as it split open once more but then she gripped his shirt, pulled him closer to her. He fisted her braid behind her neck, tangling in the loose curls still damp from cooled sweat. He pulled the tie keeping them together free. Forgetting all about his injuries, his other hand drifted down to capture her waist, fingers splayed across her side as he memorized the shape of her.

She pulled him back with her to the large boulder he had been sitting against and he reached down to grip her thighs, lifting her onto it. Her legs wrapped around his waist as he leaned in, one hand pressing her body into his as the other planted on the rock behind her hip, supporting them. Her hands pulled teasingly in his damp hair and a moan escaped his throat. Lifting her mouth from his, she began setting spine chilling kisses along the column of his neck. He was practically panting and when she laughed into the hollow skin at the base of his throat, a growl purred out of him and he grabbed her chin to pull her lips back to his. Her hands roamed down his chest and abdomen before slipping under his shirt, her cool hands on his too hot skin willing him to press his hips against her open legs. The pressure and fabric rubbed against his cock, blinding him with pleasure. She moaned into his mouth and he claimed every second of it before she pushed him away slightly to pull his shirt over his head. They were both breathless as he fumbled with the buttons of her shirt. Taking his hands in hers, she set them on her ribs, just below her breasts, and then held his heated gaze as she took her sweet time removing each button on her dark flannel, one by one. When she was finally free of the shirt, she went to reach behind and undo her bra when he said in a deep voice, "Allow me."

Giving him a wry smile, she leaned back, hands resting behind her on the boulder, putting herself on display for him as the sleeves of her shirt pooled at her wrists.

"Always the gentleman," she said. Goddamn if it didn't make him nearly lose his mind. Her wild curls fell back when she tilted her head up as his hands gave up resisting temptation and splayed across her soft abdomen, pressing into the smooth olive skin before drifting around her side and up her spine to the clasps at her back. He felt the goosebumps spread across her skin and sharply inhaled as he unhooked her bra.

She lifted her arms into her lap as he slowly dragged the straps down, tossing the garment aside. He leaned back to take in the smattering of freckles across her chest and stomach, beautiful, round breasts tipped with perfectly hard nipples.

"Is it enough now?" her sensuous voice poured into his ears, breaking him from the trance he was under.

"I don't think I could ever get enough."

And then he couldn't help himself. His hands were on her again, palming the soft flesh of her breast, ravishing that sweet mouth of hers, capturing each whimpering moan that escaped as he rubbed his thumb across her nipple. He was lost in the moment. There were hands on him, her tongue against his, her skin under his hands, the way her hands slipped under his waistband and then he gasped as she grasped his cock. Holding him tight in one hand, she set a slow pace stroking, melting his last brain cells. Her other hand worked the waistband of his sweatpants down, freeing him as they fell to the ground and he stood naked before her. She pressed her hand against his chest, giving him one last tantalizing stroke before removing her hand from him and sending him near diving after her touch.

Her emerald eyes were set ablaze as she studied him, his cock throbbing under her scrutiny and he unconsciously gripped himself as she stood, peeling off her skintight leggings. Seeing her standing before him, naked, he stroked himself once, desperate for the feel of her skin on him. She grabbed his other hand, leading him down to the bed of soft pillows and blankets he had laid for them, never imagining this scenario. Kneeling in front of each other, bare, the sounds of their breath joining the crackle of energy between them.

"Noah, I…"

"I know," he said gently, rubbing a thumb across her cheek and then palming her neck. She shivered under his touch and he said, "We don't have to do this."

"No, that's not it. I just…" She scanned his face, her lower lip trapped under teeth. "I want this."

He nodded and when he went to kiss her again he took his time, savoring the taste, the rough calluses on her hands from years of sparring as they ran across his stomach, up his back and then down his spine. He broke their kiss to nestle into her neck, breathing in her sweet vanilla scent mixed with the salty sweat and crisp cold air of fall. One hand remained in her hair and the other gripped her waist until she grabbed it, dragging his touch down and he followed like his life depended on it. Slipping a finger in, he groaned at the slick warmth before drifting further in, the tightness gripping his finger almost sending him over the edge. Her fingers wrapped around him and he shuddered, moaning.

"Fuck, Z."

Digging her nails into his back, she pulled him down between her legs, pumping once before guiding him to his fingers still sliding in and out, mesmerized. He removed his touch, gripping the soft skin of her inner thigh instead, and meeting her gaze as she smiled up at him and he drove in slowly, the tight grip around his cock pulling a loud groan from his lips. A sultry, breathy laugh floated up from below him, setting a fire within him. His thrusts quickened as his hand slid from her thigh, pressing into the smooth flesh of her lower abdomen while he pulled out completely, a gasp escaping her lips as he sank his thumb in and out. Thrusting back in fully, he began circling his thumb on her clit in time with the steady, rhythmic pace he set. Her nails dug into his forearms as she leaned her head back, eyes closed, and let out a filthy curse, causing a rough chuckle to rise from his chest. He quickened his tempo in her and on her, pressing a little harder into her abdomen, a moan released from her as her muscles started to tense around him. He hissed at the feeling, pumping harder as a soft gasping inhale sounded before her purring moan took over every thought in his mind and she came around him, wetness dripping out around his cock. He whimpered out a groan as his own release quickly followed. His pumping slowed and then stopped as he leaned forward, placing both hands beside her face before kissing her damp forehead a few times, his breath still trying to come back to him.

"That was…" she whispered, as breathless as him and he smiled against her forehead before pulling out and rolling beside her, propped on one elbow as he traced a finger along her delicate curves in the warm light of the cave setting them in a golden haze. A sleepy smile appeared on her lips as her eyes remained closed, as if replaying and committing what happened to memory.

"Izzy?" She turned to him, one eye open, her dreamy

smile stopping his heart. "That was phenomenal."

Her smile widened, her teeth grabbing at that lower lip as she nodded her head in agreement. He laughed and rolled over onto his back, staring at the ceiling of the cave while his heart found its way back to a normal pace. His eyes drifted closed momentarily and then opened when he felt the warmth of her soft skin against his own, blanket being pulled over their connected bodies and her head resting against his chest.

And in that moment, his fate was sealed. As long as she was in this city, he was never leaving. Even if it was the signature on his death warrant. His heart did a double beat as if it knew it would be.

CHAPTER THIRTY
Izzy

Izzy woke up with her head resting on a warm rock and the sound of birds chirping, the volume growing at a steady rate.

No, wait.

She opened an eye and the *rock* moved underneath her. Sitting up, the memories of the night before rushed back. Noah's bare chest glowed in the faint cave lights he had left on overnight, goosebumps appearing in the absence of her heat on him. Her naked heat. She smirked, looking away to her phone and the source of the bird chirping. Her alarm. 5 a.m. Fuck, they had fallen asleep in this cave. They would need leave soon.

She turned back to Noah and studied his chest in more detail. Everything the night before had been in a blur, happening so fast she couldn't take in the details. He had what Vahagn called a 'functionally strong' build—broad shoulders, chiseled obliques, with the strong back and arms of someone who was no stranger to work. Across his chest was an array of tattoos—some smoky looking swirls licking up his neck with details hard to make out in the dim, a fleur de lis on his right pectoral, and the most beautifully stylized shrimp on the left. She snorted and he opened an eye at the sound.

"Admiring the view?" he drawled in that deep, scratchy accent that made her toes curl. As he took in her still naked body, he growled, wrapping his arms around her waist, and pulled her back to land in the comfort of their makeshift bed. She squirmed and rolled around to face him, giggling as she placed her hands over his tattoos.

"Just making a mental map. That's all," she said.

His eyes were closed but his smile and chuckle gave her heart a stutter.

"Did I hear birds earlier?" The words were slow, methodical, eyes still closed and hands pressing her firmly to him.

Failing to resist the urge she kissed the shrimp tattoo she had been tracing and said, "My alarm. It's five. We fell asleep. We need to make our way back to my apartment soon."

He groaned and rolled on top of her, caging her beneath those taunt arms.

"How soon?" he asked against her lips, starting a seductive assault of kisses down her jaw, neck, and lower.

She moaned as he licked her nipple but despite the growing desire to explore sleepy, sexy Noah more, she grabbed his shoulders, dragging him back up to face her. His golden eyes burned as she gave him a stern look.

"Soon, Noah."

His heated gaze flicked to her mouth, the longing there smothering her, but he nodded and rolled to her side, pulling the cover of blankets off his body.

What a view, she thought as he walked over to the

clothes strewn around the boulder. More tattoos covered his back and she had the urge to get him out of this cave to explore them more in the daylight.

Shit, they were in a cave. She was in a *cave*.

As she scrambled out of the covers as well, shivering at the chill in the air, she said, "You do actually know how to get back to the apartment, right? I don't even know where I am."

He let out a low chuckle, "Yes, Izzy. I know how to get us out of here." He flashed her a grin before pulling on his navy shirt and she tilted her head.

"How do you even know about this place?"

His jaw tightened, that grin vanished. It caused an alarm bell of panic to flicker through her but she shook it off as he said, "I studied French American history pretty extensively and when I found myself in a new city knowing no one with nowhere to go, I remembered how these caves were all over the city and used as cellars. I had to scour the area for entrances that hadn't been concreted over or boarded up, but eventually I came across this old library and took a gamble. Turns out living in caves is just *too* Brom Stoker for The Society."

Izzy nodded as she finished dressing and checked her phone. Of course, no signal. They were hundreds of feet below ground. She couldn't wait to tell Vahagn about this place.

Vahagn. Her heart clenched. He *had* to have made it out last night but without service, she couldn't confirm. That's part of why they needed to get out of there as soon as possible.

She looked up to see Noah, dressed and packing away their makeshift bed.

"Noah?"

"Huh?" he said, not looking up.

"How did you get in so good with Dr. Beechum so

quickly?"

He paused, just for a moment, but Izzy's panic alarm went off again and she frowned. Goddamnit, had this been a mistake?

"We have a mutual friend in the academia world so I approached him to see if he needed any assistance while I was here."

Izzy bit her lip. Fucking him didn't entitle her to every one of his secrets but she couldn't ignore the nagging feeling she was missing something.

Noah finished packing the bedding back into the crate and grabbed the lantern, lighting it and turning to her, "Ready?"

She studied the lines that seemed to suddenly appear on his face but nodded. A loud click echoed through the expansive room of the cave and darkness cascaded around them, nothing but the soft glow of the lantern lighting the way.

"We will have to climb all those stairs back up but we are only a few blocks from your apartment."

She raised her eyebrows at him as she brushed past to open the door and start their ascent.

"Keeping tabs on me, Broussard?"

He snorted. "I live across the street, remember?"

"Convenient."

"Yes, very," he said while he brushed his knuckles down the back of her thigh as she climbed, sending shivers up her spine.

⚜

Thankfully, the trip back to her apartment was uneventful. She was actually a bit alarmed by how smoothly they made it back. Trying to take in as many details of the old library once they emerged from below had Noah promising to bring her back some day so she could explore. The intricate carvings within the wooden railings, the high ceilings, and the endless bookshelves had her nodding her head with her mouth open while he laughed and beckoned her on.

She swore he was still laughing as she punched the key code into the front door and the lock clicked opened. They shuffled in quickly and made their way up those marble steps to her hallway.

Only then did she start to recognize the vibration of her phone in her pocket.

It's repeating, persistent buzzing against her as she walked up to her door, unlocking it.

She pulled her phone out just as she pushed the door open, and didn't realize someone was in her apartment until Noah said, "What the fuck?"

Because sitting on her couch, his face full of anguish, eyes red and swollen was Lando Denalo.

❧

CHAPTER THIRTY-ONE
Izzy

Lando Denalo had not left his apartment in the sky since immortals announced their presence in the city almost twenty years ago. Not even to go down to the lobby and say hi to Larry, the doorman. Everyone else around him did his bidding, even his own daughter, his only remaining family.

What the fuck was he doing in her apartment?

Anger and confusion overwhelmed Izzy at the unexpected intrusion.

"What the fuck are you doing here, Lando?"

Noah stood behind her shoulder, a steadying hand on her lower back.

"Isabella, I have been so worried!" Lando's accent came out barely distinguishable through his sob.

Izzy glared at him.

"I don't need you worrying about me, Lando. Now get out."

She stepped aside, motioning to the door.

"No, *mi bella*, when you didn't come home last night I was so worried they had got you too and…"

Her blood ran cold. "Too?"

Lando's face crumbled. "Oh, Isabella." His sob racked through his body, making him look so frail.

"No, Lando. What do you mean 'too'?" She knelt before him, her hands around his shoulders, shaking him slightly. This was like talking to a child.

"Oh, *mia zazzera*, Vahagn. They got Vahagn. They dropped him off at the back door this morning." His sobs trembled through her arms and she glared at him.

"Okay, where is he then? Did they hurt him bad? Will he need to see the doctor?" Lando had a private doctor on call for himself and his crew. Because obviously.

Lando's sobs deepened and her scowl intensified, frustration setting in, before she felt a warm, comforting hand on her shoulder. She spun to see Noah offering her a hand, his face tight, avoiding her gaze as he pulled her up from the ground. Putting both his hands on her shoulders, his eyes met hers, pity within those molten pools. His next words shattered her.

"They never deliver their victims alive, Izzy."

She didn't comprehend him and pushed his arms off, backing away. The sunlight coming in from the windows started to feel too bright, too warm.

"No. What do you mean?" Her gaze bounced between Noah and Lando, a sharp pain starting to grow in her chest, halting her ability to breathe, to speak, to think, to hear.

"Izzy," Noah reached a hand to her, "please. Please don't make me say it."

She backed away another step and looked to Lando as he sobbed, "He's dead, Isabella. Vahagn is dead."

Dead.

Vahagn.

Her Vahagn. Her salvation in this desolate fucking city. Her protector and her companion. Her brother. Her *family*.

The room became suffocating as she sank to her knees, clutching her chest.

Murmurs of voices drifted around her but nothing registered in her except the last image she had of him, *'You're the best thing to have come storming into my life, Z',* and dead, dead, dead. The vice grip on her chest squeezed, the edges of her blurred vision faded to black until she felt hands around her shoulders and a voice yelling, "BREATHE! IZZY, BREATHE!"

Oxygen flooded into her lungs and all at once she coughed, sobbed, screamed into the void. Noah cradled her into his chest, rocking her gently as her world fell apart.

Visions threatened to pull her under. She heard Vahagn's hearty laugh surround her. His wickedly beautiful smile beneath his burly beard flashed before her eyes. Him racing her up the stairs, winking at her from across the table, shoving Charlie out of her apartment. Memories became an unrelenting assault, ripping away at her psyche, weaponizing her emotions.

More talking filled the space around her but her mind was at war with itself. His last words played on a loop she couldn't escape.

You're the best thing to have come storming into my life, Z.

She screamed again, gripping the sides of her head to silence the agony coursing through her skull, and the grip around her tightened as she made out the sound of a door opening and closing. So similar to the sound that echoed in the space of his absence as he disappeared into that warehouse.

How dare he leave her. How dare he walk into that

warehouse *expecting* this, leaving her with words like that to torment her. And he didn't even give her a chance to reply. He vanished from her life.

God, and all the while she had been hiding out underground having mind blowing sex with a man who had worked for The Society?

Noah continued to hold her, rocking her until suddenly she became repulsed by his touch. She pushed, scrambling out of his reach and away from him to sit with her back pressed against her bed, gaze wide upon him.

"Izzy," he pleaded, like he could see the war in her eyes, the betrayal she felt. He *knew*. He knew this could be the outcome. Would be and he said it would all be okay. He had lied to her.

"Did you know?" The words grated in her throat, raw.

His eyes narrowed and he tilted his head.

Her voice strained with maddening urgency and effort. "Did you know this would happen?"

"Izzy, no."

Her gaze was vicious on him. "What do you mean no, Noah? You were there. You were *one of them!* Did you know this would happen?"

His face fell, shoulders slumped as he sat back on his heels, hands clasped in his lap.

"It was always a possibility," he said, barely a whisper. "It could have been any one of us, Izzy."

"But it wasn't, was it? It wasn't just any of us. It was Vahagn." Her voice broke as another sob escaped her and she looked away to her bookshelf, spotting one of Vahagn's many gifts up there. A perfectly balanced dagger engraved with her nickname —*zazzera*. Z. The handle looked like bronze ropes wrapped around it. She never carried it for fear she might lose it.

"Like a mop!" He had exclaimed when she scrunched her face at the present. His smile had lit the room that day, even as she threatened to use him as target practice with it.

Squeezing her eyes shut, she slammed her head against the mattress behind her. There was a shuffling as Noah crawled over next to her, keeping his distance but still close enough for her to feel the warmth of his skin radiating into her arm.

"If I could go back, Izzy," he swallowed audibly, his voice above her as if he spoke to the ceiling, "If I could go back, Izzy, I would take his place. Without hesitation. I want you to know I would do anything to erase this, if I could."

A tear rolled down her cheek and she felt the gentle scrape of his thumb against it, wiping it away. They sat there for a few moments in silence, hot, heavy tears rolling down her cheek as Noah continued to catch them.

"I know," her words escaped in a rough whisper and a rush of air tickled her face as Noah sighed. He grabbed her hands, giving them a gentle squeeze and the act alone threatened to pull her back under. Vahagn would've been like this. Had their roles reversed, he would have comforted her like this. She turned her head to look at Noah.

"I just… I don't know what to do without him, Noah." Her lower lip trembled.

He offered her a sad, understanding smile. "I know, Z. I know."

Her heart felt empty, head heavy as she took a deep breath and said, "Can you take me to him?"

Noah assessed her for a moment before nodding once and standing, offering her both his hands. She took them, allowing him to pull her up. They stood before each other, staring into the other's eyes for a several heartbeats before making their way to the door and up to Lando's apartment.

❖

Izzy didn't recognize the guards at Lando's door, only noting it was more than the usual two. The men didn't blink in their direction as she and Noah made their way through the heavy ornate door.

The rich smell of coffee mixed with a layer of bleach, burning her nostrils. Lando stood over a heap covered in white sheets on his giant dining room table, whispering prayers in Italian while clutching a golden rosary in his big, rough hands. The image halted her. That wasn't just a heap on the table.

That was Vahagn.

A sob choked out of her but she kept her spine straight as she drifted over to the table. Noah stood by the door, the ever-present security of his gaze on her edging away the clouds of grief threatening to swallow her.

When she made it to Lando's side, he stopped his prayer to look into her eyes, sorrow woven deep in the etches of his face. He took one of her hands in his and squeezed, a grimace creasing the lines in his forehead as if preparing for her to snap at him. But she was so tired. So very tired. She tore her gaze from Lando's and looked to the sheet. The white looked innocent, pure. Vahagn would laugh at it.

Nothing innocent to see here, Z, he would say to her, elbowing her ribs as she would likely roll her eyes. Tears stung as she willed the thought away. That hollow feeling in her chest fractured as she reached for the sheet, glancing to Lando. He gave a solitary nod and she pulled it back. Just enough to see his face. It was enough to knock all the air out of her and she sank into a nearby chair. He looked so... serene. Like he had accepted his fate and gone willingly. Like he simply fell asleep and never woke up again. She knew better than to inspect closer but the peace on his features sent her anger into another level. He had known. He went to that warehouse expecting this outcome and wasn't even surprised by it in the end.

And for what? To free Noah because she said they needed to? She pressed her palms roughly into her eyes, grimacing at the ache growing in her chest. The air felt stifling.

Her soul began succumbing to the despair pressing in on her when she heard shuffling and grunts from the front door. She threw her hands down, eyes taking a bit to focus on the giant masses scuffling in the kitchen. She squinted. Noah held someone in a headlock. A mop of black hair shook under the hold and her heart stopped.

As if sensing her recognition, steel blue eyes met hers across the room and her hatred became a tsunami crashing through every last pillar of control she held in her feeble grip.

Noah moved and Charlie was thrown face first onto the floor with a knee in his back, hands bound in an inescapable grip. He roared against the restraint. "Lando, call the kid off!"

Lando sat at the kitchen island, sipping a coffee, eyes still red and puffy as he watched the whole scene unfold, a look of indifference painted expertly over his grief.

"Ah, Charlie, you know as well as I do, *mio figlio*, that I simply cannot do that." He waved a dismissive hand and turned his gaze back to the kitchen wall across from him, sipping his coffee.

Fury and grief whirled within Izzy's head and she couldn't decide if she needed to fight, flee, or scream. Her body chose a different path entirely as words came out in a tense whisper, "What… the… fuck… is he doing here?"

Everyone froze as she rose to her feet, hands trembling, knees threatening to give out. Her body willed itself over to where

Noah knelt into Charlie's back. Golden eyes burning with defiance and intent met hers as she dropped her knees to the floor next to Charlie's head. He strained against the pressure behind him to look up at her, the ocean eyes she used to seek in a crowded room to feel something now filling her with nothing but pure, unadulterated rage.

Izzy nodded to Noah. He gave Charlie a tentative release as he eased off him, shoving him back to the floor before standing up next to her. Charlie made cautious work of rising enough to fall back against the cabinets behind him, running a hand through his raven hair and glaring at Noah before turning his gaze to her.

"Z, I'm so sorry. I had—" His words were interrupted by her hand smacking his face sideways. Red bloomed on his cheek a second later and she watched his jaw clench, eyes turning a murderous shade of midnight as he turned back to meet her blazing gaze.

"How dare you call me that," she seethed and he winced, recognizing his mistake.

Cocking her head, her hollow laugh echoed in the room, a ruthless sound filling her soul. "What, Charlie? Not a fan of a woman putting her hands on you? No quid pro quo for you?"

A clatter sounded from the island behind her followed by a soft swear in Italian.

"Isabella," Lando said, his words a restrained growl. Charlie's gaze flickered to the man sitting up there and a moment of genuine fear sparked across his face. She raised a hand to stop Lando and Charlie quickly returned her gaze, giving her a slight glare. She smirked.

"You know, I knew deep down you never actually loved me. I convinced myself you did because what else was I going to do? Accept the reality that I was sleeping with a man who hated me? Who hated women?" A thump and another swear sounded from behind her, legs of a stool scraping across the floor. "But you know what is the saddest part, Charlie? I think you thought you loved me. I think you thought love was fucking and fighting and controlling and nearly beating the object of your affection within an inch of her life because you were afraid." His eyes narrowed on her but she wouldn't be silenced. Not now. Not ever again. "You were afraid that if I saw who you truly were, I would leave. So you did everything in your power to prevent me from leaving. I was fully under your well-crafted spell. That was until Vahagn found out." The sound that escaped her felt hollow, somewhere between a laugh and a sob. "He was going to kill you and I told him not to. I saved your life! And how do you repay me? You murder the *only* person I had in this stupid, fucked up world." Her face crumbled but she held his stare. He looked away. She scoffed and stood, brushing her knees off and stepped forward so he was forced to look up at her.

He refused to meet her gaze as she said, "You'll get what you're owed in the end, Charlie."

Before she could second guess her actions or words, she drove her knee into Charlie Valentini's beautiful fucking face.

✦

CHAPTER THIRTY-TWO
Izzy

"Y**ou fucking bitch!"** Charlie snarled as blood poured out of his face. For a fleeting moment, the image entranced her.

Everything after blurred as her own blood pulsed erratically through her veins and black speckled the edges of her vision. She had hit Charlie. Twice. She had made him bleed. She had told him her truth and made him bleed.

As she stood there in shock, she searched the depths of herself for an ounce of remorse. None came. *"What a shame"*, Vahagn's sarcastic voice sounded in her mind. The world started spinning and she thought she might fall.

A firm grip wrapped around her arms, pulling her back, away from Charlie. Lando leaned a strong forearm into his chest, holding him in place. Fuck, Lando. He knew everything now. He knew what Charlie had done to her, what she suspected he had done to Vahagn. His entire organization crumbled before him. Yet she felt nothing.

Lando said something to the person behind her. Noah? He guided her through the living room, past that ostentatious fireplace hanging from the ceiling, into a dark hallway. They passed several more doors she knew were bedrooms and en suites, all the way back toward a spiral staircase at the end of the hall.

"What… what are they going to do with him?" The words trembled across her lips. She hated herself for that.

"Climb. We will talk outside."

She obeyed. She felt detached from her body as she circled her way up to the door at the top. Beyond was Lando's rooftop patio.

Teak wood fencing surrounded the entire space, electric razor wire topping it the only detail to suggest something evil lurked beyond. This rooftop represented all the bravery Lando could muster in a world where vampires were rampant.

Noah's hand pressed into her lower back, guiding her to a round wicker couch under a pergola. The sun sat high in the sky, midday, but what did it matter when her whole life laid dead on a table below her?

The tremors started in her hands and before she knew it, she was being forced to sit in the plush circular cushion, her teeth chattering as her body quaked uncontrollably.

Noah squatted down in front of her, taking her face in his hands as he studied her. She couldn't stand the look on his face. Such sorrow and understanding. Fuck.

She pressed her eyelids closed but it was no better. The image of Vahagn's peaceful expression. Never changing. The inescapable permanence of it all came crashing down on her and she wept in convulsive waves. Noah climbed onto the couch behind her, wrapping his legs and arms around her as she shattered in his steady hold.

After a few minutes, the shaking subsided and she was able to breathe enough to form words.

"Is Lando going to kill Charlie?" Her words came out hoarse.

Noah's lips were right at her ear as he said gently, "I don't know. Not yet. He said he was going to question him some more. Get some answers to see how deep this goes." How deep his betrayal went. He didn't have to say it, Izzy knew this had to be a catastrophic blow to Lando.

"What—" The words choked her. "What am I supposed to do now?"

Noah let out a long exhale, his hold tightening around her.

"Keep living. Painfully, at first, but keep living. Vahagn would want you to keep living." His voice trembled.

They sat there for a time as Izzy tried to piece together a future without the one person who had loved and supported her unconditionally. When pink hues started to tinge the sky around them, a golden haze set in the air, she finally stirred out of his grasp to pull her phone from her pocket. She had ignored all the texts and missed calls, most of which were from Lando. A few from Charlie that had her pulse quickening as she quickly scrolled to Barry's name. She pulled up his contact information and pressed Call.

"Yessssss queen, where the fuck have you been?" Club music played in the background which meant he was likely either in the lab or at home.

"Barry, can you come over tonight? There— Something happened and I—" She swallowed the sob that tried to escape. "I could really use a friend."

The music on the other end stopped and she could

make out the shuffling of papers, closing of a laptop. "Oh honey, I can be there in ten. Fifteen if you need me to come prepared."

The click of the lab door locking rattled through her and she didn't know what to say, how to say what she needed. She didn't know what she needed.

Barry knew though. Barry always knew. "Okay, so fifteen minutes. Can you wait that long? Is someone with you? Vahagn? Was it Noah?"

Tears poured down her face and fuck, was she not done crying already? Would it ever end? She couldn't get the words out and it sent a new panic through her. As her sobs started to choke her, Noah's fingers wrapped around hers, pulling the phone to his ear and saying in a calm, grounding voice, "Barry, it's Noah. I'm with her but she could really use all the support she can get right now."

Izzy couldn't hear his response but Noah dropped his forehead to her shoulder as he said roughly into the phone, "Yeah."

He pulled the phone away and tucked it back into the side pocket of her leggings.

"He will be here in fifteen. Is there anyone else you want me to call?" he asked.

She shook her head, twisting around to face him, wrapping her legs around his waist. He looked as devastated as she felt. Was this like reliving his brother's death? No. He hadn't even gotten a chance to mourn that loss. A chance to break down and scream. Had he ever even had friends to lean on?

He had been alone. Her heart broke as she held his face in her hands.

"Thank you," she whispered, the words raspy from emptying her reserve of tears.

He closed his eyes. "Please don't thank me."

Before she could respond, Gio's frantic voice drifted from the rooftop door.

"Izzy? Izzy, are you up here?"

She surveyed the sheltered expression on Noah's face before pressing a soft kiss to his lips and calling out over her shoulder, "I'm here."

She disentangled from him and as she walked toward Gio's open arms she peeked over her shoulder to see Noah slumped forward, hands cradled between his legs.

CHAPTER THIRTY-THREE
NOAH

The way Noah saw it, everything was fucked.

And it was all his fault.

He had walked into this woman's life and simultaneously, it had imploded. Like everything else he ever touched.

True to his word, Barry had arrived fifteen minutes after getting off the phone with Noah, two bottles of tequila and a bag of weed in hand, along with a small feast of junk food. Where the man had gone to acquire such a bounty of goods, no one knew, but as he poured and passed out shots, Noah peeped a small, sad smile on Izzy's face. Barry threw a shot into the bonfire, preached, "Pour one out for my homie, my love, my friend, Vahagn," then tossed back his own.

Noah stayed on that couch under the pergola, the cool kiss of the night air chilling his body. He observed the others as they sat around a steel fire pit, passing a joint and a bottle in countering concentric circles. Smoke billowed in the air and the smell of burning wood ripped through him as memories of screams, cries of anguish, and pleas fought their way to the surface.

A loud pop from a log in the flames jolted him back to the present. He wiped the bead of sweat from his brow.

As the vices softened the sharp edges of pain, Barry, Gio and Izzy began sharing stories of Vahagn. The clear night sky offered a sparkling backdrop to the somber little celebration of life.

"One time," Izzy started, giggling before she could even get the memory out, "he wanted to bake a king cake." Her eyes shot across the fire to Noah, likely thinking of the correlation between Mardi Gras, New Orleans, and him. His lips tugged upward, still sore from the nasty split in the middle. "But where were we going to find a tiny baby to bake inside it? So, instead he rolled the smallest little baby joint I have ever seen and wrapped it in plastic to shove in the dough." Giggles drifted around the fire as it crackled in time with the shifts in mood.

Barry's eyes grew wide. "I remember that! Lando got it in his slice! I still can't forget the image of his giant sausage fingers trying to light the damn thing. He ended up burning his fingers and chased Vahagn around the penthouse to give him a noogie." They all bent over laughing. Just as they started to settle, wiping tears from their faces, the man himself appeared in the doorway, holding a platter of food.

"I don't know what's so funny about real sustenance but you need to eat something other than junk, *mia famiglia*." His Italian accent seemed heavier as weariness wafted off him.

Barry made a gesture with his index finger and thumb that set them all off again. Lando gave Noah an exasperated look.

He shrugged in response but couldn't help the grin that tugged at the corner of his lips.

Barry let out a heavy sigh, running a light hand over his

hair like it had even moved in his fit of giddiness.

"You know, I never did get him to fuck me." The statement came out so matter of fact it took Lando off guard as he set the food down on a small wooden table, falling into an empty seat in shock.

Gio turned to Barry, one eyebrow cocked. "I did."

Barry's gaze grew wide as he leaned over, grasping her hands.

"Tell me everything!"

"Oy vey!" Lando exclaimed covering his ears and sending them all back into a fit of giggles.

When they had finally caught their breath enough to eat, Izzy's gaze settled on Noah and she drifted over.

"You know you can come sit with us," she said as she handed him a plate with a fried rice ball, some marinated antipasto, and a few rings of calamari next to a red sauce.

He never would've pegged Lando as the type to cook his emotions. But then again, they all had their surprises to keep.

She sat down next to him, her thigh pressed against his, the itch to reach out and grab it overcoming his ability to think. His grip tightened around the plate.

He cleared his throat and said, "This isn't my place right now and that's okay."

As he started to dig into the food, she started talking, her eyes on the others around the fire, Lando having joined them in sharing stories and laughing.

"He told me the other night, before we had known you were missing, that he thought you might actually be deserving of me. You know, since he thought we were together." Her eyes twinkled, reflecting the strung lights around the pergola that had automatically come on when the sun disappeared and darkness fell.

It had been a surreal feeling, being out in the darkness. But once the initial sensation of fear dissipated, he looked up to the moon, closed his eyes, and felt… peace.

"The thing is," she continued, still watching the others. He had set the plate down, too enthralled in what she was offering him. "You're going to have to decide if you think you are deserving of me." She glanced to him then before nervously adding, "Not that I think I'm a prize or anything but… his opinion meant something to me. And you," she turned to him then, gripping his thigh, "You mean something to me too."

His heartbeat skipped and skittered in his chest as he stared into her eyes, forest green in the darkness around them, and he felt the rush of all his thoughts and emotions at once.

I care for you. I can't care for you. You don't need me. Shouldn't want me. I want you. I need you. I love you.

He could barely breathe as the thoughts circled his mind like sharks in the water as he bled out, his heart having been ripped from his chest and handed to her.

Before he could respond though, she gave his leg one more squeeze and stood. She started walking back to the fire, but then stopped. Turning back to him, she stared at her hands as she wrung them together.

"You'll stay with me tonight, won't you?" Her words tumbled out tentative from her soft lips, like she didn't know how they would land.

And before he could over think his own cascading thoughts, he said with a surety he hadn't felt in over a year, "Always."

CHAPTER THIRTY-FOUR
Izzy

The evening slowed down after a few others from Lando's crew came up to drink to Vahagn, giving words of condolence to Izzy. Each one made her want to throw up. Apparently she had been as much a pillar in his life as he had been in hers, a fact known to all in the organization. At some point, she had become overwhelmed and drifted over to lay back on the circular couch next to Noah. He sat as sentry while she gazed up at the stars.

When had everything gotten so fucked? When had it all gone completely sideways? It started well before they had waltzed into a Society ridden warehouse on a quest to save a man she barely knew. And here he was, sitting next to her. Filling the empty space in her heart that threatened to swallow her whole.

She slammed her head against the soft upholstery beneath her. There were no more tears, only a cruel stinging ache behind her eyes.

"Gio and Barry are heading downstairs to watch Game

313

of Thrones on mute with the soundtrack of Magic Mike playing." Lando's melodic voice sounded heavy, exhausted. He let out a soft chuckle, "Said it reminded them of Vahagn."

Izzy peeked over at him, his features pinched in pain.

He continued, "He… his… we moved him downstairs." Down to the morgue. Because this fucking building had a morgue. That's what happens when its owner is a gangster. Its occupants gangsters, too. People die. A vicious circle for a damned life.

"Okay." That was all the response she could muster. Everything about her felt hollow even with the copious amounts of alcohol and weed in her system. It worked for a bit. There had been laughter, genuine laughter. But the drop started and she feared the crash at the bottom, her mind clawing at empty air to stop it.

Lando's gaze flickered to Noah before turning on his heels and heading down the stairs.

She felt the cushion shift as Noah laid down next to her, hands behind his head. A soft sigh escaped his lips.

"I can't remember the last time I saw the stars without looking through a window."

She turned her head to look at him but he kept his gaze on the sky, his lips partly open as his eyes drank in the stars and moon in the clear midnight above. He looked younger then, a boyish wonder on his features even with all the fresh cuts and scrapes on it. His jaw tightened before he turned to her, a gentle smile pulling at the split in his lip, lights gleaming in his golden eyes.

"Tell me about your brother," she said. The way his face hardened in an instant had her regretting the words. She was prying but she had to escape the thoughts about Vahagn. Talking about him like this was the last night they would ever do so again. She couldn't stand the thought.

Noah stared into the space over her shoulder as he spoke, "He was nothing like me." This thought prompted a smile from her but he kept his gaze averted. When was the last time he had talked about his brother? When would he have had the chance?

"He was incredibly brave, inserting himself into situations without a forethought. That's how he ended up… where we were. He saw the direction things were going and he just walked into The Society and demanded a role." He shook his head and narrowed on her gaze. "I was resistant. I had questions. He always said I was too calculating for a bayou boy." He grinned but it quickly fell as he continued, "Ultimately, that's why he drew me in to join. They needed someone who would look at the angles, who could gather information and then form an idea. Calculate." The last word came out through clenched teeth.

She couldn't resist herself as her hand reached out and her fingers ran through his hair. His eyes fluttered closed at the touch. When they opened again, she was scorched by the burn within them. She wanted to say something. Anything. But what could she say?

He continued on, blinking his gaze back to the sky through the slats of the pergola. "At first, I was so angry at him. For dragging me, us, into that world. Using my mind, using me, for a goal that seemed to be insurmountable. How were two orphans from New Orleans supposed to dismantle an international organization?" She felt the frustration in his words. He ran a hand down his face.

"Anyway, that night, I didn't even know if he escaped or…" His throat bobbed as he swallowed. "On the barge is where

I overheard what happened. The building he had been in had completely crumbled to the ground. 'A raging success' the barge workers toted. 'Should've been like that at every building, then it would've worked,' they said." He scoffed. "I spent the rest of that night coming to terms that I was officially alone in this world." Silver lined his eyes as he looked at her. "I had consulted with Dr. Beechum some when I was in college so when I saw that arch on the horizon I decided to come here. At least I knew someone here. I would get a job, blend in, and figure out where to go next. What to do next."

Her gut wrenched for him. He was alone. He had been alone this whole time and couldn't even tell anyone why he was alone. He never even got a chance to celebrate his brother's life. All he got was an evening of mourning on a boat to some random destination. Alone.

He reached out and traced the line of her jaw, the gesture so soft from someone who should be hardened by the cruelty of this world. Sighing, he pulled his hand away, glancing up at one of the cameras along the fence.

"Anyway, it's been long enough now. I can accept what happened."

Her nose scrunched. "Can you?" She propped herself up on an elbow, facing him. Before he could answer though, the lights on the patio flickered and she rolled her eyes. Lando was watching them. Noah looked to her curiously, unaware of the old man's imposing nature.

"Come on, let's take this back to my place where there is a bit of privacy." She glared at the camera as she took his hand and led him toward the exit. His grip resisted behind her and when she glanced back, his gaze was set on the sky, taking it in like he would never get the chance again.

CHAPTER THIRTY-FIVE
NOAH

Noah woke with a sharp inhale, stretching out in the vast warmth of Izzy's bed. Which was empty. His eyes flew open and he sat up with a start. The morning twilight cascaded the room in an eerie glow but there was not a soul in the apartment. His quickening pulse stole his breath as he tried not to panic. This couldn't be happening. This can't happen. He rushed to the door, noticing it had been left unlocked and threw it open just in time to see the stairwell exit click shut. Not stopping to think, he rushed after.

Izzy stood at the top of the stairs, pushing open the door to Lando's penthouse landing when she met his eyes with a burning gaze. What the fuck was she doing?

"Izzy?" But she was through the door before his words could reach her. Cursing, he sprinted up the stairs, his lungs burning from the effort and the adrenaline pumping through him. She didn't wait for him, didn't acknowledge him beyond that singular moment in the stairwell, as she pushed past the guards at the door and headed into Lando's penthouse. No, she headed straight for the gym. Where Charlie was being kept prisoner. Fuck.

Noah jogged to catch up to her before matching her stride.

"Tell me what's going through that mind of yours." His words pleaded with her, breathless as his body fought to find a normal breathing rate. The dim lighting in the space made it difficult to make out her expression.

Her gaze fixated on the office door, pace unrelenting. "It's better if you don't know."

His steps faltered. Benji had said those same words to him. He had wanted to know how their revolt would end, what the outcome would look. *It's better if you just don't know, you'll worry too much, Noh.*

He reached for her arm, twisting her to face him when they were several meters from the office door. Her expression filled with rage and hurt and fear and he didn't have the words to make it all go away.

"Z, stop for a second."

The sharp edges on her face softened but she still pulled out of his grasp.

"No, Noah. I have made up my mind." She backed away before turning on her heel and stalking into the little office in the far corner of the gym. He followed, never more than a step behind. The air felt dry and static, like the slightest bit of tension would ignite the whole space. When she pushed into the small room he heard the low, rumble of a laugh from Charlie before the man said, "Hello, gorgeous. Ready for round two?"

Charlie sat bound to a metal chair in the middle of the room, cameras focused on him from every corner. He had been bloodied up some but nothing compared to what Noah had experienced. Fingers absentmindedly rubbed on the sensitive split in his lip. His stomach dropped and his hand stilled. Nothing like what had been done to Vahagn.

Charlie continued to laugh like there was some inside joke between him and Izzy. Her footsteps fell soft on the floor as she approached the man, then slapped him across the face. His eyes flickered with rage as he spat blood on the ground at her feet before sneering up at her.

"Still a bitch, I see." A hint of sorrow pinched the edges of his blue eyes. A juxtaposition, like he couldn't quite convince himself the words were true. Noah moved on silent steps to the corner of the room, observing Izzy as she moved around the office like it was her home.

Pulling Lando's leather roller chair over, Izzy sat down, facing Charlie as she said, "Shove it, Charlie. We all know how much you hate me, hate women, blah, blah, blah." Her hands accented each word with a mesmerizing flourish. Until she set them on her knees and leaned forward, right into the man's face, "Quite frankly, the repetitive dialogue is getting real fucking old so let me cut to the chase."

That's when Noah noticed the dagger she reached for in the harness around her chest. Fuck, why hadn't he checked her for weapons? Noah started toward her but her eyes pinned him in place as she flipped the dagger in the air, catching the handle without looking. Turning her attention back to Charlie, she examined the blade as she said, "It would be so easy to kill you. I'm not even sure it would hurt anymore. Me, that is." A violent emerald gaze flicked to Charlie, whose jaw visibly strained against his clenched teeth. "It would definitely hurt you; I would make sure of that."

"Just fucking do it then, Izzy. I've lost everything

already." Charlie's words were strained. Rage flooded Izzy's features.

"You've lost everything, Charlie? Because from my side of things, you stole everything from me. Everything!" The point of her dagger pressed lightly into his chest. Noah held his breath, gripping the side table he leaned against. "At what point do you grow up and take responsibility for the choices you've made? The people you've hurt?"

Charlie clicked his tongue against his teeth as he looked out the window, avoiding the rage in her stare.

"It was real for me, you know." His voice faltered a bit. Izzy's brows furrowed. "I just… didn't know what to do. I'd never felt the emotions I felt for you. They drove me crazy."

This staggered Izzy as she sat back, letting her dagger hand fall into her lap. Noah stood up, hands clenched in fists. Wavering respect is all that kept him rooted in place.

"What?" she said. Her words lost their bite.

Charlie turned to her and Noah shifted uncomfortably. He didn't think he should be watching this moment. He also knew there was no chance in hell he would leave.

"I genuinely loved you Izzy. Fuck, I still do. But I meant what I said that last night; I never deserved you. You reminded me of that. Vahagn reminded me of that. Pretty boy over there reminds me of it every fucking time I see the way he looks at you when he thinks you won't notice. So yeah, I ruined everything I ever cared about. Please just put me out of my goddamn misery already." Surrender radiated off the man as he sat back in the metal chair, stray strands of black hair cascading across the vulnerable expression on his face. This was a resigned man, given up and laying his soul to bare before him. His last words.

Izzy assessed him, a mix of shock and confusion on her

face. A moment later, her look softened and she nodded once.

"Good, but first you are going to help me," she said.

A steely look of indifference, a mask, etched onto Charlie's face as he tilted his head quizzically. Noah stepped forward then, respect for the moment be damned.

"You're going to help me take down The Society once and for all."

CHAPTER THIRTY-SIX
Izzy

"Are you fucking serious, Z?"

Izzy whirled around in her chair and for a second she saw Vahagn standing in front of her, gripping her shoulders, looking as if she had grown an extra head. But then she blinked and those eyes peering into her soul shifted to a golden hue.

She swallowed. "Yes. I'm serious."

Noah scanned her face, his lips pursed and his grip gentle yet firm on her shoulders. She liked that this close she could see the specks of freckles hidden against his deep tan skin, peppering his cheeks below those haunting gilded eyes. A wave of sadness rolled through her. Then he pulled her against his chest, one arm wrapped around her waist as the other tangled into her hair, pressing her face into his neck. She breathed in the woodsy smoke scent that clung to him, like a smooth glass of bourbon on an autumn night. Charlie grunted from his spot in the chair.

Noah whispered in her ear, "What's the endgame, Z?"

She choked when her initial thought almost slipped from her lips. Pulling back from his grasp, she barely recognized the man before her. Just like that he shifted into a warrior, readying himself for battle. A soft confidence radiated off him in a way that grounded her, liberated her of her apprehensions, melted away to reveal this cold, calculating soldier before her.

Footsteps sounded at the entrance of the office and she turned to Lando standing in the doorway, no doubt having seen and heard everything on his camera feed. She knew a guard alerted him of her presence the second she pushed through the front doors. The fact he hadn't barged in to interrupt set her on edge. What was *his* endgame?

The older man held his clenched fists at his side, staring daggers into Charlie.

"Lando, we're going to need some weapons and a crew," she said.

Breaking his mental assault on his prisoner to meet her gaze, he nodded. "Everything, Isabella. All of it, it's yours." She couldn't decipher the look warring on the old man's face as he shifted his focus back to Charlie. His anger felt understandable. His sorrow for Vahagn rubbed her wrong because what had he expected would be the result? But the disappointment? It felt almost like Charlie let him down by coming back. Izzy shook her thoughts away.

Pain etched into the lines of Noah's stoic expression. She could feel herself pulling him back into the thicket, dragging him into some insane idea blind. *Just like Benji would have done*, she thought. Reaching for him, she said, "Noah, you don't have to be a part of this. This is my battle."

His stony visage seared through her. "This is as much my battle as it is yours, Z."

She swallowed the bile rising in her throat. They needed a plan. A plan to take down The Society. Leading the way out of the office, she headed to the table of weapons on the back table of the sparring ring. Lando had more placed strategically throughout the penthouse but here she could sit in familiarity, as her world shifted and tilted off kilter. Where was she supposed to begin?

She leaned on the table, Noah at her side watching her.

"Am I making a mistake?" she whispered.

His stare intensified and she counted the breaths she struggled to complete before he finally spoke.

"No. But… we do need a plan. We can't just barge in there again. They will be expecting it."

She nodded slowly, lips in a thin grimace. "You've done this before. What do we do?"

He let out a long exhale and walked over to the window, overlooking the city and letting in the warm glow of the morning light.

Running a hand through his hair and rubbing the back of his neck, he said, "Our best time to attack is going to be during the day, for obvious reasons. But today would be ideal. They won't expect you to have organized anything that quickly. Beyond that, you're going to want a distraction. Something so big it'll force them out. Force them out, thin the group, and then attack."

He turned to her and she met his gaze, pondering his words. Soft orange light glowed around his silhouette. Her eyes widened.

"I've got an idea."

Marching back into the office, Lando seated at his desk watching Charlie, the prisoner's head bent in indignation, Izzy approached a set of bookshelves. Both men looked to her as she pulled a volume and the shelf clicked, opening with a whoosh. A cruel smile creased her cheeks as she peered at the contents within.

Noah came to her side and paled.

"Izzy…"

Before them a hidden closet opened with an arsenal of weaponry that would send Lando straight to prison if the cops even cared anymore. At the forefront, a wooden box of explosives sat, beckoning her to use them. She turned to Noah, grin disappearing as she watched panic ripple through him. Putting a hand on his arm, another shudder went through him and she squeezed gently.

"Hey." His golden eyes met hers. "You do not have to be a part of this. It's too much to ask for you to be a part of this."

"No." He swallowed and turned to her, taking her hand in his. "No, I just… have seen how this story can end. But I want…" he squeezed her hand, nodding his head, "I want to help you with this."

Her heart sank. There was a good chance he might hate her for the plan she had. She hated herself for it.

"Noah, I'm so sorry."

He searched her face and as it dawned on him what she was thinking, planning, she watched him shift to a sad resignation. That stoic mask fell over his face again as he turned back to the cache before them, dropping her hand in the process to cross his arms over his chest.

"Do you think this will be enough then?" he asked.

She stared at his profile, the hollow feeling in her chest cracking deeper. The lump in her throat caught and she swallowed it down. This gamble could cost her everything. But she turned to the armory, keeping her empty hand at her side, and said, "It's going to have to be."

Noah nodded. "Then let's get to work."

❖

Charlie turned out to be an amenable informant. Something told Izzy it had to do with the bruise blooming on his left cheek that looked a lot like the result of a fairly subdued right hook from one Orlando Denalo.

"During the day, they take shifts sleeping but have a small team that keeps watch. Used to be humans but…" Noah's sentence trailed off, shifting uncomfortably where he stood against the countertop in Lando's kitchen. He cleared his throat to continue, "They realize how vulnerable they are during the day. The guard stations are not only in the warehouse but also in the basement that connects to several surrounding buildings, each with their own guard detail. It's also how they get their… cargo in and out." The air in the room shifted as the information sunk in. A glance between Charlie and Lando caught Izzy's eye. Her brow narrowed on the two men.

"How long?" The question burned through her as she focused on Charlie in the seat across from her. She had flat out refused to sit at the table like nothing had happened. As if her whole world didn't completely fall apart there but she felt far too anxious to sit down at the island in Lando's kitchen.

Charlie looked down at the dark stone in front of him. He swallowed and a muscle strained in his jaw as he glanced back up at her.

"That night… when Vahagn came and… removed me from the situation." His gaze flashed to Lando sitting at the table, the old man studying him, assessing every word that tumbled out his swollen mouth. The glass in his scarred hands groaned against the pressure he exerted on it. Blue eyes returned to hers. "That's why I disappeared for so long after. They wanted to initiate me and make sure I was willing to cooperate."

Izzy swore and pushed against the counter in front of her. That night he held her life in his hands had been *months* ago. He had broken into her apartment since then. She had *let* him into her apartment since then. She was a fucking fool.

"Show me the tattoo." Izzy startled as Noah spoke.

Charlie's gaze narrowed on him but he pulled the collar of his t-shirt down enough to show the glimpse of a golden fleur de lis tattoo on his left pectoral muscle, intricately woven into the vines around it. In nearly the same location as Noah's.

Izzy whirled her gaze on Noah, eyes wide. The air grew cooler as he ignored her attention and said, "He's telling the truth."

"Yeah, and what about *you?*" Izzy couldn't stop the words coming out.

A muscle tightened in Noah's jaw but he still refused to look at her. Anger coursed through her. Anger and hurt. Everyone appeared to have been in on the secret comings and goings of The Society except her and Vahagn. It already got one of them killed. Her glare became a permanent fixture on her face as she turned back to Charlie.

"About how many are we talking?" she asked.

"At least one hundred in The Society total, that doesn't include whoever has made the change since their arrival. And the numbers rise weekly with new shipments from the south coming in," Charlie replied.

His gaze drifted to Noah at her side and she couldn't resist a sidelong glance. He remained stoic, unflinching under the scrutiny. No wonder The Society wanted him around.

She tore her eyes back to Lando, sitting at the counter. The lines on his forehead grew deeper. "Lando, how many do you have in your command these days?"

"Only about thirty, Isabella." The man sounded weary,

his accent losing its jovial flourish.

She sighed. Not great odds. But not impossible.

"Okay…" Gathering some confidence to inspire it to the rest, she said again, "Okay. This can work. If we are strategic. I only need one person with me. It'll look too suspicious if there is a big group of us traipsing toward their headquarters, even during the day. Charlie is coming with me. Lando, you'll lead the rest to the location Noah gives you. He can decide if he wants to join you there or stay out of this like I suggested."

"I go with you," Noah said at the same time both Lando and Charlie interjected.

"I go with you, *mia bella.*"

"I'm not a part of this!"

Izzy frowned, her nostrils flaring at Noah. He gave her an equally intimidating look but she would deal with him in a minute. Without breaking her silent battle with him, she spoke to the others around the island.

"Lando, my plan doesn't work if you are with me. I need you to *command* your crew and they won't listen to me. Charlie, you became a part of this when you decided to join The fucking Society instead of take responsibility for your actions."

A flicker of rage flashed in Noah's eyes but his mask remained. It tugged at her heart to look away from him. She couldn't decide if it was fear of missing a significant sign or something else. But she needed to confirm the other men understood the message. She wasn't fucking around with them today.

"We don't have a lot of time so we all just need to get our shit together and be on the same page. You're just going to have to trust me," she said. Her gaze flickered to the window, the sun rising higher in the sky. Time. There was never enough of it.

Tears pricked at the back of her eyes and she blinked them away as Charlie broke through the silence.

"You're going to get me killed, Izzy," Charlie pleaded.

Chin held high as she stared down at him, she practically growled, "Good, saves me the hassle then."

"Why are you even taking him with you, Isabella?" This was Lando's version of pleading. Question her. Get her questioning herself.

"Because I am going back into that warehouse and ending this once and for all."

All the men slowly turned to face her. "*Fout tonè,*" Noah murmured under his breath when he met her gaze before looking to the ceiling, sending out a silent, worthless prayer she imagined.

"This is a suicide mission, isn't it?" Charlie accused.

Her lips tightened. He wasn't entirely off base. If she had to go down in order to see the end of this plague on her city, she would willingly pay the price. But she didn't want to risk Noah in the process.

"Noah, you'll meet Lando outside the—"

"No, I'm coming with you," Noah interjected.

She scowled. "*No,* you're going to meet with Lando out—"

He stared her down, a slight twinkle of amusement in his golden eyes. What was he playing at? Her stomach fluttered despite her brain's inability to choose danger or desire.

"I'm coming with you. It's not up for discussion." For being a Southern gentleman, he was real fucking insistent.

Her glare intensified and the corners of his mouth ticked up, his gaze falling to her lips then back to her eyes. A frustrating strand fell across his brow and he didn't sweep it away.

She growled in exasperation. "Fine. Noah and Charlie

come with me. Everyone else will go with Lando."

"Good plan." The half smile on Noah's lips set her blood on fire. Who was this man? Time. She didn't have time to figure out.

Turning to Lando, she said, "Lando, gather your people. We need to be ready to move in an hour."

"*Si*, Isabella." His tone was all business again. This reprieve, a glimpse of the caring man she knew, tucked away as his face hardened.

"Charlie, you're going to describe every inch of that warehouse to me and if we get there and you're lying, I will chop your dick off right where you stand. Understood?" She pulled her dagger out, examining the sharpness.

Hatred flashed across his face at the threat but he said through clenched teeth, "Understood."

"Good," she gently smacked his cheek with the handle of her blade, just to watch the rage consume him. "Let's get started."

✦

Standing in the alley across from the warehouse they had just escaped from felt bizarre. Especially seeing it lit with the bright midday autumn sunlight. Any other day, having two solid rocks for men standing on either side of her would've provided a modicum of comfort.

Not that day.

As she stood monitoring the quiet activity across the road, her mind wondered to which of the two marked men behind her would plunge a knife in her back once they got inside. The secrets between them all were compounding, building with every second. Doubt grew and the uneasy feeling that followed had her turning around, studying them both. They were examining the building with equal looks of displeasure and resolve. Like there was an opponent in the ring and they were readying themselves for the battle to come.

"Okay, once the distraction is in motion, I give us about ten minutes to get in, place the bombs, and get out. We will focus on the basement and lower levels and let physics do the rest for us." Because her genius plan involved the limited supply of explosives Lando had in the armory. "We stick together while we're in there because…" She met both their gazes then.

"You don't trust us," Noah drawled plainly, looking again across the street.

Yep, that about summed it up. She sighed and turned back to the building. She had been brooding over that tattoo on his chest—the *same* tattoo The Society had branded on Charlie's chest—the entire time Charlie explained the layout of the warehouse. She hadn't been able to take her eyes off the spot until Noah let out a cough, grabbing her attention, and tilting his head at her.

For some reason she hadn't fully accepted his past until that moment. When it became tangible. Had he actually been kidnapped the other night or just brought back to the duty he ran away from? Did they actually rescue him or lean right into a trap? Were they doing the same thing at that very moment?

Here she stood ready to waltz into a warehouse crawling with immortal thugs to blow it up with the help of… two mortal thugs. Both with ties to these ever-living assholes. Her grandparents had to be rolling over in their figurative graves.

The soft brush of Noah's hand against her arm sent shivers down her spine. How had this been the hand fate had dealt her? Tears threatened to spill over as the reality of everything that had happened came crashing down in the moments before the battle, that hollow pit in her chest cracking open again.

"I'm so sorry," she whispered to him as a thundering boom reverberated across the city, rattling the windows in the buildings and rumbling the air around them.

"Holy fuck," Charlie whispered from behind her. "You blew up the old library."

A tear sprang free as she surveyed the chaos that started to erupt within the warehouse. She figured in about five minutes the building would be damn near empty and they would get to work placing the bombs they each had in packs on their back.

A hand squeezed hers and she turned her head to see Noah's grip in hers. When she met his sad gaze, he nodded to her and let go. She wiped the tear from her cheek and returned to see the motion inside the warehouse hit a crescendo. Immortals on every level scrambled throughout the building, making their way down to the underground pathways. Within a couple more moments, the warehouse looked like a ghost town.

"Alright, let's go." There was a surety in her voice that surprised herself. Inside, she was shaking.

They made a swift pass across the street, keeping low. Noah tentatively pushed in through the same entrance they had come in the night before, scanning the area. An eerie quiet had descended in the expansive space. Noah nodded his head and she and Charlie followed on.

Noah didn't hesitate to start setting the bombs as they made their way into the vast opening of the warehouse and across to the basement access, checking the railings that led to the levels above. His work looked meticulous. He didn't pause to think, just placed the explosives and moved on.

"Charlie and I will go down and set the last ones in the basement and then we need to get out of here," she said to Noah. Charlie nodded, disappearing through the door.

Noah gripped her arm before she could start down the stairs after him.

"No. We're staying together, Z," he said.

She gulped. She didn't want to drag him back down to his captive confines with no guarantee they would be able to escape. That's why it had to be her and Charlie. She would sacrifice that much. Meeting his gaze melted her resolve though. Fuck, she didn't want this to end.

"Please, give me this much," Noah's voice turned rough, the timbre of his whisper skittering against her skin.

"I don't need to see this shit right before I die," Charlie growled from the stairwell, looking away from them. "I don't even want to know what he did to deserve special nickname privileges."

Nickname privileges? What was he talking about?

Z.

Oh. Noah had been using her nickname and she... hadn't even noticed it. It had felt so natural. So much like having Vahagn there encouraging her. Her heart clenched as she turned to follow Charlie down the stairs, Noah in tow. All she could focus on was placing one foot in front of the other down the dark stairwell as her thoughts spiraled. Could she trust Noah? With this plan? With her heart? With her life? Hadn't she done so this entire time despite everything in her telling her to run fast and far away? Couldn't she let him explain himself?

If they survived this.

These were thoughts for if they survived this. She could examine her feelings then.

Noah set a few explosives in the stairwell as they descended and Charlie pushed open the bottom door into the basement when an abrupt sense of dread flooded her. Still, they continued to work through the dank area. A chill went down her spine as she observed Noah, strategically placing explosives in areas to make the biggest impact, against support beams, near doors and flammable objects. He had done this before.

Shit, he had done this before.

Once finished, he raised his empty hands to Izzy and nodded his head toward the exit. Making her way there, she suddenly realized she had no idea where Charlie had gone.

"Charlie!" she whispered a shout across the basement. Various crates and barrels sat stacked throughout and the lighting left much to the nightmares of her imagination. Her whisper seemed to be absorbed into the creepy darkness.

"Charlie, where the fuck are you, you stupid asshole?!" She rounded a stack of crates and stopped cold.

Someone had Noah's hands bound behind his back with a dagger to his throat.

No, wait. That was Charlie sneering at her from behind him. Her rage consumed her in a flash and her hand flew to the dagger at her side, fingers wrapping around the onyx hilt.

"What do you think you're doing?" The words bit the air between them. The traitorous fool and she had led him here. God, she felt like such an idiot.

"Taking back what is rightfully mine," a callous, cool French accent answered from behind the shadow of the crates stacked by the door. The man who emerged could've walked off the runway and into this disgusting basement, immaculately dressed in a well-tailored black suit, black dress shirt. Complete with the exact build and face that stole the hearts of women and men everywhere.

"What do you mean, *rightfully yours*? Who are you?" Her eyes flickered between the dagger at Noah's neck and this handsome man.

"Meet Emilien Dumas, his royal highness of this shit storm of a world," Noah growled out before Charlie pressed the dagger against the skin on his neck, a slight stream of blood trickling down.

"Now, now, Noah, those are such… hateful words for someone who once so fondly worked for and supported my mission." Emilien whistled at Charlie and he released Noah with a shove. Noah started to make his way to her but Emilien whistled again, stopping him in his tracks. Her heart stopped. What was he doing? They needed to run. Now.

"Tsk tsk tsk—I'm afraid your holiday is over, Noah. Time to go *home*," Emilien purred, stepping toward him.

Noah's expression pained as he never took his eyes off Izzy but still he remained stationary. Panic rippled through her, hand shaking against the handle at her fingertips.

Emilien fucking Dumas. The mind behind this disaster they all found themselves in. Standing in front of her. Talking about Noah like he was some valuable object, lost but now found.

"What do you want with a deserter anyway?" Her words were clipped, anger and fear vibrating through her. "Release him and we will be on our way. We won't stop you."

Emilien tilted his head at her, a cruel smile forming on his beautiful mouth.

"He is not merely a *deserter*, as you say. He has crimes to answer for and work to continue, in an effort to repay his *debt* to me."

A muscle ticked in Noah's jaw but he kept his eyes on Izzy as she surveyed him.

"How much is his debt? We can pay it. Let us pay it and we can leave and pretend we were never here." Only then did Noah break their gaze, his head dropping as he closed his eyes.

The laugh that escaped from Emilien echoed through the basement, cooling her skin.

"This debt can only be repaid in *blood, mon amour.*" Each word came out slow, tinged with a sensual undertone that felt like claws scraping across her back.

God, these fucking foreign men and their pet names for her. She ground her teeth together.

"Don't you have enough mortals to feed from? What makes him so special?" she asked.

"Ah, he didn't tell you?" Emilien stood next to Noah, pacing around him like he was surveying cattle for slaughter. His hand dragged across his chest, hovering over the fleur di lis tattoo above his heart.

"Noah here is *très extraordinaire* to my cause." The twinkle in the man's hazel eyes as he dug his nails into Noah's chest, set her rage aflame. Her grip tightened around her dagger and the drag of metal against leather sounded as she unsheathed it. Then a seductive female French voice floated across the basement.

"Funny, Emil. I have the same sentiment."

Emilien's cruel smile vanished as all the color drained from his face. The most beautiful woman, his equal with long, soft brown waves and piercing pale blue eyes, came out from the hallway leading to one of the underground pathways. Both exits were now blocked by French assholes. *Merde.*

The noise that came out of Emilien next was a cross between a cry and a choke as he said, "Adette." He released his hold on Noah, focused seared into this woman, Adette, as she walked around the crates. Izzy heard her footsteps behind her.

"Hello, darling," she cooed over Izzy's shoulder. "It's been a while."

CHAPTER THIRTY-SEVEN
Izzy

Emilien took a tentative step forward, as if the floor would crumble under him.

"*How?*" he asked, barely speaking above a whisper as shock seemed to overcome him. Whoever this woman was, he had not expected to see her here. This distraction Izzy needed.

"*Mon coeur,* that's hardly the most pressing issue, *n'es-tu pas d'accord?*" The woman, Adette, had a stronger accent than Emilien's but a cruelty underlined her words. No translation needed for the animosity roiling off her.

To everyone's surprise, Emilien fell to his knees, despair washing over him. Adette rolled her eyes and turned to where Noah stood. His gaze flickered to the building exits as he straightened, bracing for the impact of her menacing stare.

Fuck. The building. The building they had just lined with explosives. Their time was drifting away.

Izzy's heart rate quickened and she noticed Adette's gaze shift to her, eyes dilating for a moment before she focused back on Noah.

"It sure has been a journey to find you, *Monsieur* Broussard," the woman cooed.

Noah raised his chin but his steely gaze did not falter. Adette slid her eyes down him, smirking.

"It was a shame to learn the fate of your brother… and your failed attempt at a coup. Alas," she looked to Emilien, "here you stand. Alone. *Triste.*" Her eyes twinkled and she turned to Izzy.

"*Et tu, mon ami!* Did you enjoy my special present?" Amusement lightened the words.

Present? What was this deranged French woman talking about?

Adette's inhuman laugh ricocheted around them.

"You never could put it together, could you? *Dommage.* I thought you were a smart girl." A click of disapproval punctuated her words at Izzy before she continued, peering over at Emilien on the floor, the man silenced by this woman's sheer presence. "My dear husband played his cards too 'fast and loose' as you Americans say."

Husband? Izzy didn't have time to unpack all this. They didn't have time. She inched toward Noah.

"I thought you were *dying,* Adette! I was willing to try anything to stop that," Emilien pleaded from the floor, words expelled in a gasp.

Pure fire raged in Adette's gaze as she glared at him, a snarl forming on her lips.

"And look where that has gotten us, Emil?" She held her arms out and walked in a slow circle. Izzy took another step toward Noah, a breath remained trapped in her chest. Just a little closer.

Emilien's jaw set. "And *how* has it gotten us here,

Adette?"

She stopped, her back turned to him, letting her arms fall to her sides. Emilien slowly rose to his feet, finding the strength to stand. Adette turned around to face him, a faint hint of regret on her face.

"I had accepted my fate that day in the doctor's office. I was ready to spend the rest of my *life* with you, *mon amour*."

"And what about my life?!" Emilien's voice boomed out around them and Adette flinched as the words hit her full force.

Izzy would need a long discussion with Noah later to process everything she learned as the disgruntled couple argued. So long as they made it out of this death trap before detonation. Which was in—her gaze flicked to a wall clock above the doorway—approximately four minutes.

The anger on Emilien's face seemed to temper by the sadness in his voice as he continued his verbal assault on his wife.

"You got to accept your fate, your timeline, the rest of *your* life. But what was I supposed to do? How was I supposed to *live* without you? To *survive* without you?" he pleaded, his tormented expression pulling at Izzy's heart strings. No, she would have no remorse for this man. She shifted closer to Noah.

Adette scoffed at his words. Izzy was nearly at Noah's side. He gave her a sidelong glance, then looked to the underground exit. It would be their best bet. Ascending the stairs would take too long and what awaited them in two minutes was worth avoiding.

"It appears you figured that out perfectly fine, Emil." Sheer contempt rolled off the elision in her words.

"You made me leave; I had no other choice!" The conversation continued. Emilien's words turned frantic, on the verge of an implosion.

Adette's cool demeanor finally broke as she yelled, "You gave me no choice!"

Izzy's hand grazed Noah's and he squeezed tight. The clock was ticking.

"I gave you *everything!*" A near sob escaped Emilien's lips.

"*Tu as joué à Dieu*, Emilien, and I did not want that for my life. For us!"

Together, Izzy and Noah backed away from the scene unfolding before them, toward their escape, their salvation. Emilien's gaze narrowed on Adette, fists clenched.

"And how about now?" the man seethed through his tight jaw.

Adette's surprise was unmistakable.

"I..." She swallowed her words, looking to the floor. "Once I figured out your plans after leaving, I... needed to stop you." Her gaze met his, the anger between the two palpable. "You cannot do what you want to do. It is not natural, not right Emilien."

Izzy and Noah were a few steps from the underground exit when Emilien broke his gaze from Adette to look to the spot where they had once been standing. Finding it empty, he scanned the warehouse and found them at the door.

"No!" His voice bellowed across the space.

Acting on instinct, Izzy pulled her dagger out, it's beautiful floral etching sliding across her fingers. She pinched the steel tip between her fingers for a millisecond before flinging it across the space. The violets flew through the air, Izzy feeling a moment of loss as it disappeared from her grasp.

Right into Adette's heart.

Not stopping to see what happened next, she and Noah

sprinted through the exit. It was a short, concrete hallway with a sloping floor that spit them out into a damp, gray parking garage. A loud boom shook through the space from behind them. Right on fucking time, the explosives detonated.

"Hurry, Z," Noah encouraged from a few steps behind her. She chanced a glance over her shoulder, meeting the worry in his golden eyes, glowing despite the dim lighting.

There was no moment to think as they ran, the sound of their footfalls and roar of her heartbeat all that echoed in her ears. Her lungs burned and her legs ached but she pushed toward the ramp that would take them out of this underground hell. Sunlight beckoned from around the corner, renewing her will to push on despite her body's adamant protests. Another boom, a delayed detonation, sounded and she sprinted faster up the steep incline as a cloud of smoke and dust rolled ominous behind her.

Only once the warmth of the sun's rays hit her skin did she collapse onto the street, sobs racking through her body as she released a feral scream. Her sides flared as she sucked in oxygen, catching her breath in quick pants.

A moment later, she found the courage to open her eyes to the daylight, turning to Noah.

Except he wasn't there.

Panic ripped through her body as she scanned up and down the street, looking for him as smoke billowed in the air around her. Coughing, she yelled out his name, covering her mouth with her shirt as she searched the street. She peered back into the thick haze filling the parking garage ramp behind her. Nothing but a gray abyss wafted below.

"Noah!" Her scream scraped hoarse against her throat before it disappeared into the darkness.

Silence responded.

She paced in front of the entrance, counting down. She would give him five seconds. Five seconds and she was going in after him, damn his likely protests. He could only be mad at her if he was alive.

"Three, two, one, fuck it," she said and began marching down the decline, plunging into the murky air. A firm hand gripped her arm and pulled her up, twisting her around. Another feral scream pressed against her clenched teeth when Lando said, "*Mi amore,* Isabella, oh God you're okay, *grazie mille!*"

His voice carved a pit in her stomach. Tears stung her eyes, the smoke making them water more.

"Noah," she whispered into Lando's chest. He put her head in his hands and looked into her eyes. His own happy gaze fell as he scanned the street in another futile search. Gio motioned them on from down the road, urging them to keep moving. He gave her a wave and turned his attention back to Izzy. Soot stained his brow, a small cut above his eyebrow.

"Isabella, we must go. The smoke is getting thicker and soon we will not be alone out here," Lando said.

She tried to pull out of his grasp, to object but his grip tightened. No matter how much she fought him, he continued to drag her away. Away from the warehouse. Away from the destruction they had caused. Away from her heart she felt splitting in two with each step.

She resisted every footfall back to the building but Lando refused to relent. All the way to his penthouse apartment, they silently battled each other, only stopping the moment he pushed her into a chair at his giant dining table. The table where Vahagn's body had laid. How many would it hold before this was done?

"Lando, we have to go back!" She started to stand but

his hand pushed her shoulder back down. He sat next to her, placing a glass of amber liquid before her. She didn't want this. She wanted to leave. She needed to find Noah.

"No, *mia zazzera*, we cannot. It's gone." His eyes looked to the door as she vaguely registered footsteps coming in. He gave his head a slight shake and the footsteps disappeared into the gym. His focus returned to her. "Now, tell me what happened."

Despair ripped through Izzy as she frantically looked out the window, to the smoke filling the streets below. Then she relayed what happened. From Charlie's betrayal to Emilien's arrival to the strange interaction between Emilien and Adette.

"She called him her husband?" Lando's brows furrowed as he looked out the window, taking a sip of the bourbon.

Izzy's head drifted up and down, the drink before her untouched. There was no point in trying to numb her feelings. It wouldn't be able to touch the agony roiling inside her. What did it matter? What did any of this matter anymore?

"And Noah? Did Emilien say why he needed him? Or what the book had to do with any of this?" he pressed, his voice eager for her response.

Exhaustion flooded through her veins. Her bones felt heavy. She shook her head, her mind feeling foggy. "No. I think Adette was getting ready to explain but Emilien seemed surprised to see her there. Or even to see her alive at all, it seemed."

Lando rubbed his chin as he continued to survey the city through the windows. Izzy followed his gaze, wondering, *hoping* Noah was out there and they had just gotten separated. He would walk through the door any moment. Covered in dust and debris, rubbing the back of his neck as he flashed her a crooked grin. He was probably hiding in another cave. Not the one... it was gone now. Collapsed under the rubble of the library.

Izzy squeezed her eyes shut.

She stayed at the table until the glow of the setting sun set the city on fire.

She stayed there until darkness descended, the streets lit by the eerie tinge of the full moon in the sky.

She stayed there until she felt a sudden, gut-wrenching pain sear through her heart. She gasped, palms splayed on the table as her eyes flew open and a scream tore from her soul through her lips.

CHAPTER THIRTY-EIGHT
Izzy

Beams of sunlight shot through the windows and it felt like the most egregious attack on her senses she had ever experienced. Groaning, she rolled onto the floor, taking the covers with her and wrapping them over her head. Her covers. From her bed. In her apartment. She peeked an eye out from under the linen and scanned the room. Empty.

That emptiness settled in the pit of her stomach as the events of the past few days came crashing down on her. Consuming her. Choking her to the point she crawled, blanket and all, to the kitchen to grab some water. She chugged three glasses, the covers held around her like a cloak, before a thought started creeping in that something felt terribly wrong. Besides the obvious, her thirst only continued to *worsen* the more she drank.

She shuffled to the bathroom, squinting at the bright lights as she rummaged through her drawers for a thermometer. Surely, whatever this was could be explained by a fever. A stress fever. Stressful people were unhealthy. As she turned to head back to the living room, she caught a glimpse of her reflection and stopped.

The deep purple circles under her eyes seemed the least alarming, understandable even, all things considered. But her teeth. Something was in her teeth. She leaned into the mirror, eyes adjusting to the God-awful glare from the light. Had Lando done something to beef up their solar panels?

The thermometer clattered to the floor, falling under the vanity. But she couldn't be bothered to bend down to retrieve it. Because those were fucking fangs where her normal, rounded, *human* canines should be.

A drop of blood bubbled to the surface as she ran a finger over one. A drop that splashed with artistic grace into the pristine porcelain sink as her hand started shaking.

How is this possible? Her thoughts began reeling as she attempted to piece together how this could have happened. The shaking coursed through her body and she gripped the edge of the sink to keep herself upright. If Noah were here, she could ask him. Surely he would know. Her heart ached. *Noah.* As the dark hands of depression started to wrap around her mind, a thought dawned on her. Noah would know… and maybe that's because he read it somewhere.

Running across the living room to her closet, she glared at the sunlight and then hissed at herself for doing so. She knelt before the loose floorboard in the back corner. It took her a minute to pry it open, her hands still trembling, numb. Flinging the board up and behind her, she dug out the soft cloth parcel within. Her vision blurred as she flipped through the pages her and Noah had already researched, deeming the information fairly useless. But there had to be something in there. The Society had attacked her for it. Taken Noah for it. Killed Vahagn for it. Her vision started to blur again but she kept flipping through the book, not worrying about protective gloves or tearing pages as she scoured the decorative script for something, anything that could explain what the fuck happened to her. And why The Society cared about it so much.

An image blurred past and she had to flip back a few pages to look at it. It was... a soldier... with fangs. Just like hers. How had they missed this?

A piece of paper fell out of the gutter of the pages. With shaking hands, she picked it up, laying the book atop its protective coverings as she read the elongated handwritten script on the torn piece of paper. Noah's handwriting.

New training grâd?

Something about strength beyond measure???

The paper fell to the floor. When had he added these notes? They kept all their research in one notebook so no one could stumble across it. Most days she kept that notebook in her safe at work. She grabbed her leather bag tossed in the corner and rummaged through it, making sure she hadn't missed something. Grabbing the notebook inside, she flipped through and came across a section of torn pages.

"What the fuck," she whispered into the dark. She picked the book back up, scanning the section he must have translated and summarized for her. She continued to leaf through its contents. Another loose page stuck out and she plucked it from its space.

Thirst for a special blend of wine? The duguð here—têma?

Is that general? Why would a general have a special blend of wine? Mægenfæst? That's... vigor...

Her mind spun as she watched the words sink to the floor next to the other note. She scanned the rest of the pages of the tome, desperately in search of the crumbs Noah left behind for her. Another folded piece of paper fell to the floor. She tried to figure out which page it fell from when she saw her name on the top corner of the note.

Izzy -

I can't decipher this whole book in the dark of your closet, even with the full moon outside, but I think you were right, there was something off about the reign of Charlemagne. Cweldeht swât - that's corrupted blood. Between the pictures and what I've been able to translate, I think the crusaders under his rule were vampires. I don't know how he did it or

Or? Or what, Noah! Fuck. She sank back against the rust brick wall, pressing the back of her head behind the clothing hanging above her, blocking out the intrusive sunlight streaming in from the windowed wall to her right.

Her lower lip trembled. Charlemagne had reigned over a great portion of the European Union with a band of fucking vampires. Her breath caught and her heart lurched to her throat. How could that have even been possible? How had that truth been erased from history? Shoved under the rug to place this religious leader on a pedestal?

She groaned and shoved her head back against the brick. Grimacing at the pain, she bit her lip. The blood started to flow quickly from her fang. Her fucking fang.

Because she was a fucking vampire.

"Izzy?" Gio's rich voice rang across the small studio apartment, briefly muffled by the wall of bookshelves.

"Fuck," Izzy murmured, a new panic striking her into action. She scrambled to shove the book back into its protective coverings. The floorboard slid into place as Gio's voluptuous form stepped into the closet. In a flash, she rushed to Izzy, kneeling on her level.

"Oh, Izzy, we've been so worried." Izzy watched the stream of tears cascade down her smooth, tan cheeks. The droplets fell heavy off her dark lashes and trickled down to her neck. Izzy knew Gio was talking because she saw the muscles in her throat work. But her vision became fixated on the flow of salty water as it traveled over an artery. The blood pumped through it. Something primitive clicked in Izzy's brain and before she knew what she was doing, her hand wrapped around Gio's neck. She hauled her up and against the wooden wall behind her. Baring her teeth, Izzy reached foreword to sink them into Gio's soft flesh.

Instead, pain flashed across her skull as Gio's elbow collided with her temple. Izzy stumbled backward and snarled, ready to pounce.

Gio's hazel eyes widened and then she scrambled out of the closet, slamming the door shut behind her with a curse.

Izzy roared a feral sound, foreign to her own new, improved hearing. Nothing made sense to her beyond plunging her teeth deep into that pulsing artery and draining it.

"Lando, something's wrong. You need to hurry!" She heard Gio say on the other side of the door. Izzy tried the handle. It moved an inch so she put more effort into it the next attempt, ripping it free from Gio's hold.

The woman met her gaze, wide eyes, plump limps drooped in fear and hurt. A shard of regret pierced Izzy's heart but it couldn't overpower her one desire: to drink Gio's blood.

Before Izzy could act on that thought, Gio smacked her across the face with a flat wooden bat, a weapon from Izzy's own collection. The force sent Izzy to the floor, dazed by the surprise attack. It gave Gio enough time to escape through the still open front door of her apartment. By the time Izzy had gathered her wits and went after her, she found the hallway empty.

Letting out a quiet, frustrated scream, Izzy tossed her door shut and stalked around her apartment until her own blood stopped boiling. Then she slumped to the floor and wept. What the fuck was wrong with her? She needed Vahagn. He would know what to do in this moment. What to say to make her calm down and see that everything wasn't truly and royally fucked like she believed. Her chest clenched around her lungs and she struggled to breathe.

Her panic attack rose like the incoming tide within her. The last time this had happened it had been Noah who helped calm her down, bring her out of it. But he was gone too.

Everyone she loved left her in the end.

This sparked a rage within her. Maybe he hadn't left her. Maybe he had been taken like Vahagn. Like Vahagn…

Jumping up, she sprinted to the door, pulling on her boots in a fury. She wrenched the door open. On a second thought she ran to her bookshelf, grabbing the dagger Vahagn had gifted her. Her fingers roved over the black etched *Z* in the steel. She turned to leave then stopped. Reaching up, she pulled out a copy of Moby Dick, the fabric spine worn and the decorative embossing peeling away in spots. She flipped it open to chapter forty-one. Carved into the pages was a perfect cut out of a handgun, the firearm held snug within. She pulled it out and shoved it into the back of her pants. As she went to close the book a heavy weight pressed into her chest. She pulled the golden cross out from beneath her shirt, sliding her fingers over the heated metal. Tears blurred her vision and before she could second guess herself, she ripped the chain off her neck, threw it in the empty space carved in those pages, then strode out of her home, leaving that piece of herself behind too.

CHAPTER THIRTY-NINE
Izzy

Hope felt fickle in the grandeur of recent life events. Yet it was the emotion Izzy clung to as she walked back to the warehouse. An impossible scenario played in her mind at least a dozen times as she weaved through the shadows, hood pulled over her face.

"Way to leave me behind, Z," Noah says, smiling as he scoops her into his arms, kissing her like she's the air he needs to breathe. She smiles into his lips and playfully bats as his arms to let her down.

"You should keep up next time, Broussard," She responds as he lowers her the ground. His eyes never leave her own, his smile setting her heart off beat.

Those golden eyes twinkle as a wry smile plays at his lips, those scarred lips. Beautifully imperfect, damaged disaster.

"There won't be a next time."

Her heart lurched at the thought. *There won't be a next time.* Shaking her head free of the make-believe memory, she stepped over the rubble serving as the new entrance into the warehouse. Or what remained of it. Before her a mess of metal, wooden beams, and bricks lie strewn across the buckled concrete floor. It looked like an abandoned construction project. Pulling a bandana over her nose and mouth, she scanned the debris looking for anything, *something* to ease the ache in her heart. A sign to feed the hope flickering in her soul. Not to mention the pounding headache infiltrating every corner of her brain.

Immortality was already a real fucking bitch.

Making a slow ascent of the metal stairs that somehow remained intact in the charred room, she surveyed the expanse of the warehouse with each step. At the top, she nearly fell back down as a group of men stood before her, each looking more disheveled than the next. One looked particularly distraught, sitting on the ground. Emilien.

"You have some fucking nerve," Charlie growled, stalking toward her.

The shell of the man known as Emilien Dumas put a hand out, his accent having lost its luster as he said, "Save it, Charlie."

Charlie's pursuit halted but the scowl on his face sparked a new wave of emotion through her.

"That's a bit rich, coming from the man who fucking betrayed us all." Her plan to remain civil dissipated as the words sliced through the air between them. She didn't care at this point.

"Now, now, Isabella. Let us not poke the bear, *oui?*" Emilien said from the ground, looking as exhausted as he sounded. Some fucking nerve alright.

Her glare narrowed on Emilien. "I'm surprised you're even still here. Like a damn cat, you've lived yet again. Don't you have a marriage to reconcile?"

He couldn't be much older than her, at least when he

had taken his supposed cure to mortality. Still, his eyes looked weary at her words, like the brevity of an endless life without his reason for living had taken a greater toll than he cared to admit. To anyone.

"Why are you here, Isabella?" Emilien said, wiping a hand over his mouth, exhaustion weighing down his words.

I hoped to find Noah and leave this city.

The thought surprised her. Was that what she wanted? Would Noah be here? Had she expected him to be here, unscathed? Like it had been planned. Just another ruse, scheme in disguise as destruction.

Her thoughts spiraled in her mind, making her feel dizzy as a pain wrenched through her empty stomach. Her gaze bounced to the rest of the men standing around, gaze catching the skull tattooed on the neck of one man. She quickly averted her eyes and straightened her spine. "I came looking for you."

Emilien's eyes widened. "Oh? So, you expected we wouldn't die in your elaborate scheme? *Et prie de dire?* Please tell us why?"

Shifting the leather strap on her shoulder, she ignored his condescension and said, "I have something you want."

His eyes flicked to the bag hanging off her side.

"And I believe you have the means to something I want," she added, hope elevating her tone.

He cocked his head at this. "*Est-ce vrai?*"

"*Oui,*" she said, tentative.

"And what is it you want, Isabella?" Her name rolled off his tongue like a ball of yarn through the playful paws of a kitten, clawing and genial.

Before her stood a broken man, evident by the coat of dust over his clothing and skin, the haggard set to his expression.

But the monster within still lived as he straightened his broad shoulders, clasping his hands at his chest like he was about to give a sermon to a devoted crowd. The only thing that gave him away was the worn, sad look in his eyes, expressing the toll this had all taken on him. Decades of building a facade only for it to come crumbling down by one woman.

Izzy flashed her stupid fangs at him, those weary eyes widening. Even Charlie looked shocked. And maybe a little queasy as he stepped back from her.

No one deserving seemed to die in this city.

A crooked, evil smile spread across Emilien's face, the men standing around him darting their gaze between their boss and her, leery of what would happen next.

"Well, well, well, *mes amis*. Seems we need to welcome *Mademoiselle* Ciampi to The Society."

❧

CHAPTER FORTY
Noah

The heavy pounding in his temple served as a stupid way to assure Noah he was, in fact, not dead.

What a sweet reprieve. He sluggishly blinked his eyes open. At least he thought they were open. Wherever he was, it was fucking dark. And damp. The musty, earthen scent of dank rot hit him. He felt queasy. Faintly, he registered his body moving. Not quick, but a constant, steady hum emanated from the floor under him, pulling at his center of gravity. A sliver of light crept in from a rusted metal grate above him. He moved to wipe at the dryness scratching his eyes but winced when he met the resistant bite of rope around his wrists.

Okay, not great prospects. Death looked like a warm summer's day at this point. He closed his eyes, picturing the blue sky with its puffy clouds, the trees full of green leaves, flowers buzzing with life, the soft, cool grass underneath his fingers, the freckles on Izzy's nose scrunching as she smiled up at him... his eyes flew open.

Izzy.

Blinking urgently to rid his eyes of the crust blurring his vision, he searched the space for her. All he could see around him were shelves of chemicals and mechanical supplies.

"Z?" he whispered, a panicked note in his voice.

Silence.

"Fuck," he groaned as his gaze slid up to the flaking metal above him, shutting his lids to conjure up the memories of when he had last seen her.

They were sprinting out of the building as explosions went off behind them. Too late. They had left too late. Panic wrenched through him as he watched Izzy's arms pumping in time with her stride, exuding strength and determination. The surprise arrival of Emilien's wife had been a wrench in their plan. He heard footsteps behind them as they ran but he didn't dare look. He just kept Izzy in front of him, following her. Always following her. The light of the exit beckoned for them and they both pushed to the end. But instead of going forward, he careened sideways, surprise taking over all his senses and reflexes. His attacker took the opportunity to cover his mouth before he could yell out and then… blackness.

That was it.

Noah sighed, contemplating what kind of bad luck one man could accumulate in a lifetime to find himself kidnapped and hunted at such a predictable rate. Faint French and English voices leaked in from above. They grew louder until they were right on top of him. He stilled.

"*Non,* the plan has not changed, *d'accord?*" A female voice urged. French. Emilien's wife, Adette.

"*Et que dire de…?*" This voice, male, Noah didn't recognize.

"Noah is the plan, *bon?*" Noah's eyes popped open but he held his breath, listening closer.

"Mais comment?" The male sounded as shocked as Noah felt.

"Combien de fois dois-je t'expliquer cela? He is the sickness and the cure. Our investors were concerned about the longevity of the project. Well, *voila*, problem solved." Investors? Project? Noah's head throbbed and another wave of nausea washed over him. He missed whatever she said next as a clattering sounded in the distance.

The footsteps above shuffled away until he couldn't hear their conversation anymore. Noah sucked in a deep breath, filling the lungs he had abandoned while eavesdropping.

He is the sickness and the cure. What did that mean?

He pressed his eyelids shut, dropping his head to his chest.

"Above anything else, you never let them drink from you and vice versa, okay?" Benji had said to him, on numerous occasions.

"Yeah, obviously", he would snap back. Benji always brought out this side of him. The side that made him feel forever six years old.

"No, seriously." Benji would meet his gaze, the sincerity in his eyes enough to make Noah swallow his pride and take pause.

Benji had known then. Or had an idea but never told him.

And what good had keeping that secret gotten him? Killed.

Noah scoffed at the idea, smiling cruelly to himself, pulling on the scar forming on his lips. Because of course. There had always only ever been two outcomes. Captured and collected like a rare species or killed.

What now? What path did he take now, tied to a fucking chair on what he decided had to be a boat, likely another barge, heading from one organized crime syndicate to the next?

Izzy's emerald eyes twinkled in his mind, a memory from that night in the cave when they had laid next to each other, sharing the fractures in each other's souls.

How had the greatest night of his life marked the beginning of his downfall? He had been stupid enough to hope. To dream a future that wasn't running or avenging his brother's death or dismantling an egotistic psychopath with a taste for blood. A future somewhere untouched by The Society where they could argue the merits of historians versus anthropologists, collect memories of industrial architecture, and watch the sunsets outside without the nagging fear each one represented.

Despair sunk deep into his core, his bones growing weary and heavy in the chair. Nausea tore at the empty pit in his stomach. His head hung lower and his eyes felt hot, blurring at the edges.

"Cheer up, Noh. This is hardly a place, or hell, a position to cry in."

Noah blinked the tears in his eyes away rapidly, glaring at the person in the open doorway in front of him. Great, now he was hallucinating.

"Unless, of course, those tears are of joy at seeing your big brother alive and well," the man drawled in the New Orleans accent that always marked them as boys of Bourbon Street to anyone who heard it.

Surely to God, this was a fucking hallucination. He blinked again, the boat rocked to the side, and the image of his brother cleared.

"Welcome to The Antisociété, brother," Benji Broussard said, a wry smile on his faintly scarred face.

✦

EPILOGUE

"*B*ordel de merde," Adette whispered as she leaned against the closed door of her cabin on this *maudit* boat. This was the first moment alone she had found since starting this journey to the cursed city that was St. Louis. She felt an odd reprieve to be on the way back to New Orleans, like there existed an ounce of home in that place. Anywhere, anymore.

Her idea of home had died decades ago, along with her fantasy of a life that knew true love and fulfillment. All of it ripped away by the blackened greed of her husband.

Emil.

And yet, here she found herself in her dark, dismal cabin on the verge of tears at seeing him. Her anger had been all consuming in the moment, burying that little spark in her heart. The very heart that cruel bitch of a woman flung her knife into before sprinting away like a coward. She's lucky the building exploded before Adette could chase her down. Glancing to the decorative blade on her desk, cluttered with maps and plans, she leaned her head back against the door behind her and sighed, rubbing her hand over the scar tissue already starting to dissipate on her chest. In the end, she left the city with what she came for: Noah Broussard.

A matching genetic novelty to his brother, Noah would provide the missing piece to her research to eliminate the appalling vampiric requirement of immortality. Just as the investors wanted. A clean aesthetic for forever.

A soft knock behind her startled her back to reality. *Henry.* It was their normal meeting time. She wasn't sure she wanted to see him but found herself too exhausted to come up with an excuse. Besides, she sighed, she needed his blood after her recent injury. Her body craved it.

"*Oui*, Henry. Come in," she said, standing from her position on the floor and brushing off her green linen pants.

"Adi, are you okay?" Henry said as he walked into her cabin. His violet gray eyes shone with concern behind his wire glasses, a mess of orange waves atop his head. Not the attractive equal to Emilien, who had once stopped traffic on the Liienstraße in Munich, but at least he was here. He was kind and he understood her. Let her make her own choices in life.

"Yes, Henry. I am fine. Just tired." She motioned to the bed as she started to undress. A comfortable move of a woman who had known love and safety in a relationship and yet, it still caused Henry to tense as he sat stiffly on the edge of the small mattress.

"You know I am here for you. Whatever you need, all you have to do is ask," he said, averting his gaze to the metal beams in the dimly lit space.

She sighed. He always reassured her of his loyalty to her, to their cause. It usually put her at ease. Tonight, it made her want to toss her oil lantern against the wall and watch the whole thing go up in flames. She pinched the bridge of her nose.

"*Oui, je sais*. Please, just… lie back. Get comfortable." She tried to temper her ire.

Henry removed his boots and pants but kept on the cotton t-shirt and boxers underneath. The English were so modest. It made Adette uncomfortable when they had first moved to Oxford, so repressive after her lifetime in Paris. She rolled her eyes, releasing her chestnut braid and combing her fingers through the silky strands. The moon painted silver lines in the midnight waters outside the small window over her desk.

She climbed into the bed with Henry, the small mattress creaking beneath the movement. Forced to snuggle up next to him, she cradled within the nook of his chest. He kissed the top of her head, a hand rubbing her arm. A tear threatened to fall at the touch.

"Are you ready?" she whispered the question to him, watching the lantern on it's soft sway side to side from the hook by the door. His hand stopped.

"Erm, yes. Do you, um, let me take off my shirt. So it doesn't stain," Henry said, shifting beneath her.

She rolled to the side to allow him to sit up and pull the beige fabric over his head. He had the muscles of a lifelong academic. Nothing like the body Emilien had, sculpted and refined in the early mornings spent at the gym or rowing the canals before work.

Henry laid back down, removing his glasses and setting them on the small side table next to the bed. His dusty lavender eyes stared to the wooden ceiling. She rolled back against him, pressing a kiss to his neck.

"Just for tonight, *d'accord*. Then I will go back to the reserves." The words were thick against the saliva pooling in her mouth.

Henry simply nodded and squeezed his eyes closed. The visual tickled her anger again and she slipped into the role of predator with ease. Opening her mouth to a wicked smile, fangs exposed, she plunged them into the soft, pale flesh of Henry's neck, not stopping even as he yelped in pain.

This story continues with

LOVE YOU MADLY

Can't wait to see you on the river

❦
ACKNOWLEDGMENTS

Thank you so much for reading this story! The idea people want to read the words that come from the made-up scenarios in my mind will never seize to be surreal to me. I apologize for any and all emotional damage with that ending. I can't promise I won't try to do it again.

This story came about on a summer day, driving a country road in rural Kentucky, letting the algorithm in my music app choose the songs for me. Noah Kahan's version of "If We Were Vampires" popped on and I stopped the song to record a voice memo about a normal scientist who is madly in love with the woman he married and she's dying. What would he do to save her? Emilien Dumas was born that day and the rest is written on these pages. Or is it? My original draft was from his point of view…

Self-publishing is a wild experience because you feel like you're doing nothing and everything all at once. A huge thanks goes out to a wide selection of people who supported me in all the shades of myself that were exposed in this endeavor.

Thank you to all the authors who let me slide into their DMs and pick their brains (P, N, E—you're GEMS!). This community is full of such supportive and selfless individuals. I never expected any of them to respond, let alone fill me with such priceless knowledge and support.

To Jess – One comment. That's all it took on a random video on Instagram for us to forge this beautiful friendship. You are one of the most important people in my writing process. Your comments and support are what made this story. Cheers to many more shared stories and experiences on this wild adventure together. I look forward to one day sitting next to you at a signing event.

To the early readers of this story:

Diane, librarians are my favorite type of people and you're the gold star of the mix. Our every interaction fills me with creative energy.

Tiff, I hope this book gave you a slice of home. You're the only one who will see the sprinkles of us within these pages.

Karen, books rekindled our friendship. Books that inspired me to write again. Your insatiable appetite to read means I cherish every bit of your feedback.

Stacey, rarely do I meet someone south of the Mason-Dixie willing to be brutally honest with someone, so when you said you loved this story, I knew you meant it. I'm sorry for what I did at the end.

Emily, kindred spirits are rare to find in this world for weird horse girls who dream big and also cry a lot. You're my kindred spirit. I feel your unwavering support from across this vast country. Every description of food was also for you.

Ally, you have this incredible ability to make me feel like the most confident person in the world. I actually do not think I could've come this far without you cheerleading along the way, from reading extremely raw, unedited sex scenes to this whole goddamn book. I owe you the world.

To every single person who decided to take a chance on an unknown author and sign up to read my advance review copy. Every time I look at this list of names, I feel like the Grinch as my little heart grows more and more. Authors couldn't exist without readers like you. You're all amazing. I apologize for the typos.

To the Paul Sawyier Public Library, St. Louis Public Library, and all libraries across the country. Public libraries are one of the last pillars in this country of what good our governments can do when they start thinking about their communities as priceless investments. Look up your local public library and see what it offers; all their services are either free or low cost and available to everyone. Imagine what our country could be if we applied those same principals across the board. So much talent is hidden behind barriers that are insurmountable by most. Support your community, support your local library.

To the members and speakers at the countless groups and workshops I've attended as I navigate a whole new world. The learning curve is steep, but the resources out there are endless and amazing. I panic five times a day about how to tackle this endeavor and I'm always surprised to find answers and more available online for free.

And last, the biggest thanks goes to J. You've loved me on all my best days and all my worst. You've never stopped supporting and believing in me, even on days when I was pretty certain I did not understand my native language well enough to string together a sentence. I married my best friend. Thanks for letting me be the sole author you read. I **love you, forever**.

ABOUT THE AUTHOR

Growing up in the St. Louis metro area, Cortni dreamed of escape. She found it in the pages of books and fantasizing missed conversations and interactions. It took her over a decade to harness that skill into writing a novel but we all get where we're going in the end.

When not writing, she can be found on her small (read: tiny) farm in rural Kentucky with her incredible partner, two lovingly awful herd dogs, and a horse that is an absolute menace.

STAY UP TO DATE WITH UPCOMING PROJECTS!
www.authorcortnimarie.com
IG: @AuthorCortniMarie